Also by Raine Thomas

Daughters of Saraqael Trilogy
Becoming
Central
Foretold

Firstborn Trilogy
Defy

The Prophecy (An Estilorian Short Story)

SHIFT

Firstborn Trilogy Book Two

by Raine Thomas

Published by Iambe Books.

This book is an original publication of Iambe Books.

This book is a work of fiction. Names, characters, places and incidents are either the product of the author's imagination or are used fictitiously. Any resemblance to actual persons, living or dead, or to actual events or locales is entirely coincidental.

Visit the author's website: http://www.rainethomas.com
Cover design by: Nimbi Design

This book is dedicated with deepest thanks to Melissa and Melody, two "Mels" who have become the most amazing Estilorian fans out there.

You've both inspired me more than you'll ever know!

Acknowledgements

Words can't express the gratitude I hold to those people who helped make *Shift* happen. First and foremost, thanks so much to all of my fans. Your response to *Defy* rocked my world! You made writing *Shift* such an amazing experience.

My next big round of thanks goes to my husband, Kevin, and my mother, Diane. You're both pillars for me even in my weakest moments. I love you both so much!

Thanks a bunch to my writer pals, Roy "TC" Bronson and Bethany Lopez, for agreeing to beta read *Shift* and helping me make it the strongest story possible. You both awe me.

Additional thanks go to my friend, Sundée Himburg, who has been there for me as a beta reader since before the Daughters of Saraqael books were published. Thanks for asking such great questions as you read!

Thank you, as well, Devan Edwards of Nimbi Design, for the gorgeous cover for *Shift*. I think you might have created the best one yet.

Last but not least, thanks to my daughter, Faith, for doing everything possible to make me remember what it's like to be a child. You've inspired me and my writing, and I'll always be grateful that I have you in my life!

Author's Note

A warm welcome to those readers who are new to the Estilorians! Please note that the Firstborn trilogy serves as a follow-up to the Daughters of Saraqael trilogy. For an overview intended to bring new readers up to speed or refresh the memories of those who have already enjoyed the Daughters of Saraqael trilogy, please read the following Glossary. Happy reading!

Glossary

Estilorians (Things You Need to Know)

Daughters of Saraqael – Amber, Olivia, and Skye, triplets born to the Corgloresti, Saraqael, and their human mother, Kate, as a result of a ritual outlined in a powerful scroll. They're the first and only half-human Estilorians, which allows them to carry children...something full Estilorian females can't do. Amber is avowed to the Gloresti elder, Gabriel; Olivia is avowed to the Gloresti, James, and Skye is avowed to the Gloresti, Caleb.

Estilorian – A being that physically resembles a human, appearing no older than 40 human years old (most look like humans in their late teens or early twenties). Estilorians can fly, and have specific powers based on their class. They can live forever without aging if they're not mortally wounded. Their eyes, wings and markings—if they have any—are always the same color, and identify their class.

Estilorian Plane – About two millennia ago, the nine Estilorian elders created a separate plane of existence to remove themselves from humanity, making their kind the objects of human myths and legends. All Estilorians live on this plane, and humans cannot travel to it. Estilorian society hasn't evolved like human society, and doesn't have such modern inventions as electricity, vehicles or modern weaponry.

Estilorian Classes (Alphabetically)

Corgloresti – *Soul Harvesters* – Identified by their silver eyes, wings and markings, these Estilorians travel between the planes of existence to facilitate the transfer of dying human souls to the Estilorian plane via The Embrace…the only method full Estilorians have to reproduce.

Elphresti – *Lords of Wisdom* – These Estilorians, identified by their black eyes, wings and markings, maintain the highest levels of authority among their kind. In human terms, they would be considered judges or beings in similar positions of authority.

Gloresti – *Defenders* – Gloresti bond with Corgloresti who are on the human plane to protect the Corgloresti. Gloresti are highly trained to defend and are identified by midnight blue eyes, wings and markings. Aside from the Corgloresti, the Gloresti is the only class that can travel to the human plane, but only in emergencies.

Kynzesti – *Elementals* – Having half-human mothers, the Kynzesti are identified by deep blue-green eyes, wings and markings. Unlike other classes, they are only created through biological childbirth. The youngest of all Estilorian classes, the extent of their powers and abilities is largely unknown.

Lekwuesti – *Hospitality Ambassadors* – The Lekwuesti are identified by lavender eyes, wings and markings. Their primary focus is assisting their fellow Estilorians. They form exclusive pairings with other Estilorians to provide them items of "creature comfort," such as food, clothing, accessories, furniture, etc. All other Estilorians rely heavily on this class.

Mercesti – *The Dark Ones* – Once lauded for their skills in strategy and innovation, this class is identified by red eyes, wings and markings. The nature of the Mercesti changed dramatically when Grolkinei assumed power by killing the class elder, Volarius, out of hatred and rage. Estilorians now convert into Mercesti if they kill or intend to kill another Estilorian for any reason other than defense. Because they are formed largely of beings that used to belong to other Estilorian classes, some Mercesti maintain remnants of their former skills and abilities.

Orculesti – *Advisors* – Identified by dark green eyes, wings and markings, the Orculesti function as advisors regarding humankind. They work with paired Corgloresti and Gloresti to provide a mental connection between them when they are separated by the planes of existence. This class can read the thoughts of other Estilorians who aren't strong enough or trained enough to prevent it, and use their mental powers to suppress the thoughts and abilities of others.

Scultresti – *Creators* – The Scultresti are identified by brown eyes, wings and markings. This talented class creates all forms, including those that Corgloresti assume on the human plane when they transition there. They also create new Estilorian forms for human souls to inhabit when they are Embraced by Corgloresti, and are responsible for producing new animal and wildlife on the Estilorian plane.

Waresti – *Warriors/Lords of the Flame* – Identified by burnt orange eyes, wings and markings, the Waresti are dedicated to the overall protection of Estilorians from the Mercesti and other dangers. The most physically strong of all Estilorians, these warriors are markedly muscular and highly skilled with weapons and all forms of attack.

Wymzesti – *Intuits* – Incredibly charismatic, the Wymzesti have deep purple eyes, wings and markings. With the ability to read body language and intuit actions based upon past behavior, this class can predict events before they happen. Like the Orculesti, this class has the ability to manipulate thoughts and decision-making of those who aren't strong enough to resist them.

Kynzesti Family Tree

Parents: Amber and Gabriel
Children (in order of birth): Clara Kate, Joshua, Zara, Corliss, Riley, Kiera

Parents: Olivia and James
Children (in order of birth): Sophia, Keane, Leigh, Elle, Will, Paige

Parents: Skye and Caleb
Children (in order of birth): Tate and Tiege (twins), Nicholas, Abigail and Adam (twins), Grace, Quaid, Emma

Glossary of Terms

adelfi – A term of respect applied to Olivia and Skye, the sisters-in-law of the Gloresti elder, Gabriel.

adelfos – A term of respect applied to James and Caleb, the brothers-in-law of the Gloresti elder, Gabriel.

archigos – A term of respect reserved only for the class elders.

Avowed – The strongest connection two beings can have. An avowed pairing is made when two beings exchange heartfelt vows of love. It results in shared thoughts and feelings and can never be undone.

Central – The primary area where most Estilorians live, similar to a capitol city. Floating above the ocean and surrounded by heavy enchantments, Central is inaccessible to Mercesti. Also called *home base.*

Elder – The oldest and most powerful member of an Estilorian class; an elder must have inherent abilities that blend cohesively with the other elders.

Kragen – A beast that crossed over to the Estilorian plane when it was formed; humans called these creatures "dragons."

kyria – A term of respect applied to Amber, the wife of the Gloresti elder, Gabriel.

Mainland – All of the area outside of Central/home base. This area is not protected like Central, and as such is sparsely populated by Estilorians other than the Mercesti.

Markings – Estilorians develop markings on their skin, similar to tattoos, when significant events occur. For example, Gloresti develop a midnight blue marking when they pair with a Corgloresti, and the Corgloresti receives an identical silver marking. Also, Estilorians may have markings around their eyes, indicating they have a second ability.

Prologue

DONALD, LIEUTENANT OF THE WARESTI, HEARD THE MOAN FIRST. HE wasn't as knowledgeable about emotions as his two commanders and class elder, *archigos* Uriel, yet even he recognized the suffering conveyed by that sound.

He and a patrol of twenty Waresti were conducting a sweep of some caves within an ocean-side cliff, intending to rout out any Mercesti residing in them. A Corgloresti transition point was located not too far away. Thus, Donald needed to secure a mile-wide perimeter, clearing it of the Dark Ones. No sense risking the Mercesti finding a Corgloresti's vulnerable form and attempting to destroy it, after all.

Glancing at Isaiah, the Waresti in the group with the keenest hearing, Donald used hand signals to communicate.

Did you catch the origin of that noise?

Yes, sir. North tunnel.

Donald nodded. Signaling that the warriors all move in silence, he took the lead and treaded carefully into the tunnel, his sword drawn. Although the moan sounded feminine, Mercesti weren't above using trickery to try and lead others into a trap.

The tunnels were dark. Donald didn't conjure a light, not wanting to alert anyone to their presence. Mercesti could see in the dark, giving them an advantage in this environment. Waresti, however, had also developed good night vision over the centuries. Donald progressed with quiet confidence through the inky tunnel.

He heard another muffled groan and the sliding of a body along a gritty surface. When he rounded the next bend, he spied a huddled form on the ground. All he could make out was a glimpse of white skin and a long length of dark hair.

Fan out. Check the tunnels, he communicated to his warriors. He wasn't about to risk being taken unawares by skulking Mercesti.

When they moved to obey the order, Donald focused again on the small being crouched before him. He realized that his initial impression of a female had been correct. From what he could determine, she was unclothed and shaking violently.

Even these observations didn't prompt him to lower his defenses. He decided to introduce himself, hoping to put the female at ease.

"I am—"

She screeched as though he had sliced off one of her limbs. Her hair covering her face like a dark web, she flung her arms out as though warding him off and scrambled to press herself against the closest cave wall.

He tried to explain that he and his warriors meant her no harm, but her screaming drowned him out. The horrible sounds careened crazily off the rock.

"We will not harm you, female," he declared in a loud voice.

By then, most of his soldiers had returned, giving the all-clear. They also stared at the demented being on the floor as though unsure what to make of her.

"I am Donald, lieutenant of the Waresti," he continued. "We will help you if you have been injured or require assistance."

Her next wail wasn't quite as piercing. He took that as a positive sign. Over the next several minutes, he spoke to her in a calm voice, explaining that they would take her to Central and that someone there would ensure she was well tended. Eventually, the screaming stopped.

"Would you be more comfortable in clothing?" he asked.

Slowly, the female lifted herself, causing her hair to fall away from her face. Donald saw that much of her head, neck and upper body were caked in dried blood and dirt. A noticeable stench clung to her and it wafted closer to them when she moved. Bruising along her sides indicated that her ribs had been broken. He wondered if she fell down the cliff and crawled into the cave for shelter. Whatever had happened, her form had been severely mistreated. It seemed a miracle she survived.

But that wasn't what had Donald's normally impassive face falling into stunned lines. He lowered his sword and noticed his warriors doing the same with their weapons. They exchanged looks of bafflement.

The female on the ground was Kanika, the leader of the Mercesti.

PART I:

SHIFT

Shift [*v.* shift]: To put something aside and replace it by another or others; change or exchange: *to shift friends; to shift ideas.*

Chapter 1

IN THE FORM OF THE PANTHER, SOPHIA STALKED HER TARGET. THE FOREST provided many shaded and grassy nooks, and Domino was an admirable opponent. The three-year-old panther could remain still for hours. His spotted fur also gave him excellent camouflage, so Sophia used her heightened sense of smell to find him.

When she got within springing distance, she lowered into a crouch, her back legs digging into the ground for better purchase. Then she pounced.

Domino sensed her the moment she left the ground. He shifted to accept her weight as she tackled him. Her paws wrapped around his torso. Then she opened her powerful jaw and went for the soft part of his neck.

He quickly flipped their positions, using his greater strength to dump her onto her back. Her feline instincts had her wrenching herself to right her center of gravity. This resulted in them taking a long, tangled tumble down the side of a grassy hill.

At the base of the hill rested several of Domino's siblings. They watched for only a moment before leaping into the fray.

"Sophia!"

She froze, her ear caught between Domino's teeth. Rolling her eyes in the direction of her mother's voice, she tried to ignore the heavy weight of Domino's haunches where they rested on her right side. The panthers around her also grew still, hearing the maternal censuring tone and paying it heed.

Busted, Sophia thought.

She rolled out from under Domino and rose gracefully onto all four paws. Her mother stopped at the edge of the walkway leading from their home into the surrounding forest. The rose-colored sundress she wore swelled over her very pregnant belly and stopped just short of her bare feet. Her long, curling brown hair, worn with just a few loose daises tucked into it, gave her the look of a woodland goddess from the human fairytales she used to read Sophia as a child. Her lime green eyes held a warning that her curving lips belied.

Knowing she would get a lecture, Sophia padded closer. When she spotted Quincy watching in the distance, sunlight gleaming on his wavy blond hair and the many silver markings tattooing his muscular arms, she wanted to sink into the earth. Thank goodness panthers didn't blush, she mused, ignoring the racing of her heart that she considered normal when Quincy was involved.

She obligingly sat near her mother's feet and looked up. The light green and dark blue leaves decorating the outside of her mom's eyes gave her beautiful face a gentle appearance, but Sophia was only too aware of the fierceness of which her mother was capable.

Fortunately, her mother was a sucker for animals.

Even as her mom opened her mouth to speak, Sophia leaned forward and nudged her hand with her muzzle, urging it to the top of her head. She paired the nudge with a blink of her wide, panther eyes. As she intended, she succeeded in distracting her mother, who lowered herself to her knees and rubbed Sophia's head.

"Don't think this gets you out of a tongue lashing," her mother said in her soft, pleasing voice. "You ditched your training session again."

Figuring it couldn't hurt, Sophia licked her mom's cheek. That provoked a laugh.

"Look, sweetie..."

Sophia huffed, knowing what was coming.

"I know you prefer to spend your time in your laboratory or here with the panthers," her mother continued, "but weapons training is so important. Not so long ago, you saw just how important."

She referred to the recent experience that shook their usually uneventful lives. About two months before, Sophia's cousin Tate snuck away from the protected area encompassing their homes and ended up getting snatched by the kragen, Nyx. It took almost two weeks—and a battle against some truly scary Mercesti—to get her back.

Sophia had been among those who left in search of Tate. She didn't think it would help matters to point out that she fared just fine without a weapon of any kind. Her mother probably wouldn't take kindly to the reminder of the danger she'd been in, regardless of the outcome.

"I know that there will be things that happen outside of our control," her mother said. "Tate didn't plan to get herself stranded so far from home, but she was able to rely on the skills we taught her to survive. I want you to be able to do the same, and that includes having the ability to wield weapons effectively to defend yourself and others."

Sophia huffed again. In her mind, there was more than one way to defend against threats. Weapons were the most archaic way and of no interest to her. She felt that she could solve any number of issues through the equipment in her lab much better than could be resolved on a battlefield.

In point of fact, she was working on developing a serum to combat the effects of Nyx's toxin, a serum that could be administered to anyone who would be around the kragen on a regular basis. Now that Nyx was a seemingly permanent resident in the area, Sophia worried about one of her younger siblings or cousins—all of whom loved to play with the large creature—accidentally coming into contact with her paralyzing toxin.

Unfortunately, she recently realized that she wasn't progressing much with her efforts. She decided that she needed more information from Nyx's Estilorian friend, Zachariah. The enigmatic Mercesti male had developed an antitoxin that could be administered after the toxin had been introduced. Sophia hoped to extend his efforts to develop something more proactive. In effect, a vaccine.

"I'll never get a moment's rest if I don't think you can protect yourself if anything ever happens to you," her mom said.

Guilt rushed through Sophia at the words. She could only imagine how much stress she had put her parents through during her absence while rescuing Tate. Hanging her head, she gave her mom an apologetic look.

Her mother shook her head in response. "Just don't forget again, okay?"

Sophia nodded, causing her mother's hand to lift up and down.

"Now, since it's surprisingly warm today considering autumn has arrived, those of your cousins who *did* participate in today's training are going to head over to the waterfall for a swim. Why don't you go get changed and join them? It's probably the last swim you'll have until late spring."

The idea of a swim with her family sounded enjoyable, and it might give her a chance to chat with Zachariah about the antitoxin. She nodded again.

Her mother got awkwardly to her feet and winced as she stretched, rubbing her belly with one hand as she pressed against her lower back with the other. "Phew. I'm ready for this baby to arrive. My back is killing me."

Sophia debated shifting back so she could help her mother, even though she'd be naked when she did. Then her mom smiled and caught her gaze.

"I'll be fine, sweetie. You can wait to shift until you get to your room. Besides, Quincy is still watching."

Despite her concerns about her mother, that gentle reminder was enough to have Sophia dashing in her panther form into the house. Being seen naked by Quincy was the very last thing she needed.

Quincy started down the hill as soon as Sophia loped away. He had seen Olivia's grimace when she stood up after speaking with her daughter. As both a friend and the Estilorian who served as the obstetrician for Olivia and her sisters, Amber and Skye, he was concerned by her obvious discomfort.

"Do you need any assistance, Olivia?" he asked.

He stopped a couple of feet from her, studying her for physiological indicators of how she felt. He knew that these last days before the projected due date were particularly wearying on the expectant mother. Her energy and abilities weakened as she prepared for the birth. It was one of the reasons that Olivia and her sisters had remained behind when their firstborn children recently ventured away from the protected homeland.

Her pupils and breathing were normal now, he was pleased to note.

"I sure do," she answered with a grin. "Can you get Sophia to quit skipping out on her training sessions?"

His lips twitched. "Are you sure you don't have something less challenging for me? Maybe a previously unknown pain, or a dire threat to your person I could possibly avert?"

"I can hear you," Sophia called out.

The irritation in her voice had Quincy grimacing. "Sorry," he said loudly toward the open door of the house. Then, more quietly, he said, "Oops."

Olivia smiled and waved it off. "Sophia deserves the knock. She's terrible about participating in the training sessions and she knows it." Her voice rose in volume when she added, "I'll never let her leave home again if she doesn't start taking this more seriously."

"Yeah, yeah…I get it," Sophia replied in a grumble.

Quincy shook his head. "Well, let me know if you experience any signs of the baby's impending arrival, okay? If you'd be more comfortable with me sticking around here instead of joining the others at the waterfall, I'd be happy to."

"You're very sweet, Quincy. Thanks." She once again ran a hand over her belly. "But I think we're still okay for now."

"All right. Then I'll go wait for Sophia and the others near the training paddock. You know how to find me if you need me."

"Absolutely." Olivia smiled and turned to walk back into the house. "And if you happen to give Sophia another lecture on the importance of learning to defend herself in hopes it might penetrate her hard head, I wouldn't mind a bit."

"Sure thing," he said.

As he walked toward the training paddock, he considered Olivia's concern for Sophia's well-being. It very closely mirrored his own. He clearly remembered the challenges he and Sophia faced together in their pursuit of Tate all those weeks ago. Sophia had nearly been killed. The fear and anguish he'd experienced while treating her injuries surely reflected what Olivia would have felt in his place.

Why wouldn't it? he mused now. After all, they both loved her.

He supposed the biggest difference was that Sophia didn't have any idea how he felt about her. And he had yet to figure out how to change that.

Chapter 2

WHEN QUINCY REACHED THE TRAINING PADDOCK LOCATED GEOgraphically central to the homes occupied by Olivia, Amber, Skye and their families, he spotted Zachariah. The large Mercesti male was alone, leaning against one of the wooden fence posts surrounding the paddock. Dressed in his usual ensemble of a black tank, black pants and black boots, he looked like a perfectly-honed human military soldier. Of course, Quincy knew after spending a great deal of time among humans that Zachariah's wild-looking blond hair would never make the military cut. He stood with his arms crossed over his chest, his sharp red eyes not missing a thing.

When Quincy came to a stop and said, "Good afternoon," Zachariah nodded in return. It was as cordial a greeting as the unemotional and ornery Mercesti ever issued.

It was hard to know how to relate to Zachariah. Once the Gloresti second commander, he had been mentally assaulted and forced to kill the Gloresti he supervised, causing him to convert to a Mercesti. The experience sent him into seclusion for more than fifty years. Only when he encountered Tate and got involved in saving her life almost two months ago did he decide to rejoin Estilorian society.

Despite the fact that Zachariah had paired with Tate as her protector in a Gloresti-Corgloresti style pairing, he wasn't going out of his way to integrate himself into the family dynamics that existed before his arrival. In fact, he did very little at all to make others comfortable.

Still, Quincy knew that Zachariah was dedicated to Tate's safety. If nothing else, in light of his own feelings for Sophia, this gave Quincy a sort of affinity with him.

Even as that thought entered his mind, Quincy spotted Tate emerging from her family's home. She was hard to miss with her mass of colorful curls. They spiraled in shades of brown, light blue, deep blue-green and glittering dark blue all the way to the middle of her back. She currently wore it down since they were going swimming, rather than in its usual high ponytail bedecked with colorful beads and feathers.

Unlike Sophia's graceful stride, Tate bounced when she walked. She also nearly always wore a smile, and her dimple peeked at them now as she neared. Her enthusiasm and positive energy were contagious. Quincy grinned back at her.

"Hiya, Quincy," she said cheerfully. "Coming swimming with us?"

"What the bloody hell are you wearing?"

The question came from Zachariah. Quincy realized the Mercesti had moved away from the fence post and uncrossed his arms. He glowered at Tate, not an unusual expression for him.

"A bathing suit," she said, glancing down at herself and shrugging as if she didn't understand the question. "And sandals."

Zachariah strode over to her and grabbed the towel she wore over one shoulder. Tate's swimsuit consisted of a green halter-style top that stopped a few inches beneath her breasts and a pair of striped, low-waisted boy shorts. When Zachariah paused for a moment after removing the towel and gave Tate's curvy, well-toned form a longer study than was proper, Quincy almost laughed. The other male was still unused to the human wardrobe choices often worn by the Kynzesti and their half-human mothers.

The sound of voices turned his attention as others emerged from the nearby homes and headed toward the paddock. Quincy spotted Tate's twin brother, Tiege, and the Lekwuesti, Ariana, cutting across the flower garden beside the twins' home. From the other direction came *archigos* Ini-herit, who was staying with *archigos* Gabriel's family for a while. His presence right now surprised Quincy. The emotionless Corgloresti elder wasn't normally one who engaged in something like swimming for entertainment.

When Quincy heard Clara Kate's voice coming from the direction of Sophia's home and watched the two cousins walk together out of the forest, he suddenly understood.

No one knew exactly what occurred when Gabriel's firstborn daughter transitioned to the human plane a few months ago and spent time with

Ini-herit while he was in his human form. But it was clear there had been more to their relationship than the Corgloresti elder now remembered. The fact that Ini-herit hadn't retained any of his human memories had definitely affected Clara Kate's behavior since their return.

Now, Quincy's class elder watched C.K. as if trying to analyze her. Quincy knew that Ini-herit's lack of emotion was particularly ingrained due to his millennia of existence. Yet the elder seemed to be trying to move beyond it.

"You will not be going anywhere in this—outfit," Zachariah said, once again drawing Quincy's attention.

The Mercesti whipped the towel around Tate, wrapping her upper body in the cloth. Then he put a hand on her shoulder and began ushering her bodily toward her home.

"I'm going swimming, Sparky," Tate argued, trying to twist away from his grip. "We wear bathing suits to swim."

"You are practically naked. You should not be walking around others like this."

Tate rolled her eyes. "Since when have Estilorians ever given much concern to modesty? By all that's holy—this is my *family* you're talking about here. Well…and Quincy. But he's practically family, and he's seen me naked lots of times."

Quincy's eyebrows shot up. When Zachariah flashed a lethal glare at him, he cleared his throat and held his hands up in the universal sign of peace. "I'm their physician," he explained.

Turning his gaze back to Tate, Zachariah shook his head. "The others are all wearing more fabric than this," he ground out, striding toward the house with Tate's arm in his grasp.

Their argumentative words were cut off when Zachariah opened the door to her home, thrust her inside and then followed her in, closing the door behind them. Quincy could only imagine the words they exchanged. As he considered Tate a close friend and loved her dearly, he inwardly winced over her position.

"I don't know why Tate puts up with him," Ariana said. "She's a fully grown female. She can wear whatever she wants."

Quincy refrained from comment. Tiege reached out and rubbed her shoulder, as did Sophia. Ariana had suffered a great deal at the hands of the Mercesti class a couple of months ago. She was still recovering. Zachariah hadn't been one of those who abused her, but Ariana wasn't yet at a place where she could separate him from his class. She gave him a wide berth and viewed him in a notably harsh light.

"I just hope they finish this particular argument soon," Sophia said, adjusting her towel so it rested more firmly on her shoulder.

Quincy took care not to stare at her too long, though it was a hard thing. She wore a blue one-piece swimsuit that flattered her petite and feminine form and highlighted her deep blue-green eyes. Her long, straight blonde hair was unbound, softening her appearance to a point that made his chest ache.

"Me, too," Clara Kate said. "I'm ready to swim."

She avoided standing near Ini-herit, Quincy noticed, and she had yet to meet the elder's gaze. It was very unlike her usual forthright and confident demeanor, which concerned Quincy.

"Here they come," Tiege observed.

Everyone watched as Tate walked out of the castle first, followed by Zachariah. She now wore some kind of robe that ended mid-calf. Quincy choked back a laugh when Tate caught his gaze and rolled her eyes again. Still, her smile was wide and he knew she didn't really mind the wardrobe update.

A few more Kynzesti who were old enough to do so also made their way to the paddock, and then they all headed into the forest. Quincy walked a few feet behind Sophia, not wanting her to figure out that the only reason he was going was to keep an eye on her. The waterfall and spring were within the protected area of the homeland, but after what had happened to Tate, he didn't want to take any chances of Sophia coming to harm.

As if she read his thoughts, Sophia glanced over her shoulder. The sunlight glimmered on the deep blue-green butterfly-wing markings around her enchanting eyes. His heart rate sped up as he tried to think of something to say when she looked at him. Nothing remotely appropriate came to mind. Panic started to set in.

Then, much to his surprise, her gaze latched onto Zachariah.

He watched with further bafflement as she slowed her pace to walk beside the Mercesti. Zachariah's expression didn't change when he glanced down at Sophia, whose head didn't even reach his shoulders. He did lift a questioning eyebrow, though.

"I wanted to chat with you about the antitoxin you created using your blood," she said. "I've been concerned about the possibility that Nyx could poison one of us—accidentally," she tacked on when his eyes narrowed. "What if we create a form of vaccine so that we could all become immune? That way, there won't be that risk."

Quincy blinked. There was a time when Sophia would have come to him regarding one of her experiments. They had spent hours together in her laboratory or in his medical lab. Of course, it had been a number of years since the last time he felt that he had enough self-control to be alone with her for very long.

Zachariah was quiet for a moment, his gaze considering. "With the right equipment," he said at last, "it could probably be done."

Sophia smiled. The sight of it had Quincy's gut clenching. She used to smile at him that way.

"Great," she said. "Would you be willing to work with me on it? I'll need to retrace what you did and see how we can adapt it to be effective on full Estilorians and those of us who are mixed with human DNA."

"Ooo...sounds fun!" Tate said. "I love watching Soph in action during her experiments." She gave her cousin a wink.

Zachariah shrugged. "I can work with you on it."

Quincy waited for Sophia to turn to him, figuring she would surely ask him for his assistance, too. After all, no one knew the properties of human, Estilorian and combined DNA structures like he did.

But she didn't. She thanked Zachariah and then moved up to continue her conversation with Clara Kate. She never even looked at Quincy, a fact that brutally pained him.

He couldn't help but feel in that moment that her heart would be forever beyond his reach.

Chapter 3

WHY DIDN'T QUINCY OFFER TO HELP?

That thought ran through Sophia's mind as they walked back home from the waterfall. She had been thinking about it since she talked with Zachariah about the vaccine. There was no doubt that she'd need Quincy's assistance, as well. She didn't have nearly the knowledge he did when it came to anatomy and genetics.

Yet he hadn't said a word. She'd lingered like a dolt next to Zachariah, thinking Quincy would ask if she'd like his help. She had even mentally rehearsed a blasé response that she thought made her sound less than pathetic when she accepted his help.

All for nothing.

It just reiterated to her how much they had grown apart over the years. Ever since she had assumed her fully grown form at the age of thirteen, Quincy had distanced himself from her. Sophia reasoned that it was because she was so odd-looking compared to the rest of the Kynzesti. Unlike her kin, she was rather small and fair in coloring. While she hadn't ever thought of Quincy as superficial, his reaction when he returned from a transition to the human plane and saw her in her mature form for the first time definitely spoke volumes. He had barely been able to look at her. Things between them hadn't been the same since.

She tried to convince herself she didn't care. Just because she had begun to think he might be getting past his disgust over her appearance didn't mean she was right. Sure, he gave her that quick kiss a few weeks ago, but he was probably just trying to distract her.

"What are the elders doing here?" Ariana asked in a nervous voice as they reached the training paddock.

Glancing around and blinking to clear her thoughts, Sophia spotted all of the class elders—aside from Ini-herit—walking toward her Uncle Gabriel and Aunt Amber's home. That was quite odd.

She couldn't help but remember the last time the elders visited. Then, it had been to deliver the news about members of the Mercesti class prowling the mainland in search of what they would later discover was the Elder Scroll. It had also resulted in Tate sneaking away and getting snagged by Nyx.

Ini-herit's silver eyes flashed, indicating he had received a thought from his fellow elders. "They have something important to discuss," he said. He looked at Clara Kate and added, "They have asked you to come."

"Okay," she replied with a nod.

It must be difficult for her cousin to be around Ini-herit, Sophia thought, in light of what obviously sat unresolved between them. Yet, true to C.K.'s personality, she pushed aside her own feelings to focus on the bigger picture.

"I'm sure it's just a check-in," Tiege said. He watched Ariana with concern.

Sophia realized that Ariana, someone she had come to consider a good friend over the past six weeks, was worried that the elders would demand that she take them to recover the remaining two pieces of the Elder Scroll. One of the rare full Estilorians with a second power, Ariana could find anything. Because of this, she was the only Estilorian on the plane who could identify the location of the Elder Scroll pieces. Such an endeavor would require her leaving the area of protection, something Sophia knew her friend was not prepared to do.

"They wish to speak with all of you, as well," Ini-herit said, his gaze sweeping over Ariana, Tiege, Tate, Zachariah, Quincy and Sophia.

Sophia's eyes widened. She exchanged glances with her cousins, taking care to avoid Quincy's gaze. They all started toward Uncle Gabriel and Aunt Amber's home while their younger cousins and siblings broke away from their group to return home.

Why would they possibly need me? Sophia wondered as they walked. She could understand Clara Kate being invited to the table as the eldest Kynzesti. And if the elders had, indeed, come to discuss retrieving the two remaining pieces of the Elder Scroll, it also made sense that they wanted Ariana there.

The rest of them, however, didn't seem necessary for such a meeting.

Aunt Amber's paired Lekwuesti, Blue, stood inside the front door of the castle where her aunt and uncle made their home. Her aunts, as well as her mother, had invited their paired Lekwuesti to come to the mainland to live with them in their homes if they wanted to, rather than remain at Central. Each of the Lekwuesti had gratefully agreed to do so.

"Please feel free to change before meeting with everyone on the back terrace," Blue said as they entered. "I placed dry clothing for each of you in the guest rooms."

"Thanks, Blue," Tate said with a wink. "I hope you picked something appropriate for me."

The large Lekwuesti grinned. "I know you, don't I?" Then his smile faded. "I suspect they'd like y'all out there sooner than later, so go on up now."

Sophia trailed after Tate and Clara Kate to the rooms upstairs. C.K. walked with purposeful strides to her bedroom while Tate and Sophia went to the room beside hers. They shared it whenever they stayed the night.

"What do you suppose this is all about?" Tate asked as she closed the door and began disrobing.

"I have no idea," Sophia said. She walked over to the bed she usually used and found a russet-colored sundress waiting for her, complete with undergarments. "I can't imagine why they'd need to meet with all of us."

"It's weird. I'm kind of nervous, actually."

Sophia nodded in agreement. Tate hung her damp swimsuit over the footboard of her bed and used her towel to finish drying off. Sophia did the same. She didn't have any qualms about her nakedness around her cousin, though she couldn't deny the flash of envy she experienced over her larger cousin's much curvier build...especially when she reached for her own two-cup-sizes-smaller bra.

Sighing, she finished dressing and joined Tate in exiting the room. Her cousin had also been provided a sundress, Sophia realized. Unlike hers, however, Tate's shimmering, full-skirted sundress stopped above her knees, revealing the amazing legs she had inherited from her mother.

When they stepped out into the hallway, Sophia saw Zachariah glance over from where he leaned against the wall. He focused on Tate's legs. His gaze lingered for a long moment and then moved up...slowly. His expression was hard to read, but Sophia thought he looked irritated.

"The Lekwuesti picked that for you to wear?" he asked.

"Yes," Tate said, sticking out one of her legs and displaying the red strappy sandal that coordinated perfectly with the dress. "Do you like it?"

"I do not," he said in a tight voice. "We need to discuss your wardrobe choices."

"Again? Look, Sparky, we need to go and meet with the elders—"

He moved away from the wall and took Tate's elbow. "They can wait a minute longer."

They disappeared into the available bedroom just as Clara Kate stepped out of hers. Her navy blue sundress was tailored more like Sophia's. The thin straps displayed her cousin's impeccably toned shoulders and biceps in a very flattering way. Her dark brown hair framed her face and fell around her shoulders in such beautiful, natural waves that they could have been painted with a brush. Sophia smoothed her stick-straight hair and tried to stop comparing herself to every other female around her, but it was surprisingly difficult.

And when Quincy rounded the corner and caught her eye, then looked away after only a brief glance, she knew why.

"Where are Tate and Zachariah?" he asked. "Tiege and Ariana are already downstairs."

"They're—" C.K. began.

"Here," Zachariah interrupted, opening the bedroom door. He strode out, followed by Tate. His face was an expressionless mask.

Sophia fell into step beside Tate as the males and Clara Kate took the lead. Her younger cousin grinned like a simpleton. She attempted to tuck some of her seriously out-of-control curls behind her ear without much success. If possible, her hair seemed even more mussed than it had a few minutes ago.

"Why do you endure Zachariah's lectures about your wardrobe?" Sophia asked her in a low voice, no longer able to stop herself. "Any time you wear something he finds objectionable, he gets all over you about it."

"Oh, yes," she agreed. "He sure does."

Even more perplexed, Sophia pressed, "Why don't you tell him to leave you alone?" That was what Tate normally told anyone who criticized her unique fashion sense.

"Why would I want to do that?" Tate asked.

Before Sophia could pursue the baffling conversation, they reached the outdoor terrace. The double wood-and-glass doors leading out to the terrace both stood open, so they walked out and headed toward the seats around the veranda. The seating was arranged in a circular formation to promote conversation. Tables between some of the chairs contained glasses of colorful juice.

As the sun lowered and a breeze kicked up off the neighboring sea, the temperature cooled considerably. Fortunately, the Lekwuesti elder, *archigos* Sebastian, had the ability to generate a form of energy to surround the terrace that kept it from getting too cold.

"That will be all, Blue, thank you," Sebastian said as they took their seats.

Sophia watched Blue bow and close the doors as he stepped out. She selected a chair beside her father, who was seated beside her mother. It was a large, cushioned seat, so she tucked her legs up beneath her. Quincy sat beside her. She hated that her pulse thrummed over his nearness, especially when her attention should have been on more important things.

"How are you feeling, Olivia?" he asked, leaning forward to see around Sophia.

Of course he sat where he did so he could keep a close eye on her mother, Sophia thought, grinding her back teeth in frustration.

"Like a beached whale, quite frankly," her mother replied. Her father reached over and took her hand, giving it a squeeze.

Quincy smiled, the expression causing Sophia's heart to race yet again. She cursed herself and deliberately ignored him. Looking around, she realized the only one who hadn't taken a seat was Zachariah. He stood a couple of feet behind Tate's seat, leaning against the railing encircling the terrace. No one told him to sit, knowing he wouldn't.

At last, Jabari spoke. "We have some news that we felt best to impart upon all of you at once," the Elphresti elder said. "In light of what occurred a few weeks ago, it seemed only right to include all of you in this and all future discussions related to the Elder Scroll."

Sophia sat straighter. So this *was* about the Elder Scroll. She noticed Ariana stiffen. Tiege started to reach for her, then stopped himself, appearing uncertain.

This time, it was the Waresti elder, *archigos* Uriel, who spoke. "We have discovered that the Mercesti leader, Kanika, is alive."

Silence followed the announcement. Sophia felt her lips part over the unexpected news. They had been told that Kanika died at the hands of Eirik and Deimos, two of the Mercesti males who had captured Ariana and Tate. She survived the attack?

"That can't be."

Everyone looked at Ariana. Her words barely qualified as a whisper, but they all heard her. Sophia noticed Quincy tense as he gave Ariana a careful study. When Sophia also looked at her friend, she realized how pale she had become. Her lavender eyes moved across the terrace but didn't seem to focus on anyone or anything. Her breathing was erratic. The pulse in her neck indicated an accelerated heart rate.

Quincy leaned forward in his chair. Sophia's concern mounted over his expression. "Ariana—" he began.

"It can't be!" Ariana interrupted in a near-scream. "I've seen what Deimos can do. I've *felt* what he can do. You don't know. None of you know!"

She surged to her feet. Quincy hurriedly stood up, as well. Sophia soon realized why.

He was just in time to keep Ariana from hitting the ground in a dead faint.

Chapter 4

"YOU HAVE KEPT ME WAITING LONG ENOUGH, METIS," EIRIK GROWLED.

"I do understand your annoyance, Eirik, but the delay was unavoidable. You knew this plan would involve some patience on your part. It is not exactly straightforward."

Eirik watched the Estilorian he knew as Metis walk past him with a hand extended. She reached for the unpredictable and savage Mercesti male, Deimos, who had traveled with Eirik in his recent search for the Elder Scroll. Deimos flashed sharp teeth as Metis ran her hand over his long, dark hair, but he wasn't threatening her. In fact, his expression was as close to adoration as Eirik had ever seen.

He didn't know much about their odd relationship. He had stumbled across the pair when he was hunting the Mercesti leader, Kanika, with the intent of killing her and taking her place. Their fates had been intertwined ever since.

"I am sorry to leave you out here, my sweet Deimos," she murmured. "I promise I will send you a special treat to feast on this evening."

"Never mind him," Eirik snapped. He might be forced to endure the wild male's presence as he pursued his goal of assuming the powers of an elder, but he didn't have to like it. "I want to know your plan to draw out Ariana and the Kynzesti female who can dissolve illusions."

The two females were the essential keys to finding what remained of the Elder Scroll. If it hadn't been for the two of them, Eirik wouldn't even now possess the first scroll piece. Metis knew this and had implemented a plan to get the females outside of the area of enchantment that currently protected them. Unfortunately, she had yet to reveal the specifics of her plan to him.

"Tate," she said.

"What?"

"The Kynzesti female you seek. Her name is Tate."

He didn't ask how she knew. She currently had access to far more information than he could ever hope to gain. Knowing this made him want to slay her with his cursed krises right where she stood. Instead, he clenched his fists and nodded.

"Good to know," he managed to say past his clenched jaw. "Your plan?"

"Is already in action," she said. "You will have to hold onto your patience for a while longer. As I collect more information, I will share it with you." She gathered her cloak more closely to her body. "Now, if you will excuse me, I must return before those with me become suspicious. They believe I am resting."

Fury lashed through him when he realized she didn't intend to tell him anything new. "I do not appreciate being left out here awaiting your whim to visit with updates."

"Well, we both know there is no avoiding that, now, is there?" she said with a taunting lift of her chin.

He reached out and grabbed her around her slender throat, ignoring the animalistic response it provoked from Deimos. He met her red gaze with his own, making sure she read him clearly.

"You may be in a position of leverage right now," he said, squeezing to the point she gasped for breath. "But never doubt what will happen should you cross me.

"Bring the females to me."

Quincy tried not to look as surprised as he felt when Sophia entered the bedroom he was using to treat Ariana. His surprise intensified when he realized she was alone.

The bedroom, which seemed spacious a moment ago, suddenly felt much too small. As Sophia stepped in and drifted closer to the bed, her beautiful eyes focused on Ariana. They were filled with concern. Her scent, which always reminded him of a fragrant, moonlit night, floated up to him. He felt his thoughts abandoning him.

Well, except the one where he wanted to grab her and kiss the frown from her spectacular mouth.

"She just had quite the shock," she said softly, reaching down and picking up Ariana's hand. "The poor thing. She's so cold."

He knew that she and Ariana had become friends over the past few weeks. The Lekwuesti female had been rather distant with others following her ordeal, but she had opened up with Sophia. Quincy figured that she perceived Sophia to be the least intimidating of everyone due to her petite size and overall unruffled demeanor. The irony of that misconception certainly wasn't lost to him.

Words flew through his head as he tried to think of a response that didn't involve him making a fool of himself by rambling on about his feelings for her. He was saved when Ariana's eyelids fluttered open.

"What happened?" she mumbled, trying to sit up.

"You fainted," Quincy responded.

He didn't mention that he had intentionally removed her from the terrace and let her awaken on her own without healing. He hadn't wanted her to be overwhelmed by the presence of the others. She'd likely be embarrassed enough about her faint as it was.

Moving beside Sophia, he checked Ariana's pulse. He tried to ignore the softness of Sophia's hair brushing against his bicep.

"I don't think you're eating enough or getting enough rest," he said. "That combined with the news of Kanika's survival sent you right into a form of shock."

Swallowing audibly, she caught Sophia's gaze. "They're going to want me to find the other two scroll pieces now, aren't they?"

"Yes," Sophia said. "You're my friend, Ariana…you know that. I have to be honest with you. After you fainted, they asked me to speak with you about the scroll."

Quincy's eyebrows rose. This made a lot of sense. Trying not to be too obvious, he stepped away from the bed to give the females the chance to talk. Hopefully the one-on-one interaction would be more successful in getting through to the Lekwuesti.

"I knew it," Ariana said. Her eyes filled with tears. "Sophia, I can't."

Sophia gave Ariana's hand a fortifying squeeze. "I know you're frightened. It sounds as though whatever awful experience Kanika went through left her with blank spots in her memory. I understand how traumatic it must have been for you, too. But, Ariana, I also know how strong you are."

Quincy's lips curved. Sophia was a remarkably smart being. She knew what angle to take.

"I know more than most that physical strength isn't everything," she continued. "And I know you're stronger than Eirik and Deimos combined." When Ariana wiped her tears and shook her head, Sophia added, "The plan is that you never encounter them again, anyway. You won't be alone on the trip for the scroll pieces. *Archigos* Uriel intends to escort you personally, along with as many Waresti as he can spare. They won't let any harm come to you."

Tears continued to leak from Ariana's eyes as she slowly sat up. Sophia moved to sit beside her on the bed.

"If you don't go," Sophia said gently, "the elders will have to resort to the intrusive mining of *archigos* Ini-herit and Uncle Gabriel's minds in hopes they can pull out the memories of the locations of the other scroll pieces."

"Why can't they just do that?" Ariana asked, wiping again at her cheeks. "Retrieving memories without the risk of confronting Eirik makes more sense."

Sophia looked at Quincy. Although his breath seized momentarily over having her direct attention focused on him, he understood.

Clearing his throat, he answered, "The amount of power required to retrieve these single memories could cause permanent damage to *archigos* Ini-herit and *archigos* Gabriel. It's highly likely that their cognitive functioning will be affected in some way. There's also a possibility that they'll be left with no memories at all."

Ariana blinked at that. "Oh," she said in a small voice. She looked at Sophia through the fall of her black hair. "You must think me the lowliest of cowards."

"Of course I don't," Sophia chided her. "As you said, none of us knows what you went through. I understand why you aren't eager to venture back out."

"You may say you don't think I'm a coward," Ariana said, her words hitching on a sob. "But the fact is, I am. Sophia…I can't face Eirik and Deimos again."

It felt like a long walk back out to the terrace. Sophia was highly conscious of Quincy walking quietly beside her. Ariana had asked them for some time alone to collect her thoughts and neither of them wanted to deny her that.

Sophia was surprised that Quincy didn't try to make some excuse as to why he couldn't walk with her. She thought of how he deliberately stepped away from her when they stood so close at Ariana's bedside. Although he tried to be discreet, she knew he hadn't wanted to be near her any longer than necessary. She imagined he saw Ariana's return to consciousness as a welcome reprieve from having to converse with her, a thought that now had her throat and eyes burning.

You will not *cry*, she told herself fiercely. *Suck it up.*

"It was good of you to come and talk to Ariana," he said after a moment.

She thought his voice sounded strained, as though he forced himself to say the words. She wanted to snap a response back at him, but was suddenly weary. Her temper drained away. Shrugging as they approached the terrace doors, she replied, "It didn't do any good. But thanks."

All eyes turned to them as they stepped outside. Sophia tried not to flinch over the expressions of hope on her Aunt Amber and Clara Kate's faces. Swallowing hard, she decided to get right to the point.

"She's not ready yet."

There was a collective sound, almost like a sigh, as everyone processed the announcement. Sophia took her seat, appreciating the pat of understanding that her dad gave her shoulder when she did. She watched all of the elders exchange glances and figured they were also exchanging thoughts.

In the end, there were nods from each of them. Aunt Amber frowned. Her worried expression made Sophia feel like a failure for not having convinced Ariana to try.

"Then we face a difficult decision," Jabari said in a grave voice. "Kanika was tortured by Eirik for her knowledge of the scroll. Any number of other beings could be at risk of the same treatment. Although the Waresti are hunting Eirik and his followers, we must take immediate action to ensure those scroll pieces are not found by anyone else. We must take Eirik's unholy motivation away from him. In short, we have no choice but to proceed with the memory extraction...and pray that it is successful."

Chapter 5

"I DON'T UNDERSTAND," TATE SAID, DRAWING QUINCY'S ATTENTION. SHE twirled a sparkling, dark blue curl around one finger as she thought about Jabari's announcement. "Even if Eirik gets the three scroll pieces, he won't be able to make it work, right?"

"That is correct," Jabari replied. "But he doesn't know that. I suspect that even if he was told that, he would choose not to believe it."

Uriel added, "Eirik is dangerous because he has a vision of what this scroll will do, and he will never let go of that vision, regardless of how warped and incorrect it might be. Any being who stands in the way of that vision risks a fate like Kanika's. Or worse."

"Is there some way to deactivate the scroll's power?" Clara Kate asked. "I know you mentioned that it was created by all nine of the original elders, and because Volarius—one of those elders—is now dead, it can't be destroyed. But what if you combined your powers to try and reverse or counteract the scroll's properties?"

"I wish that was possible," Jabari said solemnly. "Without Volarius, there is no altering the scroll's inherent properties."

They all considered this in the ensuing silence. Quincy snuck a glance at Sophia. She was deep in thought, pulling at her lower lip with her fingers, as was her habit. Only when he found himself envisioning capturing that lip gently between his teeth did he turn his gaze from her. He couldn't help but wish that he could look at her for more than a few seconds before such thoughts entered his mind—especially at such inappropriate times—but that hadn't been the case for a long time now.

"What's the real harm in letting Eirik find all three scroll pieces?" Tate asked. Quincy belatedly realized that she had moved so that she sat beside her twin on a divan. He guessed she had seen Tiege's distress over Ariana's faint and sought to comfort him. "You're saying that even if he gets all of the pieces, he won't be able to use them."

"A sound question," the Orculesti elder, *archigos* Malukali, responded. "It is correct that Eirik can't use the power of the scroll on his own. It wasn't designed that way. Because the idea behind the Elder Scroll was to create a ninth elder in the event one of us was lost, the scroll's power is only activated by the coming together of eight specific minds and souls."

The elder's words touched on a memory at the far edges of Quincy's mind. Something about the coming together of eight different paths...

"Eight? So, all of the remaining elders?" Tiege asked.

"No," Malukali replied. "We didn't want the activation of this powerful artifact to come down to something as obvious as our joined abilities. The new elder was meant to work for his or her role. Part of the scroll's success depends upon the challenge that is overcome to claim it."

"Who are the eight, then?" Sophia wondered.

Knorbis answered, "There were no specific beings in mind when we created the scroll. We focused on the traits of the individuals. Those traits would have to be joined to imbue the new elder with his or her abilities. The necessary traits relate to each Estilorian class: strength, loyalty, intuition, creativity, compassion, ingenuity, hospitality, leadership and faith."

Again, Quincy felt that nudge. *The aligning of eight.* What was it that stuck in his mind about that number?

"Well, if those eight beings don't ever come together, the scroll will never be a danger, right?" Tate surmised.

"I think it's safe to assume that Eirik will never stop searching until he finds the eight beings needed to harness the scroll's power once he has it reassembled," Gabriel said. "And if we stop Eirik, there's always the risk that someone else will step in where he leaves off. We need to recover the scroll ourselves to avoid anyone else trying to use it."

"Is there a way that you could perform the ritual without the physical scroll?" Sophia asked. Quincy was glad for the excuse to look at her again, even though he knew that made him exceedingly pathetic. "If you know someone who would make a great elder, couldn't you just perform the ritual and void the scroll's usefulness or something?"

"I'm afraid not," Jabari said. "The physical scroll is what contains the power. And we no longer recall the words penned on it. When we initiated the protocol that erased our knowledge of the locations of the scroll pieces, we made sure to erase the ritual words, as well."

"Of course you did," Amber said dryly.

"It was deemed safer for all of us," Malukali explained. "No one could possibly pull the locations of the scroll pieces or the ritual words from our minds if they weren't there to find."

Quincy couldn't deny there was a certain logic to that. Of course, all of their precautions hadn't prevented Eirik from learning of the scroll's existence, and he seemed to be doing quite well at circumventing their efforts to keep the locations of the scroll pieces a secret.

"Despite our precautions," Knorbis said, "when Malukali and I performed a scan of Gabriel's suppressed memories, we were able to glean a portion of the words on the scroll piece that he hid. The words tie directly into the joining of the eight."

Malukali nodded and recited, "*To unfurl the force herein, Eight journeys must now begin; Once separate and undefined, different paths somehow align.*"

The blood drained from Quincy's face as the words echoed in his mind. He was momentarily pulled back to a memory he had long ago buried...the memory of an adventure that had ultimately led to his best friend's death.

"We're hopeful that since we were able to recover this much the first time, we can access the memory of the piece's location without unduly impacting Gabriel's mind," Knorbis said.

Although he wasn't sure how, Quincy managed to say, "That won't be necessary."

Everyone turned to look at him. He saw a few expressions of concern and imagined he didn't look much better than Ariana had before she fainted. He turned his gaze to the cliffs in the distance and took a deep breath to center himself.

Then he said, "I know where the scroll piece is hidden."

Sophia had never seen Quincy so visibly upset. His complexion was pale and his silver eyes couldn't seem to focus. She fought the urge to reach out and comfort him, knowing he wouldn't welcome it.

"How do you know where the scroll piece is hidden?" Ini-herit asked. As usual, the elder's tone was without inflection, but Sophia sensed his curiosity.

"I've seen it," Quincy said. He ran a hand down his face as though to compose himself. Still, he had to clear his throat before he continued, "It's in the ancient library."

"Do you mean the library where our dad found the scroll that he used to try and save our mom's life?" Aunt Skye asked, her light blue eyes wide.

"Yes, I—" Quincy stopped himself and clenched his jaw, looking toward the door leading back inside the castle. "I need a moment."

He got up and left without looking at anyone, closing the terrace doors behind him. Sophia's heart wrenched with realization.

"Quincy was with our dad in the library?" her mom asked, exchanging a look with her father.

"Yes," Knorbis said. "As you know, they were best friends. When Saraqael said he needed Quincy's help to save Kate, Quincy helped him. They went together in search of a possible cure for Kate's illness."

Sophia found herself unable to look away from the doors through which Quincy exited. She knew he had been friends with her grandfather. It only now occurred to her, though, that he rarely discussed their relationship. She was rather stunned by how much he was still affected by her grandfather's death after all this time.

"They had no way of knowing that the scroll Saraqael found would result in his death," Malukali said in quiet tones. "But Quincy still feels..."

Sophia closed her eyes when she fully understood the weight Quincy carried. She hadn't realized the depth of feeling he kept inside. He always acted so normally—interacted so typically with everyone—that she hadn't ever guessed there was so much more beneath the surface. What else was he keeping contained from everyone?

How much more did he feel that she had never bothered to try and discover?

"Well," Malukali finished, "I have spoken with Quincy at length about this, and I will talk to him again. But he has just given us an invaluable piece of information."

"Why didn't he just tell us about this in the first place?" Tiege asked. He sounded irritated. "He could have saved Ariana a lot of stress."

"He didn't realize what it was that he read all of those years ago,"

Malukali answered. "I could tell that Quincy's memory was prodded by the wording I recited."

Unfortunately, Sophia thought, that hadn't been the only memory prodded.

"Okay," Aunt Amber said. "So let's get someone to the library as soon as we can. Once we get that scroll piece, we don't have to worry about Eirik getting his hands on it. We'll have plenty of time to work on the last piece."

Sophia noticed that her usually unflappable aunt looked relieved, and realized that she was probably thrilled that they had bypassed the dangerous thought-mining her uncle would have had to undergo to locate the scroll piece. Her uncle noted her reaction, too. He reached over and took her hand. It made Sophia consider the fact that Quincy had no one to comfort him like that.

"We don't know where the library is," Uncle Gabriel said.

Aunt Amber frowned. "Huh?"

Looking around at all of them, he explained, "The library is protected by the same kind of enchantments that protect Central and our homes. Its location is contained on a map."

"Where's the map?" Clara Kate asked.

Archigos Zayna spoke up for the first time. "It was entrusted into the care of an Estilorian who has been removed from society for a number of centuries. His name is Hoygul. Hoygul the Scultresti."

Chapter 6

QUINCY WAS UNSURPRISED BY THE APPROACH OF MALUKALI AND Knorbis. The two elders with the strongest mental abilities were married and did nearly everything together. In truth, he envied their close relationship.

That didn't make him feel any more hospitable toward them at the moment.

"May we come in?" Malukali asked when he answered the door to his cottage.

"Of course," he replied automatically, stepping aside and allowing the couple to enter.

He had decided to retire to his cottage rather than return to the gathering at Gabriel's. It had just felt like too much to participate in the conversation. Knowing that Malukali could easily intercept his thoughts, he had conveyed what he remembered to her and asked her to make excuses for his failure to return.

She and Knorbis now moved inside, walking over to the sofa situated in the small gathering area just to the left of the entrance. An arched doorway at the rear of the gathering area led to his bedroom. The bulk of the cottage was comprised of Quincy's clinic, however. A door to the right of the front entry led to the clinic, as did a second door from outside. Because the cottage was located very near to the central training paddock, it received quite a few visitors, especially if Gabriel or Amber weren't around to heal injuries.

Quincy knew the polite thing to do would be to offer the elders something to eat or drink, but he didn't want to encourage an extended visitation. Instead, he took one of the two chairs adjacent to the couch.

"How can I help in the retrieval of the scroll piece?" he asked, deciding to get right to the point.

"You can't," Malukali replied. "You know very well that Saraqael's next grandchildren are due at any moment."

He flinched at the reference to his friend, but couldn't argue.

"You're needed here, Quincy. You are the most qualified Estilorian to deliver the Kynzesti."

Knorbis added, "Zayna knows the way to Hoygul's cottage. She just left with Uriel and a host of Waresti to get the map to the library. Then they'll retrieve the scroll piece and bring it back here."

Quincy frowned. "Here? Why would we endanger those who live here by bringing such a thing among them?"

"It will only be temporary," Malukali explained. "We need a heavily protected area to contain the scroll piece while we gather the others. Once the scroll is again assembled, we will determine what to do with it."

"I don't like it," Quincy said, but he knew there were few options. "That aside, does *archigos* Zayna think she'll be able to find the exact location of the scroll piece within the library? I found it completely by chance all those years ago, and I couldn't tell her where it is even if I tried."

"No," Knorbis agreed, "you couldn't. A being's memory of the library's location is erased once he leaves it. Similarly, the contents viewed there are usually erased. The fact that you retained this particular line in your memory, even though it was suppressed, is very curious."

"I'm not sure that particular enchantment works," Quincy argued. "Saraqael retained full knowledge of the scroll he read even after leaving the library."

"You reported seeing a flash of light as Saraqael read the scroll, correct?" Malukali asked.

"Yes."

"Was there a glow emitting from the scroll piece you read?"

He allowed himself to return to the memory, though it pained him. Eventually, he nodded.

The elders exchanged glances. Then they again looked at him. Malukali's dark green eyes were filled with compassion.

"Saraqael's fate was sealed when he read the scroll that ultimately resulted in Kate's pregnancy and the existence of their three daughters," she said.

Reaching out, she touched his hand. "Quincy, we believe that you retained the information contained on that piece of the Elder Scroll because your fate is in some way connected to it."

He wouldn't have been more stunned if Saraqael walked in the door right then and wished him good day. Blinking several times, he said, "You think I'm one of the eight?"

"We can't be sure," Knorbis said, his brow drawn in concern. "But we've discussed it, and this is really the only explanation that makes sense. The fact that you detected the scroll's energy when you read it and retained the words, well..."

In the silence that followed, Quincy looked from one elder to the next and tried to process this news. They were saying that he would somehow have to participate in the ritual that would allow a new elder to assume his or her powers. They were also saying that he had been as equally fated to visit that library as Saraqael had been.

"This is a lot to take in," he said at last, rubbing the bridge of his nose to fight off a burgeoning headache. "Is there some way to confirm this theory once the scroll piece is brought here?"

"Yes," Malukali said. "We will watch the scroll piece's reaction when you touch it. It will tell us what we need to know. And we believe that Hoygul's map will provide Zayna with the information she needs to recover the piece." She paused, then asked, "Will you allow me to use my abilities to ease your grief, Quincy?"

He considered it for a moment. The emotional oblivion she could provide would be welcome compared to the still-potent guilt and sorrow currently seated in the center of his chest.

"No, but thank you," he said eventually. "I'd really just like to be alone for a while."

The elders stood. "Very well," Malukali said. "I also wanted to let you know that Knorbis and I will be going to visit Kanika. We're hoping that we can do something to help ease her emotional trauma. While we're there, we'll make note of any lingering physical issues she may still have. May we consult with you about these when we return?"

"Of course," he said, walking them to the door and opening it. "I would be happy to help."

"Thank you." Malukali touched his arm as she walked past him and out into the night. "I'll be here for another hour or so if you change your mind."

"I appreciate it."

He ushered them out, then closed the door and rested his forehead against it. Not even ten seconds later, another knock sounded on the door. He felt the vibrations like shock waves through his already aching head, and jerked away from the wood with a vicious curse.

"Um…should I come back?" he heard from the other side of the door.

Sophia.

Even as his heartbeat accelerated at the sound of her voice, he wondered what cruel twist of fate would have her seeking him out right now when all he wanted was solitude.

Opening the door, he resigned himself to whatever destiny awaited him. "Sorry about the, uh, language," he managed to say in greeting.

She waved that away as she walked past him into the gathering area, lowering the hood of her cloak as she passed. The crisp nighttime air clung to her hair and clothing, adding to the mysterious scent that was distinctly her own. He breathed it in like a healing balm.

"It isn't as though I've never heard the words before," she said as she sat on the sofa. "You've heard Tiege and Joshua when they're training, haven't you?"

Despite himself, he smiled briefly. "I suppose you're right."

When he just stood in front of the closed door staring at her, she tilted her head in question. Abruptly regaining control of himself, he took the steps necessary to get to the chair placed furthest from her. In his current mental state, he didn't trust himself to get any closer.

Her eyes moved from him to the seat closer to her. She issued a small sigh before catching his gaze and saying, "I'm sorry that you had to revisit what was obviously a painful memory today, Quincy. I've never for a moment stopped to consider how my grandfather's death must have affected you."

He didn't know what to say. He certainly hadn't expected this when she knocked on his door.

"It's made me realize that I haven't been a very good friend," she continued. "We were so much closer when I was younger. When I assumed my fully mature form and we grew more…distant, it was easy for me to assume it was because of my appearance."

She no longer held his gaze, but looked at her hands folded in her lap. A pink blush colored her cheeks. He wondered with a great deal of embarrassment how long she had known that he found her the most beautiful being on either plane of existence and began to wish he hadn't opened the door to her knock. His headache resumed as his stress level rose.

"What I never considered," she said softly, "was that it was my personality, and not my appearance, that you suddenly found so unappealing."

Quincy felt like he had just been body-slammed into a rock wall.

"Today has made me realize how self-involved I've been," she added as he struggled to catch up with her ridiculous and incorrect deductions. "If I hadn't been so focused on adjusting to my adult form and accepting how different I am compared to the rest of my family, I might have had more perspective related to the change in our friendship."

She once again caught his gaze. "I'm sorry for judging you in such a harsh light, and for failing to uphold my half of our friendship. I should have made more of an effort to communicate with you when I sensed that things were changing between us. If I had, perhaps we could have gotten things back to the way they were. And I might better know how to offer you comfort at a time like this."

After wondering whether he had somehow managed to cross into yet another plane of existence, he blinked to clear his head.

"Sophia."

"Yes?"

"For someone so intelligent, you've never been so wrong."

She frowned. He could all but see her remarkable brain puzzling out his meaning. It suddenly occurred to him that his best friend had been willing to die for love, but he himself hadn't been willing to face Sophia's rejection or the possibility of casting out by her family because of his love for her.

Well, there was no time like the present to change that.

He stood up and moved closer to her. She also got to her feet, which he anticipated. Because she was so much smaller than most of those around her, she had never been comfortable having someone hovering over her. She took a step away from him when he advanced, inadvertently moving closer to his bedroom. He couldn't deny that the room's convenient proximity flashed through his mind.

"I can't really blame you for the conclusions you've drawn," he said.

His voice was lower than usual as he stepped closer to her. He watched her eyes go from narrow with concern to wide-eyed with confusion as she took another step away from him.

"After all," he continued with another step toward her, "you've been provided deliberately clouded concepts upon which you based your hypothesis."

Here, her pupils dilated. Her breathing quickened. She stopped retreating and instead gazed up at him with her lips slightly parted. Then he did something he never allowed himself to do: he focused on her mouth with every intent of kissing her until she knew unequivocally how he felt about her.

A knock on the door shattered the moment.

"Quincy?"

Tate's muffled question came from the other side of the door just as she opened it to let herself in, something she had always done. Quincy took a step away from Sophia, who moved just as quickly in the other direction. Then they both turned guilty gazes to Tate, who studied them with raised eyebrows as she breezed into the room, followed by Zachariah.

"Oh," she said. "What did I interrupt?"

"Nothing," Quincy and Sophia replied at the same time.

Tate's grin went wide as she easily read the lie in their words. "Hey, that's great," she said. "It's been a long time since I interrupted nothing."

Chapter 7

"NO," ZACHARIAH SAID. "YOU HAVE THE FORMULA COMPLETELY WRONG. We already went over this."

Sophia used a towel to wipe sweat from her face and neck as Zachariah scratched through the notes she had just made and began adding his own. Her flush was due more to embarrassment over failing to pay proper attention to him than it did the amount of heat in the room.

She hadn't slept much last night after leaving Quincy's cottage. Her mind had been filled with the memory of the intensity of his silver eyes as he leaned toward her. Had he been about to kiss her? Why would he do that when he didn't even like her?

But did he like her? Did he possibly—she was kidding herself for even dreaming it—even *more* than like her?

No, she had mostly convinced herself. She still remembered how adamantly he told Tate that he didn't think Sophia was pretty just a few weeks ago. Her appearance hadn't changed in five years and wouldn't ever change again, so he couldn't possibly be attracted to her.

So what had last night's interaction been all about?

"I'm sorry," she said now, carefully avoiding Tate's knowing gaze from where she sat in the lab's window seat sketching on some parchment. "You're right. Let's take it from where we left off with the plasma proteins."

Zachariah ran a hand through his already wild hair, a sure sign he was aggravated. "There are at least a thousand plasma proteins, and I said before that although Nyx's toxin enters the bloodstream, it really only has its impact when reaching the nerve endings."

Sophia nodded and pulled at her bottom lip in consideration. Then she said, "We know the antitoxin worked for Tate even though you designed it to work on you. Therefore, the genetic differences in a full and part-Estilorian's blood appear to be negligible when accounting for how Nyx's toxin interacts with it."

"We need to know more about the differences between human and Estilorian blood in order to know why the antitoxin I created worked for both of us," Zachariah pointed out. "I have never studied human anatomy, so I am unable to proceed with the formula."

Sophia stiffened. "Well, I have. We've mapped the stages at which it affected the eosinophils—"

"Quincy!" Tate suddenly called out. She had stood up on the window seat and called down toward the courtyard from the high open window. "We need you!"

"Tate!" Sophia gasped. "What are you doing?"

"Get down, you demented female," Zachariah said irritably. He walked over to the window seat and gripped Tate around the waist, lifting her as though she weighed nothing and returning her to the ground.

Ignoring him, Tate said to Sophia, "Do you need Quincy to make this go easier?"

Sophia opened her mouth to snap out a "no," only to consider her cousin's ability to tell when someone was lying. Pursing her lips, she lifted her chin in curt acknowledgment of Tate's point and then glanced surreptitiously at her reflection in the mirrored surface of her triple beam balance. Her cheeks were flushed and damp tendrils of hair stuck to her temples. She was what Tate would call a hot mess.

Her shoulders slumped in defeat. Here she was, convinced that Quincy didn't like her, yet she tried to adjust her appearance to make herself more appealing to him.

She was pitiable.

She answered the door when a knock sounded. Quincy stood on the other side of it. She noted that he wore a navy blue tank with matching pants, a color she loved on him because, when paired with his many silver markings, it reminded her of a night sky.

"We need your help to create an inoculation to Nyx's toxin," she greeted him.

His eyes met hers for an extended heartbeat of time. What was it she couldn't read in that gaze? She simply had no idea. And his meaningfully-issued response only confused her more.

"I'm all yours," he said.

Metis had a more difficult time escaping the next time she went to meet with Eirik and Deimos. It was sometime between midnight and dawn when she reached their temporary shelter among the trees.

The air was so cold that her breath plumed around her head. The loud crunching of her booted feet on the dead leaves carpeting the ground heralded her arrival. When she arrived, Eirik was awake and standing outside the rocks covered by a canopy of wide branches and leaves that he had erected with his limited abilities.

They had decided that keeping his location hidden, even from other Mercesti, was essential in light of the scope of their plans. This arrangement was much easier for her, she had to admit, since she had respectable shelter.

"I come bearing good news," she said as she stopped a few feet from him.

"You had better," he said in his deep voice. "I grow tired of waiting."

And she grew tired of his griping, but knew better than to voice that thought. She had to bide her time to achieve her goals. For now, Eirik played a key part in making sure things went as she planned. There was also the fact that he was probably the only being on the plane who could appropriately deal with Deimos in her absence.

"Very soon, we will have the lure needed to draw the Lekwuesti and Kynzesti females to you."

"How soon?"

"By tomorrow or the next day."

He considered this in silence. She wondered—not for the first time—whether he was debating whether to slay her rather than continue to trust that she was upholding her part of their plans.

"Did Deimos enjoy the gift I sent him yesterday?" she asked to break the silence.

Glancing over his shoulder into the shelter where Deimos lay sleeping, Eirik gave a short grunt. "He enjoyed the hunt. She was a worthy bit of prey." He looked back at Metis. "His violence is escalating. The female was hardly more than a mass of torn flesh when he finished with her."

She waved that away. "He cannot help what he is. I have assured him that he can have the two females you seek once we are through with them. He will cooperate with our plans."

Eirik's eyes narrowed. "You had better do whatever you have to in order to ensure that. He has tasted the Lekwuesti now. I expect it will be nearly impossible to keep him off her when she is back with us."

She didn't allow her concern to show. Any sign of weakness would spell disaster. But she could silently acknowledge that she worried over Deimos' increasing aggression.

"He will be fine," she said. "He can make use of the Kynzesti female if needed."

"I require her abilities, as well," Eirik snapped. "Allowing Deimos to kill her would—"

"Who said anything about killing her?" she interrupted coolly. "Just allow him to relieve some of his aggression through her if he requires it. I will instruct him to feed on animals while you search for the scroll."

Eirik shook his head. "You fail to recognize the bloodlust in your own creation. I will tell you once again: you had better do what you can to control him. I might need him to transport me with his unusual abilities at some point. But if he interferes in my plans, I will kill him. Then I will return and do the same to you."

She stiffened, but nodded. As she turned to leave, she wondered how he would react to the knowledge that she intended to kill him first.

Quincy's contributions resulted in Sophia and Zachariah developing a formula for an inoculation to Nyx's toxin for both full and part-Estilorians. It only took them a few hours of brainstorming, after which Zachariah ended up carrying Tate from the lab. She had been bored into sleep.

Sophia, however, was energized. It had been a long time since she worked with Quincy on something so deeply intellectual. She remembered now how attractive she had always found him when he was engaged in something that stimulated the mind.

Okay, she had always found him attractive regardless. But this...*wow*.

She was sure her smile radiated from her face after she bathed and changed and made her way downstairs to find out what her family was having for supper. When she heard a host of voices—including those of beings who weren't related to her—coming from the dining room, she took it in stride. Having impromptu guests was very common with the three family homes being so close together.

"The issue has definitely become more paramount in recent weeks," she heard Sebastian say. "Tate was stranded without the benefit of a paired Lekwuesti to provide her with sustenance or clothing. Fortunately, she has learned the skills needed to stay alive on her own, but if she had been injured to the point of immobility..."

Sophia walked into the room as the elder trailed off. All eyes shifted briefly to her. She realized that her parents and aunts and uncles were also there, along with Quincy, Ini-herit and Jabari. She knew that Zayna and Uriel had gone to Hoygul the Scultresti, while Malukali and Knorbis had traveled to the home of Kanika.

"Should I come back?" she asked, trying to ignore her grumbling stomach and the platters of sandwiches and fruit on the table.

"No, Sophia," her father said. "This topic relates to you. We'd appreciate your input."

As she nodded and took a seat next to her dad, she wondered about Quincy's presence. Then her mother made a pained face and Quincy's sharp gaze quickly assessed her. Sophia understood. With the baby due any time, he wouldn't go far.

"We're talking about the need to pair you and the other firstborn Kynzesti with Lekwuesti," her mother said as Sophia took half of a sandwich and some cantaloupe.

That made sense. Sebastian's example was valid. Tate had been stranded thousands of miles from home without the ability to connect with a Lekwuesti for food, shelter or clothing. Yes, she had drawn on important skills that she learned from her parents and aunts and uncles to survive, but her ordeal would have been far less difficult if she had already been paired with a Lekwuesti.

"I think it's a great idea," Sophia said. "We're all mature enough now to appreciate the weight of the exchange of vows that a Lekwuesti pairing entails, and to honor the once-a-day limit on hospitality requests."

There were nods around the table.

"I think that the pairings should take place at Central," Jabari said, surprising Sophia.

"Agreed," Sebastian said. "We should allow the Kynzesti to pick their paired Lekwuesti, much as we allowed their mothers to do. It would be too much of a security risk to have so many Lekwuesti brought within the protections around your homes."

Sophia took a sip of water to wash down the bite of sandwich she had just eaten and tried not to gape. She would be traveling to Central? Holy crap.

"Zachariah won't let Tate travel to Central without him," Aunt Skye mused.

"It would only be for a couple of days," Sebastian said. "She would have protection."

Aunt Skye's eyebrows rose. "Zachariah will only sleep if he's on Tate's bedroom floor and blocking the door," she pointed out. "His latent Gloresti instincts have been fully awakened by their pairing."

"A Mercesti can't travel to Central," Uncle Gabriel said. "The protections prevent it."

After a moment, Aunt Skye nodded as if to herself. "Zachariah can. I'll take him there." She was referring to her ability to teleport, which wasn't inhibited by the protections if she knew where she was going. Quincy started to speak, so she quickly added, "*After* the babies are born."

"You will be unable to use your abilities for at least a month after the babies arrive," Jabari said. "We all know how the births drain your powers."

Aunt Skye sighed. "I know. But it's either we wait until then, or someone manages to convince Zachariah to allow Tate to leave for a couple of days without him."

Everyone exchanged looks. Sophia figured they were thinking exactly what she was: there was no way they'd convince the hard-headed Mercesti to let Tate leave. He'd probably kill himself trying to get to Central.

Eventually, Jabari nodded. "It appears there is little choice. Sophia, Tate, Tiege, Clara Kate and Zachariah must travel to Central after the next Kynzesti are born and Skye has recovered her abilities."

Sophia watched her parents exchange glances with each other and her aunts and uncles. She knew that, outside of Aunt Skye's brief teleport, none of them would be able to travel to Central because they needed to stay with their newborn children. They were likely all exchanging thoughts about this difficult reality.

Her gaze met Quincy's. He looked at her with quiet intensity. She blinked, uncertain of the significance of that look. Why did she feel as though she was missing something?

"Very well," her mother said then, turning her attention. She covered Sophia's hand with her own. "We agree. Our firstborn children will travel to Central once the babies are born."

Chapter 8

QUINCY EMERGED FROM HIS COTTAGE THE FOLLOWING DAY WITH Sophia at the front of his mind. This was hardly unusual. But the news yesterday about her traveling to Central made him fixate.

The Kynzesti had yet to be formally introduced to Estilorian society. So far, only the elders and the top ranks of each class had even met them. There were a number of reasons for this, not the least of which being that the elders wanted time to understand their abilities. In light of their elemental natures, the Kynzesti were unpredictable. Thus, putting them in the midst of other Estilorians without knowing what to expect was considerably unwise.

Now, however, it appeared the firstborn Kynzesti were deemed ready to integrate into Estilorian society. Quincy couldn't help but equate that with his recent personal acknowledgement that Sophia was, indeed, now a mature female with the ability to make decisions about her own future. He was both thrilled and terrified by that realization.

It was time for training in the paddock, so he decided to walk over and check it out. He occasionally participated in weapons training. Today, since he had gotten very little sleep the night before and still felt sluggish, he decided to observe.

As he walked, he caught a glimmer out of the corner of his eye and spotted Nyx getting settled in the shade of a tree. Sunlight reflected off her large, black, serpentine body and her diamond eyes. Although he was getting more accustomed to the kragen's presence within the homeland, she was still a rather fearsome creature to behold.

Tate stood on the outskirts of the paddock, so Quincy walked up to stand beside her. She wore a dark orange training tank with brown pants and boots, a rather conservative look for her. Her colorful, curly hair was bound on top of her head in a messy bun. She gave him a bright smile when he approached.

"Hiya, Quincy." She stepped closer and linked arms with him, a friendly and familiar gesture. "Came out to make sure Sophia participates in today's training, right?"

He grinned back at her. "I don't know what you're talking about."

"Lie," she said with a wink. "Yeah, I dragged her out this morning. Sparky keeps getting me up earlier and earlier for my training since he wants me to learn to fight better on my own. I headed over to get Soph as soon as my torture session was over."

That explained why she wasn't in the center of the paddock with Zachariah, Tiege, Ariana, Sophia, Clara Kate and a number of other Kynzesti old enough to participate. Everyone was stretching and otherwise preparing themselves for the training ahead under Zachariah's assessing eye. The Mercesti had taken an active role in defensive and offensive training of the Kynzesti since pairing with Tate. Because he was new to the family dynamic, he more easily spotted the holes that existed in the training that the Kynzesti had received over the years.

"Sparky got some of Nyx's toxin earlier," Tate said, her eyes focused on Zachariah. "Sophia should be able to process the inoculation using the formula you created."

"That's great."

"Yeah." She looked at him. "You'll do what you can to ensure it has a good likelihood of working, right?"

"Of course."

She sighed. "Good. Sparky won't let the serum be tested on anyone but him."

Just then, Zachariah indicated that it was time to begin training, so everyone gathered around him. The Mercesti was as expressionless as usual as he scanned the group. Quincy supposed he shouldn't have been surprised by Zachariah's selfless commitment to test the inoculation on himself, but he was.

"Today we will train in hand-to-hand combat," Zachariah said. "Be sure to take advantage of your opponent's weaknesses. If you do not, they will never learn to overcome them."

There were a few nods as he began pairing them off. He didn't pair Ariana with anyone, Quincy realized with a concerned frown. The Lekwuesti female's spirits had improved somewhat since learning that at least one of the scroll pieces had been located. Standing face-to-face with Zachariah now caused her to lose some of her color.

"Let him work with her," Tate said quietly before Quincy interfered. When he caught her gaze, she added, "Our efforts to help Ariana get through her trauma haven't done much good. Maybe she needs another kind of help."

Quincy wasn't so sure, but for the sake of his friendship with Tate, he nodded. His gaze moved to Sophia, who was paired with Tiege for training. She wore a hunter green training tank and pants. He'd be lying if he didn't admit that part of the draw getting him out to the training paddock was the sight of her in the conforming clothes, though it made him feel lecherous to admit that even to himself.

"You fear me," Zachariah said to Ariana. Quincy realized they had moved closer to him and Tate and away from the others because Ariana backed away from her opponent. "Use your fear to defeat me."

"I can't," she said in a nearly inaudible voice. She trembled.

"You can and you will," Zachariah argued. "I am coming after you calmly and in control. Those such as Deimos will not."

Ariana flinched at the name of the male who had attacked her. She glanced over her shoulder as though seeking a route of escape. Quincy barely fought the urge to help her. She looked like a doe in the sights of a vicious predator.

"Do not turn your attention from me," Zachariah snapped. Ariana's wide lavender eyes flew back to him. "You have been here for six weeks, yet you still harbor fear. Do you want to learn to protect yourself from an attack or not?"

"I—I—"

"You were pinned," he said, grabbing her arm and using one of his booted feet to sweep her legs out from under her. They fell together onto the grass. He now held her down, his hips between her legs. "Use your waist as a pivot to gather space and momentum—"

"Get off me!" Ariana screeched, bucking against him.

"—to roll us both over," Zachariah continued as though he didn't see or hear her terror. "Then use your elbow to disable me."

"Get off me, damn you!"

"The temple and the base of the cerebellum—"

Ariana screamed. All other activity ceased as everyone watched the spectacle. Quincy moved forward, disturbed by Ariana's dramatic reaction and Zachariah's heedlessness to her fear.

"—are the weakest points accessible to you. If you strike me in either of those places with your elbow with enough force, you will render me—"

"I said, get off me!"

"—unconscious or possibly kill me." Zachariah stayed where he was, holding her down as she thrashed uselessly, spouting curses and crying. "If you want me off, get me off you. I have just told you how."

"Get off of her, Zachariah," Tiege said. He now stood beside the couple. Seeing the angry fire in Tiege's eyes, Quincy prepared himself to intervene.

"Like this," Zachariah said, ignoring everyone except Ariana, who was now sobbing. He shifted so that there was room between their bodies, as though she had swiveled her hips and waist like he instructed. "Then grab my wrist like this and flip us." He demonstrated and rolled with her. "Bring your elbow up as you roll and hit me—"

She lashed out, but rather than strike him with her elbow, she tried to punch him.

"You Mercesti demon!" she screamed, trying now to kick him and strike him however she could. Tiege grabbed her around the waist and pulled her back. "*I hate you!*"

Zachariah got to his feet. Several lines of blood welled just beneath his left eye where Ariana scratched him. He looked completely unaffected.

"Next time, use your elbow like I showed you," he told her. "It is the strongest part of your body. Your nails will only aggravate your attacker and likely get you killed."

"You really are unbelievable," Tiege said. "Come on, Ariana." He turned and guided the distraught female away from the training paddock.

The crowd around Zachariah looked on in shock and uncertainty. Tate moved closer to him and reached up to touch the cuts on his face, but Zachariah shook his head at her and she withdrew. Seeing her hurt expression, Quincy's anger surfaced.

"Just what do you think you're doing?" he demanded, stepping in front of

Zachariah. "Ariana has been victimized—forced to endure things that no being should have to—at the hands of your class. You have no business attempting to aid her in dealing with her trauma."

Zachariah's jaw clenched, but he didn't respond.

"Doesn't he?"

Quincy glanced with surprise at Clara Kate. She stood with her arms crossed and a considering look on her face.

"Zachariah was also victimized by the Mercesti," she pointed out. "He was forced to do things that—"

"Enough," Zachariah interrupted, not looking away from Quincy. "She can hate me all she wants so long as she learns to be more than just a victim." Now, his gaze moved to Sophia, making Quincy stiffen. "It appears you have no partner now, Shifter."

"I'll spar with her," Quincy offered when Sophia's eyebrows rose.

"You will not," Zachariah said, turning to stride back into the center of the training paddock. "She needs a challenge, not a head-patting."

The insult had Quincy balling his hands into fists. He considered pitting himself against the Mercesti instead, training be damned. Then he caught Tate's eye and knew he had to restrain himself. He wondered, though, what he would do if Zachariah pulled a similar stunt with Sophia as he had with Ariana and had a vision of ripping the other male's head from his shoulders.

Zachariah turned and looked at Sophia, who had yet to move. "What are you waiting for? Prepare to defend yourself."

Sophia realized that everyone had given up the idea of sparring with each other and had instead decided to watch her training session. Clara Kate caught her gaze as she walked past. Sophia answered the silent question in her cousin's eyes with a curt nod. She would do this.

Still, she couldn't deny that her heart raced nervously as she approached the large Mercesti. Ariana had gotten his face pretty good with her nails, making him look even more intimidating than usual.

The memory of Ariana's screams ran through Sophia's head as she approached him. She may have understood what Zachariah was trying to achieve with her friend, but his methods were dubious. She worried over Ariana's mental state and considered telling Zachariah to stick it so that she could go check on her.

Unfortunately, the Mercesti was stubborn. She knew she wouldn't get out of this.

"You are smaller than your kin," he began as she neared him, "but you have more strength than any of them. You have to learn how to properly harness it."

What was he talking about? she wondered, trying not to get so close to him that she had to crane her neck to meet his gaze. Then he positioned himself in an offensive attack stance.

"Defend," he said.

That was all the warning she got. He swung out with his boot and nearly clipped her in the head. He followed that up with a back-hand strike. She barely avoided the blows by ducking and weaving. While she recovered from her awkward dodge, he planted his boot on her hip and sent her sprawling.

"Get up," he instructed. "Always keep moving."

She was already doing that, thank you very much. Irritation and embarrassment had her surging back to her feet with the intent of giving him a swift kick anywhere she could reach. He ruined her plan by going low and sweeping her legs out from under her. Her breath left her in a painful whoosh as she once again hit the ground. When he followed her ungraceful fall with another shove in the side from his boot, her irritation transformed into anger.

"Kicking her while she's down—" she heard Quincy growl.

"An enemy would do far worse," Zachariah interrupted. "You need to move more quickly," he said to Sophia as she got back to her feet. "You have yet to use your true strength and abilities to properly defend yourself."

She opened her mouth to give him an earful as anger flooded her, but he stopped her with another kick. This one, she managed to avoid with a spin. She tried to kick him as she moved to his side, but he grabbed her foot and shoved her right back to the ground. This time, she rolled and avoided his follow-up kick.

"You are learning," he said. "But I want more from you, Shifter."

When she got to her feet, he sucker-punched her. One hard hit to the side of her head. Even as the pain registered and she staggered, she heard outraged exclamations from her family.

"She's so much smaller than you! How dare you strike her like that?"

"Can't you see she's not strong enough to defeat you?"

As the words swirled around her, Sophia's anger flashed into fury. Not big enough? Not strong enough? How about a bear? Would that be big and strong enough?

And this time, when she lashed out at him, it was with the arm of a bear. She ripped through fabric and muscle as her claws and power struck him. This time, he was the one who fell.

Everyone watched with astonishment as Sophia's arm returned to its normal state after her partial shift. She felt the amazement on her face as she looked at a severely injured Zachariah getting back to his feet with Tate's assistance. He would need Uncle Gabriel or Aunt Amber's healing help…and soon.

"Why the bloody hell did you not do that in the first place?" he asked.

Suddenly wanting to throw her arms around him, she replied, "I didn't know I could."

Chapter 9

WHILE SOPHIA AND CLARA KATE WENT IN SEARCH OF GABRIEL OR AMBER to heal Zachariah, Quincy headed toward the flower garden beside the home of Tate and Tiege. He wanted to check on Ariana. His mind was fully occupied processing the events that had just occurred, so he didn't see his class elder until he almost walked into him.

The elders still within the homeland had been meeting at Gabriel and Amber's home about the plans once the Elder Scroll piece was brought back. They must have concluded their meeting, however, since Ini-herit now stood under a tree with his gaze centered on Tiege and Ariana. The couple was seated a fair distance away on a wooden bench beneath a trellis covered in ivy. Tiege's hand rubbed soothing circles on Ariana's back as they talked, but their words were too quiet to be heard.

How strange that Ini-herit just stood there watching them, Quincy thought. It was almost as though he was studying them.

That thought saddened him. His elder had gone through so much to try and relearn and experience human emotions, all to no avail. Now it seemed he was trying to figure out what he could by studying those who did experience emotion. He probably didn't even realize that his behavior would be seen as strange by most others.

"Did your meeting go well?" Quincy asked as he approached.

"Very little was decided," Ini-herit replied, not shifting his gaze. "Until the scroll piece is recovered and the other elders have returned, there is not much sense in spending time strategizing. We were putting together some initial thoughts."

"I see," Quincy said, though he felt a little lost.

"It appears that today's training session was eventful."

Frowning, Quincy said, "Yes. Zachariah has no subtlety or consideration for others. His thoughtlessness today set Ariana back in her recovery."

"Hmm."

"Do you think differently?"

Ini-herit shrugged. "I am not usually the one others ask about issues pertaining to emotion."

Quincy couldn't argue that, and he didn't want to make his class elder uncomfortable. Uncertain how else to respond, he just nodded.

"However," Ini-herit continued, "I am curious whether you have seen the Lekwuesti female exhibit an emotion other than fear and sadness since her arrival here."

"I..." Quincy trailed off. "Now that you mention it, I suppose I haven't."

"Yet today, she expressed anger toward Zachariah."

"Well, yes. A lot of anger, actually."

"You have worked among humans in the medical field for many years now," Ini-herit observed. "Are there not stages to the healing and recovery process for victims of traumatic experiences?"

Seeing where the conversation was going, Quincy's brow creased. He reluctantly acknowledged, "Yes. And anger is one of those stages."

Ini-herit nodded as though to himself. "Perhaps she was uncomfortable expressing her repressed anger to anyone else here. All of you have been nothing but helpful to her as she recovers. No one is forcing her to move forward with recovering the scroll pieces, despite the importance of that task. And no one is pressing her to overcome her fears...which essentially leaves her facing them alone."

"She feels guilty and angry," Quincy said as understanding dawned. "Zachariah gave her an outlet for those emotions."

The elder didn't reply. They both watched as Tiege cupped the side of Ariana's face. When he started leaning toward her with the obvious intent to kiss her, Quincy turned away. It was clear that Ariana wouldn't need his assistance at this point. The elder turned with him and they started walking back toward the paddock.

"But Zachariah doesn't know anything about human emotions," Quincy said, still trying to rationalize what he saw. "He orders Tate around like she can't think for herself and objects to nearly everything she wears, dragging her off to lecture her every other moment. For heaven's sake, he just thrashed Sophia—a much smaller being—during their training session without a second thought."

The training paddock came into sight. Gabriel was even then placing his hands on Zachariah's chest as Tate looked on with tears in her eyes. Sophia had her arm around her cousin's waist and appeared more pale than usual. Blue-gray light flashed, causing Zachariah to issue a searing curse as his wounds healed. Because he was a Mercesti, the blessed healing didn't come without pain.

"Did he now?" Ini-herit murmured.

Quincy started to respond, but stopped himself. He was full of questions now, when before he had been so sure about everything.

Ini-herit stopped walking, causing Quincy to also stop. The elder's silver eyes were depthless as he said, "It seems to me that emotions cloud judgment. I caution you not to draw conclusions about Zachariah's actions until you know him better."

His gaze shifted to the paddock. Clara Kate was looking up at them, but she glanced away when he turned in her direction. His voice was quieter when he added, "Always know, Quincy, that a being does not have to experience or exhibit emotion to know how his thoughts and actions impact others."

It took a couple of hours for Eirik to reach his destination. He left Deimos behind in their mockery of a shelter. If the fiend was gone when he returned, he really didn't care.

Metis was taking much too long to fulfill her end of their bargain. She wouldn't provide him with any details, making him question her honesty. The fact that he didn't share the bulk of his plans with her was irrelevant.

Much as he had suspected, the two Mercesti he sought were just where he left them a few weeks ago. Bertram and Tycho were practically useless without leadership. They had all but fallen over themselves to please him over the years just so that they had some form of direction in their meaningless lives.

While Eirik normally would have considered them too weak to serve him much purpose, they had provided him with one of the keys he now knew he needed to recover the Elder Scroll. If it hadn't been for them, he was loath to admit, he would never have discovered the piece of the scroll he now had.

When he had cast them out of his group of followers for taking unapproved liberties with the Lekwuesti, Ariana, who was helping him find the scroll, Bertram and Tycho captured the lost Kynzesti who he now knew was named Tate. They had figured that he would allow them back into the fold if they presented him with such a rare and valuable captive. Fortunately for them, they had been correct.

Although he hadn't known exactly what he would do with the unusual female, he was only too aware of the leverage she provided him. As a Kynzesti, she had blood ties to the Gloresti elder, Gabriel. What would the elders be willing to do to spare her life?

Unfortunately, he hadn't been given time to answer that question because Zachariah entered the scene. Eirik still wondered about the other Mercesti's motives. Zachariah claimed to only be interested in the hunt of the Kynzesti female, but Eirik thought there must be more to it than that. The former Gloresti commander had been impossible to read, however. Then, while Eirik was negotiating with Zachariah for the exchange of the Kynzesti for the services of the Lekwuesti, everything had gone to hell.

In the end, it had been Tate who shattered the illusion protecting the scroll piece from his view. It had only required her contact with the illusion to dissolve it. He now knew that he required Ariana to locate the scroll piece and Tate to get through any protections surrounding it.

As for Zachariah, he was a clear competitor. He had placed himself between Tate and Eirik's cursed kris, taking the deadly strike himself. This told him that Zachariah was a step ahead of him regarding finding the scroll pieces. The other male had obviously known that the Kynzesti female could see the truth in lies, and he had tried to spare her life so he could make further use of her. He must have also known that the scroll was in more than one piece—something Eirik only discovered after the fact. Which meant Zachariah was a dangerous and well-informed opponent.

In light of this, Eirik wasn't content waiting for Metis to fulfill her mysterious plans. If Zachariah was out there seeking the scroll and already had that much knowledge about obtaining it, there was no more time to be wasted.

As he approached from the air, Eirik discovered that the site where he had obtained the scroll piece was now barren outside of the mountain, the trees and the two Mercesti camping there. He landed and extinguished his wings, then eyed the two males sleeping side by side with unconcealed contempt. He briefly reconsidered his decision, but knew he had little choice but to move forward.

"Wake up," he ordered.

Bertram and Tycho both jerked awake and got to their feet within seconds, redeeming themselves at least a little. When they had drawn their swords and realized who stood before them, they quickly lowered their weapons and fell to one knee.

"We are at your service, my lord," they said.

"Then get up."

They rose. He studied them as he weighed how much to share with them. Bertram was shorter than most males, his wiry build giving him an advantage against larger opponents…never a bad thing. His dark, unkempt hair fell past his shoulders, reminding Eirik a bit of Deimos. There were deep scars on his face, but since Eirik bore his own facial scars, this made no impression on him.

Tycho was taller and notably more muscular than his companion. His hair was dark blond and even longer than Bertram's, but no more maintained. His red eyes never stopped moving. Eirik knew that of the two, Bertram was generally the one who gave the orders and Tycho was more unpredictable.

"You must recover the Kynzesti female that you gifted me," he said.

They both blinked over the command. Then they exchanged glances. Eventually, Bertram spoke.

"If I might ask why—"

"You may not."

They exchanged another glance over his tone. He crossed his arms and stared down at them, daring them to press him.

"But she was taken from here by a kragen, my lord," Bertram said. "If she is even still alive, she is within the protections around her homeland by now."

"Your point?" Eirik asked coldly.

Bertram stared at him for a long moment. Tycho looked at Bertram. Eirik saw the smaller male weighing their options. He was smart enough to know that to deny Eirik was to ensure their deaths.

Finally, he bowed his head and said, "Just that…we will get to work trying to find her right away."

Eirik contained his satisfaction and nodded. "I expect you to make haste."

"Yes, my lord. Where may we find you so that we may bring her to you when we find her?"

Pausing, Eirik considered how to answer. In the end, he saw no other option than to give them the truth.

"I cannot be certain where I will be, depending upon how soon you locate the female. However, you can begin by looking for me in the forests surrounding the home of Kanika…the supposed Mercesti leader."

Chapter 10

KNORBIS AND MALUKALI TRAVELED TO KANIKA'S HOME WITH A HOST OF Waresti. It took them nearly two days of flight time to reach their destination. Neither of them minded, however. As long as they were together, they were content.

"Judging by the reports sent to Uriel by lieutenant Donald," Knorbis said as they ate a light lunch on the last leg of their journey, "Kanika's behavior has been rather unpredictable."

Malukali sensed the responding thoughts of the Waresti around them, and filtered them very naturally as she ate the slice of cheese that her husband handed to her. His words were entirely for the benefit of their company. The two of them knew each other's thoughts and feelings better than any other two beings possibly could.

"You will want to be sure you're on guard," he continued. "Donald indicated that she responds better to females." Here, he frowned. "Unfortunately, the one Waresti female with whom she had the best relationship has gone missing. She apparently never returned from a recent scouting assignment. Donald and his team are still looking for her."

More thoughts flowed around them. Again, Malukali filtered them. After centuries of having the thoughts of all Estilorians running through her mind, she had learned how to sort them without it requiring much concentration.

"We hope that Kanika will listen to what we have to say, thus beginning to ease her from her trauma-induced state," Knorbis said.

Although the majority of the Waresti with them were well-aware of these facts, a few of them had only just joined them. Knorbis felt it best to give everyone the same warning. Malukali could only appreciate the consideration he was giving Kanika's mental state by issuing these instructions.

"Of course, *archigos*," replied the lead Waresti, Esteban. "We will keep our distance so that you may approach the Mercesti leader without interference."

"Thank you."

Knorbis caught Malukali's gaze. She smiled over the look in his deep purple eyes. Since they were focused on helping Kanika, it had now been a number of days since they last had a chance to be together in an intimate way. As a result, her husband's thoughts had begun to stray into the inappropriate realm. In fact, his current thoughts had her cheeks flushing.

Focus, darling, she thought with amusement as she bit into an apple slice.

I'm trying. But you don't make it easy.

I'm not doing anything.

You're breathing.

She laughed at that, unable to help herself. She didn't care that the Waresti around them watched her with uncertain expressions. When Knorbis leaned down and kissed her, she met him halfway.

They hit the air not long after that, reaching Kanika's holding within a couple of hours. Although the elders had offered to protect Kanika's home with similar enchantments to those surrounding their own homes, she had refused. The other elders, after all, had protected their homes largely from the Mercesti. From whom would she be protecting herself? Her own class?

In the end, only the air around her home had any enchantments on it. Beings could only enter if they walked through the main gate.

Lieutenant Donald stood at that gate when Knorbis, Malukali and their escorts arrived. He wore a concerned expression.

"Greetings, *archigos*," he said, bowing deeply with his right arm crossed over his chest. "Thank you very much for making this trip."

"Of course, lieutenant," Malukali said. "How is Kanika?"

Turning to lead them into the large stone mansion, Donald replied, "Not as well as one should hope, I am afraid. She spends the majority of her time in her bedroom, refusing to see us. Ever since Gwendolyn went missing, we haven't had a female here who could help ease her discomfort."

Malukali nodded in understanding. "I hope she will at least speak to me. I can always reduce her anxiety if she requests it. She needs to talk about what she went through if she is to begin healing."

There were a number of Mercesti inside the home alongside the Waresti. The thoughts that she picked up from them were generally distrustful of her and Knorbis' presence. This wasn't unexpected in light of the fact that they were in Kanika's home, but Malukali had to wonder whether the high number of aggressive Mercesti males contributed to Kanika's continued distress. She could only imagine how hard it would be to try and govern a class when members of that class had turned against her in such a violent way.

They reached the double doors leading to Kanika's bedroom a moment later. Donald knocked.

"Yes?"

The voice belonged to Kanika, but it definitely sounded strained. Malukali opened her thoughts to try and gauge the mindset of the female on the other side of the door. She was surprised when she encountered unusual resistance. Frowning in concern, she wondered if the trauma had been even more impactful to Kanika's psyche than she feared. She exchanged a look and thought with Knorbis.

"I have brought *archigos* Malukali and—" Donald began.

The door flew open. Kanika stood in the doorway, her long, black hair unbound and unbrushed. "Why did you not say so?" she demanded.

The nightgown she wore barely covered her, and Malukali couldn't help but find it an unusual wardrobe choice in light of the recent abuse she suffered. Then again, it seemed the Mercesti leader was far from in a rational state of mind.

"I apologize," Donald said with a slight bow. He gave the elders a look that clearly said, *See what I mean?*

"Hello, Kanika," Malukali said, giving her a small smile. "I am sorry it has taken us so long to get here."

"I should think you would be sorry," Kanika said, making Malukali blink in surprise. Then she waved a hand in apparent dismissal. "I will get my robe and you will join me for tea. We have much to discuss."

Knorbis touched Malukali's arm. "I will leave you two to have your discussion."

"Nonsense," Kanika said as she walked back into her dimly-lit chamber and picked up the robe that lay over the back of a chaise near her bed. "I wish to speak with both of you."

She appears stronger in spirit than Donald depicted, Knorbis mused with some confusion.

I can sense that he's also puzzled by her behavior, Malukali returned. *But what do we know of her mindset? I can tell something is different. Her thoughts are terribly jumbled. I have heard of humans undergoing something of a mind-split when they are extremely traumatized. Perhaps that is what occurred here, though I have never seen this among Estilorians.*

He didn't argue. Kanika emerged from the room in her robe and brushed past them. Her movements were almost what humans called manic, lending credence to Malukali's guess. Malukali and Knorbis turned to follow her. Donald trailed behind them, along with a handful of Waresti. They ended up at a library. A Mercesti was setting a small table with tea and biscuits.

"We will meet alone, Nigil," Kanika said authoritatively, and the male bowed and exited the room. Seeing that Donald and his Waresti had walked in, Kanika's eyes widened. "I will not talk with these—males in here."

Her voice trembled. Malukali turned and gave Donald a nod, indicating that she and Knorbis would be okay. After a moment of hesitation, Donald bowed and left the room along with the other Waresti.

"Thank you," Kanika said, placing a hand on her chest and taking one of the seats situated around the small table holding the tea set. "I am sure you must think me without sanity. I know that I am not making much sense these days."

"Please don't worry about it, Kanika," Malukali said gently as she and Knorbis took the other two seats at the table. "We know that you have endured much. We want only to help you."

Kanika sighed. "Again, thank you." She reached for the teapot. "I hope you will both join me in a cup of tea. I have found that such mundane tasks help calm me."

"Of course," Knorbis said.

Malukali knew that he, like her, wasn't thirsty since they had only just eaten lunch a few hours before, but they weren't about to upset the fragile female right then. When Kanika handed them cups and saucers, they accepted them.

"Sugar or cream?" Kanika asked.

"No, thank you," Malukali replied. When they all had their tea, she asked, "How are you feeling, Kanika? Is there anything we can do for you?"

The other female fiddled with her saucer, appearing uncertain. "I have been having trouble remembering things," she said in a quiet voice.

"We can help you with that," Knorbis said. He exchanged a look with Malukali. "It would be painless and…we could avoid bringing forth any of your more painful memories."

"You can?"

"Yes," Malukali confirmed. She started to reach out to touch Kanika's hand, but the Mercesti pulled away. Understanding, Malukali returned her hands to her teacup. "We have the ability to pull forth memories that have been suppressed by trauma."

There was a long pause as Kanika considered this. To occupy herself in the silence, Malukali took a sip of her tea, noting its floral aroma. It smelled familiar, but she couldn't quite place it.

What's in this tea? she thought.

Knorbis tasted it so he could answer her. Malukali's head felt strange. It was when she started to see two of her husband and her tongue grew thick in her mouth that she realized she hadn't drunk tea at all. They had just ingested a beverage made of the highly toxic koimoumai flower.

As darkness and fear claimed her, she had the final, certain thought that she would never see her husband again.

Chapter 11

AS AFTERNOON APPROACHED ON THE DAY AFTER THE TRAINING SESSION, Quincy walked in the front door to Sophia's family home. He had long ago learned that knocking was unnecessary. The Kynzesti and their parents all came and went between their homes as they pleased. It made for a warm and welcoming family environment within the homeland, even if it was very different from what an Estilorian usually experienced.

Estilorians didn't have issues with privacy, but there was a certain expectation regarding the respect of personal space. There wasn't such a concept when it came to the Kynzesti homeland. Family was family, they said, and Quincy had always been the equivalent of family.

While he was honored by this distinction, he knew now that this contributed a great deal toward him failing to express his true feelings to Sophia. His love for her had begun when she was so young, as had his undeniable attraction to her. She had captured his heart with her unquenchable curiosity and sharp intelligence, then had all but slain him with her beauty when she grew into her mature form.

He had known that she—never mind her parents—wouldn't understand his intense feelings for her back then, and he had wisely kept them to himself. But now that Sophia was old enough that his admission might not be seen as creepy or result in his death at the hands of her father, he had no idea how to begin to get her to think of him as anything other than an extended family member.

"Hi, Quincy," Olivia greeted him as he walked into the kitchen. Her green eyes caught his and she smiled, making the dimple in her left cheek appear. "I was just sitting down to a little snack. Can I interest you in anything?"

"No, but thanks," he said, returning her smile. "I'm here to see if Sophia needs any assistance with the inoculation she intends to create today."

"Oh, yes," Olivia said with a soft laugh. "You know Sophia. She's been hard at work on it since before the sun graced us with its presence this morning. I'm rather surprised she hasn't come running down with a loud declaration that she's finished yet."

"I'm sure it's just a matter of time," he said.

"I'm sure you're right, especially with Zachariah up there helping her out. He really seems to know what he's doing." She stacked cheese on a slice of pear and added, "I don't know how he dragged Tate out of bed so early to get her to come over here."

Quincy hadn't ever experienced it before, but he recognized the jealousy that surged through him at the mention of the other male.

"Zachariah is here?" he asked mildly.

"Yes. He said something about testing the inoculation today. Sophia was very excited to see him this morning."

Clenching his hands into fists, Quincy nodded. "Well," he said in a deliberately level voice, "Guess I'll head on up to the lab and see if there's anything I can do to help."

"Quincy," Olivia said, reaching out and touching his arm. "Is everything okay?"

"It's fine," he replied. But even he heard the underlying tension in his voice. Frowning, he added, "I just don't understand why everyone seems okay with Zachariah's treatment of Ariana and Sophia yesterday. He *punched* your daughter."

"I see." She nodded. "Well, I can't say that I would have wanted to witness that. I'm sure I would have been as bothered as you. But Sophia came home from the experience more enthusiastic about her abilities than I've ever seen her. Knowing that she can complete a partial shift and not lose all of her clothes in the process was very…freeing for her." She smiled. "So, even though the methods were unlike anything we would have done, Zachariah managed to accomplish something remarkable."

He supposed he saw her point.

"You love Sophia," she continued, making him start. "Much as you love all of our children. It's understandable that you feel protective."

The feeling that struck him as he once again realized Sophia and her family would only ever see him as a close friend or surrogate family member was difficult to bear. He looked at the ground and cleared his throat. The thought occurred to him that the only way they might begin to shift their thinking about him was if he came clean about how he felt.

"You're right, Olivia," he said. "I do—"

"Get out of here!"

Quincy stopped mid-sentence as Sophia's voice, followed by her laugh, bounced into the room from the stairs leading to her laboratory. She arrived just seconds later, followed closely by Zachariah and Tate. She wore a practical mauve tank and khaki capris, her hair up in a bun. Her cheeks were pink and laughter filled her beautiful eyes.

"There's no such thing as a mermaid," she said.

Her eyes were on Zachariah as they entered the room, but she looked away and spotted Quincy. Her smiled faltered. "Oh. Good morning, Quincy," she said.

He couldn't help but notice how stilted and formal she sounded compared with the more easy-going tone she used with Zachariah and Tate. "Good morning," he replied. "Have you completed work on the inoculation, then?"

"Yes," she confirmed, reaching over and stealing a piece of the sliced cheese in front of her mother. She deftly moved her hand when her mother tried to swat it. "We were actually on our way to see you at the clinic. You have the best implements to use to inject it, and we'll want you to monitor the effects."

Was that the only reason she would seek him out?

He couldn't stop that thought from entering his mind even as he forced a smile. "Sure. Let's go and see how you did."

Sophia was a mass of nerves as they walked as a group to Quincy's cottage. She had worked very hard on this inoculation. She *really* wanted it to be successful.

She told herself that it was her thoughts about her experiment and not Quincy's nearness that had her jabbering like a crazed being as they crossed the forested path outside of her family's home and approached the central training paddock and Quincy's cottage. She absolutely didn't wonder whether he thought that her ability to partially shift was cool or yet another sign of her weirdness. He had left the training paddock and not returned after she shredded Zachariah's chest, so that was answer enough, she supposed.

"...we should know right away if it works," she said before pausing for breath.

Reaching over, Tate rubbed her arm. "I know, Soph. You've mentioned that about four times already."

Seeing Quincy give her a brief, questioning look, Sophia shut up.

"Hey, are you going to test Sophia's inoculation?" Clara Kate asked.

She and a number of others, including Ini-herit, stood in the training paddock. Judging by the sweat covering all of them, they had been training pretty hard for quite a while. Clara Kate sheathed her blessed butterfly swords and started toward them, though no one responded to her.

"Cool," she said. "I want to see how it goes."

Noticing that the Corgloresti elder followed C.K., Sophia's eyebrows rose. He sure did seem fascinated by her, even if he couldn't make heads or tails of her.

"Okay," Sophia said. "We're headed to Quincy's."

They all walked the remaining fifty feet to the cottage. Quincy opened the door on the clinic side and moved so that everyone could walk in. Despite the fact that the structure was a cottage by design, the clinic was spacious. They were all able to fit in the exam room where Quincy kept his medical tools without being too crowded.

"Let me have the serum," Quincy said to Sophia.

She handed him two vials.

"I thought we were testing this on Zachariah," he said with a frown as he took the vials.

"We are," she replied, her chin lifting. She was certain he would argue with her next statement. "And on me."

There was a pause when it did appear he might argue, but eventually he just asked, "Why?"

Her defensiveness eased at his calm tone. She shrugged. "The serum needs to be tested on both full and part-Estilorians. Since I created the formula, I should be the second one who tests it."

"It would seem to me," Ini-herit observed, "that another Kynzesti would be a more appropriate test subject."

Sophia frowned at the elder as Quincy hurriedly said, "He has a point. If anything goes wrong, we need you to be able to help fix it."

But Sophia knew that Ini-herit didn't say something unless there was a significant reason why, and her instincts flared. "That isn't what you meant, is it?" she asked him.

"No," he replied. "I was referring to the fact that your DNA differs from your kin."

She wondered how the elder had drawn that conclusion. Yes, she could shapeshift and it was an unusual ability, but all of them had second powers as well as the ability to control an element. His statement made little sense.

"Sophia—" Quincy began.

"No," she interrupted, holding up a hand. "I want to hear this." She didn't turn her gaze from Ini-herit's. "What makes you think my DNA is different from my kin? Do you know why I have such a different ability from everyone else? Why I was the only premature Kynzesti? Why I'm smaller and my hair and skin colors are so much fairer?"

"Sophia—" Quincy started to say again, but Ini-herit interrupted him.

"I imagine it is because your mother was struck with a cursed weapon while you were still in her womb."

Never in a million years would Sophia have predicted that those would be the words to leave the elder's mouth. For a moment, the only sound she heard was the sound of her blood pulsing through her head. Her vision tunneled until all she could focus on was Ini-herit's unemotional silver eyes. A sharp, uncomfortable stinging sensation flushed up the back of her neck. Eventually, she looked at Tate, whose face was pale and her eyes wide.

"Is he lying?" she managed to ask.

Tate's gaze grew watery, answering the question. But she slowly shook her head.

Feeling as though she wasn't really standing there, Sophia swallowed hard. Then she looked at Ini-herit and said, "You're saying that my DNA is cursed? That I'm even more of a freak than I thought?"

"Sophia—" Quincy began for the third time.

This time, she cut him off with a look. "You've always known," she said, her tone biting. "You, of everyone, know our DNA. You *knew* I was different because of that curse."

She read the truth all over his face. And then she finally, after all these years, realized why he saw her as such an abomination.

Because she was one.

Turning, she ran from the cottage. She ignored the hands that reached out to stop her, ignored the cries for her to wait. Deciding that she might as well be around creatures that felt more like kin to her at that moment than any being in the homeland, she shifted into her panther form and fled.

Chapter 12

DOMINO SEEMED TO KNOW THAT SOPHIA NEEDED COMFORTING. SHE RAN straight for the panther's den and found him napping. It took only one nudge with her muzzle and a soft cry to get the cat's attention. He opened a yellow-green eye, studied her for a moment and then got to his feet. Without even engaging in his normal grooming upon waking, he bounded off into the forest with the clear intent that she follow.

She gladly did so. In her panther form, she was half-controlled by the panther's instincts. She had enough awareness to know what she was running from, but not enough to care.

That suited her just fine.

They raced through the forest, moving in a northern direction toward a part of the homeland she hadn't ever explored before in this form. Her sharp eyes, heightened hearing and improved sense of smell made it an amazing experience. The autumn leaves covering the ground crunched beneath their paws, releasing the sweet and homey scent of organic decay. The cool air added a crisp and invigorating element to each inhalation. She saw the bark of the trees they passed with exceptional clarity, even noting movement if there were birds, squirrels or insects among the tree branches.

She focused on these sensory images as they ran to avoid facing the reality that awaited her once she inevitably lost the shift. The knowledge that she was different had always bothered her. Now she had to deal with the fact that the reason she was different was so awful that her parents hadn't ever told her about it.

Freak. Mutant. Aberration.

Much as she tried, she couldn't stop the thoughts from running through her mind even as she worked to escape them. If she had been in her Estilorian form, she suspected she would be a bawling mess. So she vowed to maintain the shift as long as possible.

Domino appeared tireless, springing ahead of her with a goal of some sort. She eagerly followed, welcoming the adventure. Eventually, they entered a small clearing. Domino stopped running, prompting Sophia to do the same thing. They both had to catch their breath after such a long sprint.

As she collected herself, Sophia noticed an enticing aroma in the air. Curious, she turned in the direction of the scent and padded over to it. Domino went with her. She realized the odor was coming from a grouping of green plants that nearly reached the top of her panther head.

It smelled so good that she couldn't fight the urge to taste it. Domino gently pulled some of the leaves from the plant and chewed them. Sophia quickly followed suit.

Whatever properties were in the unusual plant quickly had Sophia's mind growing hazy. Her blood sang, giving her the urge to flop on the plants and roll around...so she did. She vaguely realized she was forgetting why she was there and what had so upset her in the first place. That was when she understood that Domino had led her there on purpose.

Smart kitty, she thought with a great deal of enthusiasm before she couldn't think at all.

Quincy forgot all about testing the inoculation after Sophia left. The moment she sprinted away, he turned to his elder with fury slashing through him.

"Why would you tell her that?" he demanded, for the first time in his existence not caring that he sounded disrespectful.

Ini-herit looked back at him with a placid gaze. "She would have received skewed results if she had proceeded to test the serum on herself. As a scientist, I thought she would appreciate the—"

"Sophia isn't *just* a scientist," Quincy interrupted. His chest and throat were tight with searing anger. He couldn't tell whether he was more upset with his elder or himself. "She has feelings, damn it. You've just made her think that she's somehow less than everyone else because of her differences."

When that provoked no reaction, Quincy cursed and stormed out of his cottage. He walked over to Sophia's clothing and picked it up from the ground. Whenever she shifted, her form used energy to convert from Estilorian to animal. During the split-second in her shift where her form was nothing but energy, she always lost her clothing. Since he intended to go after her, he knew he'd have to bring the clothing with him.

He started in the direction of her paw prints at a jog. They passed near her home, so he reasoned out where she'd gone. Before he started down the path leading to the panthers, the door to the house opened.

"Hi, Quincy," James said as he and Olivia emerged. He raised an eyebrow. "Do I want to know why you're holding Sophia's clothing?"

Glancing down, Quincy realized he had Sophia's bra and panties in one hand and the rest of her clothing in the other. Feeling his face flush, he quickly balled everything up so the undergarments were no longer visible.

Clearing his throat, he explained, "The experiment started off on rocky footing." When James and Olivia approached and stopped a few feet away, he said, "*Archigos* Ini-herit told her about the cursed arrow."

Olivia inhaled sharply and lost all of her color. James reached out and pulled her against his side, looking nearly as shaken.

"Oh, my God," Olivia breathed. She looked at James as her eyes filled.

"Where did she go?" he asked.

"I think she's with the panthers." Quincy lifted her clothes. "I was about to go after her."

James nodded in understanding. "Thank you, Quincy. We were about to go and meet with the elders. Zayna had difficulty reasoning with Hoygul and she's heading back without the scroll piece. We have to figure out what to do." He exchanged a look with Olivia. "But now…"

Quincy's mind jumped from one concern to the next. The Scultresti elder had failed in her attempt to get the map to the library, which meant the scroll piece was still out there and potentially accessible to Eirik. He didn't see how that was possible. Why would Hoygul defy his elder when it came to something so important? Why didn't Zayna try to force the issue and use her power to retrieve the map?

He thought back to his own experience with the odd Scultresti male all of those years ago. If it hadn't been for Saraqael's quest to save the woman he loved, Hoygul never would have shared the map with them. Quincy wondered if he might have more success if he approached the Scultresti, but he doubted it.

Shaking his head, he returned to his more immediate concern. "Let me go and retrieve Sophia. I'll talk to her about this and help her process it."

James frowned. "I'll come with you. She must be upset with us for keeping this from her. She has a right to feel that way."

Tears trailed down Olivia's cheeks. She didn't comment, but her grip on James' hand was tight enough to turn her knuckles white. When she jumped a little and rubbed her belly with her free hand, Quincy gave her a questioning look.

"I think it would be best if you stayed with Olivia," he told James. "The baby is very close to arriving. I'd feel better if I knew you were with her in case she goes into labor."

Clearly torn, James looked at Olivia. "I don't—"

"I promise, I'll bring her back as soon as possible," Quincy interrupted. The need to go after Sophia tugged at him. "Let her get her anger out with me rather than you. Go and find out what the plan is regarding the scroll piece, and once you're done, Sophia will be back and you can talk to her about everything."

The couple exchanged looks and thoughts. Eventually, James reluctantly nodded. "Okay, Quincy," he said, catching his gaze. "Please let her know…"

Even without the words, Quincy understood. "I will."

Before they could change their minds, he turned and hurried in the direction of the section of forest where the panthers dwelled. He knew Sophia very well. She had likely gone straight to Domino.

The panthers lived in a rather vast part of the protected forest near Sophia's family home. Over the years, with a few of the panthers having prowled the plane only to return with mates, the cat population had grown to nearly thirty. It was easy enough for Quincy to make his way to Domino's den.

The cat's sister, Cleo, slept there still. Quincy used a wise amount of caution when approaching the female. Although the panthers were all tame by their standards, an animal was an animal. No sense risking a claw swipe or bite.

"Cleo," Quincy said. He had to repeat her name several times before she opened her eyes and yawned. Her wide mouth revealed sharp, yellow teeth. "I need you to take me to Domino and Sophia."

The panthers born of the bloodline leading back to Olivia's panther friend, Aurora, and her mate, Titan, all possessed a heightened level of intelligence. He knew Cleo, as one of their grand-cubs, understood him.

"Please. It's very important," he said, allowing his concern to filter through his tone. "Sophia's upset and I need to speak with her."

Cleo rose and stretched, then scented the air and the ground. Within a minute, they were off and running.

Quincy wished he could fly to Sophia. The thick trees wouldn't allow for an extension of wings, but even more importantly, the heavy enchantments in place around the homeland—necessary to contain the unpredictable powers of the Kynzesti—also prevented it. So he kept up with Cleo as best he could, ignoring the burning of his lungs and the sheen of perspiration that formed as they progressed.

The sun was low in the sky before they reached a small clearing. He heard the sound of movement before he saw them. Taking a few seconds to catch his breath and center himself, Quincy wondered what to say. He knew Sophia would be furious and upset.

Finally, he decided he would say whatever he thought would help get her through this. If she decided to lash out at him, well, it wouldn't be the first time. He could handle it.

Cleo hurried straight into the clearing, so Quincy now followed her. When he got within sight of the three cats, he blinked in confusion. They were all rolling around among a clump of rather matted-looking plants. Sophia was stretched almost her full length on a bed of the crushed greenery.

"Sophia?"

She rolled slumberously and looked up at him. Her deep blue-green eyes stood out against her blonde fur, making his breath catch. Even in this form she was spectacular.

Then she started to rise. Her sleek grace and controlled power was apparent in every movement. Much to his surprise, however, she didn't just rise up on all four paws. Instead, she dissolved the shift.

He felt his jaw slacken. His pulse thundered in his ears. With the last rays of golden sunlight dappling her naked skin, she looked every bit like a goddess from human mythology.

"Hello, Quincy," she said. "I wondered if you'd come."

Chapter 13

"SOPHIA."

That was all Quincy managed. He couldn't command his limbs to move. His eyes were so focused on her in all of her magnificence that he hadn't blinked in over a minute. When she approached, he had the insane urge to run. This was way too much temptation for him.

And it was so far outside of Sophia's usual behavior that he thought she must be possessed.

"You'll have to forgive me, Quincy," she said as she reached for her panties. They practically fell out of his hand and he had to adjust his hold on the rest of her clothes. "I believe whatever plant that Domino introduced me to affects cats in an unusual way. It's lingering even after my shift."

Her words finally eased him from the spell she had cast. Deliberately not focusing on her body as she began to dress herself, he looked into her eyes. They were glassy. Her cheeks were flushed. She had to hold onto his arm as she put her panties on, telling him her balance was at least somewhat compromised. Then she giggled, the sound definitely unnatural for her.

"You're drugged," he said in disbelief.

"I am?" she asked, her face transforming into a smile. "How lovely."

He looked more closely at the plants. "That's *nepeta cataria*—catnip. It affects some cats like a drug might affect a human."

She took her bra from him with a sound of acknowledgement, apparently unconcerned over her condition. He started to say something else, but realized she had brought the fastening of her bra to the front and was trying to get the hooks to catch. Her movements were deliberate and focused. And unsuccessful.

Cursing, she handed the bra to him. "Help me with this, would you?"

He must be dreaming. He *had* to be dreaming.

"Sophia..."

She rolled her eyes. "Just hook it for me, Quincy. Surely you can manage that, even if it requires you touching someone as freakish as me."

Now he frowned, his temper rising. If for no other reason than to get her covered so his blood could cool off, he tossed her other clothes onto a log, grasped her arms and began putting the bra on her, praying he was doing it right.

"Stop calling yourself a freak," he said.

"Why?" she retorted, though her tone was calm in contrast to his irritation. "You obviously think of me as one. You haven't been able to look at me for longer than a few seconds at a time since I turned thirteen and assumed this form. And I heard you tell Tate I wasn't pretty."

She turned her back to him and moved her long hair over her shoulder so he could clasp her bra in the back. The deep blue-green crescents running along her shoulder blades marked where her wings would emerge whenever she wanted to extend them. Like the rest of her class, she also bore a symbol on the back of her neck marking her as a Kynzesti: a deep blue-green sun with gold, light green, light blue, dark blue and blue-gray flames...a blending of their bonded parentage.

When his fingers brushed against the soft skin of her back as he fumbled with the clasp, they both reacted. He clenched his jaw against the desire to touch her more. She shivered.

He finally got the bra hooked. Rather than let her turn around, however, he moved closer to her, pressing himself against her back. He heard her breath catch. Settling his hands on her shoulders, he bent down so his mouth all but brushed against her ear.

"As I tried to explain when you visited me in my cottage," he said softly, "you couldn't be more wrong. I don't look at you for too long because I'd never be able to hide how powerfully you affect me." Now, he did allow his lips to brush against the sensitive skin of her ear. Her breath quickened. He allowed his hands to glide down the smooth length of her arms. "I told Tate that you're not pretty. You're *spectacular*. Sophia, since the moment I first saw you in your fully mature form, I've had to restraint myself from touching you like this. Every moment you're near me is blissful torture."

She turned. He lowered his hands, but held her gaze.

"You're not a freak," he said when she just continued to stand there staring at him in the indigo twilight. "You're a wonder. More special than any other Estilorian. Your abilities are unique and amazing, and something to be proud—"

She interrupted him by reaching up with both hands, grabbing him by the back of the neck and bringing his lips to hers.

Just as the effects of the catnip eased, Quincy's addictive touch and potent words had their own impact on Sophia's senses. The feel of his warm body pressed against her half naked back had been beyond description. Combining that with his lips against her ear, whispering such incredible words in his musical accent, had nearly made her knees buckle. She began to think she was more heavily drugged than she thought, and he was merely a hallucination speaking words she had long dreamed to hear.

Almost as if to prove that had to be the case, she decided to kiss him. Unfortunately, that only told her she was utterly wrong.

At first, he stiffened in shock. But he quickly sank into the kiss, making her realize just how little she knew about this particular activity.

His warm lips moved tenderly against hers, telling her that her urgent pressing of her mouth against his wasn't quite right. She deliberately relaxed, focusing on every sensation as his hands moved to cradle her, one hand against the small of her back and the other at the base of her neck beneath her hair. Every touch sent delicious waves of pleasure coursing through her. It was even more potent than the charge of energy she experienced when she shifted.

A soft moan built in her throat as his lips moved against hers. She felt his hand move from around her neck to the side of her jaw. When he traced the delicate skin there, it sent another shiver through her.

"Open for me," he whispered.

When she obediently parted her lips, he kissed her in a way that put even her most lucid dream kisses to shame. His tongue touched hers, introducing a whole new layer of sensation to the experience. She suddenly understood why this was seen as such a huge moment in someone's existence. It was *amazing.*

Before long, the kiss took on a sense of urgency that frightened her. Yet she found herself making even more noises of approval in the back of her throat. Combined with his touch, she thought she might ignite into a pile of cinder.

He broke their connection when they both needed to catch their breath. The abrupt parting brought with it a healthy dose of sobriety.

When she pulled away, he didn't stop her. They stood staring at each other for a long moment. She easily saw the emotions that he had been keeping from her all of these years. He clearly struggled to keep his eyes on her face, verifying what he told her a few minutes ago. She suddenly saw the last five years in an entirely different way.

And it broke her heart.

Moving over to the log holding her clothes, she dressed in the moonlight, feeling his eyes on her the entire time. She wondered if he would speak, but wasn't surprised when he didn't. He knew her well enough to understand that she required time to process information, especially regarding new discoveries.

When she was once again dressed, she faced him again. "I really wish you had told me this sooner, Quincy."

His silver eyes caught the moonlight. She read the regret there. "I should have."

"You understand now that in the span of half a day, I've learned that you've kept two life-altering pieces of information from me," she said levelly. "You've kept them from me for years, despite the fact that I had a right to know both."

He started to say something, then stopped himself. Eventually, he just said, "Yes."

"You've shattered any trust between us," she said, feeling emotion burning behind her eyes and fighting against it.

"I know," he said quietly. "I'm sorry, Sophia. I won't offer you excuses. But I will ask you if you think there's any chance I can rebuild that trust."

She hadn't ever felt such an overwhelming mix of emotions as what coursed through her right then. Anger had her wanting to lash out at him and insist there was no way she would ever trust him again. But because he finally held her gaze for longer than a brief moment, she saw how much her words impacted him. There was no way she would be able to sift through everything she had just learned in such a brief span of time.

Though she knew it wasn't the answer he wanted to hear, she gave him the truth.

"I don't know."

Chapter 14

"HOYGUL FEELS THAT THE SCROLL PIECE IS SAFER IN THE HIDDEN LIBRARY than it would be outside and in the possession of an individual," Clara Kate said.

She sat next to her mother on one of the large logs around the outdoor fire pit not too far from the training paddock. When Quincy and Sophia returned, it was to find everyone getting ready for a gathering around the fire. The families usually did this a couple of times a month, letting the kids roast marshmallows and stay up past their usual bedtimes. At the moment, the younger kids all played a game in the distance, freeing their parents and older siblings up for this conversation.

Quincy sat with Tiege and Ariana on a log next to Clara Kate and her parents. Tate sat beside her parents with Zachariah standing behind her. Jabari, Sebastian and Ini-herit took up the next log, leaving Sophia seated beside her parents on the other side of the fire.

Knowing his guilt was all over his face, Quincy tried not to look at any of them. It had been a very painful and quiet walk back with Sophia.

He'd really made a mess of things now.

Gabriel looked over at him. "Quincy, when you dealt with Hoygul, what convinced him to give you and Saraqael the map?"

Bringing his focus to the issue at hand, Quincy responded, "Saraqael told Hoygul about his quest to save Kate. Hoygul and Saraqael got into an odd conversation about Hoygul's writing…the stories he was forced to leave behind on the human plane when the planes were separated. He asked if humans still studied his work under the name Homer, and whether Saraqael could tell him who Odysseus' love was."

"Penelope," Clara Kate, Sophia and Olivia all said at the same time.

"Yes," Quincy said. "As soon as Saraqael answered him, Hoygul agreed to give us the map."

There was a moment where the only sound was the fire crackling. Quincy noticed a few looks shared between the parents of the Kynzesti and the elders and imagined they were exchanging thoughts.

Though he knew he shouldn't, he glanced at Sophia. The firelight made her already beautiful features even more striking. When he found himself remembering how unbelievable she tasted, he forced himself to turn his thoughts. That was when he realized she was looking across the fire in his direction.

His heart rate picked up. Was she also thinking about their kiss?

Then he clued into the fact that she wasn't looking right at him, but beside him. Feeling like an idiot, he also looked over to see what had captured her attention. Ariana sat wringing her hands and staring into the fire. Her face was pale, but she appeared calmer than in recent days.

"Hoygul's point that the scroll is safer in the library is a valid one," Jabari said, turning his attention.

"However," Gabriel added, "Hoygul's home isn't exactly secure. While it isn't easy to find and it's surrounded by a jungle that most beings won't willingly pass through, it isn't protected in the same way as Central or the homes of the elders."

"Why not?" Tate asked.

Ini-herit answered. "It was not seen as necessary. Very few know that Hoygul holds the map to the ancient library. Nearly as few would have any interest in traveling there. Most Estilorians, in fact, are unaware of the library's existence."

"How did you find out about it, Quincy?" C.K. asked.

"I, uh, was told about it by commander Raphael," he replied.

He tried not to flush when he felt his elder's gaze settle on him. He hadn't been exactly forthcoming with his class commander regarding his reasons for wanting access to some of the oldest and most powerful texts on the human plane. He suspected that after Saraqael died, his elder found out that Quincy had basically deceived the commander.

"Do we have any idea if Eirik knows about the library?" Sophia asked.

"Uriel is communicating regularly with his scouts," Gabriel said, "but they haven't discovered Eirik's location. It appears that he's laying low rather than rebuilding his forces."

"We have no reason to believe that he knows about the library yet," Jabari added.

The "yet" wasn't lost on any of them. Quincy considered what might happen if Eirik somehow learned about the library. Hoygul would likely be brutally tortured, if not killed, for the powerful information he held.

"I don't understand why you just don't make Hoygul give you the map," Tiege said with a frown. "You're elders. Why should he have a right to refuse you?"

Jabari sighed. "The map is not a physical item," he explained. "It is passed to a being through Hoygul's abilities. It's almost as though the map becomes a part of you."

That was a fairly accurate description, Quincy thought. Saraqael had been the one to receive the map to the library. After Hoygul used his skills to activate the map, Saraqael flew there as though a homing beacon had been inserted into his head. Quincy, on the other hand, had received an internal "map" that only worked while inside the library. It ultimately led to the scroll Saraqael used to save Kate. If they hadn't worked together, they never would have found it.

It appeared that Hoygul had a strong sense of protectiveness toward the items in the library and didn't want to take any chances. That was what made him such a great map-keeper.

"Because the map requires Hoygul's cooperation to obtain," Jabari continued, "there is no *forcing* him to provide it."

"Besides," Sebastian said, "he's only doing what we empowered him to do in the first place."

Quincy considered Eirik and his penchant for torturing others. While it wasn't something the elders would ever resort to, he suspected there might, indeed, be a way to force the map out of the Scultresti male. It was a true concern.

Tiege's expression darkened. "That still makes no sense to me. You said yourselves that Hoygul is the only way we have to get to the library before Eirik does."

"Not the only way."

Ariana's words were soft but clear, especially since they issued from right beside Quincy. Her lavender gaze remained focused on the fire. When Sophia got to her feet, Quincy glanced at her. She walked right toward him, making all of the thoughts vaporize from his brain.

Her gaze never met his. The deliberateness of it hit his heart like a viper's strike. She walked past him and then knelt in front of Ariana. Her scent, like a mix of night blooms blended with crushed exotic spices, floated up to him as she took the other female's hand.

"You're right, Ariana," Sophia said. "You can find the scroll piece."

"How could you ask her to do that, Soph?" Tiege demanded. "She's—"

"She's strong," Sophia interrupted, not looking away from Ariana. "And she's more courageous than she knows." A tear slid down Ariana's cheek. "But what I know most about Ariana is that she cares about others. It's why she became a Lekwuesti when she assumed her Estilorian form upon transitioning to this plane. It's why she'll do this…because she won't want what happened to her to happen to anyone else."

"There must be another way."

"No, Tiege," Ariana said. She finally looked away from the fire and turned to catch Tiege's worried gaze. "I don't think there is. I understand why you're resistant to my doing this, and I thank you for it. Every part of me wants to resist it, too. But Sophia's right."

Quincy's eyebrows rose as he realized what she was saying. He felt the surge of hope and excitement that circled through the group.

She was willing to go and get the scroll piece.

Then she turned back to Sophia. "You say that I'm courageous, but I'm not. I'm terrified and selfish enough that I want to spend the rest of my existence here. I'll admit that the only reason I'm considering doing this at all is because I fear falling short of your opinion of me. I treasure the friendship you've shared with me, Sophia."

"I understand. I feel the same," Sophia said.

Quincy heard the emotion in her voice and ached to reach out and place a comforting hand on her shoulder. Then his heart dropped into his stomach.

"Will you come with me?" Ariana asked.

"Of course," Sophia replied without a moment's hesitation.

A rush of conversation struck up then, but Quincy barely heard it. He watched Ariana reach out to hug Sophia and knew—because he knew Sophia—that there would be no swaying her from this course. Fear raced through him as he watched her stand and turn in her parents' direction.

Olivia and James both rose as they objected to Sophia's agreement to leave the homeland, but they stopped talking when she faced them.

"Mom and Dad," she said in a calm tone as she stepped closer to them, "I need you to let me do this. I want to do it for Ariana and for the lives it will save." She turned and waved toward Tate. "Tate will have to go to dissolve the illusion around the library once Ariana leads us there. Tiege isn't going to let Ariana and Tate go without him, even if he has to use another illusion to sneak away like he did last time."

Quincy watched Caleb and Skye exchange looks with each other and their children as they all considered this. The gravity of the situation was hugely apparent.

"Zachariah will go wherever Tate does," Sophia continued, "and *archigos* Uriel already promised to send us with a host of Waresti. I won't be alone."

She stopped right in front of her parents, who both reached out to touch her shoulders. Quincy saw the conflict on their faces, yet knew they weren't going to deny her. The outcome they all sought—stopping Eirik from reassembling the scroll—was too important. Any risk Sophia and the others took by traveling with heavy protection to the library was far outweighed by the need to guarantee the safety of all Estilorians.

"You're right, honey," James said, pulling Sophia into a hug. "But I'm not happy about it."

"I know, Dad," she said.

Her gaze slid to Quincy's when she pulled back from the hug. He opened his mouth to speak. There was no way she was doing this without him. He would ask commander Raphael to come down to watch over Amber, Olivia and Skye while he traveled with the others, just as he had done before. Yes, that would—

"Uh oh," Olivia said.

Everyone turned to look at her. Quincy surged to his feet. He knew that he wouldn't be going with Sophia, after all.

"What is it?" Jabari asked, also getting to his feet.

"My water just broke," Olivia replied.

PART II:

DISTURB

Disturb [dih-**sturb**]: To interrupt the quiet, rest, peace or order of; to interfere with or hinder.

Chapter 15

SNOW SWIRLED THROUGH THE BITING AIR AS METIS MADE HER WAY TO Eirik and Deimos. She hated traveling in such inhospitable weather, but she knew that Eirik wouldn't tolerate another day without news from her, and it wasn't as though he could just walk into where she currently lived without getting captured or killed.

She had given serious thought to severing their agreement. He was so arrogant that he would fall easily if she decided to end his life. He didn't trust her, but he would never suspect her true capabilities.

The fact was, however, that she had very little practical knowledge about the Estilorian plane. Although she had been taught about the world outside of the cavern where she was raised, she now knew that the reality was far more overwhelming than mere stories. She didn't yet understand the differences between the classes and how they all interconnected, since the only being she had ever known before Deimos entered her life was her creator. Hearing about a Lekwuesti's ability to conjure clothing or already-prepared food was one thing. Experiencing it was quite another.

No, if she wanted to use the Elder Scroll and assume a position of esteem and importance on this plane, she needed to know more about it first. Eirik had already taught her much, as had those beings currently residing with her. Given just a bit more time, she knew she would no longer have any need for Eirik at all.

He suddenly stepped out from behind a tree, making her start and clutch her cloak more closely to her neck.

"I see you have been waiting for me," she said, her voice sounding both loud and dampened in the snowy wilderness.

"For far too long," he said.

Despite the temperature, he still wore nothing more on his upper body than a furred vest. This was paired with his usual black leather pants and knee-high heavy boots. His long blond and red-striped hair was in its usual spiked half-ponytail, but the snow was beginning to make it appear wet and limp. A snowflake landed on his long eyelashes. The white fluff didn't soften the look in his eyes in the slightest.

"I have achieved success with my plan," she said.

Now, his face showed interest. "You have the two females?"

"No," she said, shifting her weight as her feet grew numb. "I have secured the leverage we need to bring them here."

"This is taking too long, damn it," Eirik snapped, his frown fierce.

"I know that you are impatient, but the scroll is not going anywhere."

"How do you know that? For all we know, the elders have collected any remaining pieces of the scroll while you keep me here following your lead like a sheep."

If only he knew.

"I am certain that the elders have not retrieved the other scroll pieces," she said. "My recent efforts have given me extensive insight into their plans and actions."

"Is that so?"

Not liking his narrowed eyes, she added, "You know very well who my company is these days. They talk, I listen."

He stared at her in silence.

"Where is Deimos?" she asked, not allowing herself to grow intimidated.

"I have decided that you will not see him again until you present me with the females."

Outrage rushed through her. "What?"

"Two can play at this game, Metis," he said. "If you will not keep me apprised of your plans, I will withhold the only thing of any importance to you. Until those females have been delivered to me, Deimos is mine."

Sophia was allowed to attend her sibling's birth. Although she'd been asking to witness one for years, she hadn't ever been granted permission. It was an intense experience, her parents had explained, that required the utmost concentration of both parents and the being delivering the baby.

Having a young, excitable child with a million questions in the room could lead to someone becoming distracted and, thus, disastrous results.

This time, she had finally been deemed mature enough to watch. Although her mind raced with questions, she held her tongue. Like her relatives, she sat and watched the proceedings in silence.

Well, not utter silence. Sebastian had conjured soft music. It served as a calming factor, she supposed.

The delivery room was located on the second floor of Quincy's clinic. Sophia hadn't ever been up here before. He kept the room sterile and ready for use, especially so close to delivery. There were three beds that rose or lowered as needed. Although it had yet to happen, there was always the chance that all three sisters could deliver at the same time. For this reason, Quincy had ordered three birthing stations when the clinic was built.

An assortment of medical implements lined the counter near the bed where her mother now rested. Having conversed with Quincy at length about this process, she knew that he faced unique challenges on this plane regarding monitoring the baby. On the human plane, he had explained, they had something called electricity. The electricity allowed for the operation of what humans called machines, and these machines were used to monitor the mother's heart rate as well as the baby's. They could even tell when a contraction was coming.

Such was not the case here. Quincy spent a lot of time monitoring a device that he had created to measure the birthing mother's blood pressure, as well as a stethoscope to listen to her heartbeat. He frequently held both of his hands on her mother's belly, though what he gauged there she had no idea. She only knew that she had never seen him so focused.

Her dad stood beside her mother's bed, holding her hand and talking to her. Although Sophia and her relatives could all hear through the barrier of lavender light that Sebastian generated to keep any germs from spreading to the birthing area, none of them spoke to keep from being distracting. Sophia knew her aunts and uncles could all communicate with their thoughts, so they didn't really need to speak anyway. For the first time, she wished she had that kind of connection with them.

"Here comes another one," her mother said, adjusting herself on the bed to try and make herself more comfortable for the next contraction.

Just like the others had, this contraction caused her mother to issue low moans as she breathed her way through it. Quincy held his hands on her belly as her father rubbed her lower back. Sophia hated to see her mother in such pain. She seemed to grow paler with each passing minute. Based on what she'd learned, Sophia knew her mother would be pushing her body beyond limits considered normal for a human birthing. This experience would all but bring her to death's door.

"That was definitely more intense," Quincy said when the contraction passed. "We're getting closer. Time to check the baby's progress."

Her mother nodded wearily as her father wiped her brow. She settled back on the bed as Quincy positioned her legs and lifted the sheet covering the lower half of her body so that he could conduct his examination. Sophia realized that he treated her mother with something akin to reverence. Everything was done with care and consideration for the birthing mother.

"You're about seven centimeters," he reported as he again lowered her mother's legs. "You're doing great, Olivia. You'll be able to start pushing soon."

His accent wasn't as noticeable when he was so controlled, she realized, watching him walk over to a sink to wash his hands. That was kind of a shame, she couldn't help but think. She had always loved the lyrical quality of it.

Her mind went back to their kiss. She hadn't ever expected to feel that way. She couldn't believe the range of feeling that another being's touch could evoke. Okay, *Quincy's* touch. She could at least be honest enough with herself to acknowledge that she wouldn't have felt quite the same exhilaration and passion with just anyone.

But there was so much more involved here. He had kept some truly major things from her. After speaking with her parents earlier, she knew that they had asked everyone not to tell her about the fact that she had been affected by a cursed Mercesti weapon. They hadn't wanted her treated any differently because, they said, she wasn't different in any way that mattered. They had worried that she would feel alienated or set apart, which she admittedly did.

So maybe she could give Quincy some grace about that one. He was merely honoring her parents' wishes, and she knew that her parents had done what they thought was best. It had hurt to learn the truth, of course, but her mother's tears and fierce hug when she returned home told her that they would have spared her that feeling if they could do it all over again.

But the other huge, gargantuan omission by Quincy, well...that was all on him.

How could he have kept his attraction to her a secret all this time? He had caused her immeasurable hurt and confusion over the past five years. The close friendship they'd nurtured before she turned thirteen had been changed forever by his treatment of her thereafter. When she thought of the many times he made excuses to avoid being alone with her and how awkward and ashamed that made her feel, she wanted to march into the delivery room and give him a piece of her mind.

As though he sensed her thoughts, he glanced over and caught her gaze. He started to smile, but whatever he saw on her face had the expression faltering. Instead, he turned back to his tools, picking up the stethoscope.

Sophia felt another gaze on her. When she glanced sideways, she realized her Aunt Skye was watching her. Her aunt's light blue eyes moved thoughtfully from Sophia to Quincy, and Sophia's face suffused with heat. Her aunt was remarkably intuitive.

Rather than risk giving anything away, Sophia looked back at her parents.

Time passed quickly. Her mother's contractions grew closer together. Her moans got louder, bordering on cries of agony. Sophia knew her father absorbed what he could through their connection to try and alleviate some of her pain. They were both flushed and sweating despite the cool temperature in the room.

Then Quincy did another exam and nodded. "It's time."

Sophia realized her aunts and uncles sat a little straighter. Not knowing why, she did the same, leaning toward the lavender barrier to watch the proceedings more closely.

Quincy once again lifted her mother's legs, bending them at the knee and instructing her to move closer to the end of the bed. She did so with her father's assistance, remaining in a sitting position. Quincy raised a couple of wooden handles on either side of the bed that Sophia hadn't noticed before. She wondered about their purpose until her mother reached out and grasped one on either side.

"Okay, Olivia," Quincy said, sitting on a stool at the foot of the bed, positioning himself between her legs so that he could assist with the baby's delivery. "You need to push with the next contraction. Focus on me."

Where his tone had been soothing and encouraging before, it was deadly serious now. Sophia watched with awe as his eyes began to glow with silver light.

The baby's Estilorian energy wasn't fully joined with its part-human form inside the womb. Similar to the way a human soul transitioned into an Estilorian form as it was Embraced and brought to the Estilorian plane by a Corgloresti, the unborn baby required a concentrated amount of faith by both of its parents and the Corgloresti delivering it in order for the birth to succeed.

In light of this uncertain element to the process, Sophia well understood why her mother and aunts all wanted Quincy's help. Outside of his medical knowledge, his unsurpassed faith was invaluable.

"Here it comes," her mother said with a deep breath.

Sophia gripped the arms of her chair as she watched her mother catch and hold Quincy's gaze when the contraction hit her. Her father rubbed her back and issued words of encouragement as her mother grimaced and pushed.

Quincy's eyes glowed like stars. Pure silver light radiated from beneath the sheet covering her mother's lower body. The intensity on Quincy's handsome face had tears pricking Sophia's eyes.

He was performing a miracle.

Several heart-stopping moments later, a soft cry erupted. Tears trailed down Sophia's cheeks as Quincy grinned and held up a towel-wrapped newborn to her exhausted parents.

"Congratulations," he said. "It's a boy."

Chapter 16

OLIVIA AND JAMES NAMED THEIR NEW SON DEVON.

Quincy took care of cleaning the mess that inevitably resulted from birth as the couple bonded with their newborn. The initial moments immediately following the birth were precious and essential. After the baby was named, both parents whispered words that fully bonded them as a family, not unlike a pairing vow. To seal the vow, they kissed the baby at the same time.

The flash of deep blue-green light that resulted caused the Kynzesti marking on the back of the baby's neck. Loud bawling ensued, which Olivia promptly subdued with shushing and cooing noises. The offering of her breast for the baby's first meal also helped.

Only after Quincy made sure the area was sterilized and Olivia and James were ready did he give Gabriel the nod to send a thought to Sebastian so that the barrier could be removed. When it faded, everyone hurried forward.

"Congratulations, Dad," Gabriel said with a grin, clapping James on the back. Then he leaned down to kiss Olivia's cheek. "You did great, Liv."

Amber moved forward to use her healing energy on Olivia. Although the power required for the birth drained the mother of her abilities for weeks afterward, Amber and Gabriel could provide some amount of physical healing to expedite Quincy's efforts.

Words of congratulations and support were exchanged among the family members as Quincy gathered his implements and a bag of soiled linens to bring to Sebastian for sterilization and cleaning. He was surprised when he sensed someone standing by his elbow. He was even more surprised when he realized it was Sophia.

He wanted to greet her, but her deep blue-green gaze was focused on him and his tongue just lodged to the roof of his mouth.

Fortunately, she spoke first. "Thank you, Quincy. I had no idea how powerful this entire experience would be. What you can do...well, it's amazing."

Turning his gaze to the counter, he was finally able to command his voice. "It was nothing."

"Don't say that," she said, her tone more forceful than he would have expected. It caused him to look at her again. "You should never downplay your abilities."

She had no idea how much her words meant to him. For a brief energized moment, they simply stood there looking at each other. When her gaze moved to his mouth, he knew she was remembering their kiss. That, of course, made him think about it.

Again.

Noticing that it had grown very quiet, he finally looked away from her. He realized that everyone in the room now stared at them.

"Ah..." he began, his face growing warm. He trailed off, not having a clue what to say.

"I was thanking Quincy," Sophia said, moving closer to the bed. "I've never experienced anything like that. It was absolutely beautiful."

Just like you, Quincy thought, and wanted to hit himself in the head for being so pathetic.

"Would you like to hold him?" Olivia asked, shifting the sleeping baby toward Sophia.

Sophia's face lit up. "Sure."

She accepted the bundled baby, holding him gingerly and with obvious awe. The tender and unguarded look on her face had Quincy longing to reach out and touch her. As she lowered the blanket to look on her brother's features for the first time, her expression changed. She looked stunned.

"What is it?" Quincy asked, hurrying over.

She caught his gaze, her eyes wide. "He's blond," she said. Her eyes filled with tears and she looked back down at Devon and smiled. "I'm no longer the only blond Kynzesti."

It was late the next day before Sophia joined those of her kin training in the paddock. She normally would have found an excuse to avoid it, especially in light of her exhausting experience the day before, but she was about to embark on a dangerous journey in search of the second scroll piece. It made sense that she prepare as much as possible.

"Hey, Soph," Clara Kate greeted her with a grin. "Congrats on becoming a big sister again."

"Thanks," Sophia said, returning the smile.

She received similar congratulations from other members of her family, though she only vaguely heard them. She had just noticed Quincy walking over to Aunt Skye and Uncle Caleb's home. Ini-herit walked at his side.

The last time she saw Quincy speaking alone with his elder, he had been preparing to leave because of something she said to him. Was he about to do the same thing now?

Seeing where her attention had turned, C.K. said, "Oh, yeah. Zayna and Uriel arrived late last night. And it sounds like Knorbis and Malukali will be getting back today. I'm sure they're going to make plans for you all to head out as soon as possible."

"Oh," Sophia said. She couldn't deny the relief she experienced when she realized she hadn't once again chased Quincy away.

"Indeed they will," Zachariah said, drawing her attention. He tossed a bo at her, which she caught one-handed. "So we should stop the chit-chat." His red gaze swept the small crowd and settled on Tate. "On this journey, you will face injury and death.

"Prevention against either of those outcomes begins now."

Sophia couldn't ever remember being this sore. Even a warm bath didn't ease the stiffness of her muscles after Zachariah's vigorous workout. She dressed in a long-sleeved top and pants with boots, since the temperature had dropped, and then made her way downstairs.

Her parents waited for her in the kitchen. Her mother nursed Devon in a rocking chair situated in the eating area and looked up as Sophia entered.

"Hi, sweetie," she said, attempting a smile. It obviously masked her worry, though. "Your dad is ready to go with you to meet with everyone."

He stood up from his place at the table and moved to her mother's side. "Just send a thought if you need anything."

His comment was issued out of more than just typical courtesy. These early days after Devon's birth were meant to be spent within close proximity of both parents. The baby was developing the faith needed to maintain his new form. His parents were the ones who would help him do that. Both Olivia and Devon needed care and attention right now to ensure their well-being.

"We'll be okay," her mother said. "Amber and Skye will be here soon. Sophia, I'd love a hug."

Smiling, Sophia walked over and fulfilled her mother's request. "This won't take long. We're just going to chat with everyone about the plan."

"For now," her mother said. "But before I'm ready, you'll be leaving on this quest. I don't know when I'll see you again."

"It'll be fine, Mom."

"That's what they always say."

The meeting took place in her Uncle Gabriel and Aunt Amber's home. Sophia and her dad were the last to arrive. Everyone else waited in the large family room.

Tate sat on the raised stone hearth beside a crackling fire. Zachariah leaned against the wall beside the fireplace with his arms crossed over his chest and his eyes moving from one spot to the next. Sophia had learned that he had a very assessing mind. Since one of the core class attributes for Mercesti was strategizing, she figured this worked well for him.

Ariana and Tiege sat beside each other on a loveseat near the fireplace. Their hands were linked, a fact that made Sophia's eyebrows rise. Apparently their relationship was progressing. She wasn't quite sure what to think about that.

"Welcome, James and Sophia," Jabari said. "Please make yourselves comfortable."

"Thanks," Sophia murmured, settling on the sofa next to Clara Kate. Her father moved over to stand beside her Uncle Gabriel and Uncle Caleb.

"We're glad to have everyone back," Jabari said. Then he added, "Well, with the exception of Malukali. But we do understand why she would remain behind when Kanika is still so unwell."

Sophia followed his gaze to Knorbis. The Wymzesti elder gave everyone a small smile and nod, but it didn't reach his eyes. He seemed tired and a little distracted, she thought. But then, the two elders were so close that it had to be difficult to be apart for any length of time. It made her wonder why he had left his wife to come here.

"We appreciate you making the trip back so quickly to help us strategize, Knorbis," Jabari said, answering her question. "The news that you learned from the Waresti guarding Kanika just impresses upon us how important it is that we move forward."

"Knorbis and Malukali found out that Eirik knows more about the location of the second scroll piece than we thought," Uriel explained from his position standing near a window. "Malukali received several disturbing Mercesti thoughts while at Kanika's. She and Knorbis felt it best that Knorbis come back to share this information directly."

"There is always the possibility of Mercesti with mental abilities intercepting our thoughts," Knorbis said. "We didn't want someone giving Eirik valuable information."

"He apparently knows that the second piece is in the ancient library," Uncle Gabriel said. "Knorbis said that they've also learned that the map to the library is being held by Hoygul, which puts the Scultresti at risk."

"We need to move forward with doing what we can to acquire the scroll piece before Eirik does," Jabari said. His gaze moved to Ariana, then continued around the room. "Ariana and Tate will need to use their abilities to get the piece. Zachariah, Tiege and Sophia will aid them. Uriel will lead the Waresti who will accompany them for their protection. The trip shouldn't take more than a week or so, depending upon exactly where on the Estilorian plane the library is."

"We should leave tomorrow at daybreak," Uriel said.

Sophia tried not to goggle. Tomorrow? She was only just starting to wrap her head around the fact that she was going to be a part of this, and he wanted to leave the following day?

"You still have enough of a connection to the scroll to be able to locate it, right?" Uncle Gabriel asked Ariana.

The Lekwuesti nodded, her expression grim. "Eirik sliced me with the sword that Volarius wore during the scroll's creation ceremony. I'll be able to draw on that connection to the scroll to find the remaining pieces. It would be helpful to know more about the library so that I can focus on getting to that piece first. If Eirik knows about it, we need to be sure he doesn't get it before we do."

Sophia smiled over the determination she heard in her friend's voice. It was very encouraging in light of the rough emotional road she had recently traveled.

"Quincy, will you speak with Ariana about what you remember from your visit to the library?" Jabari asked.

Surprised because she hadn't known he was in the room, Sophia glanced in the direction of Jabari's gaze and saw Quincy sitting at a checkerboard table against the wall. He briefly caught her gaze.

"Of course," he replied.

Flushing, she turned back around as Jabari said, "Thank you. As some of you know, Sebastian intends to travel with you since the Kynzesti haven't yet had an opportunity to visit Central and pair with a Lekwuesti. He will assist you with your hospitality needs."

"I believe it would be wise for me to go, as well," Knorbis said. "I might be able to be of some assistance if something goes awry at the library. Although my memories were erased, I did design it with Sebastian and could recall something when we get there."

"Very well," Jabari said. "And perhaps Malukali can join you if Kanika recovers."

Knorbis nodded. Sophia once again thought that he looked strained. He definitely missed his wife, something that made her heart go out to him.

"We will all meet tomorrow morning in the training paddock to see you off," Jabari concluded. "Let's put an end to this."

Chapter 17

QUINCY DIDN'T SLEEP MUCH THAT NIGHT. HE COULDN'T BELIEVE THAT Olivia and James were going to let Sophia leave. Didn't they realize how much danger she faced?

Every time he closed his eyes, he thought of Sophia in Eirik's clutches. He remembered the horrible and vicious creature, Deimos, who had attacked Ariana and Kanika and killed a number of other females. Thinking of Sophia against such an opponent terrified him.

The thought that she could shift into a stronger form was all that kept him sane. Of those traveling to retrieve the scroll piece, Sophia was probably the most able to defend herself against one of these fearsome opponents. In light of her small size, there was a lot of irony in that statement.

Since he wasn't sleeping anyway, Quincy got up before the sun rose and connected with his Lekwuesti for some tea and toast. He figured that was the most his system could handle just then.

A couple of hours later, everyone else finally started stirring. The sun was just cresting the horizon when everyone gradually made their way to the training paddock. Quincy absolutely had to speak with Sophia alone. There was still so much to say. He knew he wouldn't be able to sleep at all if she left without knowing how he felt about her.

As he passed Skye and Caleb's home, Tate's voice captured his attention, causing him to slow down. He glanced toward a covered terrace on the side of the castle and saw Tate engaged in a heated discussion with Zachariah in the shadows.

"I always wear them, Sparky," Tate said. "You can't dictate how I style my hair on top of everything else!"

"I can and I will," Zachariah argued. "You must leave the beads and feathers behind."

Quincy figured that wouldn't go over well. Tate was very rarely without her elaborate hair decorations. She had worn them since she was a child and considered them a standard part of her daily attire. When he saw her cross her arms and lift her chin, his suspicions were confirmed.

"I'm quite capable of making my own wardrobe decisions," she snapped. "I've been doing it for years. If you don't like my hair, too bad."

Zachariah reached out and grabbed her by the shoulders, giving her a little shake that had Quincy frowning and considering intervening. "This is not about my opinion regarding your hair, damn it. This is about sense. I have millennia more experience than you about such things, and you will listen to me."

Tate snorted. She didn't appear at all concerned that Zachariah looked like he wanted to choke her.

"Bloody hell," he said with another shake. "Do you not realize that it was the damn feathers and beads that led them to you?"

Quincy's eyebrows rose in surprise and comprehension. Zachariah was referencing the two Mercesti, Bertram and Tycho, who had captured Tate and brought her to Eirik almost two months ago. Quincy watched Tate's demeanor change as realization sank in for her as well. She reached up and touched her decorated ponytail, easily removing a brightly-colored feather.

Zachariah took it from her and held it in front of her face to punctuate his point. "These will create a trail leading the enemy right to you. Go and remove them. Now."

Tate lowered her gaze. "Okay, Sparky." She looked and sounded quite defeated.

She turned and walked back inside. Zachariah's gaze stayed on her until she closed the door behind her. Then he studied the feather for a moment, apparently lost in thought. He brought it closer to his face, as if catching its scent. Quincy saw an expression pass briefly across the other male's features that looked strangely like regret. He figured he imagined it. From what he had experienced so far, the Mercesti cared only about doing his job.

When Zachariah put the feather into a pants pocket and then turned to follow Tate into the castle, Quincy hurried to get back on the path to Sophia. A minute later, he spotted her exiting her family's home. She was by herself, a fact that thrilled him. He figured her parents weren't far behind, however.

"Good morning, Sophia," he greeted her, hurrying to catch her before she walked closer to the training paddock and those beings who might overhear them.

He thought he heard her sigh from beneath the hood of her cloak before she stopped walking and turned to face him. A few tendrils of her golden hair caught in the cold breeze and blew across her cheeks, but the rest had been confined in a bun. She adjusted the hood to make more of her face visible.

"Hi, Quincy. Are you seeing us off?"

"Yes." Nerves almost had him stopping there, but he'd spent far too long backing away from expressing himself to her. "I wanted to speak with you for a moment before you leave."

"Okay. I'm listening."

He swallowed, not very encouraged by her unemotional tone. Knowing he was pressed for time, he said, "I hope you'll take care while you're gone. You're very brave for doing this. I'll worry about you the entire time you're away."

She shrugged. "It'll only be a week, maybe two. You heard Jabari."

"Yes," he said, keeping his tone as level as hers. "But the babies will have all been delivered by then."

Her lips parted. He saw her processing this and the implications of it. Eventually, she closed her mouth and shrugged again.

"I suppose that means you'll be leaving again for an unknown period of time to harvest more souls?" she said. She could have been commenting on the weather for all of the inflection she put into the words.

"Well...that depends."

"Depends on what, Quincy?" she asked. "Or are you going to keep this to yourself, too?"

He winced at the sharp point, but knew he deserved it. "It depends on several things, including how everything stands between us. Before you go, I want you to know how I feel about you. You're right that I've kept things to myself, and I know now that I waited a very long time to say this. I can only hope I didn't wait too long."

Her face went from expressionless to puzzled. Before she spoke, he went on, "I love you, Sophia. I always have."

She stepped away from him, her face washing of all color. Moving forward out of instinct to see if there was anything he could do to help, he came to an abrupt stop when she held up her hands to ward him off.

"Holy light, Quincy," she said, her voice raspy. "I've only known since yesterday afternoon that you don't think I'm an abomination upon all Estilorians after believing that for more than five years. And now you're springing this on me just before I leave on this important journey?" She shook her head, looking at him as though she didn't recognize him. "You might just have the worst ability to express yourself of anyone on the plane."

"I thought—"

"What did you think? That I needed this on my mind right now? That the pressure of coming up with a response to your declaration of love was a great way to send me off?" She tugged her hood back into place, shielding half her face from him. "Well, you're wrong, Quincy."

And then she turned with a whip of her cloak to head toward the training paddock, leaving a shattered mass where his heart had been.

She didn't even tell him goodbye.

Clara Kate found him going an intense round with a sand-filled punching bag shortly after everyone left to retrieve the scroll piece. She was also dressed for training. She walked up to the punching bag and held it in place.

"Thanks," he said. Then he moved into another series of strikes.

"Got a lot of power in those punches today," she observed after a few minutes. "Working something out?"

Quincy paused, bouncing on the balls of his feet. "You could say that," he said before resuming.

Several more minutes passed with the thudding against the punching bag the only sound. When he paused again, Clara Kate caught his gaze. "It sucks to be left behind while the others do this huge thing, doesn't it?"

Stepping away and reaching for a nearby towel, Quincy wiped sweat off his face and neck. "Yeah," he said, figuring that was as safe an answer as any.

"It sucks even more when one of those who left is someone you really care about."

At first, he thought she meant Ini-herit. But the Corgloresti elder hadn't left, so that couldn't be right. As he drank some water he had left nearby, he considered her words.

"You know?" he asked at last, catching her understanding gaze.

"I've suspected," she clarified.

Because her eyes and expression reflected no judgment, he relaxed a bit. Shrugging, he put his cup to the side and then sat on the ground to stretch. She sat beside him.

"Your suspicions are spot on," he said.

"Well, it'll sure be interesting to see what kind of reaction Zachariah has when he finds out you're in love with Tate."

His eyes widening, he turned to her with an aghast expression. She burst out laughing and he knew then that she had been joking. That loosened up even more of his tension. He found himself grinning and shoving her in the shoulder.

"Ha, ha."

"I'm sorry," she said, though she didn't look it. "Yeah, I've been pretty certain about your feelings for Sophia since we went on our recent trip together. You expressed far more concern over her when she shifted and left our campsite than seemed necessary."

"Ah."

"Then I started paying attention to how the two of you interacted. I could see that carrying her in the harness was having an effect on you."

Now, embarrassment flooded him. "Geez, C.K. Give a guy a break."

She reached over and rubbed his hand, then gave it a squeeze. "Look, I just knew that it wasn't the most comfortable experience you'd ever had. It was easy enough to see that it wasn't because you didn't want to be touching Sophia."

He realized that she wasn't trying to be funny this time, so he let his defensiveness fall away. Releasing her hand, he reached down to grab his feet so he could stretch his quadriceps. "Yeah, well, Sophia saw it exactly the opposite way."

"What do you mean?"

"I mean that up until I talked with her yesterday, she was apparently convinced that I loathed the very sight of her."

Clara Kate's expression reflected the shock he felt when he first discovered this. She then grew thoughtful. "Hmm. Knowing Sophia like I do, I'm a little surprised."

"Why is that?"

"She rarely draws a conclusion with so little evidence to support it."

He snorted at that. "In her mind, she had all the evidence she needed. When I tried to tell her the truth, she blew up at me. She seems to think that I only told her how I feel so I could make her current trip more stressful."

"Oh, Quincy," she said, her eyes full of compassion. She reached up and rubbed his arm. "I'm really sorry. I know this doesn't help, but I do know how it feels to love someone without knowing exactly how they feel about you in return."

"It sucks," Quincy said.

"Yeah, it does."

They both turned at the sound of a throat clearing. Ini-herit stood behind them. Quincy hadn't even heard him approach and found that quite unnerving. Also unnerving was the elder's intent stare. He was focused on Clara Kate's hand where it rested on Quincy's shoulder. She seemed to realize this at the exact same time he did, as she quickly snatched her hand away.

"Yes, sir?" Quincy asked, hoping this didn't turn into yet another awkward situation. He'd had quite enough of those to last him a lifetime, thank you very much.

"I have come to inform you that Amber is in labor."

Instantly, everything else ceased to hold as much significance. Yes, the others had left on their important mission, but there were life-changing events occurring right here.

Quincy nodded and got to his feet. "Great. Please let her and Gabriel know that I'll meet them at the clinic." Glancing at Clara Kate, he asked, "So…you want to see your new brother or sister brought into the world?"

Chapter 18

"WHAT ARE WE DOING HERE, BERTRAM?"

Glancing up from his inadequate meal of a handful of walnuts, Bertram watched Tycho pace. They weren't really sheltered from sight, so the agitated movement as well as the fairly loud question made Bertram frown.

"Would you keep it down?" he snapped in a loud whisper. "And stop the pacing. The only thing between us and the one we are following is a couple of barren hills. For the love of darkness, any Estilorian taller than six feet could stand at the top of a hill and spot us even without the pacing. So knock it off already."

Although he hissed in complaint, Tycho dropped to the ground beside his companion. "I do not understand why we were asked to do this scouting by Eirik," he said.

At least his voice was a few decibels lower, Bertram observed. "It is not our job to understand."

He didn't add that he had been having similar questioning thoughts since Eirik's unexpected appearance. Back when they brought the Kynzesti female to Eirik to earn his favor, their leader made mention of some kind of scroll. Outside of that, they had no idea what he sought, and no amount of questioning had produced the information.

"He tells us next to nothing and now wants us to bring in the Kynzesti and Lekwuesti females for him. I suspect that he will then do whatever he wants with them and shut us out again."

"Our lord is honorable to his loyal followers," Bertram argued. "When we do this, we will be indispensible in his eyes."

Tycho considered this. "Do you suppose he will be inclined to share part of whatever it is the two females can find with their abilities?"

"Probably not," Bertram answered after a moment. That was why he had been questioning his lord more and more frequently in recent days.

They were distracted when the being they tracked suddenly appeared in the distance, surrounded by Waresti. Bertram waved at Tycho. The two of them quickly flattened themselves in the high grass. They had created camouflaging suits of stitched-together pieces of grassy earth and now hoped their efforts paid off. Lying as still as they could, they watched as the group gathered to depart. Although they were too far away to be heard, they were obviously about to take flight.

"Are you seeing what I am?" Tycho whispered.

Frowning, Bertram wondered what his companion meant. He looked among the group and couldn't see anything unusual.

Then two of the males parted. Standing right in the center of the others were the two females Eirik sought.

"Yes," Bertram said.

"Why do you suppose they are bringing the females outside of the protections surrounding their homeland?" Tycho wondered. "All this time, I thought we would have to capture someone and coerce them to get us through the protections."

Bertram considered the possibilities. They had followed the Wymzesti elder from Kanika's home, figuring he would lead them to where the two females resided. Once the elder disappeared from their sight, they set up camp, knowing that eventually someone would emerge from the area of protection. They then planned on capturing that individual and convincing him—or her—to either get them within the protected area or bring the females outside of it.

There had been concerns. Waresti patrolled the area, as did a large, black kragen and some fierce looking panthers. But as converted Waresti, Bertram and Tycho had survived many centuries on their abilities to evade detection.

Now, their efforts had paid off. They watched as the group extended their wings to take flight. A huge mass suddenly flew out of the forest. Apparently the kragen would be going with them.

"Is that a pair of red wings I see?" Tycho asked.

Tilting his head, Bertram saw the wings in question right beside one of three sets of deep blue-green wings. When some of the crowd lifted into the air, Bertram and Tycho were able to see to whom the wings belonged.

"Zachariah," they said at the same time.

"Why would he be within the area of protection?" Tycho mused. "Could he have been taken prisoner?"

"No," Bertram said as he thought it through. "They would never bring a prisoner within the protected homeland of the Kynzesti. He is in league with them."

Tycho frowned, clearly not seeing how this could be possible. Bertram was equally perplexed. But he knew that Zachariah was the former Gloresti second commander and, as such, had been relatively close to the Gloresti elder. Perhaps that had allowed him to convince them that he should be permitted within the homeland.

"I have no idea how he managed it," Bertram said, "but all this means is that Zachariah is another obstacle for us to get through to acquire the two females."

Tycho glanced at him. "We will be risking our lives to do this."

"I know."

"It strikes me as foolish to put ourselves at so much risk for Eirik's benefit."

Bertram nodded, coming to an immediate decision. "Agreed. I think that if we are going to put ourselves at such risk, it should be us who experiences the reward."

His eyes narrowing in understanding, Tycho said, "We will draw Eirik's wrath by defying him."

Bertram shrugged and began thinking of how they would follow the now-airborne group without getting caught. "Eirik seems to think that whatever scroll these two females can find is worth any price. That tells me that if we get it instead, Eirik's wrath will not be a concern."

"Very true," Tycho said. He got to his feet. "Let's go."

Quincy took his time arranging the delivery room to his specifications as Amber walked around to ease her discomfort. Gabriel sat on a stool watching her in case he was needed. As this was her seventh time going through this, they were all very familiar with what worked best. Unlike Olivia, who preferred to rest during labor, Amber preferred action.

"I'm glad you're here," Amber said to Clara Kate through the lavender barrier as she walked past it. "Don't be too surprised if you hear words coming out of my mouth that you normally wouldn't, though."

Clara Kate laughed. "No worries, Mom. Better you than me."

Quincy glanced at C.K. and shared a smile with her. His smile faded when he turned back to his tools and set out a device meant to monitor body temperature. They actually didn't know yet whether female Kynzesti would be able to reproduce. The exams he could conduct without the scanning equipment available on the human plane told him that Kynzesti females did have the right reproductive organs. However, none of them had ever menstruated.

He knew this concerned their parents. They had hoped, with their daughters being one-quarter human, that they might also be able to bear children. Only time would tell.

Amber stopped walking and grasped the edge of a bedrail, squeezing her eyes shut in obvious pain. Gabriel got to his feet and hurried to her side as she started breathing through the contraction.

"Back?" he asked.

She nodded as she concentrated on her breathing. He rubbed her lower back to help ease the pain of the contraction.

This went on for another two hours before Quincy determined that Amber was ready to push. He and Gabriel helped her get settled on the bed in a sitting position. Her face was flushed from her efforts and, Quincy knew, embarrassment over her exposed position. No matter how many times they went through this, she was still uncomfortable with it. He found that endearing.

"Okay, Amber," he said as he brought his stool over and sat down. He began summoning his Corgloresti power as he instructed, "I want you to close your eyes and practice your visualization techniques."

Of the three sisters, Amber had the most difficult time with her deliveries. It had gotten better over time. But because faith was such a core element to a successful Kynzesti birthing and Amber had the least faith of her and her sisters, she required more of Quincy's energy.

He thought back to Clara Kate's birth and the first time they went through this. They hadn't known what to expect. Quincy operated largely off of instinct and what he knew of Kate's labor when Saraqael's daughters were born. He had known that it wouldn't be a straightforward human birth and had created a number of hypothetical scenarios beforehand. None of them compared to the reality.

They had come dangerously close to losing Clara Kate. He'd used a lot of his Corgloresti power during the birth, needing it to offset Amber's diminished faith. After that, they had learned ways to help Amber develop the skills she needed for future births.

Now, he waited until she opened her eyes and caught his gaze. He saw the silver glow of his eyes reflected in her gold irises.

"I'm ready," she said.

"Okay," he said. "During the next contraction, push. And focus."

She nodded. Gabriel rubbed her shoulders and leaned down to kiss the top of her head. Quincy brought forth more of his energy and thought of the little life inside of Amber's womb. Gender and physical details didn't matter. What did matter was the baby's vitality. Its will to live. Its desire to enter the world and join its family.

When Amber started pushing, Quincy held her gaze and envisioned her holding the baby. He thought of her nursing it and kissing its head. He thought of the milestones to come and the role Amber would play in helping the baby achieve them. He thought of the baby's existing family and envisioned the baby as a new part of it.

These were all things he taught her to visualize. When he felt the baby's head emerge with a vibrant current of energy, he knew the tactic had worked.

A moment later, her new son was born.

Quincy wrapped the baby in the waiting blanket and then handed him over to his beaming parents. The drain on his energy after the nearly sleepless night had Quincy moving slower than usual to take care of the rest of his routine. He knew the procedure well enough that it didn't require much thought, though.

Before long, Quincy gave the all-clear so that Sebastian could remove the barrier. "Come and meet your brother, Jack," Amber said to Clara Kate.

Quincy watched the family gather around the new baby and smiled. He had just brought another part of Saraqael's legacy into the world. It was something he eagerly anticipated every three years...though not as much as he anticipated seeing Sophia again.

Inevitably, his thoughts turned to her.

Within the span of a day, she had gone from seeing him as a miracle worker to thinking of him as a bumbling fool with no consideration for others. He now understood that by keeping his feelings to himself all these years, he'd severely damaged their friendship. He'd made the female he loved feel like she was somehow less than everyone else, something for which he would never forgive himself. He knew how much she valued his opinions when she was growing up. He should have seen how his avoidance impacted her.

Instead, he had turned a blind eye to it, fearing the repercussions of baring his heart to her.

Well, she wouldn't have to worry about him making her uncomfortable or unhappy anymore. He would accept the harvest request put to him by *archigos* Ini-herit. Once Skye's babies were born, he would be free to transition to the human plane.

By the time Sophia returned, he would be gone.

Chapter 19

IT HADN'T TAKEN LONG FOR ARIANA TO PICK UP THE TRAIL TO THE SCROLL piece contained in the library. Once they stepped outside the area of protection, she used her connection to Volarius' sword and the descriptive information she gathered from Quincy to sharpen her focus and make sure they followed the right path. After a brief discussion over their flight formation, they all took off.

Sophia flew near the front of their group because she was there to offer Ariana support, and Ariana had to be in the lead. From what Sophia understood, Ariana's ability was different in the air than on the ground. The Lekwuesti explained that while flying she felt a sort of "pull" in the right direction. Only when she was on the ground could she actually see the path leading to the item she sought.

Ariana had been able to tell as soon as she tapped into her second power that the scroll piece was quite a distance from the homeland. Uriel made the decision to begin their journey by flying to cover more ground. He sent scouts ahead to keep an eye out for Mercesti so that they wouldn't be spotted. He didn't want word getting back to Eirik regarding their efforts.

Although conversing while flying was difficult due to the wind, Sophia occasionally checked on Ariana to see how she was doing. So far, her friend was holding up rather well.

Without conversation to fill the time, Sophia was left with her thoughts. She pondered how frustrating it was that they hadn't had an opportunity to test the inoculation she created for Nyx's toxin. That thought, of course, led her to remember why they hadn't tested it and what ended up occurring instead.

Damn Quincy and his amazing kiss, she mentally grumbled. She didn't stop to consider how telling it was that she focused on Quincy and not the fact that she had been cursed before birth.

It didn't mean anything because she had enjoyed his kiss, she told herself as she scanned the ground. She'd been attracted to him for years, after all. When she was younger, she'd even learned that what she had was called a "crush."

Well, he'd crushed her heart, all right. She was still reeling from the events of the past few days. Just how much had he expected her to process at once?

Deliberately pushing him from her mind, she thought of the Elder Scroll. The artifact had the ability to turn an otherwise "normal" Estilorian into an elder. What a ridiculous thing to create, she thought. What other outcome could there possibly be than someone trying to get it and use it for their own purposes?

Of course, back when the scroll was created all those millennia ago, things had been much different. Still, she had to believe that selfishness and greed had always been a part of life.

"We will rest up ahead," Uriel announced.

Sophia almost sighed with relief. Flying wasn't as physically draining as it was spiritually. It required one's faith to extend and use one's wings. For her, a being who relied more on logic than faith, she had to admit that flying made her weary.

They landed on the outskirts of a forest and then hiked until they reached a large clearing. Noon sunlight filtered between the trees and warmed the air to a point where Sophia almost didn't need her cloak. Still, she kept it on, not knowing when they would fly again.

"Do you see the trail?" Uriel asked Ariana as she settled herself on the grass.

"Yes." She lifted a hand and pointed. "It's that way, just as my senses told me in the air. The energy is getting stronger, but we're still a fair distance from it."

When the Waresti elder nodded and walked over to talk with his warriors, Sophia sat on the grass beside Ariana. She noticed Tiege standing nearby and wondered if he'd join them, but he was listening to whatever Uriel said.

"How are you doing?" Sophia asked.

The Lekwuesti gave her a small smile. "I'm terrified. I just want to get this over with so we can return to the homeland."

Understanding, Sophia nodded. "I'm in complete agreement. We'll get through this together, okay?"

"Thank you, Sophia. I don't know what I'd do without you and Tiege."

Smiling, Sophia said, "Yeah...about that. What's up with the two of you?"

The Lekwuesti blushed and glanced around to see if anyone was near. Seeing they were alone, she turned back and grinned.

"He kissed me," she whispered, her face all but glowing. "It was the best experience of my entire existence."

Sophia's heart wrenched. This was the kind of hushed, exciting conversation that she had always envisioned having with her sisters or Tate and Clara Kate. She'd taken a big step into womanhood, one they always giggled about when they were growing up. Now that she'd actually had her first kiss, though, she didn't think she'd ever share it with them. How could she possibly explain that Quincy had kissed her after lying to her for so many years...and that in that single moment, his deceit hadn't mattered at all?

What kind of hypocrite was she?

"I'm thrilled for you, Ariana," she said, plastering a smile on her face. "You and Tiege make a perfect pair."

"I appreciate you saying so." Her blush intensified. "I'm actually planning on asking *archigos* Sebastian if he will allow me to formally pair with Tiege as his Lekwuesti."

That made Sophia blink. "Oh. His paired Lekwuesti?"

"Yes." Ariana frowned. "Is that odd?"

"Um..." Sophia considered her words. A pairing where Ariana saw to Tiege's hospitality needs seemed terribly unromantic. But then, who was she to judge? "I think it's great. Since we'll all be paired to Lekwuesti soon, anyway, you may as well put the idea out there."

Ariana nibbled on her lower lip. "Do you think Tiege will accept my offer?"

"He'd be a fool to refuse."

When Ariana flashed a bright smile, Sophia couldn't help but be happy for her. At least she could help navigate the matter of someone else's heart, she reasoned, since she was failing so miserably with her own.

* * *

"They went into that forest," Tycho said.

He and Bertram had flown separately, remaining as close to the ground as possible and as far in either direction as they could from the group containing the two females while still keeping them in sight. This had allowed them to evade detection, though Bertram had barely escaped the diamond gaze of the black kragen when she conducted a wide sweep. He had no idea why or how a kragen was in league with this group, but he didn't intend to fall prey to it.

"Yes," he said, scanning the trees. "We should drop back. This is too close to be able to see where they end up emerging. The last thing we want is for them to take flight without us seeing where they are going."

Not arguing, Tycho joined Bertram in traveling back the way he had come, stopping when they crested a rise in the landscape. When they turned back, more of the forest was visible.

"Were you able to get close enough to get any clues about their destination?" Bertram asked.

"Not yet. They have a host of Waresti guarding the perimeter of the forest. They aren't communicating by hand signals, either."

"Damn."

Bertram had hoped they could get ahead of the group to somehow lay in wait. Even better than capturing the two females and forcing them to find the scroll that Eirik sought would be having them find it and then simply taking it from them. Exactly how they would do that with them being so well-guarded was a concern, but Bertram had been certain they could figure something out.

Now, it seemed he would have to devise another plan.

"Very well. What were you able to observe?"

"There are fifty Waresti, three Kynzesti, two Lekwuesti, one Wymzesti and Zachariah. And the kragen, of course. The female Lekwuesti took the lead while in flight. It appears Uriel consults with her frequently, just as Eirik did when she was leading him to his goal."

"You spotted the Kynzesti female who shattered the illusion?"

"Yes. She no longer wears any decorations in her hair, but the unique coloring is distinctive enough to identify her. Not to mention that spectacular form of hers."

Bertram knew well enough what Tycho wanted to do when he finally got his hands on the Kynzesti who had escaped them. Keeping him in control was going to be a challenge...but one he didn't need to consider just then.

"Okay. I can understand why they would have at least one other Lekwuesti with them to see to their hospitality needs. Outside of that, however, their group is oddly compiled."

"I thought the same thing. But then, we do not really know what kind of scroll they are searching for. Perhaps the various skills of these individuals are needed to acquire it."

Frowning, Bertram said, "Well, we will have to make this work to our advantage. Our biggest obstacles are the Waresti and the kragen."

"And Zachariah."

That was one more element, Bertram supposed. It once again made him wonder about the Mercesti's involvement. "True," he acknowledged.

They pondered their options in silence. As far as Bertram saw it, their only chance was to somehow get the females away from the others. It seemed an insurmountable task. Regardless of the odds, though, he knew they could be no worse off for trying.

"Very well," he said at last. "We will observe and see if one or both of the females we seek step away from the group so we can grab them. If that never comes to pass, we should try and take one of the other two Kynzesti. Trust me...the females will come to us one way or another."

Chapter 20

SOPHIA FELT A LITTLE REFRESHED FOLLOWING THEIR AFTERNOON REST, but by the time they flew another few hours, she was exhausted.

When the sun began to set, they found another forested area that would offer them respectable shelter and protection for the night. If it hadn't been for the fact that their glowing wings stood out in stark contrast to the night sky, making them much easier targets for Mercesti scouts, Sophia thought they might have continued on even longer. Thank goodness for luminescent wings, she decided.

Because it cooled off, the Waresti started a small campfire. Sebastian created a few tents and a number of blankets for them to use when they were ready to sleep. He and Ariana began preparing some food for supper.

Sitting on a log away from the chaos near the fire, Sophia tried to keep her mind off Quincy. It was rather difficult, especially considering the niggling feeling of guilt that sat at the back of her mind. She couldn't help but picture his face when she issued her response to his declaration of love.

But she'd been right, hadn't she? Here she was, dwelling on that when she should have been over with Ariana making sure her friend was okay.

Sadly, Ariana looked steady and determined. It was Sophia who felt off-balance and scared.

"Hey, Soph," Tate said, gesturing to the log next to her. "Care for some company?"

She really didn't, but couldn't see why she should say so. She shrugged to avoid getting pegged with a lie.

"Cool." Tate sat down and stretched out her long legs. "What a day."

"Yeah," Sophia agreed. She spotted Zachariah standing in the gathering shadows of the trees a few feet away and knew he was maintaining a watch over her cousin. "We've never flown this long before."

"I know. I feel ready to drop. Hopefully some food will help."

Glancing at the center of the campsite where lavender light flashed, Sophia nodded. Whatever the Lekwuesti had conjured up smelled wonderful.

"Are you all right, Sophia?"

Blinking with surprise, she automatically replied, "Sure."

Tate raised an eyebrow. Sophia knew the lie had probably blasted from her and felt herself flush. "Sorry."

"Don't worry about it. Is it something you want to talk about?"

"Not really."

"Soph?"

"Yeah?"

"You're lying to yourself."

Sophia sighed. She didn't need Tate's second power to tell her that. "I'm sorry," she said again. "I suppose I should talk about it with someone."

Tate gave her an understanding look. "I'm not trying to pry. Just offering a shoulder."

"Thanks, Tate." She took a breath and then blurted, "Quincy kissed me."

"He did?" Tate's smile beamed from her face. "Well, geez—it's about time!"

Sophia's lips parted in shock. "You knew?"

"Of course I did," Tate said cheerfully with a wave of her hand. "He's been over the moon about you for years."

Getting slowly to her feet, Sophia stared at her cousin and considered how carelessly she had just dismissed what Sophia could only think of as a betrayal. "You *knew* and you didn't tell me?"

Tate's expression fell. "I'm sorry, Soph. I just thought it would be best—"

"Why is it everyone else gets to decide what's best when it comes to my feelings?" Sophia interrupted, not caring that her voice rose and she drew the attention of the others. "Didn't you ever consider how I would react, finding out about this after so much time? After all these years of thinking much worse about Quincy's opinion of me?"

"It is not for Tate to share someone else's feelings," Zachariah said from behind her.

Furious with her cousin, furious with Quincy, and especially furious with herself for feeling so out of control, Sophia whirled on the Mercesti.

"As if I should listen to anything you have to say on the subject," she snapped.

If she expected a reaction from him, she was in for a disappointment. He merely stared back at her.

"Soph—" Tate began, reaching for her.

"Leave me alone, Tate. I've had enough of being deceived by everyone I trusted. I need some time by myself."

"Do not go far," Zachariah warned.

Lifting her lip in a snarl, Sophia turned and ran. She shifted into her panther form and bounded into the forest, knowing that she wasn't truly escaping anything.

"I see you are beginning to regain consciousness."

Malukali gazed up at Kanika with eyes that felt like they had been scraped with glass. She was once again in a state of numbness. And still, the Mercesti leader spoke to her.

"Do not worry. This time you will not be harmed. I wanted to let you know that your husband has agreed to aid me in my plans. Apparently your screams were enough to obtain his cooperation."

Malukali tried to blink. Where was she? Why couldn't she form any real thoughts?

An image of a teacup flashed through her mind, but it faded as quickly as it entered.

"You may be wondering why I am doing this. As there is no one else I can tell, I will share it with you. Mind you, if I get any sense that you are getting closer to full consciousness, I will have to take action. It would not be a good thing to have the Orculesti elder inside my head, I have been told."

Her words made little sense. Malukali attempted to turn her head so that she wasn't staring into Kanika's face, but movement was impossible.

"Before I begin, you should also know that we have broken a number of your bones in our bid to encourage your husband to cooperate. You should not fight too hard to free your mind unless you wish to feel the pain that will accompany it."

The words barely registered in Malukali's hazy mind.

"My name is Metis. I killed the Mercesti female whose form you now see. Well, in fairness to my dear Deimos, he did most of the work. He does so enjoy his time with females."

Kanika...she wasn't Kanika?

"But in order for me to assume her form, I had to be the one to finish the task. She has been dead for some time."

Kanika was dead.

The thought brought with it a brief flash of insight, but Malukali was unable to hold onto it.

"Eirik was near when Deimos and I made the kill. He had been hunting the Mercesti leader himself. He gave me quite the education about how things work on the Estilorian plane. I have only been free to roam it for a short while, you see."

No, Malukali didn't see. Where was Knorbis?

"I was kept from you...from all of you. My creator wanted to keep me all to herself. If I had allowed her to live, I am sure she would regret that decision."

Murderer. She was in the care of a murderer.

That realization brought with it a stinging pain in her eyes. Her vision blurred.

"I see you have enough of your awareness to express sympathy for me. Do not expect the same in return. Although I was schooled in human emotions by my creator, I do not experience them myself. If I see any further signs of your recovery, I will dose you again."

Teacup. Falling.

"Where was I? Oh, yes. My creator, Tethys. Before the creation of this plane, she had the lack of sense to fall in love with a human male. When she could not conceive, as no Estilorian female can, the male abandoned her for another. As a result of her experience, Tethys wanted to find a way to create a female Estilorian with the ability to reproduce. I am the result of her efforts."

Females who can reproduce...

"Tethys was a failure. I cannot reproduce. What I can do, I discovered after I killed Tethys, is assume the forms of those I kill. Changing forms is a painful process, however, so you will just have to trust me on this."

Kanika...no, not Kanika...lifted an eyebrow.

"I am still debating whether I should attempt to kill you and assume your form. Tethys advised against such an act, believing I was not strong enough to go against an elder. Only because I had such difficulty assuming this aged and powerful Mercesti female form did I decide to consider my creator's warnings. Tethys was centuries old, after all, and I bested her. But my creator was not very powerful."

Malukali's captor paused for a moment, her eyes unfocused. Then she continued, "Deimos was my own attempt at creation. Unlike Tethys, I allow him a certain amount of freedom. His appetites do require me to keep him largely within my control. If the Waresti discover him, I doubt they will let him live."

Waresti...Uriel.

A twinge of pain in Malukali's leg made her draw in a sharp breath.

"And that, I believe, concludes our session for today."

A small prick in the arm.

"Next time, I will explain how your husband is going to make me the next elder."

Chapter 21

DESPITE HER IRRITATION OVER ZACHARIAH'S UNWELCOME ADVICE TO stick close to camp, Sophia wasn't stupid enough to ignore it. She wanted to be alone, not get herself captured or harmed by any Mercesti who might be in the area.

She ended up shifting into an orangutan and climbing a tree located a far enough distance from the camp that she couldn't easily hear anyone. Once up in the tree, she shifted into her harpy eagle form to make use of the bird's heightened eyesight. She realized as she scanned the immediate vicinity that the Waresti had established a perimeter. There were a number of them about a hundred yards in any direction.

She considered the idea of shifting back into her Estilorian form, since maintaining a shift—even while just sitting—took a toll on her energy. The idea of sitting naked in a tree, however, didn't seem like a ton of fun. On top of that, she could more easily control her emotions while in the form of an animal.

Maybe that's why she enjoyed it so much.

Now that she'd had some time to get over the initial astonishment of Tate knowing about Quincy's feelings for her, she could acknowledge that she had been wrong to lash out at her cousin. She had even been wrong to lash out at Zachariah, as he had spoken nothing but the truth. How many times had she issued a lie in Tate's vicinity throughout their lifetime? Too often to count. Yet from the time she was old enough to understand her second power, Tate hadn't ever revealed Sophia's secrets.

Sophia shouldn't have expected any less of Tate regarding Quincy's feelings. She might feel as though her cousin owed her a greater loyalty, but that wasn't fair. Tate and Quincy were good friends. And Zachariah was right. It wasn't Tate's place to tell her how Quincy felt.

It was Quincy's place…and so far, he had failed miserably at it.

Even as that thought flashed through her head, Sophia wondered whether she was still being hypocritical. Tate said she was lying to herself. Just how far did that lie extend?

She had been trying to convince herself that the kiss in the forest had occurred only because she was under the influence of the plant she had eaten. That was definitely a lie. There had been many times over the years that she had daydreamed about kissing Quincy. The plant had merely given her the courage to act upon something she wanted to do.

She had also waged an argument with herself that the only reason she found Quincy so attractive was because he was one of the few males she knew to whom she wasn't related. Yet another lie.

Her attraction to him extended to before the age of thirteen, if she was being truly honest with herself. The Kynzesti matured more rapidly than humans, after all, and she had spent a great deal of time with him. She had always loved the curve of his mouth and the line of his brow, especially when he was concentrating. There was also the fact that he worked hard at maintaining a physical form that devastated her senses.

But what had attracted her from a very tender age was his keen intelligence and his eagerness to share it with her. So why had he been so willing to share his knowledge and so reluctant to share his feelings?

"I still don't understand why I can't have even *one* feather in my hair."

Sophia gave an internal wince when she heard Tate's voice. Of all the places in this forest her cousin and Zachariah could go to have yet another spat, why did it have to be close enough that she could hear it? She had grown so weary of their bickering.

"You have not listened to a word I said," Zachariah countered.

Ugh. They were getting closer. Sophia heard their footsteps and soon watched them enter her range of vision. Tate had her arms crossed over her chest and a frustrated pout on her face. Zachariah followed her with his usual blank mask of an expression. Sophia wondered what form she could assume to get out of the tree she was in without them noticing.

"Oh, I've listened," Tate said as they got within feet of the tree. "I just chose to—"

"Far enough," Zachariah interrupted.

Then he grabbed Tate, spun her around and kissed her.

If Sophia had been in her Estilorian form, her jaw would have proverbially hit the ground. Even in her emotionally-subdued state, shock and confusion rolled through her.

Tate, however, didn't appear at all caught off-guard by Zachariah's passionate assault. She slid into the kiss with ease and enthusiasm, telling Sophia that this was a well-practiced form of encounter for them. Her cousin's hands moved from Zachariah's muscular chest up to behind his neck and the back of his head, where she wound her fingers into his already disheveled hair.

Zachariah's hands, well...they had Tate making sounds that explained to Sophia just why they were doing this so far from the hearing of others. She knew if she hadn't been in the eagle form that her cheeks would have been on fire.

She suddenly thought back to the conversation she'd had with Tate after Zachariah pulled her into the guest bedroom at Clara Kate's to "lecture" her about her clothing.

"Any time you wear something he finds objectionable," Sophia had argued, "he gets all over you about it."

"Oh, yes," Tate had said in a tone that Sophia now realized was filled with feminine appreciation. "He sure does."

Sophia *so* got it now.

They finally broke apart after a couple of minutes of serious making out. Sophia felt like a forced voyeur and wished she could shift into a tree so she didn't have eyes or ears.

"We really," Tate panted, "have to come up with some better argument material than my wardrobe."

"Why?" Zachariah's response was barely audible since his mouth was currently doing something to Tate's neck.

She made a sound between a gasp and a moan. She forced Zachariah's head back up so she could kiss him again. He didn't seem to mind the rough handling. When they broke apart this time, she replied, "Because the weather is cooling off. My clothes are going to be less skimpy."

"A bloody shame," he said.

For a moment, they just stood there staring at each other. Then he kissed her again. This time, there was something less urgent about it. In fact, if Sophia didn't know the Mercesti better, she would have called it tender.

When they parted, Zachariah reached up and framed Tate's face with his hands. He rubbed a thumb across her cheek.

"I do not like it when you cry," he said in a quiet voice.

Sophia blinked. She felt like she was watching a stranger with her cousin.

"I know," Tate said softly. "I'm sorry, Sparky. But I've hurt Sophia."

Cursing the sharp vision that allowed her to see the tears that filled her cousin's eyes, Sophia debated whether or not to shift so that she could run up to Tate and apologize for being so stupid. If it hadn't meant being naked in front of Zachariah—and admitting that she had been watching them this entire time—she would have.

"She will forgive you," he said, wiping away Tate's tears as they fell. "Unlike you, who appreciates spontaneity and reacts quickly to change, your cousin requires time to process things."

Sophia realized in that moment how much she had misjudged Zachariah. As open-minded as she considered herself, she knew that she had lumped him in with every other Mercesti she had ever heard about. It had been easy to believe that he didn't have feelings himself or insight into the feelings of others since he never showed them. She should have known that Tate, who saw through any lie, wouldn't willingly pair herself with someone who didn't care about her or others.

The realization had her questioning herself and other conclusions she had drawn.

"Just because I know Sophia will forgive me doesn't make me feel any less guilty," Tate said, her arms encircling his waist as he continued to wipe her cheeks. "She's like a sister to me. I love her and Quincy. I just want them to be happy."

Sophia wondered if it was possible to spontaneously shift into a troll just because she felt like one.

"It's hard, you know? Being able to tell when someone's lying."

"I know," he said. He pulled her close, pressing her against him with her head tucked under his chin. "On the other hand, it did allow you to see through me."

"Yeah," she sighed. "I wonder what you look like with red eyes and no Gloresti markings."

So, Tate saw Zachariah as the Gloresti commander he had once been, Sophia realized. That sure explained a lot. It also told her a great deal about the ornery Mercesti's true character.

"What you see is the only me worth seeing," he said.

Tate pulled back. She reached up to touch the side of his face. "I love you, Sparky," she said.

Even in her eagle form, Sophia felt her breath catch at the words. She thought of Quincy and how he had said just that to her before she left. She also considered the fact that she hadn't even told him goodbye.

"Do you think the time will ever come when you can say the same to me?" Tate asked.

Her cousin's softly-spoken question made Sophia realize that she and Zachariah actually had something in common. They both had wonderful beings in their lives who loved them and they were too stupid or stubborn to let them know how they felt in return.

Nakedness be damned. She had to shift back and tell Zachariah that he was being a prize idiot, just like she was.

Suddenly, he shoved Tate from him with such force that she flew with a squeak over a nearby hedge of shrubs. A series of unladylike curses ensued. Anger on behalf of her cousin had Sophia changing her mind and her strategy. If Zachariah was so opposed to reciprocating her cousin's feelings that he felt it necessary to manhandle her, well, she would show him a thing or two while in her panther form.

"Tate?"

Ariana's voice stopped both Tate's complaining and Sophia's internal tirade. Zachariah had obviously heard the approach of the female and had tossed Tate from him to try and keep their relationship a secret.

"She needed a few moments of privacy," Zachariah said in his cool voice as Ariana got within sight of him.

The Lekwuesti eyed Zachariah warily. Moving in a large circle, she made her way around the tree where Sophia lay and headed toward the group of bushes hiding Tate.

"That isn't what it sounded like to me," Ariana said, not removing her gaze from him until she got behind the bush. "Tate, are you all right?" she asked when she had disappeared from Sophia's range of sight. "I heard you shouting."

Zachariah stiffened. Sophia figured he had just realized that Ariana was going to question what she had seen and heard. Then Knorbis approached.

"Hello, Zachariah," the elder said as Tate and Ariana chatted behind the bush. His voice sounded more commanding than cordial, Sophia realized in growing bewilderment. His eyes started glowing dark purple. "You will let me pass now."

There was a moment when Zachariah's posture eased and Sophia thought he might obey. Instead, the Mercesti shook his head as though to clear it.

"I was afraid of that," Knorbis said, even as Zachariah cursed and reached for the tomahawk he kept harnessed near the small of his back.

Sophia froze in numb bafflement as the Wymzesti elder slapped Zachariah on the upper arm. The Mercesti crumpled like a felled tree. Then Knorbis walked behind the bush that hid Tate and Ariana.

Sophia heard him say, "You will both come with me."

She watched as her cousin and Ariana walked from behind the bush and followed the Wymzesti elder toward the edge of the forest. Knowing that something was very wrong, Sophia shifted back to an orangutan to shuffle quickly down the tree. Then she shifted into her panther form so she could follow them as stealthily as possible.

Maybe the elder was merely testing their defenses at Uriel's request, she thought. There was no way that the good-hearted male she considered something of an uncle would ever do them harm.

Her opinion quickly changed when Knorbis somehow induced sleep on the Waresti warriors keeping guard at the edge of the forest. She watched as the elder said something to Ariana and Tate and gave them each something that they promptly drank. The elder then took flight, the two females doing the same without a single word of complaint or question.

Well, Sophia could certainly question things. That was what she did. The results she came up with now defied all logic.

After a brief moment in which she considered running back to camp to sound the alarm, she concluded that she had to follow them now or risk losing sight of them forever. Despite the fact that she was already beyond tired, she shifted back into her harpy eagle form so that she could fly without detection in the dark.

Then she took flight after them.

Chapter 22

"MY EYES MUST BE DECEIVING ME."

Bertram didn't reply to Tycho's comment, but he felt much the same way. The Wymzesti elder had just walked up behind three Waresti guarding the perimeter and did something that had all three males sinking to the ground. Even more astonishing than that was when he walked completely out of the forest followed by the two females they sought. He said something to the females that Bertram couldn't hear from their distance and then handed each of them something. Whatever it was, the females brought it to their lips and tilted their heads back as if drinking.

A moment later, they took flight.

"We have to follow them," Tycho said. "We can definitely overpower one male."

"That is the Wymzesti elder," Bertram pointed out. "If he sees us coming, he will get inside our heads. He could order us to kill each other and we would do it without stopping to wonder why. We have to remain far enough from them that he doesn't see our wings against the night sky."

Why was the Wymzesti elder taking the two females away from the others? Was this some kind of trap?

"They sure are moving fast," Tycho observed.

A bird took flight from the forest, startling them. Bertram's mind raced as he considered the possibilities. This was all very strange. He understood why Tycho was so eager to take advantage of the situation, but rushing into something that made no sense could well get them killed.

Then a thought hit him. They had first started tracking the elder from Kanika's home. What if he was headed back there now?

He thought back to the conversation he had overheard between Eirik and the female he called Metis while he and Tycho waited in the woods surrounding Kanika's home. She indicated that she had initiated a plan to bring the females to Eirik. That plan must somehow involve the powerful elder, he decided, his respect for the odd creature raising a notch.

"All right," he said. "We should go now before the Waresti follow. I will take the east flank. We will follow the pattern we used earlier while evading the Waresti and that damned black beast. I will work on developing a plan to get the females away from the elder.

"If we want the prize for ourselves, they cannot reach Metis and Eirik."

Tiege paced beside the fire. He and Ariana had eaten together, but just when he started to talk to her about how she was feeling, she mentioned that she wanted to speak with Tate. Although he offered to walk with her into the forest where his sister and Zachariah had gone, she declined, indicating that she wanted their conversation to be private.

The idea of her walking alone into the darkening woods didn't sit right with him, but he could see this was important to her. He considered following her at a safe distance as she hurried off. He could always use his second power to disguise himself as a forest creature, he thought.

"Believe me when I say that you will never live it down if you go against her wishes," Knorbis said as Tiege edged toward the forest where Ariana disappeared.

Frowning because he knew the elder was right, Tiege weighed the options.

"Perhaps I can be of assistance," Knorbis offered. "I'll follow Ariana. If she sees me, I'll pretend I was just out for a stroll."

It was certainly better than nothing. Tiege nodded in appreciation and the elder headed into the forest just behind Ariana.

But that had been more than ten minutes ago. Possibly even close to twenty. While he didn't know what Ariana wanted to discuss with Tate, he saw no reason why it would take this long.

He considered Knorbis' advice. The elder had been married for a number of years and probably knew what he was talking about. Tiege's goal was to have Ariana fall in love with him, not get angry with him for failing to give her time and space when she needed it.

Torn, he approached Uriel. He had to wait for a couple of minutes before the elder was done speaking to some of his warriors. In that time, Tiege's concern escalated.

"What is it, Tiege?" Uriel asked at last.

Suddenly feeling like an idiot, Tiege considered keeping quiet. His clamoring intuition wouldn't allow him to, though. "Would you please connect with *archigos* Knorbis and make sure Ariana is okay? They've been gone a while."

If the elder thought the request was dumb, he didn't say so. After a moment, however, he frowned. Tiege's heart sank.

"*Archigos*," said a Waresti from the edge of the clearing, "Jason, Timothy and Duncan have not reported in."

Uriel glanced at Tiege, who didn't even wait to be asked which direction to go. He turned and ran into the forest where Ariana and Knorbis had disappeared. Although the path wasn't straight or easy to follow thanks to the thick trees, Tiege found their trail with the aid of a ball of light.

He also found Zachariah.

Nyx stood beside the Mercesti's prone form. The huge creature was very protective of Zachariah, and watched them carefully with her diamond eyes as they approached. Uriel instructed the Waresti beside him to go and check on the missing guards.

Then he held up his hands. "I will help him if I can," the elder said to Nyx, moving slowly toward Zachariah.

The kragen remained still, but watchful. Uriel knelt with Tiege beside Zachariah and felt for a pulse. "He lives," he said. He lifted Zachariah's eyelid, studying his pupils. Then he plucked a small barb from the Mercesti's upper arm. "He's been given something to render him unconscious. It must have been very fast-acting, as he didn't even get to his weapon."

Fear lanced through Tiege. He was torn between staying to see if there was anything he could do for Zachariah and thrashing through the forest like a demented being to find Tate and Ariana. He scanned the area for any clue as to what happened and was relieved he didn't see any blood.

"I believe this was a dose of somnuliam," Uriel said after sniffing the barb. "I haven't seen the plant in many centuries, but Knorbis would know where to find it."

Tiege barely grasped what the Waresti elder was saying. "*Archigos*

Knorbis poisoned Zachariah?"

"I don't want to assume anything," Uriel replied, flagging one of the Waresti who had remained behind. "Find Panakeia," he instructed. "Have her bring me one of her elixirs."

"Yes, sir."

Unable to think clearly, Tiege started walking and looking around to see if he might find evidence that Ariana and Tate were still in the area. Alarm and panic spiraled as he walked around Uriel and Zachariah in widening circles until he could no longer absorb the details around him or make any sense of them.

One of the Waresti soldiers returned and reported, "Jason, Timothy and Duncan are all unconscious, sir."

Uriel issued a curse, making Tiege's fear spike again. The Waresti elder never lost his composure. Before Tiege could dwell on that, a female Waresti hurried into the clearing from the direction of the campsite. She held a glass bottle with a vibrant green liquid inside it.

"It only takes a drop, sir," she said, removing the stopper. "Please open his mouth and I will administer it."

Uriel did as she asked, pulling Zachariah's lower jaw down. Panakeia leaned forward to carefully pour a drop of her elixir into Zachariah's open mouth.

"Back away the moment you can," Uriel warned, making Tiege wonder what he meant.

The drop hit Zachariah's tongue. Both Uriel and Panakeia hurried back. Zachariah's throat moved in a swallow.

He surged to his feet, grabbed his tomahawk and looked around with a fierce expression on his face within the span of a second. "Tate," he said, looking at Uriel.

"She appears to be gone, as is Ariana."

The elder's words had the confusion and fear that clouded Tiege's mind finally starting to clear. Anger quickly took its place.

"The Wymzesti poisoned me," Zachariah said.

Uriel frowned. "I had hoped otherwise."

"How long have I been unconscious?"

Tiege answered, "Ariana left to come and speak with Tate about twenty minutes ago."

Zachariah clenched his jaw and ran a hand through his hair. "I cannot sense her," he muttered.

Startled, Tiege realized that he couldn't sense his sister, either. He hadn't even thought to tap into their blood connection, which told him he needed to get his head on straight. He wasn't doing Tate or Ariana any good by failing to think clearly.

"What are you still doing here, you blasted beast?" Zachariah snapped, looking at Nyx. "We have talked about this. Come here."

He stalked a short distance away. The kragen padded after him, her demeanor subdued. Tiege struggled to hear what the Mercesti said. All he made out was "Tate" and "important."

Zachariah's red gaze moved to the Waresti elder. "Which direction?" he called out.

"We believe they went west."

After issuing a few more words to Nyx and sending her through the trees, Zachariah glanced back at them. "What are we waiting for?" He turned to follow the kragen.

"Wait," Tiege said as another thought occurred to him. He looked around in every direction, but sensed no movement outside of the Waresti guards. With an increasing feeling of dread, he asked, "Where's Sophia?"

Uriel and Zachariah exchanged a glance. They both turned in opposite directions and began scanning the ground as if they knew each other's thoughts. Not wanting to feel useless, Tiege also started walking again with his gaze focused on the ground. His heart felt like it beat its way up into his throat as the facts finally sank in.

Tate and Ariana were gone.

"Here," Zachariah said a moment later. He lifted a feather from the ground. "There is only one blonde eagle of which I am aware." He studied the tree next to the feather's location, then glanced over to where he had been found on the ground. "I believe she saw what happened."

"You think Sophia went after Tate and Ariana?" Tiege asked. The idea gave him hope.

"Yes." Zachariah turned. "And now we need to follow her and Nyx."

Tiege matched Zachariah's stride as they hurried to the edge of the forest so they could extend their wings with all of the Waresti traveling with them. "I haven't ever tried to connect with Sophia using our Gloresti blood. She's my cousin, so the connection is going to be diluted."

"You will get me to Tate."

Zachariah's voice brooked no argument. Tiege couldn't fault him for wanting to get to his sister. He was just as determined to get to her and Ariana, so he didn't comment. He saw the break in the trees ahead and said, "I just can't believe *archigos* Knorbis has done this. Do you suppose he thinks he's keeping Tate and Ariana safer this way? That he has an alternate plan?"

"I do not know, nor do I care," Zachariah replied as he replaced his tomahawk in its holster so he could take flight. "I am just grateful that I am already a Mercesti."

"Why?"

"Saves me the hassle of converting when I kill him."

Chapter 23

SOPHIA KEPT HERSELF AS MUCH IN THE MIND OF THE EAGLE AS SHE could. That was all that stood between her and abject terror.

She was alone, and as far as she could tell, all that stood between the most powerful Wymzesti on the plane and Tate and Ariana's well-being. Of all the possible problems she might have anticipated on this journey, this hadn't even remotely occurred to her.

Why had Knorbis done this? He hadn't converted to a Mercesti, so he apparently didn't intend to kill her cousin and friend, nor did he believe he was leading them to their deaths. Maybe he intended to use them to find the scroll piece himself for some reason. He might have foreseen something that prompted him to isolate the two females from their protectors so that he could prevent it.

That was really all she could guess. In the end, she was left with the fact that none of this made any sense and she had no idea what to do.

They weren't flying in a straight path, which worried Sophia. They had changed course a number of times throughout the day, telling her that the Wymzesti elder was either trying to throw any followers off-course or he had no idea where he was going. She had to believe the former. Knorbis didn't do things without a well thought-out plan.

Another concern, Sophia quickly realized, was that whatever the Wymzesti elder gave Tate and Ariana to drink had boosted their speed and endurance. Sophia had never seen Estilorians fly as quickly as the three of them did, which told her that the elder had ingested whatever he'd given them, as well. They had been flying for hours without any signs of tiring or intent to land.

Fortunately, the harpy eagle was a fast bird. She could reach speeds of up to fifty miles per hour and could keep pace with those she pursued without difficulty.

Unfortunately, Sophia was reaching new levels of exhaustion. She knew she wouldn't be able to hold the shift much longer.

She couldn't help but remember the time a couple of months ago when Quincy brought her outside the area of protection surrounding her homeland so he could teach her to fly. That was when Tate was taken by Nyx, and Sophia had followed her in the form of the harpy eagle just like this.

And just like then, she was going to fail to reach her cousin.

Acknowledging the fact that she was going to have to abandon Tate and Ariana when they needed her most left Sophia with a fiery ball of anguish in her chest. But she knew that to continue on was suicide. She was losing the hold on her shift while miles up in the air. Whereas before she had known in the back of her mind that Quincy wouldn't ever let her fall, now she had no such backup.

I'm sorry, she thought toward her cousin and dear friend.

Then she started looking for a place to land that might afford her some shelter while she recovered her energy. The ground beneath her was marshy flatland. Wide mounds of brown grass rose up between what amounted to little more than puddles. She would make a ridiculously easy target to any Mercesti who happened to fly by.

A fresh wave of exhaustion hit her. She briefly lost her shift, falling nearly twenty feet in her Estilorian form before managing to recover. Her vision blurred as she tightened her hold on the eagle form. She had to get to the clump of dead-looking trees she saw in the distance.

Though her speed was significantly less, she changed her course and headed for the trees. Up, down. Up. Down. She commanded her wings to move.

By the time she got to within a few yards of the trees, she stopped flapping and allowed herself to coast in, angling her wings to fit among the spindly branches that spread like skeletal hands in every direction. She tried to find some kind of grassy clearing and belatedly realized that the trees were swamped by murky water. If she landed, she might drown. There was no way she'd be able to move at this point.

Just when she decided she would have to land in a tree, she lost the shift. Her collision with the water was loud and ungraceful. The cold shock was enough to prevent her from sinking immediately into unconsciousness, however.

That meant she saw the group of beings standing nearby when she managed to drag herself to a shallow and roll onto her back to keep the frigid water out of her face.

Just before she passed out.

Bertram thought he was losing his mind.

He had been curious about the large bird following the Wymzesti elder and the two females. It changed direction whenever they changed direction, and it was an unusual golden color that caught the limited moonlight as it moved.

Although the bird was quite a distance ahead of him and Tycho, he could easily make it out against the night sky with his enhanced Mercesti night vision. Tracking it soon became their only option to catch the two females. Bertram realized that whatever the elder gave the females to drink, it caused them to fly impossibly fast.

The bird, however, had sharp vision and speed on its side. It was able to keep its distance while still maintaining their course. As the sun rose and the day progressed, the bird remained in the air without landing once. That gave Bertram another clue that there was something different about the animal. So when it veered to the left and clearly out of the flight path of the others, he wondered why.

And then the bird wasn't a bird. It was a blonde, naked female falling through the sky.

Wondering if he had been flying so long that he was in the grip of some kind of waking dream, he cupped his hand to his mouth and issued a coo-like signal to draw Tycho closer. He had a split second to decide whether to try and follow the Wymzesti elder and the two females or change course and follow the bird that might not actually be a bird. He quickly concluded that there was no possible way to reach the group. He couldn't even make them out against the horizon at that point. So he followed the bird.

Tycho quickly caught up with him, always having been a superior flyer. "What are you doing?" he hissed when he approached. "We will lose them!"

"We already have," Bertram countered. "You know that we will never catch them. Yet that bird tracked them. It seems to me the bird might be able to pick up the trail of the two females once it has rested."

"You are giving up the two females that Eirik wants us to retrieve for a *bird*?"

"Do not talk to me as though I have no sense. This is no ordinary—"

He cut himself off as they watched the bird fly into the marsh. In a blink, there was no need to complete his thought. There in the water lay the blonde female.

And she wasn't alone.

Tycho slowed to fly beside Bertram. "Okay...you were right," he said.

From their distance, Bertram couldn't make out many details about the female outside of the fact that she was fair and petite. "I wonder if she is somehow akin to Metis?"

"It could be possible. I have never known another being to shift between forms like that."

"I do not recognize any of those around her. Do you?"

"No."

Bertram considered this and shuffled it in among the other facts in his head. Then he shrugged. "Well, we have little choice now but to wait and see what this group does with her. If she is in league with them, perhaps we can negotiate a way to make use of her abilities in our quest."

"Why would they want to work with us?"

"Simple," Bertram replied. "They will not want to incur Eirik's wrath. We will explain our mission and what has happened to those who have gone against him. They will surely do what they can to support the most fearsome Mercesti in existence."

Skye's labor started just a few hours after Quincy finally fell asleep following Amber's delivery. Fortunately, Estilorians required little sleep to recharge. He was alert and ready to help bring her twins into the world.

Skye was a talker. She kept her nerves level by talking with her sisters and their husbands through the lavender barrier. She chatted with Caleb, who wasn't much for idle chit-chat, especially at such an intense time, and she always drew Quincy into the conversation.

"What do you think of the names I've picked out, Quincy?" she asked from the bed. At the moment, she was sitting up in it. "Willa and Wesley."

He grinned. She always went with the same first letter when she named her twins. "I think they sound perfect. As long as you have another boy and girl set of twins this time."

"Oh, I will," she said with a bright smile.

She was right. Willa and Wesley arrived into the world without incident. Fortunately, Skye's faith was so strong that Quincy's efforts were practically unneeded.

He began his routine cleanup as the happy parents engaged in the important bonding that would need to continue over the coming weeks with their babies. Only when he made an unusually loud rattling noise with his tray of instruments did he realize that it had gotten rather quiet. Glancing over his shoulder, he saw Gabriel exchanging glances with his wife that said all was not well. Amber held Jack, since the close contact was needed this early in the baby's life. Olivia also held Devon.

"Quincy, I'd like to remove the barrier now," Gabriel said.

His heart feeling too heavy to pump blood, Quincy swallowed and nodded. The light faded a moment later.

Still holding his tray of instruments as though not knowing what to do with them, he watched as the siblings gathered around the bed. They congratulated Skye and Caleb and took a moment to bring all of their children together, briefly touching their heads together and generating a synergy that only existed for the Kynzesti. None of them knew exactly what it meant or how it worked, but they had instinctively done it since their firstborn children arrived.

"What happened?" Quincy asked when he couldn't wait any longer. "I'm sorry, but I have to know. Is everyone okay?"

Now, Gabriel briefly closed his eyes and then opened them to look around at everyone. "I didn't want to say anything until we had done our ritual. It wouldn't have been right.

"I received word from Uriel a little while ago. Something has happened." He looked at Skye and Caleb. "We don't know why, but Knorbis has taken Tate and Ariana away from the group. He poisoned Zachariah and used his power to induce sleep on some Waresti guards."

Skye gasped, her face pale. "No. Knorbis wouldn't do that!"

"It appears he did."

Then his gaze shifted to Olivia and James. Without Gabriel saying a word, Olivia's eyes filled with tears. Quincy felt his grip on the tray loosening as he braced himself for the blow.

"I'm so sorry," Gabriel said, pulling Olivia into a tight hug. "Sophia's gone, too."

Chapter 24

KNORBIS WAS A BEING WHO HAD MASTERED CONTROL. WHEN ONE SPENT several millennia sorting through near-constant visions of the future while trying to live "normally" in the present, one had to develop control. Otherwise, insanity would result.

He was completely out of control now. He had betrayed the trust of his fellow elders. He had used his abilities to harm unsuspecting Waresti. He had poisoned Zachariah. He had caused what was surely immeasurable grief to Tate's family and was leading an already emotionally-scarred female back into the den of those who caused her such harm in the first place.

He would never forgive himself. Every inch closer they got to Kanika's home, the lower he sank in his own esteem. But whenever he thought about changing his plan, he remembered the sound of his wife's screams.

They tortured her for an unbearable amount of time until the being guised as Kanika was convinced he would do what she wanted.

"You will use care not to project any thoughts to anyone else regarding your plans," she said to him as she circled the chair he was strapped to. Although she had given him enough of the debilitating brew she created that his mental powers were useless, his ears worked very well. "You will bring the two females to me, and I will allow you and your wife to live. I will dose you both so that you cannot follow us, but it will wear off and you can return to your lives as though none of this ever happened."

"Yes," he managed to say.

She squatted in front of the chair and held his gaze. When she reached up to touch his cheek, she studied the resulting moisture on her fingers without expression.

"I have heard of these things called tears," she said. "I have decided I do not wish to experience them. Your wife expelled a great many of them along with her screams. Remember that as well as the eager Mercesti at my disposal if you choose to disobey me."

Knorbis had no way to know whether the being guised as Kanika was somehow monitoring him now. She hadn't spoken of her abilities at all except to say that she wasn't actually Kanika and held no regard for them at all. He only knew that the idea of causing his sweet Malukali any more pain was enough to have him doing the unthinkable.

He could only pray that one day the people he loved whose trust he had betrayed would learn to forgive him.

The tray of tools fell to the floor with a crash, making everyone jump and look at Quincy. He didn't care.

Sophia was gone.

He staggered to a nearby stool and sat down. She wasn't dead. He had to cling to that. Sophia wasn't dead.

"They aren't sure where Sophia is," Gabriel explained. "They found a feather that they think was from her eagle form. They pieced together that she saw Knorbis take Tate and Ariana, and she followed them."

At least she was with Tate and Ariana, Quincy thought, though he was still reeling in confusion over why the elder would lead them away from the others. Maybe he had picked up a threatening thought from one of the Waresti and thought this was safer?

"What can we do?" Olivia whispered as she wiped her tears. "We have to do something."

Quincy managed to regroup enough to respond. "You all know how pivotal these early weeks are for the babies. Both parents must be here providing as much contact with them as possible for at least a month. Three is ideal. Your bodies need to heal after the deliveries. Exerting yourselves right now would be quite dangerous. It isn't just about your physical health."

The sisters exchanged glances. He knew they were silently agreeing with him, even if it was a hard reality.

"There are Waresti scouts looking for Tate, Ariana and Sophia," Gabriel said. "Tiege is attempting to connect with Tate and Sophia through their blood bonds, but it isn't working."

"In regards to Sophia, that might be because she's in her shifted form," Quincy guessed, his mind racing. "Her DNA is unique, and we've never had the opportunity to test the bond before. We don't know how it will work. And it could be that Knorbis is somehow subduing Tate's consciousness if he doesn't want her communicating with Tiege or Zachariah."

"I think you're right about that, Quincy," Gabriel said. "All of us elders are continuing to try and reach Knorbis. He's put up a mental barrier that I think only Malukali could get through...and she's not responding, either."

What on the Estilorian plane was going on? Quincy couldn't wrap his brain around any of it.

But he knew one thing with absolute certainty.

"I'm going after them," he said.

Everyone turned to look at him as he rose from his stool and began collecting the dropped medical instruments as fast as he could. He started creating a mental list of anything he might need to bring even as he said, "And I think Clara Kate and *archigos* Ini-herit should be among those who come with me."

"Quincy—" Gabriel began.

"You can't go, so we'll go in your stead," Quincy said, talking over the elder in his haste to get out the door. "They might need healing, and *archigos* Ini-herit and I can help with that. Clara Kate's ability to imbue weapons might also be needed, depending upon what evil is driving all of this." When he saw them exchange glances, he added, "Look...we're the only ones left here at the homeland who are properly trained for this outside of the six of you, and you can't leave. We have to go."

After staring at him for a moment, Gabriel nodded. "All right. Let's go find the others and run this by them. And Quincy?"

"Yes?"

"If any harm comes to my daughter, you'll be the one answering to me."

Tiege didn't think he had ever been this frustrated. They had flown west for a few hours before he finally acknowledged that he wasn't going to be able to connect with Sophia. For some reason, the "pull" he was supposed to feel just wasn't happening.

They landed to discuss what to do. Moonlight shone on a wide lake as they stood on the shore. The Waresti patrolled the lake by foot as well as by air. Uriel stood nearby, facing the water as he communicated an update to Tiege's family back at the homeland. Knowing the news they received was devastating, Tiege felt like an utter failure.

As usual, Zachariah paced, running his hands through his hair and muttering to himself. The activity wore on Tiege's nerves.

"It must have something to do with her altered DNA," the Mercesti said eventually. "Perhaps her Gloresti nature is too suppressed by whatever gene it is that allows her to shift."

Tiege thought Zachariah sounded intrigued despite himself. The suggestion did kind of make sense. "It's also possible that because I'm so closely connected to Tate, I can't extend the Gloresti bond to anyone else," Tiege hazarded. "I mean, our dads can't connect with us that way because they're paired with our mothers, so their bond is permanently attached to them."

"You and I both have a connection to your sister," Zachariah pointed out. "That means it can be shared."

That was true. Tate's vow exchange with Zachariah had been based on her protection, not on love, as their parents' had been. Tiege supposed that meant that only avowed pairings made the Gloresti connection permanent and singular. He wasn't sure why he couldn't connect with Tate or Sophia, but the bottom line was he couldn't.

"Where would the Wymzesti take them?" Zachariah mused.

That was another question Tiege couldn't answer. He was trying to piece everything together, but Ariana's face kept entering his mind and interrupting his train of thought. He worried about her emotional state, which had been getting stronger over these past weeks, but was still nowhere near where it had obviously once been. There was no way to know if she would get through this experience without permanent scarring.

His sister was well-trained and resourceful. For all of her vivaciousness and bright energy, Tate had their dad's ability to think things through and do what it took to survive. Ariana, on the other hand, was a Lekwuesti through and through. As such, she thought of others before herself. This, above all, had been what caused her the most turmoil in her refusal to help find the scroll pieces. She knew her choice impacted others, but she had been unable to overcome her own fear to do something about it.

Now she had...and look where it had gotten her, he thought darkly, kicking a rock into the water with his pent-up anger.

"You have a new brother and sister," Uriel said, looking over at Tiege. "Willa and Wesley."

Tiege didn't know what to say. The announcement hit him like a kick to the solar plexus. Normally, he and Tate would join their family in welcoming the new babies. They had a family ritual of sorts where each of the siblings introduced themselves to the newborns, stating what they intended to pass along to them. For the first time in their lives, he and Tate wouldn't be around to participate in that.

"Thank you for letting me know, *archigos*," he said at last.

He did what he could to suppress his emotions, not wanting to appear weak in front of the others. But he could admit that the knowledge that he and Tate had missed out on something so important hit hard. Tate didn't even know they now had a new brother and sister.

"He is going to Kanika's," Zachariah said, drawing everyone's attention.

"He is?" Tiege echoed.

Turning to face Tiege and Uriel, Zachariah asked, "When was the last time anyone heard from *archigos* Malukali?"

"I last heard from her and Knorbis just before they met with Kanika," Uriel replied.

"Prior to this, when was the last time you remember the two of them being apart?"

There was a pause as the Waresti elder considered this. Then he said, "I believe it would have been before they were married."

Zachariah nodded. "He would not have left his wife unless it was absolutely necessary. Something must have happened at Kanika's that prompted him into this course of action."

"Do you think *archigos* Malukali is dead?" Tiege asked with mounting alarm.

"No," Uriel said. "We would all definitely know if an elder had been killed."

"What if she had only been injured? Deliberately?"

"You think Kanika intentionally hurt *archigos* Malukali?" Tiege asked.

"It would seem the most effective way to gain the cooperation of the Wymzesti elder, would it not?" Zachariah responded. "Torture is a standard Mercesti practice. They would likely know that by torturing her, they will ensure his cooperation."

Tiege swallowed hard, knowing only too well that he was right. "Okay," he allowed. "Suppose that's true. What would Kanika want with Tate and Ariana?"

"The Elder Scroll."

Tiege puzzled over Zachariah's matter-of-fact response.

Uriel reflected Tiege's thoughts when he said, "Kanika was the only Mercesti commander who survived Grolkinei's rule. She has been the acting leader over her class for nearly two decades. Why would she want to find the Elder Scroll?"

"For all of her supposed power as the Mercesti leader, she is not an elder, is she?" Zachariah replied. "Perhaps she seeks to change that."

"That doesn't sound like something Kanika would do," Uriel argued. "She has never struck me as ambitious. She made a mistake and she has done what she can to make up for it."

"There is some reason that the Wymzesti elder left his wife behind," Zachariah pressed. "I should have considered that before, but when he said that she stayed to see to Kanika's mental state, I did not question it. I should have wondered why he did not just remain behind with her rather than leave her to return to the Kynzesti homeland alone. His reason of not wanting to convey the thoughts across the distance for fear of them being intercepted by wayward Mercesti was flimsy at best."

Tiege realized he was right and saw Uriel coming to the same conclusion. Looking particularly grim, the elder said, "Kanika's home is to the north of where Knorbis left with Tate and Ariana, not the west.

"We've been going the wrong way."

Chapter 25

SOPHIA SLOWLY SURFACED FROM THE DEEP SLEEP. BECAUSE SHE FELT A pillow and the softness of a mattress beneath her and warm fabric on top of her, she gradually realized she was safe at home and in bed. Everything must have been a dream.

Whispers floated around her as she struggled to open her eyes. She felt as though she needed a couple more hours of sleep, but something in her subconscious wouldn't allow it.

As her brain started to clear, she realized that soft light had turned the world beyond her closed eyelids a pinkish-golden hue. She took her time opening her eyes, not wanting to have to blink against the light of the dawn. Still, when she finally parted her eyes to slits, the sting of even the mild sunshine brought tears to her eyes.

She moaned, bringing a hand up to cover her eyes. Although she normally considered herself a morning being, the description was far from apt at the moment.

"Are you all right?"

Sophia jerked into a sitting position, instinctively clutching the sheet to her chest. Her eyes somehow managed to acclimate in an instant as she looked around for the source of the voice. It sounded female, but not any female she knew.

She realized she wasn't at home, sending her already escalated heart rate soaring. The room was about the size of her bedroom, but where hers had a single window, this one sported a set of floor-to-ceiling windows that ran the length of the room to her left. Outside the windows, she saw a small, sunlight-dappled terrace surrounded by high, ivy-covered walls. The ground was a series of graduating circles that reminded her of the inside of a felled tree. On the right side of the room sat a small desk, a chair, and a nightstand with a bowl and pitcher on top of it.

The door to the room was right in front of her, about ten feet from the end of the bed. It stood partly ajar. She thought she saw a shadow in the gap between the door and jamb, making the hair on the back of her neck rise.

"Miss?" came the voice.

Whoever it was sounded hesitant, Sophia realized. Her fear settled into a healthier range as she realized she wasn't under any immediate threat.

"I'm…okay," she responded. "Where am I?"

"You are safe. We found you in the marshes. You were clearly in need of aid."

Knowing that was true, Sophia said, "Thank you." She glanced down and realized that, although she was clean—and she really didn't want to know who had bathed her—she was still naked. She debated whether or not to try to find clothes, since she really wanted to get back in the air in search of Tate and Ariana. Should she shift, or just use her wings?

"I am Melanthe," said the female on the other side of the door.

"Oh. Hi. I'm Sophia."

"Is there anything that you need, Sophia?"

Finding the whole talking-through-the-door thing very odd and wondering where on the plane she was, Sophia tilted her head and replied, "Well, I'd like to thank you face-to-face. You don't have to be shy, Melanthe. You've already seen me at my worst and I've got the sheet to cover me now."

In response came the sound of exchanged whispers that Sophia strained to hear. She was pretty sure she detected a minimum of three voices, which just increased her curiosity. Just when she was about to use her shifting ability to give herself the hearing of an owl, the voices silenced on Melanthe's abrupt, "Just try and stop me." Sophia's eyebrows rose over the firm tone in the other female's voice…quite different from the uncertainty of a moment ago.

"Very well, Sophia. I will enter. But please try not to panic."

Why would she say that? Sophia wondered. Her anxiety rose as she—naturally—panicked. The door opened enough to admit the female, who closed it quietly behind her. Sophia had only to take a quick look to understand why she had been warned.

Her hands raised in peace, Melanthe stood against the door as though afraid to move any further into the room. Her golden-brown hair fell in soft, shimmering curls to just below her shoulders. It had been captured with ruby-encrusted combs behind each ear, giving her a very youthful appearance. The olive tone of her skin was complemented by the flowing red gown she wore. There was nothing at all threatening about her.

Except the fact that she was a Mercesti.

And that meant, Sophia realized as her fear once again surged, that the multiple beings standing outside of the room were also probably Mercesti.

"I will not hurt you," Melanthe said in her quiet voice.

It was hard not to believe her. She appeared ready to fling the door open and throw herself back out of the room if Sophia showed even the slightest discomfort over her presence. Although her heart continued to hammer in her chest, Sophia found herself more puzzled than frightened.

"Okay," she replied slowly, her mind processing this turn of events. A Mercesti who had not only rescued her, but didn't wish to harm her?

That thought made her think of Zachariah, the only Mercesti she knew. He fell into a similar category as Melanthe. He had saved Tate and, although he frequently threatened to throttle her cousin, Sophia knew he would never harm her. Maybe these Mercesti were dedicated to Kanika's ideals and the concept of transforming the class into something other than the evil plague it had become under Grolkinei's leadership.

"Are you not afraid of me?" Melanthe asked.

"Not particularly," Sophia admitted, surprising herself. She had no good reason to believe this female with so little evidence to support her claim, yet she couldn't deny that she felt at ease here.

"Even though I am a Mercesti?" Melanthe pressed.

"Even though." There was a long pause. Finally, for lack of anything else to say, she asked, "Is this your home?"

"Yes."

Sophia offered the other female a small smile to try and ease some of the tension between them. "Well, from what I can see of it, it's quite lovely."

The words more than the smile seemed to have the right effect. Melanthe's pretty face eased from strained concern into an expression of pride and contentment. "Do you think so?" she asked, sounding very much like any other hostess might when a stranger entered her home. "I would be happy to show you around if you would like."

"That'd be great, thanks," Sophia responded, though in truth she was more eager to leave and go after her cousin and friend than walk around the dwelling. Still, this female had played a part in saving her life. A few more minutes wouldn't hurt. She glanced again around the room, but she unfortunately hadn't missed spotting a clothes-bearing armoire. "I don't suppose you have a spare set of clothing around here, do you?"

Now, Melanthe's entire demeanor changed. She lost any sense of uncertainty and actually appeared pleased by the question. "I do not, but I can generate some clothing for you if you would allow me to scan your form for the proper size."

"Oh! You were once—er," Sophia stopped herself, not sure whether discussing the female's former class was taboo. She felt a flush building as she thought of how to recover from her blunder.

"That is correct," Melanthe said matter-of-factly. "I was once a Lekwuesti."

"Sorry," Sophia responded, not sure what else to say.

To try and move things along, she climbed out of the bed and stood naked beside it. Being without clothing was second-nature to her, so she didn't feel much embarrassment as Melanthe's eyes began to glow so she could do a visual scan of her form. Sophia knew, having questioned *archigos* Sebastian at length over the years, that Melanthe's Lekwuesti abilities were allowing her to take Sophia's measurements by sight. Not all Lekwuesti could do this. It depended upon the individual strengths of the Lekwuesti.

"Excellent," Melanthe said a moment later.

Although the glow subsided, her eyes continued to absorb every detail, from Sophia's hair and eye color to her height and build. Then she nodded. Walking over to the bed, she concentrated and soon brought forth a number of clothing items.

Intrigued despite the surreal feel of the moment, Sophia moved closer to the bed. The gown was a shade of deep blue-green just a bit darker than her eyes. The fitted, square-necked bodice had golden laces up the front and looked rather low-cut. It had long sleeves and a full, floor-length skirt with gold stitching woven through it.

"Is this velvet?" Sophia asked, reaching out to caress the bodice.

"Yes. And the skirt is made of a satin blend I developed. It helps maintain warmth as well as wool, but has this lovely shimmer and breathability."

"It's gorgeous," Sophia said, her eyes wide. Then she took in the undergarments beside it. "Is that a corset?"

"Of course it is," Melanthe replied with a wrinkle forming on her brow. "Do you not wish to wear any undergarments?"

"I do want to wear undergarments, but I'm not used to this, uh, particular style."

The Mercesti considered this. "Well, I did adjust the corset to be less painful but just as flattering to the female figure as the styles from centuries ago," she said. "If you will allow me to assist you in donning it, we can determine whether you want to keep it on."

If it meant the difference between having undergarments or not, Sophia was positive she would want to wear the corset, but she didn't share that comment. Instead, she obediently allowed the Lekwuesti to assist her, once again wondering why she felt so at ease when everything she'd been taught should have had her running out the door, shifting into a cheetah and never looking back.

"Mel, what is taking so long?"

The voice that rumbled through the closed door had Sophia jumping. There was such a thick, rolling burr to the words that she could barely understand them. She thought back to her past education on the history of dialects and registered that the accent sounded like what humans called Scottish.

"I am getting her dressed," Melanthe called out. "Be patient."

Sophia thought she heard a resigned sigh from behind the door and her lips curved into an unexpected smile.

"I did not hear any screeching when Melanthe made her appearance," came another male voice. "We can take that as a good sign, no?"

That had definitely been a French accent. It was getting harder and harder to be alarmed when the conversation around her was so very normal. Before she could think more about it, she realized that Melanthe had gotten her fully secured in the unusual undergarments. Looking down at herself, Sophia felt the astonishment on her face.

"Wow—I have cleavage!"

"Of course you do. You have breasts, do you not?"

"Well, technically, I guess."

Sophia had never felt more feminine. And when Melanthe helped dress her in the beautiful gown and Sophia saw the results of the corset on her clothed frame, she made the immediate decision to forever change her regular wardrobe to include the unusual undergarment.

"Thank you, Melanthe," she said. "This is the most amazing thing I have ever worn."

A smile flashed across the Mercesti's face. The show of emotion made Sophia blink. Although many Estilorians had re-learned human emotions in the nearly two decades since the daughters of Saraqael had transitioned to this plane, most Mercesti had been so removed from the rest of society—and the three half-human sisters—that they hadn't. What did that smile signify?

"You are welcome, Sophia. May I style your hair for you?"

As Sophia opened her mouth to reply, the Scottish-sounding male said through the door, "Hairstyling, too? That does it."

When the door swung open, Sophia instinctively stiffened over the introduction of strangers into her environment. The room quickly filled up with a mix of males and females...all of them Mercesti.

"You could have waited a few more minutes, Derian," Melanthe chided, her gaze moving uncertainly from Sophia to the group.

Sophia couldn't take her eyes off the large, red-eyed male who stood at the front of the group. His nearly black, wavy hair was pulled back in a short ponytail at the nape of his neck, revealing a face that was arresting both for its compelling masculine beauty and its fierceness. A colorful woven tattoo began in the center of his forehead and curved along the left side of his face, winding almost delicately beneath his eye and across his cheekbone, continuing down along the side of his neck. Since he wore nothing more than a knee-length kilt and boots, she saw that the tattoo pattern continued down along his left arm and across the left side of his muscular chest, ending in a pattern that she couldn't quite make out directly over his heart.

When she managed to quit gawking long enough to lift her gaze to his, she could read nothing in his red eyes. That only made his next words stop the blood in her veins.

"I think she is ready enough, Melanthe. Time to turn her over to us."

Chapter 26

EIRIK HAD JUST DECIDED TO KILL DEIMOS WHEN METIS APPROACHED. The crazed male that Metis pampered so much was making enough noise to bring every Waresti within a mile right to their location. Being kept from Metis had prompted the behavior, something Eirik hadn't anticipated and was unwilling to endure. It was one thing to put up with the savage's lack of hygiene and limited communication skills, but this was unacceptable.

Just as he reached for one of his krises, Metis hurried up to them. She gave Eirik a sharp glance that told him she knew what he intended as she rushed to Deimos' side.

"My dear Deimos," she murmured, putting her arms around him and petting his dirty hair as though he was a precious gift. "I know you hunger. I have not had another opportunity to find a female to offer you, but that will soon be remedied."

"What is it that drives him to such madness?" Eirik asked with disgust, debating whether or not to follow through with his plan to kill the other male and be done with it.

He didn't expect a reply and was surprised when Metis answered, "It was my mistake that made him like this. I did not fully understand the limitations of my own abilities when I attempted to create him."

Eirik was intrigued despite himself. She was a being unlike any he had ever met. "Are you a Scultresti?"

"I was at the time," she replied.

Apparently, that was as much information as he would get. Dismissing it as unimportant, he began to pace as she issued her revolting cooing noises. Fortunately, her strange connection to the beast-like male served a purpose.

The noise had stopped.

"I want to know your plan, Metis. I have waited long enough. As it is, I have had to lead your deranged companion from one location to the next around Kanika's property to avoid detection. You may have told the Waresti that you did not want them patrolling the grounds because you thought it would keep members of your class from seeking you out, but that has not stopped them. They are still searching for the female you led to Deimos."

"I understand," she said, not looking away from Deimos. "You will have the two females you seek within the next day. Likely in a matter of hours."

Eirik considered this. A few days ago, he overheard a couple of the Waresti patrols discussing the arrival of the Wymzesti and Orculesti elders. Reasoning out Metis' plan to somehow use the elders to draw out the two females he sought, he had flown back to Bertram and Tycho and brought them to Kanika's. When the Wymzesti elder left, Eirik sent the pair after him with the order that they report back as soon as they learned what he was up to. He hoped to secure the females without Metis knowing. Unfortunately, the two males who had assured him of their loyalty had yet to make an appearance.

They would be dealt with accordingly whenever he next saw them.

"How do you intend to get the females within range of this place without being seen by Waresti scouts?" he asked.

"I have arranged a location to meet them. Their impending arrival will be conveyed to me in advance and I will come and get you so that you can be with me to greet them."

He highly doubted that. "Where will the meeting take place?"

"I will determine the specific location once we are notified."

"That is not what you—"

"I know what I said," Metis snapped. "I had initially planned to meet them on the far side of the lake. There is a bridge there with shadowed niches beneath it that would be ideal for evading detection. However, the water level is beginning to rise as the snow melts. I will likely have to think of a secondary location."

"We will determine the secondary location now," Eirik said.

"How are we to know which locations will be avail—"

"If they will arrive within a matter of hours, then I will wait in a location that was recently scanned by the Waresti. They will not go back and investigate it again before the females arrive. You can simply meet me—and Deimos—there when you receive the alert."

He had her there, and they both knew it. She ran a hand along Deimos' face and nodded.

"On the east side of the lake is an abnormally tight grove of ash trees," he said. "Do you know the place?"

"Yes."

"Good. Just north of the ash trees is an abandoned dwelling. It is rotted through and has little more than three walls left. But there is enough coverage within the ruins that Deimos and I can remain out of sight." He deliberately paused. "That is, of course, assuming I can control Deimos enough to avoid us being detected."

Metis flicked her gaze to him, then looked back at Deimos. "You understand that this is only for a short while longer, do you not, my sweet Deimos? We will soon be free from this place and able to access more beings on the mainland. I might even allow you to hunt if you behave for just a short while longer."

Deimos gave her a jerking nod in response. It was apparently enough to appease Metis. She rose and turned to face Eirik.

"You will see to Deimos' protection and I will bring the females to you," she said, as though this had been her plan the entire time.

"That is what I indicated, yes."

Her nostrils flared over his choice of words, but she didn't contradict him. Instead, she gathered her cloak closer to her throat and said, "Just remember the next time that you are feeling ill toward him that it was Deimos and his abilities that got you out of the last predicament in which you found yourself. Were it not for him, we would not be having this conversation."

His jaw clenched at the reminder. "I will ensure he is safe...so long as he does what I tell him to do."

They exchanged no other words, both understanding that they each wanted to be in the position of power, but neither of them were. Metis turned and walked back toward Kanika's dwelling as Eirik glanced at Deimos with his lip curled. It might be that he needed Metis and her pet right now, but he intended to change that dynamic at the earliest opportunity.

For now, he had to figure out a way to patrol the area with Deimos in tow while avoiding detection. He may have told Metis they would stay in one location, but he knew that plans had a way of changing.

With his goal now in sight, he'd damn well be prepared.

It didn't take much to convince Clara Kate and Ini-herit to go along in search of Sophia, Tate and Ariana. All Quincy had to do was tell them what happened. Although they had both been as baffled by Knorbis' actions as the rest of them, they had decided to set out right away.

Unfortunately, Quincy couldn't leave immediately. He had to wait for commander Raphael to arrive so that someone capable was within the homeland if any emergencies arose among the newborns and their mothers. Even on an express platform from Central, the trip took a couple hours.

He spent those hours conducting exams of Amber, Olivia and Skye as well as their babies to convince himself they were all as stable as he could leave them. They had all been through this so many times by now that it was practically routine, but he wouldn't have been able to focus while he was away if he doubted for a moment that they would all be okay. In the end, he determined that everyone was doing as well as could be expected. That eased his mind somewhat.

The other part of his mind obsessed over Sophia.

Where was she? They were nearly certain she was following Tate and Ariana, but how close to them was she? What would Knorbis do when he found out she was trailing after him? Although the highly intuitive elder wasn't able to read the Kynzesti's thoughts as well as a full Estilorian's, he could possibly sense her intent to intervene.

Surely the elder wouldn't hurt her, Quincy tried to convince himself. Knorbis was a peaceful, happy male. He treated the Kynzesti like his own children, as did all the elders. There must be a logical, nonthreatening reason for his behavior.

Quincy packed a satchel with the medical supplies he thought he might need. Although he was paired with a Lekwuesti, he preferred to save the once-daily connection for things like food and clean clothing. Having his supplies immediately handy could mean the difference between life and death. He wasn't about to take any chances.

Commander Raphael arrived as Quincy secured a scabbard around his waist. Although he didn't use weapons very often, he was rather skilled with a short sword. He prayed he wouldn't have to use it.

He spent another twenty minutes briefing the commander on each of the sisters and their newborns. Fortunately, the commander was experienced and took everything in stride. Each minute at the homeland felt torturous to Quincy, knowing Sophia was out there somewhere without so much as a paired Lekwuesti to aid her. She had been missing for nearly twenty-four hours. Although night had fallen, that wasn't going to keep Quincy and the others from leaving.

When he stepped out of the cottage, he found all of the parents of the Kynzesti nearby. They stood on the outskirts of the training paddock where a group of Waresti, led by the class second commander, Alexius, had gathered. Clara Kate and Ini-herit conversed with the commander, but Quincy couldn't hear what they said. When he approached the parents, they all turned.

"Thanks again for doing this, Quincy," Olivia said.

Devon was covered in a soft blanket and resting against her chest, much as her sisters held their babies. He read the barely controlled fear in her light green eyes. It closely mirrored the feelings he was trying to contain.

"We all appreciate it," Gabriel added, his hand on Amber's shoulder. His gaze reflected the same worry. "Not being able to go ourselves...well, it's hard for all of us."

"I know," Quincy said. He would be going out of his mind if he couldn't go after Sophia. "I'll bring them all back. And we'll have the scroll piece," he thought to add.

"Feel free to let Knorbis know that we intend to kick his ass for this," James said. He tried to keep his tone light, but there was a rare hardness to his gaze. "We'll expect a full explanation of what he was thinking to put us all through this."

Quincy nodded. He looked over and spotted Clara Kate. She gave him a "come on" gesture, so he said, "Looks like my cue." Turning briefly back to Gabriel, he added, "We'll keep you updated through *archigos* Ini-herit's connection to you."

"Thanks. Be safe, Quincy."

"I will."

He turned back to the training paddock and took a few steps toward it. Then he stopped.

Not knowing what suddenly prompted him, he once again turned around and walked back to Sophia's parents. They both looked at him with puzzled expressions.

Funny, he thought as he made his impromptu decision. He had always imagined he would be more nervous than this. Terrified, even. Now, nerves and fear were the furthest things from his mind.

He looked from James to Olivia when he confessed, "I love Sophia."

"We know, Quincy," Olivia said.

"No," he clarified. "I mean, I've loved her since she was born. But I've been *in* love with her for years."

"We know," Olivia repeated, her tone and expression as calm as usual.

Blinking, Quincy looked from her to James and back again. He wasn't sure how to react. Neither of them was upset or shocked or angry. Neither demanded that he leave the homeland never to return. Neither went on and on about how he had violated their trust by falling in love with their daughter.

They did none of the things he'd feared all of this time.

"You do?" he finally managed.

"Yes," Olivia said, now giving him a soft smile. "You've always treated Sophia differently than the others because you connect with her so well on an intellectual level. That difference in treatment became more pronounced when she reached maturity."

He flushed with embarrassment and self-censure as he realized he had been transparent in his feelings to everyone except the one who mattered.

"Does Sophia know?" James asked.

Quincy thought of his failed conversation with her before she left. "Yes."

Olivia's smile widened at that. "And does she love you?"

The answer was suddenly right there. "Yes," Quincy said. "She just doesn't know it yet."

Chapter 27

"WHAT DO YOU SUPPOSE THOSE MERCESTI ARE DOING WITH THE Kynzesti?" Tycho wondered. "They have had her in that unusual dwelling for hours."

"How should I know?" Bertram grumbled. "I have been sitting here beside you this entire time."

He was hungry, tired and irritable. They had followed the group of Mercesti through the marshes until they reached a much larger swamp. That swamp was filled with an abundance of odd-looking trees. The enormous trunks of the trees reached up to high, wide branches ending in fluffy-looking, dark green foliage. A series of bridges connected the trees and the homes that had been built among them. From the sky, and even largely from the ground, the trees camouflaged the dwellings. Since the ground was nothing but murky water, the likelihood of anyone stumbling upon this place was slim.

He slapped at a mosquito large enough to carry off a small animal and cursed his lot in life.

"They maintain a regimented watch," Tycho observed.

"Yes." Bertram had already noted that. "There are likely converted Waresti among them."

"Have you ever heard of a permanent Mercesti settlement such as this?"

Frowning, Bertram admitted, "No."

"Do you suppose they even know of Eirik?"

That was an excellent question. If this group didn't know who Eirik was, they would have no reason or incentive to turn the Kynzesti female over to them. And if they didn't turn the female over, Bertram and Tycho would have no way of finding the two females Eirik sought. If they returned to him empty-handed, they might as well just stick their necks out for his krises to do their worst.

"We cannot spare much more time here," Bertram said. "I do not know if this group has ever heard of Eirik, but they are Mercesti. If they do not bring the Kynzesti female out and let her fly soon, we will intervene to get her free so she can continue after the other females. She is our only hope to get past Eirik alive."

Turn her over to them?

The comment made by the tattooed male named Derian ran through Sophia's mind, causing her anxiety to crest. Had she been a fool to let her guard down?

"Do not be an ass," Melanthe said then, making Sophia blink in surprise. The other female walked up to Derian and tilted her head back so that she could look up at him. "Sophia is our guest. We should make her feel welcome."

"She is *yer* guest," Derian argued in his thick brogue. "Ye welcome her as ye see fit and we shall welcome her our way."

Melanthe gave the large male a shove. It didn't really move him, but the effort was there. She obviously wasn't intimidated by his aggressive demeanor.

Sophia looked from the bickering pair to the other Mercesti in the room. Although she spotted a number of beings just outside the door, standing in her room were two other males and two females. One of the males was almost as tall as Derian, but not nearly as broad or muscular. He could best be described as lithe, judging by what his outfit of an eye-searing green tank and tight plaid pants revealed. His mop of copper-colored hair hung in shaggy lengths around his square face. Several pieces of hair on either side of his head had been braided and decorated with beads. Sophia noted the same colorful tattoos as Derian's lining his skin.

The other male was bald and dark-skinned. He stood several inches taller and wider than even the large Derian, making Sophia think of the giants her mother told her about in her fictional bedtime stories. Like Derian, he wore no shirt. Wide metal bands adorned each of his huge biceps. His pants were khaki colored and appeared to be made of some kind of animal skin. His boots were fur-lined and probably would have reached Sophia's breastbone if she'd put them on. Although his dark skin masked some of the coloring, he was also tattooed.

Both of the females wore flowing gowns similar to the one worn by Melanthe. The first had rich, brown hair worn in an up-do decorated with jeweled pins. Her pretty face was dusted with freckles across the bridge of her nose. She stood beside the giant and her head topped out just above his elbow. The second female was taller and her blonde hair was cut into a short style that suited her long face. It was clear by the way she stood and the well-toned lines of her build that she knew how to handle herself.

"—and that is that," Melanthe said, pulling Sophia's attention away from the group staring at her. She turned from Derian and offered a small smile. "I would like to introduce you to some friends of mine, Sophia. I assure you that they will not harm you." She darted a warning look at Derian. "Despite what impression has been made."

"Okay," Sophia replied, squelching her fear. She tried not to think of the time ticking away.

"These are my friends, Alys," Melanthe said, indicating the blonde female, "and Oria." She pointed to the brunette. Turning to the copper-haired male, she continued, "This is Verrell, and over there is Cleve. You have already deduced that this is Derian, I am sure."

"Hello," Sophia said, sweeping her gaze across the group to include all of them in her greeting. When they stared at her without responding, she added, "Thank you for pulling me out of the marsh."

"Are you a Kynzesti then?"

The question came from Verrell. She realized he was the male with the French accent. "I am," she answered.

They all exchanged glances. Her heart picked up in pace as she wondered if they would now decide to hold her prisoner to bargain for her return to her family. In an effort to protect the Kynzesti, little about them was shared with outsiders. The elders only notified the other classes about births and shared a few details about the newest Estilorian class. She could see the group taking her measure.

Unable to stand the silence, she said, "I really must go." When she saw Melanthe's face fall, guilt flooded her. "After the tour."

"Not so fast, Kynzesti," Derian said, his arms crossed over his chest.

"What brings ye out here to the middle of nowhere?"

Unsure how much she should share, she hedged, "I was following my cousin and a friend. I really need to catch up with them."

"Is that so? And why, I have to ask, are ye away from yer protected homeland in the first place?" His eyes bored holes through her.

"We're helping the elders," she said, trying to find a way to convey a sense of importance without attracting too much of their interest. Fortunately, since she had grown up with a truth-detecting cousin, she had long ago learned the art of telling the truth without telling the truth. "Since you know of my class, you likely know that we each have different abilities. The elders requested the assistance of some of us."

"What kind of assistance?" Verrell asked.

"I would prefer not to discuss it." Sophia watched them process that. When Derian's expression darkened, she held his gaze and added, "Believe me when I say that it's in all of your best interests not to pursue that answer any further."

A long silence followed. Eventually, Derian gave a brief nod of acknowledgement. Sophia couldn't help but be impressed by his restraint. The fact that he took her seriously told her that he had good instincts and that he respected the position he was in as the apparent leader of this group.

"How did ye get out here all alone without a stitch of clothing?" he asked.

Not batting an eye under his scrutiny, she replied, "I fell behind the group I'm following. I exhausted myself trying to catch them. My abilities include shapeshifting. When I assume an animal form, I shed my clothes."

"And why are there two Mercesti followin' ye?"

"What?"

"There are two Mercesti males on the outskirts of our marsh," Derian explained, making Sophia's skin prickle with bumps. "They were followin' ye and appear to be waitin' for yer departure to pick back up the chase."

Sophia had to sit down as his words sank in. Melanthe hurried to her side with an exclamation of concern, but Sophia barely registered that.

She had been followed? By whom? For how long? And why?

"What—" She had to clear her throat, as it had become so dry with fear that her words were raspy. "What do they look like?"

As Derian relayed a detailed description, Sophia felt the color leech from her face. Her head swam. Bertram and Tycho.

They had followed her.

"Do ye know them?" Derian asked.

"I..."

Sophia trailed off and shook her head. She struggled to regain her composure as shock eased into acceptance.

Despite the other beings in the room, she suddenly felt very alone...and she longed to see Quincy again with a need so painful it surprised her. Unexpected tears stung her eyes and she forced them back.

"Sophia?" Melanthe said in a quiet voice, likely noting her distress. "Do those Mercesti mean you harm?"

"If they're the two males I think they are," Sophia said at last, "they wouldn't be following me for a good reason."

"Rogues," Verrell muttered.

He glanced at Derian, who nodded once. Turning without another word, Verrell left the room with Cleve and Alys right behind him.

"Ye can wait here while we dispatch the two males," Derian said as though this was a common occurrence. "Then ye can leave."

Uncertain how to feel, Sophia just said, "Thanks."

"Would you allow me and Oria to style your hair for you while you wait?" Melanthe asked.

"Sure," Sophia said with a shrug. She supposed it would give her some reason to sit still while she tried to figure out what in the world she would do when she was finally allowed to leave.

How had Bertram and Tycho found her? Even more important, *why* were they following her? She had nothing to offer them. Tate and Ariana were the ones who—

She stiffened. They hadn't been following her. They'd been following Tate and Ariana. And the two males served Eirik, which meant he was surely involved.

"Is everything all right?" Melanthe asked. Her hands were full of Sophia's hair, telling Sophia that she and Oria either lacked the Lekwuesti abilities to style hair or they just preferred to work with their hands.

"Not really," she murmured as she finally grasped the gravity of the situation.

Fortunately, no one pressed her for more information, though they exchanged glances over her head.

She thought through her options as she waited. She wished she could figure out a way to get back home, but the memory of her homeland's location had been wiped from her mind the moment she left, thanks to the protections. Even if she could go home, that would take at least a day. Besides, the homeland had surely been alerted to what happened and help was likely already on the way.

She could head in the direction that Knorbis had gone with Tate and Ariana. The problem was that she had no idea whether he had departed from that course. It seemed probable, as he had been very evasive in his flight path. Even if she shifted into an animal with hunting abilities, she didn't have a scent or other stimuli to help guide her now.

Or did she?

Her mind returned to the moment nine weeks before when she stood on the cliff outside the area of protection surrounding her homeland. She'd been scratched by the trees in her eagerness to escape Quincy's touch and the feelings he evoked in her, so her skin bore open wounds. As she stood on that cliff, Tate was grabbed by Nyx and snapped through the air with the kragen's powerful tail. The resulting spray of blood had covered Sophia, open wounds and all.

So they had shared bodily fluids, one of the ways Gloresti bonds formed. On top of that, she and Tate were cousins, and both of them were part Gloresti. She should be able to use that connection to find Tate.

So why didn't she experience the pull and connection to Tate that she should?

She balled her right hand into a fist. The only explanation for her failure to draw on her Gloresti side was her freakish DNA. That meant, if her conclusion was correct, she would be unable to properly track Tate and Ariana.

It also meant that Eirik was soon going to be in possession of the Elder Scroll.

Verrell and the others returned just as Melanthe and Oria finished styling Sophia's hair. He looked at Derian and shook his head.

Sophia understood. The Mercesti had escaped.

Even as fear threatened to choke her, she got to her feet. She looked to Melanthe and said, "Thank you so much for your hospitality, but I really have to go."

"Of course," Melanthe replied. She looked at Derian. "Can we not offer her an escort?"

Frowning, Derian looked at Sophia. "Where is it ye need to go?"

Feeling utterly overwhelmed, she shrugged in defeat. "I have no idea," she said. Then she issued a brittle laugh. "Unless you happen to know where Hoygul the Scultresti lives."

Quirking an eyebrow, Derian said, "What do ye know? Today is yer lucky day."

Chapter 28

THE SUN WAS HIGH IN THE SKY AS KNORBIS LANDED WITH TATE AND Ariana on the outskirts of the land surrounding Kanika's home. Despite the time of day, red balls glowed in the air above her dwelling, lighting the way in a mockery of welcome.

He had never felt so wretched in his entire existence. On the other side of the trees in front of him was the dwelling where his wife lay—in what condition he could only guess. The meeting location that Metis had imparted to him when he connected with her a short while ago was a ten-minute walk from here. He had only to lead Tate and Ariana to the site and then go and retrieve his wife. Straightforward enough.

Looking at the two females as they stood in front of him with vacant stares, he knew he couldn't do it.

Malukali, he thought as anguish gripped him, *if you can hear me, please forgive me. I love you. I'll find another way to save you.*

His vision blurred as he released Tate and Ariana from the mental hold he'd kept on them since he abducted them nearly thirty-six hours ago. They slowly blinked back to awareness.

"Whoa," Tate said, swaying. The elixir he had given them to fly would wear off soon. They would have to sleep when it did. "How did we get outside the forest?"

Ariana also looked around in confusion, pressing her hands to her temples. "Why is it daytime?" she asked.

"Tate, Ariana, I'm so sorry," he said, reaching out to touch their arms. "I've taken you away from the others. They have Malu—"

"Tsk, tsk."

They all turned as a group of beings emerged from the forest. Knorbis froze in shock, then instinctively threw up what mental defenses he could. A number of the younger and weaker-willed Mercesti turned and moved back into the forest, obeying Knorbis' silent command. Everyone else stopped.

Eirik was neither young nor weak-willed, and his red eyes bored into Knorbis. "I sense your will, elder, and I feel it weakening. You have not slept in quite some time and you have already exerted a great deal of your energy getting the females here. You will not hold me long."

He was right. "Tate, Ariana—you have to leave," Knorbis said. "Hurry."

But the effects of the elixir were already taking their toll. Ariana sank to the ground. She let out a sob. Tate bent to try and pick her up, but fell to her knees.

Then Metis, still maintaining Kanika's form, stepped out of the forest. The weight of his complete failure broke through the last thread of Knorbis' concentration. He lost the hold he had on the minds of the surrounding Mercesti.

"Your wife will surely appreciate your cooperation," Metis said in silky tones.

It felt like someone squeezed a band around his heart. "Please don't hurt her."

"But you were about to release the two females," Eirik pointed out.

"I did bring them, though," Knorbis argued, swallowing against his raging fear for Malukali.

How had he let things get to this point? He was an elder with the ability to predict the future, damn it. Why hadn't he foreseen this?

Eirik made a motion with his hand and four Mercesti stepped forward, moving toward Tate and Ariana. Even as Ariana whimpered, Tate surged to her feet, her blessed nunchucks in her hands. The weapons winked with an inner light that hurt the eyes of the Mercesti.

With more courage than Knorbis could ever hope to have, Tate faced down her opponents. She didn't appear concerned that she was outnumbered. Indeed, it didn't matter.

Her blessed weapons hurt the Mercesti and she used that to her advantage. Whirling, dipping, spinning and charging as though she wasn't beyond exhausted, she had all four males backing away with injuries that ranged from a broken arm to a badly burned face.

"Enough," Eirik snapped. He looked at Knorbis. "Does she know we have your wife?"

When he saw the shock flash across Tate's face, saw her lower her weapons, Knorbis' fear switched instantly to fury. "Damn you."

"It is too late for that." Eirik now looked at Tate. "If you do not want to be responsible for the slow and painful death of the Orculesti elder, I suggest you drop your weapons and cooperate."

It both pained and relieved Knorbis when Tate tossed her nunchucks away. She still stood protectively in front of Ariana, who hadn't moved from her spot on the ground.

"You will also notice that you cannot send thoughts," Eirik said, walking over to Tate and slowly circling her. "I have taken more precautions this time, knowing I would have a Kynzesti to keep under control."

Wanting to kick himself for his lack of sense, Knorbis belatedly tried to send a thought to Uriel. He knew immediately that it didn't get through and understood that Eirik had at least one mentally gifted Mercesti capable of dampening somewhere in their midst.

"This one," Eirik added with a nod in Ariana's direction, "is already cowed." He stopped when he once again stood in front of Tate. "It will be entertaining to break you, however."

Knorbis was relieved when Tate refrained from comment. She must have known how much trouble they faced.

"You will also be coming with us," Metis said to Knorbis. "Once you have rested, you will use your abilities to help control these two females. So long as you do what we say, your wife will remain sedated and unharmed."

He should have known Metis would never keep her word. But it had been the only option he had to try and protect Malukali. Wishing he hadn't exhausted himself to the point where he could barely think, he asked, "How will you explain your absence to the Waresti in your—Kanika's home?"

"The Waresti have been contained. They will not be a problem."

Her words slammed the lid on the last sliver of hope Knorbis had that he could rescue his wife. He saw nothing but a yawning pit of darkness and hopelessness where the future lay.

A noise emitting from the forest had the hairs on the nape of his neck standing on end. It sounded like an animal in heat. When another group emerged from the woods, he realized his assumption was accurate enough.

"Ah, my sweet Deimos," Metis said, hurrying over to the males who held the straining Mercesti with some kind of harness. "I told you I would bring them to you, did I not?"

As she spoke, the howling quieted. She said a few more words that Knorbis couldn't hear, but they appeared to calm the horrid creature. Eirik reached down and lifted Ariana, who was as pale as the moon. Tears glistened on her cheeks.

"Now," he said, "unless you want me to turn you and the Kynzesti over to Deimos, tell me which way to go to get the scroll."

Ariana and I are with Knorbis. Eirik is here w—

Tiege's wings locked as Tate's alarmed and confused thoughts flashed through his head. He lost a bit of altitude before he regained control of himself. His sister's words had fear and adrenaline pumping through his system. Beside him, Zachariah looked over as though he sensed news coming.

"What's wrong?" Uriel asked from his other side.

"I just received a thought from Tate," Tiege answered, looking over at the elder. "She said that she and Ariana are with Knorbis, and that Eirik is with them."

Uriel didn't react to the awful news. Instead he asked, "Did she indicate that Sophia is with them?"

"No," Tiege said, and a fresh wave of worry hit him. "Maybe Sophia tracked them and she's hiding from the Mercesti while she tries to figure out how to help."

"Ask Tate if they're at Kanika's so we can be sure—" Uriel began.

"She's no longer accessible," Tiege interrupted. "Her thoughts were cut off."

"Her connection to you is likely being dampened by someone," Zachariah said.

Tiege hated that the other male shared this statement as though it was a simple fact and nothing of concern. Anger had him glaring at Zachariah and snapping, "Don't you care at all that they're back in Eirik's control?" When that provoked nothing more than a stare, he said, "You may not know what Eirik is capable of, but I do. Ariana was his captive for almost two weeks. I know what he did to her. He's very creative in his tortures."

"She has been trained—"

"Don't you get it?" Tiege interrupted, fury making his voice tight. "He needs Ariana coherent and healthy to get the scroll piece. She'll be relatively safe." He watched the Mercesti process this and then drove his point home. "Eirik can shatter whatever illusion surrounds the scroll piece by tossing Tate's barely conscious body at it. He knows this after the last time. He'll use Tate however he wants to in order to ensure Ariana's cooperation."

There was a long pause as Zachariah considered Tiege's words. Finally, the Mercesti looked over at Uriel. When he spoke, his voice was hard.

"You must bring us to the Scultresti's home so that we can acquire the map to the library."

"Hoygul will likely refuse to give it to us," Uriel pointed out.

"Just let him try."

Quincy, Clara Kate, Ini-herit and their Waresti escort flew for the better part of the day with only a couple of stops to rest. After communicating with Uriel, they decided to head straight to Kanika's home.

The quiet flight gave Quincy a lot of time alone with his thoughts. Was Kanika actually holding Malukali prisoner, as Zachariah reasoned? It did seem to make sense that a threat to his wife would prompt the Wymzesti elder to act so out of character. Adding to this theory was the fact that Uriel was apparently no longer receiving check-ins from lieutenant Donald and his team stationed out at the Mercesti leader's home.

Quincy found this fact particularly alarming. Sophia was following Knorbis, Tate and Ariana into a very dangerous situation. If she tried to intervene to save Tate and Ariana, which he was sure she would do, she could end up hurt or—

No. He wouldn't go there.

They stopped traveling again as darkness fell. They were only a matter of hours from Kanika's and it was hard not to push everyone to continue. But Quincy knew better than anyone how important the restorative rest between flights was in the long-run, so he restrained himself. They ended up in a small, grass-covered valley without much along the lines of cover, which told Quincy they wouldn't be staying long. That suited him perfectly.

Before he had even taken his satchel off to stretch, he noticed Ini-herit pause and tilt his head as if listening to someone. His silver eyes flashed.

Hoping that Uriel was conveying that he, Zachariah and Tiege had caught up with Tate and Ariana, he hurried over to his elder. Clara Kate moved up beside him to await the news.

After a moment, Ini-herit blinked and turned his emotionless gaze to them. “Tate and Ariana have been brought to Eirik.”

Clara Kate stiffened and drew a sharp breath. Quincy felt as though his heart flipped over in his chest. “What about Sophia?” he managed to ask. “Have they found her?”

Ini-herit glanced at Clara Kate and then focused on Quincy. “They have not, despite Uriel sending his fastest scouts after her. Those scouts have nearly reached Kanika’s, but they have not found any sign of Sophia. It appears that she has vanished.”

Quincy stared stupidly at his elder, unable to process what he’d just heard.

“We will have to change course and join the others in convincing Hoygul to turn over the map to the library,” Ini-herit continued.

“You’re going to abandon the search for Sophia?” Quincy asked. The words felt as though they sliced his throat as he spoke them.

“We must,” Ini-herit replied. “The only hope for all Estilorians is that we acquire that scroll piece before Eirik does.”

PART III:

ALIGN

Align [v. uh-lahyn]: To fall or come into a line; to bring into cooperation or agreement with a particular group, party, cause, etc.

Chapter 29

SOPHIA WANTED TO LEAVE IMMEDIATELY FOR HOYGUL'S HOME, BUT Derian refused. He intended to lead her to the Scultresti himself and had to make a few arrangements before he did. She had little choice but to wait.

Despite her fear over the uncertain path ahead of her, she could admit to being awed by the Mercesti encampment. It was deceptively large, housing several hundred Mercesti, and was built entirely among gigantic medeina trees above the waters of the swamp. Sturdy woven vines served as bridges, connecting the dwellings. Stairs curved around the outsides of some of the tree trunks, leading from homes in the upper levels to those closer to the bottom.

Only medeina trees, specially crafted by the Scultresti, could maintain their structural integrity while having multiple homes carved out of them. Sophia found the design of the encampment both fascinating and beautiful.

"How long has this been here?" she asked Melanthe. The female Mercesti had taken the lead in giving her a brief tour after serving Sophia breakfast.

"Oh, for well over a century," Melanthe replied. "We have kept it very quiet and well-protected, as I am sure you can appreciate."

"Sure."

It was really no different from her own protected homeland, Sophia mused. They passed what appeared to be a dwelling containing a variety of foods. Several Mercesti walked through the dwelling carrying baskets, which they filled with food and then brought to a wooden counter manned by a female.

"What is this place?"

"Our food larder," Melanthe explained. "There are only a handful of us with the ability to generate food, but many mouths to feed. We stockpile what food we can to ensure everyone has something to eat when they are hungry. We supplement by hunting and gardening."

"I see," Sophia said. She remembered learning that because Mercesti lost some or all of their previous class's abilities upon converting, there weren't many who could create food, clothing and shelter. And since converted Mercesti lost their pairings with Lekwuesti, they couldn't get their hospitality needs met that way. "Well, it sounds like you've developed a great community here."

"Thank you, Sophia." Melanthe nodded a greeting to a passing female as she continued, "We have had our struggles. Derian is not comfortable wearing the mantle of responsibility that comes of seeing to everyone's welfare, but he has little choice." It appeared she intended to say more, but reconsidered. Smiling, she said, "I know you are anxious to continue on your journey. I believe that Derian has finished making all of the arrangements, so we might as well get started."

"We? You're coming along?"

"Of course. I cannot let Derian go off without me to rein him in. Believe me when I say that would not be in the best interests of anyone."

Normally, Sophia would have minded her own business, especially with a virtual stranger. But Melanthe was so kind and open that she found herself asking, "Are you and Derian, um, together?"

"We are mates," Melanthe confirmed as they turned onto a bridge leading to the largest dwelling within the encampment. "And now you are probably wondering why I would love such a cantankerous male."

Sophia thought of her cousin and Zachariah. "No, not at all. Although…"

"Yes?"

"Well, I have been wondering how it is you experience emotions."

"Ah." Melanthe nodded. "I understand. Well, some of us experience more emotion than others, as is true for all Estilorians. Not all of us have been within the encampment for a very long time. There are some who only just found us. Many of those who have entered our circle over the past eighteen years were exposed to the daughters of Saraqael and came to us with an understanding of human emotions."

That made sense. Sophia knew that one of the primary focuses of her mother and aunts after the defeat of Grolkinei had been to spend as much time as they could among the Estilorians. Although the homeland was their primary base, they all traveled frequently to Central and to various places on the mainland, visiting with all of the classes and trying to help impart human emotions to as many as possible. Once their children came along, they rotated who traveled so that the children were always cared for, but they still continued their efforts.

They reached their destination before Sophia could consider this further. Melanthe opened the door and held it so Sophia could enter first.

It was some kind of gathering space, she realized as she entered and saw the large number of beings inside. There were several separate seating areas around the room comprised of an eclectic mix of couches, chairs and tables. A fire pit in the center of the space housed flickering red flames, telling Sophia that they were generated by energy and not true fire. As they were in the middle of a tree, she imagined a real fire would have been disastrous.

Only when Melanthe joined her did Sophia catch on to the fact that the room had gotten very quiet. Everyone stared at her.

Bringing a hand to her head, she checked her hair to make sure it wasn't somehow standing on end. Melanthe and Oria had pulled her hair back at the temples and created a series of small braids woven with blue-green and gold threads, pinning them at the crown of her head and leaving the rest of her hair down. It felt like it was still in place.

"Do not mind them," Melanthe said. "They are just unused to seeing non-Mercesti here."

Sophia knew none of them had ever met a Kynzesti. Not sure what to do or say, she just followed Melanthe's lead and walked through the room toward the back without meeting anyone's gaze.

They headed for a closed door. When they reached it, Melanthe placed her hand on it and waited. A moment later, there was a distinct "snick" and the door opened.

"Follow me," she said.

Curious despite her itch to speed things up and get out of there, Sophia walked through the door to find herself at the top of a spiraling staircase. Even as she stepped onto the first stair, the door closed on its own behind her. She followed Melanthe down, gaping at the elaborate carvings decorating the inside of the tree trunk as they descended. She hadn't ever seen anything so beautiful. Her younger sister, Leigh, the artist in the family, would be beside herself.

When they reached the bottom of the stairs, they walked through another doorway. This one led to a windowless room only about half the size of the one above it. Sophia detected a moist feel to the air, as well as the noticeable scent of damp wood. The room contained one large, round table in the middle with stools all around it. Each piece of furniture emerged from the ground in a way that made Sophia believe the room had been carved around them.

Around the table sat Derian, Verrell, Cleve, Oria, Alys and at least twenty other Mercesti. Sophia realized they were all garbed for battle. Their armor ranged from pieces made of thick leather to the highly complicated, lightweight armor that only very skilled Lekwuesti could generate. She tried not to gape as they all turned to look at her. She had somehow managed to inherit her own personal army.

"Have ye changed yer mind about fillin' us in on yer little adventure, Kynzesti?" Derian asked. "It would be helpful not to go into this blind."

What should she tell them? It would be plain stupid to mention the Elder Scroll. The artifact was far too much temptation for most Estilorians. But she didn't want them to be unprepared.

"Please take a seat, Sophia," Melanthe said when she hesitated, taking her by her elbow to gently guide her to a stool.

Comforted by the fact that Melanthe sat beside her, Sophia began, "The elders are attempting to recover an artifact. That same artifact is being pursued by a Mercesti named Eirik."

Looks and murmurs circulated around the table. Sophia realized that they knew who Eirik was. She had a moment of sheer panic as she wondered if they might be his allies. After all, she knew next to nothing about these Mercesti outside of the fact that they were treating her well.

Verrell quickly put her fears to rest. "A right bastard," he spat, making a gesture with this hand to punctuate the remark. "Greedy and power-hungry."

Derian nodded. "Whatever Eirik seeks is surely nothin' he should have."

Relieved, Sophia said, "You couldn't be more right about that. He's been looking for it for quite some time. He's already got part of it, and he's figured out he needs more for it to be complete. It would be detrimental to all of us if he acquires it."

"And Hoygul has the key to this artifact?" Alys asked.

"In part," Sophia replied. "Let's just say that Hoygul can get me to part of the artifact, and if I can procure to it and get it safely to the elders, Eirik will be unable to fulfill his plans."

"Reason enough for me to play armed escort for a Kynzesti," Verrell said.

There were nods and words of agreement from the others. Sophia looked at Derian. He stared back at her. She couldn't read his expression at all and she once again found herself comparing him to Zachariah. If Tate had never paired with Zachariah, would Sophia have ever believed that this kind of commitment by the Mercesti was possible? She doubted it. She would probably have done the cheetah thing and fled.

What a loss that would have been.

"We leave once Mel armors up," Derian said at last. He held up a hand when Melanthe opened her mouth. "Ye'll wear it or stay here."

Melanthe sighed. "Fine. Sophia, we should provide some armor for you, as well."

Sophia shook her head. "When I shift, I'll lose it."

"Then ye'll not be shiftin' while with us," Derian argued. "Ye need an escort and we will provide it. But ye go armored and armed."

His words caused Sophia to recall the conversation she'd had with her mother about her needing to focus more on her training and learning to defend herself in any type of situation. Had that really been only a few days ago? The memory brought a pang of homesickness and had her mentally shaking her head. Why was her mother always right?

Not seeing any reason to argue with Derian's dictate, she nodded. She marveled over the fact that this group had converted Mercesti among them with enough skills to generate so much equipment. That had another thought occurring to her.

"Are any of you converted Orculesti or Wymzesti?" she asked.

When silence again fell and everyone stared at her with stony expressions, she realized she had just committed some kind of social blunder.

"I'm sorry," she hurried to say. "I just thought, well, maybe someone could help me let my family know I'm okay."

"We have such Mercesti among us," Derian replied, his tone neutral. "But the only possible way to communicate a thought to yer family would be to send it directly to *archigos* Malukali, and she has been inaccessible for days."

Blinking in confusion, Sophia repeated, "Days?"

"Aye."

"That can't be. She and *archigos* Knorbis went out to Kanika's home to help her—"

"Kanika is dead," Derian interrupted.

"No, she's not," Sophia argued. "Everyone thought she was, but—"

"Aye, she is."

Irritated that the Mercesti kept interrupting her, Sophia clenched her hands into fists and frowned at him. "She survived the attack by Deimos. Lieutenant Donald found her more than a week ago. *Archigos* Malukali and *archigos* Knorbis went to counsel her afterward because she was in shock. *Archigos* Malukali is still there." She spoke of the incident as though the group should know about it. They certainly seemed more knowledgeable about happenings on the plane than most Estilorians.

"She did not survive it," Verrell said. "She was killed by a being who can assume the forms of others."

Sophia's eyes widened. If the two elders went to Kanika's home believing this supposed imposter was Kanika, they might have been taken off-guard. And if this being killed Kanika, she would have no qualms about attempting to overpower a couple of trusting elders. Sophia considered the fact that Knorbis had returned to the homeland without his wife. It was the first time in her entire existence that she had seen one of them without the other.

Filled with mounting horror, she looked around the table and said, "This is even worse than I thought. We have to go. We have to go *now*."

Chapter 30

ARIANA HAD GONE INTO THE VENTURE OF FINDING THE REMAINING scroll pieces with the understanding that something could conceivably go wrong. But she knew she'd be surrounded by her new friends, a couple of elders and a team of Waresti. They could certainly handle anything that arose.

Never—not once—did she think she would end up right back where she started nine weeks ago.

She wanted to curl up into a ball and will it all away. Just kill her and be done with it, she thought. But now she didn't only have herself to think about. Tate was with her, too.

Although she and Tate were both exhausted from whatever it was the Wymzesti elder had given them, Eirik told them that they had to fly. Knorbis tried to argue with the Mercesti, explaining their conditions, but it didn't do any good.

Besides, it was too little too late, in her estimation.

He had betrayed them.

"Did any of them send out thoughts before you imposed your abilities?" Eirik asked a dark-haired male dressed in a black toga before they took flight.

"The Kynzesti sent out a partial thought that indicated she and the Lekwuesti are with you and the elder, my lord. She revealed nothing else."

Eirik stared down at Tate. "Who was on the other end of your thought?"

She hesitated for a moment, but must have decided it wasn't worth resisting. "My brother."

Ariana's eyes burned upon hearing that. She knew how close Tiege was to his twin. The partial thought must have hit him like a strike to the heart.

"I shall take measures to deal with him, then," he said ominously.

What does he mean by that? Ariana wondered, exchanging a panicked glance with Tate.

Then Eirik turned his attention back to Ariana. She couldn't avoid flinching under his gaze as he said, "We have wasted enough time here. Use your power to find the missing scroll piece and lead us to it."

"Or is it *pieces*?" the female Mercesti beside him asked.

They didn't know.

Despite her fear and the fog of exhaustion coating her brain, Ariana found herself stuttering, "Th-there's only one more."

"Then what are you waiting for?" Eirik snapped. "Fly."

They all extended their wings. Ariana opened her second power to its full extent. Her mind racing, she reasoned that Tiege and the others would try to get to the ancient library as quickly as possible, since it contained the only scroll piece they knew where to find. If she and Tate were going to have any chance of surviving this, they would need the help of their friends and family. Thus, Ariana had to be sure she led them to the library.

Because there were two more lavender trails leading to scroll pieces—well, three, counting the one leading directly to Eirik and the piece he obviously kept on his person—she had to focus on getting to the correct one. Using the information conveyed to her by Quincy, she pictured a library with shelves overflowing with books and scrolls, visualizing everything from how it looked to how it smelled. She soon identified the correct trail.

"When we're in the air," she said, "I don't have the same ability to see the path."

"Then we will land periodically to ensure you are leading us true," Eirik said, looking at her with his cold, red eyes. "But you had best be sure we get there soon. You are well aware of the consequences I will impose if we do not."

Her stomach tightened in remembered fear. Oh, she knew. But as they lifted into the air, she also knew she had no choice but to take a longer route than necessary to the library so she could give their rescuers a chance to acquire the map and get there first. She had to believe that Eirik was bluffing about having a plan to intercept and stop Tiege and the others. Even if he wasn't, she knew Tiege was very capable of defending himself and was surrounded by Waresti. He was strong, she reasoned. He'd be fine.

As tears trailed down her cheeks, she prayed that she had a fraction of that strength to get through this again.

Bertram and Tycho watched from their hiding place as the Kynzesti female and her Mercesti escort emerged from the large tree village and flew west. Night was falling, but the fading sunlight still glittered on armor worn by a few of the departing beings.

They had nearly been caught spying by the other Mercesti. Their centuries of existence as former Waresti alerted them, though. Bertram thought he saw a scout on a well-hidden post among the high tree branches. Going with his instincts, he and Tycho had quickly left, making their way back across the marsh until they found a section deep enough that they could immerse themselves to avoid being seen, but close enough to see if anyone left the trees.

"I still do not see why we did not make ourselves known to the other Mercesti," Tycho grumbled as they emerged from the marsh and dripped on the boggy ground beside the water. "Who is to say whether or not they would have worked with us to acquire whatever scroll it is we are after?"

Bertram removed a leech from his arm with a look of disgust. "If we had approached them about it, we would have had to share the prize with them. This way, we can follow them and simply acquire the Kynzesti when she steps away from the group, keeping the prize to ourselves."

Tycho issued a grunt of acknowledgement. Then he said, "Where do you suppose they are going?"

Having given this some thought, Bertram answered, "They have probably made some kind of ransom demand and are taking her to the place where her family can pick her up. As they live out here in the middle of nowhere, they probably do not want to bring the Kynzesti's family to their doorstep, so they arranged for the exchange a fair distance from here. Likely they lack food, clothing and other items that they feel would be a good bargain for the female's life."

"Fools," Tycho said with a shake of his head. "They have no idea what potential they now have within their control. Eirik is surely pursuing something worth at least ten times what they are bargaining for."

"Whatever is on this scroll that Eirik seeks, it had better be worth all of this," Bertram replied as he extended his wings to take flight. "If not, this

Kynzesti's life will not last long enough to be a part of any kind of ransom exchange."

Tiege paced as Uriel relayed the map to Hoygul's home. The elder had decided to continue on to Kanika's home while Tiege, Zachariah, Sebastian and the Waresti with them went in search of the scroll piece and, of course, Tate and Ariana.

"If Knorbis went through all of this, then Malukali must be in grave danger," Uriel explained. "And if Eirik managed to convince Kanika to participate in his quest to acquire the scroll, she must be dealt with accordingly. Just as important, I need to find out why my lieutenant and those under his command are no longer responding to me."

Harold, the Waresti commander, was on his way with more Waresti. Some of those soldiers would accompany Uriel and some would remain with Tiege and Zachariah. They could arrive at any time.

Each passing minute dragged like an ant through honey. Tiege listened to Uriel's directions, but he didn't know his way around the plane well enough to understand half of them. He knew he would have to rely on Zachariah, who now nodded and asked follow-up questions of the elder, to get them there. That was not a heart-warming realization.

"Hoygul's home looks like an old, abandoned cottage on the outside," Uriel said. "That was the only illusion he would allow to be placed on it."

Why the Scultresti didn't want to be more thoroughly protected in light of the information he maintained completely defeated Tiege. He supposed he would just consider them lucky that they didn't have to dissolve yet another illusion cast by the elders on this debacle of a mission.

"If you attempt to strong-arm the map from him," Uriel continued to Zachariah, "he will refuse to give it to you. While I appreciate your sense of urgency and I know your pairing to Tate is driving you to find and protect her, you will need to push that aside when you communicate with him."

If that was true, Tiege decided that it would be in their best interests to leave Zachariah outside when they got to the Scultresti's cottage. He'd wait to mention that idea, however.

"Ini-herit, Quincy and Clara Kate are on their way to Hoygul's, as well," Uriel said. "If they get there first, it is my hope that Quincy can once again convince Hoygul to give him the map."

"Because it turned out so well the last time," Tiege muttered, but no one heard him.

As the conversation between the other two males continued, Tiege turned his thoughts to his sister and Ariana. He tried again to connect with Tate and was met with the mental wall that had come down on her last thought. The dampening preventing her from connecting to his thoughts also kept Zachariah from sensing her through their Gloresti-style bond.

He wondered how Ariana was holding up. She had been so deeply affected by her previous experience at Eirik's hands that he worried her mind wouldn't endure this. His only hope was that having Tate there might help.

What he did know was that when he finally got to them, it would be a tight race between him and Zachariah as to who would get to Eirik first.

"Harold is here," Uriel said, drawing his attention.

Sure enough, within the span of a minute, the Waresti commander and the warriors he led landed nearby. Conducting a quick scan, Tiege estimated there were nearly a hundred beings present.

"Fifty of you will come with me," Uriel announced. "If Kanika and her followers have control over her homestead, they will not have many more than that in number. It is a relatively small dwelling, and even if some of them are residing in the surrounding forest, I predict no more than seventy could occupy it."

"Do you need any provisions?" Sebastian asked.

"No. We won't be gone long and I can connect with you if needed."

The Lekwuesti elder nodded.

Uriel looked from Tiege to Zachariah. "Once we rescue Malukali, the hold Eirik has over Knorbis will be removed. I suspect he can counter the effects of Eirik's dampeners even now, but he's choosing not to because it would put Malukali at risk. Once she's free, you should be able to connect with Tate."

"Then stop wasting time talking to us," Zachariah said. After a brief pause, he tacked on, "Sir."

As rude as the statement was, Tiege couldn't help but find himself in complete agreement. They all needed to get going. Without question, getting both the scroll piece and Eirik's hostages was going to take monumental timing.

That, and a miracle.

Chapter 31

INI-HERIT CONNECTED WITH ZAYNA TO GET THE MAP TO HOYGUL'S cottage. Although the elder had been there before, his memory of the exact location wasn't clear. Once he received the details, they all headed to the Scultresti's after only an hour of rest.

Quincy followed the others, but it about killed him. All he could think about was Sophia. Was she okay? Where was she? Had she continued to track Tate and Ariana?

He hoped that she was, indeed, still tracking them. That meant he would ultimately connect with her again when they all reached the library. He vowed that even if she told him she didn't want to hear it, he would never let another day go by where he didn't tell her how much he loved her.

"It appears we will be delayed," Ini-herit said, making Quincy focus on their path.

Ahead of them churned a bank of storm clouds. Even from their distance, they saw the deluge of rain produced by those clouds. Lightning streaked to the earth, generating a low rumble a few seconds later.

"Can't we go around it?" Quincy asked.

"No," Alexius said. The Waresti second commander flew between Clara Kate and Ini-herit and looked grim. "Judging by wind speed and the span of those clouds against the horizon, by the time we flew sideways in either direction, the storm would catch us. We must seek shelter."

Fortunately, they were near a series of mountains. Finding a cave large enough to hold them didn't end up being too difficult. Within ten minutes, they all sat inside the cave with balls of light bouncing along the ceiling as the storm raged outside.

Although Quincy wanted to keep moving, he was smart enough to know they couldn't risk flying in this weather. He decided to take this opportunity to rest, not knowing when he would next get to do so. Picking a spot in a relatively secluded part of the cave, he settled down on the hard ground and closed his eyes.

Miraculously, he dozed. His dreams were filled with images of Sophia in varying states of distress. His eyes flew open on the tail-end of a dream in which she screamed out to him for help just before an arrow pierced her heart.

His own heart pounded at a gallop as he oriented himself. He realized he had rolled onto his side and faced a wall of rock. The hiss of rain continued to fill the cave.

"What was I like on the human plane?"

Quincy blinked in surprise when he heard Ini-herit speak from just a couple of feet away.

"I wondered if you'd ever ask," Clara Kate replied.

Her soft voice was nearly as close. Quincy realized the pair had also retreated to this quieter part of the cave and must believe he was still asleep so they could talk freely. Although he considered making some kind of movement or giving them another indication that he was awake, he couldn't deny a morbid curiosity over the answer to his elder's question. So he remained silent.

"I have hesitated to discuss it with you," Ini-herit said. "I did not want to cause you undue pain."

That made Quincy wince. He was sure that just by being within Clara Kate's line of sight every day, the elder caused her pain. He knew she would never say such a thing, however, and she didn't surprise him.

"You can feel free to ask me anything you'd like, Harry—uh, Ini-herit."

"Harry?"

"Um, yeah. Sorry about that. It was a nickname. Mrs. B started using it when you were little because it was easier for your friends to pronounce."

"I see."

"So, as far as what you were like," Clara Kate said in an obvious attempt to turn the conversation, "you were a straight-A student...president of the student body with a good number of friends. You were a bit like my dad was as a human, seeing as you were raised by the same foster mom. You had a southern accent and spoke in a way that reflected good grammar, and you took care to convey appropriate manners."

"A gentleman," Ini-herit concluded.

"Oh, not always."

Her tone had Quincy's eyebrows rising. *Really?*

"The storm is clearing," came Alexius' voice. "Wake Quincy so we can depart."

He abruptly forgot all about whatever had occurred between C.K. and Ini-herit as his mind switched gears. Sophia, Tate and Ariana needed them.

It was time to move on.

They barely managed to avoid the storm. Sophia was very impressed with the clever maneuvering by the Mercesti. What surprised her most was that it was the quiet female, Oria, who led them.

Melanthe explained that Oria was a very rare Mercesti. She used to be a Wymzesti and had retained a large portion of her former class's traits. She was able to guide them using heightened instincts, predicting the best path to avoid any potential problems.

"I'm seeing a trend among you," Sophia said to Melanthe as they flew side by side.

"You are referring to the fact that there are so many of us with unusual abilities for Mercesti, I assume?"

"Yes." Sophia saw Derian's eyes move between the two of them and knew he was listening from his position on the other side of Melanthe. He didn't look pleased, but from what she had seen, he never did. "I'm not trying to pry and I promise not to say anything to anyone if it's an issue. I just noticed it and found it…interesting."

"You are very perceptive, Sophia," Melanthe said with a small smile. "You pick up on things that others might miss."

Not everything, Sophia thought, her heart sinking as she thought of Quincy. How many signs had he given her over the years that she had missed or ignored? She had been so convinced of her conclusion that he couldn't stand the sight of her that when she was presented with another truth, she threw it back in his face.

Perceptive? Maybe. Flexible? Apparently not.

"Derian discovered some time ago that Grolkinei deliberately targeted converts based upon their abilities," Melanthe continued. "He sent scouts across the mainland seeking out Estilorians with powerful enough skills that those skills would likely survive a conversion. Then his mentally-gifted Mercesti used their abilities to drive those Estilorians to commit an act that would convert them."

Sophia blinked at that. What she described was exactly what had happened to Zachariah. As the Gloresti second commander, he had been a grand prize for Grolkinei. Zachariah had maintained enough of his former self after converting, however, that he refused to join Grolkinei's army and instead exiled himself for fifty years, right up until he met Tate.

"That's awful," she said.

She thought of how she would feel to be in that position…mentally assaulted and forced to kill or intend to kill another being, resulting in conversion into what others perceived to be a monster. Because she now knew Melanthe and Oria, she knew that even gentle beings who were good at their cores could be pushed to act upon buried impulses if their mental defenses weren't strong enough. Although she was curious about what Melanthe had done to convert, she would never ask.

"Derian began gathering others like him," Melanthe said, her tone subdued. "Those who refused to serve Grolkinei and opted to live in exile. And he started following Grolkinei's army. Whenever he could, he interfered with their plans, preventing forced conversions." She glanced over at him, then said in an even softer tone, "And whenever he arrived too late, he did what he could to rescue the converted."

Sophia easily pieced the rest together. The two of them had obviously met that way. She imagined they had started the encampment together, providing a place where exiled Mercesti could dwell without fear of judgment. It was all rather amazing.

"What did you used to be, Derian?" she asked. "Or am I not allowed to ask?"

The male remained silent, but Melanthe answered, "He was a Gloresti."

That surprised her. Gloresti were among the most difficult to convert because their base natures centered around loyalty and the protection of others.

"Oh," she managed. "Well, Zachariah might be happy to find out he's not the only one."

The sharp red glare she got from Derian had her eyes going wide. What had she said now?

"Ye speak of commander Zachariah?" he asked.

"Yes." She shifted her gaze from Melanthe, who looked troubled, back to Derian. "He was also forced to convert about fifty years ago."

There was a long silence. Eventually, Melanthe said, "We all thought he was dead. Derian was deeply troubled when we received the news."

Sophia nodded in understanding. "Everyone thought that." She belatedly wondered how Derian was reacting to the fact that he wasn't the only Gloresti who had been "encouraged" to convert.

"How do ye know this?" he asked.

"Zachariah resurfaced a couple of months ago. He helped save my cousin's life."

"Where is he now?"

Frowning, Sophia admitted, "I don't know. When I last saw him, he was, uh, incapacitated by *archigos* Knorbis."

"What?" Melanthe gasped.

"I don't know why or how, but *archigos* Knorbis made Zachariah fall to the ground. The elder obviously wanted to get my cousin and my friend away from him."

"Zachariah presented a threat to the Wymzesti elder?" Derian asked with a dark expression.

"Well, since the elder was after my cousin, and Zachariah is paired with her for her protection, then I guess you could say that."

She found Derian's stare disconcerting. It felt as though he was trying to pry more from her with just a look. Indeed, she almost found herself blurting more, but stopped in time.

"I believe that I might just have to press ye for more information, after all," the male said.

Sophia swallowed hard at that. A signal from Oria had all of them descending, which was a relief. She wasn't sure what she should share with Derian and what she should keep to herself. What if he or one of these other Mercesti decided they had nothing to lose in trying to acquire the Elder Scroll for themselves? The artifact had already driven other beings to some extreme behavior, after all. She felt it was better for all of them if she kept the details to herself.

As they got closer to the ground, she took in the vast expanse of green in front of them. It looked like the densest, most overrun forest she had ever seen. The trees resembled none of those surrounding her homeland.

Melanthe turned to her as they landed and said, "We walk through Hoygul's jungle."

A jungle? Sophia looked more closely at the trees and foliage and nodded in recognition. Although she hadn't ever seen a jungle, she had certainly learned about them through her mother's teachings. If it meant getting to the map leading to the library, she was willing to trek through a jungle.

"Ye'll want to stay close," Derian said, hefting the lochaber axe that he had carried with him from the encampment. "The wildlife in here will eat yc whole."

Sophia tilted her head in consideration as she followed the others into the thick foliage. "I think I'll be okay," she said. "After all, I can always eat them first."

Chapter 32

MALUKALI LEARNED AFTER THE THIRD TIME SHE WAS DOSED WITH whatever sedative the Mercesti were feeding her that she should give no indication she was awake when she managed to surface. This was a hard lesson learned.

Now, as sleep slowly eased from her mind, she focused on controlling her breathing and other responses so that she still seemed asleep to anyone observing her.

She knew she was bound to a flat surface of some kind. Her arms and legs were positioned in a spread-eagle pose and secured with tight shackles. Pain rolled through her, but she welcomed it in lieu of the numb, painless void from which she had just surfaced. She would rather hurt than be unaware…mentally nebulous.

The moment her mind cleared enough, she reached out to her husband.

Knorbis?

Malukali! Oh, thank God.

Knorbis, where are you? You aren't still here at Kanika's, are you?

No. Oh, honey—I had to leave you. I'm so sorry.

His emotion was so powerful that she feared she would ruin her plans to fool her captors by weeping. Instead, she used her own power to calm them both.

It's okay, my love, she thought, keeping her tone gentle. She had never sensed such misery and self-loathing in her husband. It frightened her. *Are you all right?*

No, he returned.

Her fear heightened. When she heard her own breathing alter and someone within the room with her made a sound indicating movement, she forced herself to smooth it back out. She used a form of meditation to help.

Metis had me bring Tate and Ariana to her, telling me she would free you if I did, he thought. *I've since discovered that Eirik is in league with her and now we're all on the way to the library.*

She couldn't even compose a response to that, she was so shocked.

I've been a fool, and I've failed you.

Please don't say that, love. I would have done the same in your place.

He hesitated, but she sensed a tiny portion of his guilt easing at her words. She knew he felt her sincerity through their connection.

I should have foreseen this, he conveyed miserably. *The fact that we are in this position is unforgiveable. For all of my power and abilities, I am here—miles from you as you lie alone and in terrible pain—leading the one being we didn't want to have the scroll right to it.*

Knorbis...how were you to think clearly when half of you has been lying here with me, even if only in thought?

There was a long pause, during which time she sensed him working hard to collect himself. She had to put herself into a deeper meditative state to keep from losing her composure and giving herself away.

I love you so much, he thought at last.

I love you, too.

She felt another layer of his crippling emotion ease at the words. Regrouping, he conveyed, *There is a male Mercesti here who can dampen thoughts. He isn't strong enough to keep you out of my mind, but he's preventing Tate from connecting with Tiege. I doubt Zachariah will be able to sense her, either. I'm too exhausted to counteract what he's doing. Can you?*

Easing from her meditation so she could try, she realized that there was still some inhibitor in her system preventing her from truly exercising her mental powers. She had connected with Knorbis due to the depth of their connection and his equally strong mental abilities, but at the moment, she couldn't even sense the other elders.

No, she said. *But I'll keep trying.*

Okay. He hesitated, but his thoughts were never guarded with her. *You should know that Eirik and Metis are using you as the motivation for our cooperation. Tate and Ariana know that you've been captured and that you'll be hurt if they don't comply.*

That made anger surge through her, telling her the effects of the dose she had received were wearing off. *Very well,* she responded. *Then I'll just have to get out of here so that you don't have to worry about me anymore.*

Ariana had never before reached this level of exhaustion. She was so tired that she began wobbling in the sky. She felt her ability to keep her wings extended fading.

"Can't go on," she managed to say. Her eyelids drooped. She shook her head to clear it.

"You will keep flying," Eirik demanded.

"Can't sense the scroll anymore," she said, putting more firmness into her voice. Her words sounded garbled.

"You will kill them if you don't take any time to rest," Knorbis insisted.

"We could all stand a brief rest," Metis said. "Even some of your followers are weakening."

Eirik gave Metis a long look. Ariana noticed Metis glance at the male in the black toga who was apparently containing their outward thoughts. He did appear very tired. Apparently agreeing, Eirik signaled with his hand and they all started descending. Ariana wanted to weep with relief.

They landed on a white sand beach beside a calm, clear blue sea. Palm trees and other tropical foliage provided shade about a hundred feet from the water, though that was hardly needed since the sun was setting. Ariana staggered blearily after the others as they walked under the cover of the trees. Out of the corner of her eye, she noticed that Tate's step was equally unsteady.

Any patch of ground would do for her to get some rest, she decided. But before she could even think about settling down, Eirik walked up to her.

"First, you and the Kynzesti will see to our needs," he said.

"Needs?" she slurred. There was two of him now. Her vision blurred. "'Fraid not."

The world went dark.

TellSparkytogotosleep.

Frowning, Tiege wondered if he heard his sister's thought correctly. It had been issued in the span of a second, all of the words blending together. The dampening clamped down again almost immediately.

Glancing over at Zachariah as they flew, he said, "I'm not sure, but I think Tate just told me to tell you to go to sleep."

The Mercesti didn't respond. Instead, he immediately slowed with the clear intent to land. As they were over a vast field of grain, their cover was nonexistent. That didn't deter him.

They ended up standing with wheat shafts waving around their bodies as the sun set. Tiege could admit to being bone-weary, so he couldn't really complain about the stop. But it was odd, and they really needed to press on.

Zachariah evidently didn't agree with that last thought, as he sank down to the ground and settled onto his back with his hands stacked on his waist. He closed his eyes.

Looking up at commander Harold, who studied Zachariah with a puzzled expression as he and the rest of their armed escort gathered around, Tiege shrugged.

"Guess he's having a nap," he said.

Quincy recognized some of the landscape and knew they were finally nearing Hoygul's jungle. They flew longer than he normally would have recommended for an Estilorian's well-being. It felt like the trip took an obscenely long time.

He glanced at Ini-herit, who flew beside him.

"No word yet," the elder said.

Normally, Quincy would have been embarrassed that his class elder knew he was about to ask again for news about Sophia, but now he just didn't care. He felt mildly guilty for asking every ten minutes like a child begging for a new toy, but he couldn't help his concern. Sophia was all that mattered to him.

"I'm sure she's fine, Quincy," Clara Kate said from beside Ini-herit. "Sophia can take care of herself. Have faith."

Oh, there was some irony: telling the Corgloresti who hadn't ever failed in an Embrace and who had brought every Kynzesti into the world to have faith. He understood what C.K. meant, though. She meant that he needed to direct his particular strength toward this undertaking to help ensure its success. That, in part, meant believing that Sophia could protect herself.

He nodded at her, turning his gaze back to the path ahead. While he knew his worry for Sophia wouldn't diminish, he could acknowledge that she knew how to protect herself. Zachariah had been right…Sophia was the strongest of all her kin. On top of that, she was extremely intelligent and stubborn as the day was long. If any being could manage on her own when circumstances called for it, it was Sophia.

That acknowledgement finally eased the tight grip of fear that had settled over him the moment he learned that no one had any idea where she was. Although he wanted to see her again more than anything, he knew he had to focus on the larger goal.

Sophia would be fine. He wouldn't accept any other outcome.

"The jungle is just ahead," Alexius said.

Quincy saw it in the fading sunlight. The vast expanse of green was hard to miss. He thought back to the time he made this approach with Saraqael.

"Are you sure the map leads us here?" Saraqael asked as they flew.

"Yes," Quincy replied. "The Scultresti's cottage is located in that expanse of greenery."

After studying the area for a long moment, Saraqael said, "We will have to walk, I suppose."

"Walk? Through that jungle?" Quincy remembered feeling as though his friend had lost his mind. "You do know that there are wild animals and insects and even plants that can kill us in there, right?"

"Sure," Saraqael said easily. "But Kate is worth any risk."

Now, as he landed once again in front of the jungle leading to the home of the eccentric Scultresti, Quincy found himself smiling. It was the first time in almost forty years that a memory of his best friend had left him with something other than the ache of guilt and loss.

I know now what you meant, my friend, he thought. *Thank you for helping me learn it.*

Chapter 33

URIEL AND HIS WARESTI LANDED ON THE OUTSKIRTS OF THE PROPERTY surrounding Kanika's home as night fell. The elder had only to conduct a comprehensive scan using his innate power to know exactly what they faced. It took him just a few minutes longer to develop a strategy to fulfill their mission.

He gathered his warriors around him, hidden from the eyes of the Mercesti by the thick forest. The Dark Ones weren't bothering to monitor this section, an oversight that Uriel found remarkably foolish.

On his right stood his second lieutenant, Enyo. She watched him with an expression that told him she was more than ready to hear what he had to say. Looking around at those selected to complete this mission, he nodded.

"The perimeter is patrolled by twenty-four Mercesti in six groups of four. They are adhering to a standard Macedonian watch system. There are ten possible entrances to the structure, accounting for doors and large windows. Each entrance has two guards. Our fallen are contained in a single room on the lowest level of the east wing," he conveyed. "It appears they have been incapacitated. My assumption is that they were given the same or similar drug as what was used to subdue Knorbis and Malukali. They are guarded by thirty Mercesti armed with cursed weapons, including crossbows and other projectiles."

"No problem, sir," Enyo said.

Not expecting anything less, Uriel continued, "I will head to the room housed below Kanika's bedroom. That is where Malukali is being held. She has ten guards."

"Yes, sir," came the reply.

One of the warriors who had conducted a sweep of the area approached. "Sir, I found these on the ground forty yards west of here."

Glancing down, Uriel saw Tate's nunchucks in the male's hand. Frowning, he reached out and said, "I will hold onto these."

"Yes, sir."

"Thank you, Sean. All of you, please give me a moment."

Uriel walked a brief distance away. Behind him, he heard Enyo making the most of their time by instructing the warriors around her. Drawing on his elder power, he reached out to Malukali's mind. Much to his surprise, since he had attempted this numerous times in the past few days without success, he connected.

Uriel?

Yes, it's me. Are you all right?

She hesitated. *Not really.*

I understand. We're outside. We're coming to get you.

They have some Waresti in their keeping. They were trying to protect me.

I know. Kanika—

Isn't Kanika.

What?

The creature that assumed Kanika's form killed her. That isn't Kanika.

Uriel blinked in surprise. What manner of being were they dealing with here?

He took a moment to send out the news to the other elders. Then he thought toward Malukali, *Okay. Are your abilities returning to you?*

A bit. I can't influence the Mercesti in this room with me, though. So far, I've only been able to connect with Knorbis, and now you. They keep dosing me.

Very well. Do what you can to exercise your power. We're coming in after you.

Tiege sat apart from the others in the field of wheat, trying to rest as Harold spoke with his Waresti warriors and Zachariah lay on the ground a good distance away with his eyes closed. The wheat stalks kept Tiege from seeing much of anything but the darkening sky above them. He found his mind drifting again and again to Ariana.

He wished he had asked her to pair with him before this all began. He'd intended to for a while now, but feared that she would only accept an offer of pairing with him in a role similar to the one Tate had with Zachariah. Tiege was half-Gloresti, so there was as much likelihood that he would be able to pair with a being for her protection as not. But he knew he wouldn't be content with the type of relationship his sister had with her Mercesti guardian.

Not with Ariana.

Even worse was the thought of her wanting to pair with him as his Lekwuesti, essentially bonding herself to him solely so that she could see to his hospitality needs. Although he knew that Ariana was a caregiver at her core, he wanted to be more to her than just an obligation.

But he hadn't wanted to pressure her by asking for something more. They'd only known each other for about two months, after all. And the things she'd been through had definitely left their mark. The last thing he wanted to do was make her uncomfortable by asking her to take steps in their relationship before she was ready, despite how much love he held for her and how eager he was to express it.

That was why he waited so long to kiss her. His attraction to her had been on-the-spot instant. Who could resist her beautiful, raven-colored hair, magnificent lavender eyes and heart-stopping smile? But he was intuitive enough to know that she wouldn't welcome advances by a male after what she had been through.

So he bided his time, learning more about her first and sharing whatever she wanted to know about him. Over time, she opened up to him about Eirik...and the cruel punishments he imposed on her when she was forced to help him find the first scroll piece.

Hearing what she had endured only convinced Tiege even more that she was the most courageous being to ever walk the plane. He didn't think he would have ever put himself in the position of possibly ending up in that kind of situation again, yet Ariana had. And in the cruelest twist of fate, she was once again in Eirik's clutches.

It made Tiege want to kill someone.

He supposed that gave him a sense of kinship to Zachariah. Although he didn't agree with the other male's methods—and still wanted to choke the life out of him over his lesson with Ariana—he now understood more of his do-whatever-it-takes mindset. Tiege knew he'd do anything to get Ariana back. Although he had resisted the truth of it for weeks, he also knew that he and the Mercesti shared an equal concern for Tate.

Violet light flashed from somewhere near Zachariah, drawing Tiege's attention. Frowning in bewilderment, he started to get up to investigate. Before he did more than rise to one knee, however, Zachariah sat up. He glanced around and caught Tiege's eye through the shifting stalks of wheat.

"Thank you for conveying the message," he said.

Blinking in surprise, Tiege nodded. That was the first remotely nice thing the Mercesti had ever said to him.

Zachariah got to his feet. He started walking toward Harold, then came to a stop. Tiege also rose. As he brushed debris from his pants, he watched Zachariah bring his left hand up and study it with an odd expression on his face.

Curious, he also glanced at the Mercesti's hand. He spotted a silver ring on his ring finger. He couldn't make out many details in the dwindling light, but the stones in it looked like they were red and deep blue-green. Wondering if the other male had always worn the ring and he just hadn't noticed, he shrugged it off as Zachariah dropped his hand and continued in Harold's direction.

"You're awake," Harold said when he spotted Zachariah. "Are you sure we're not keeping you from your beauty rest?"

Not rising to the bait, Zachariah said, "Thank you for stopping. Now I need you to wait for Tate to fully awaken so that we can fly to her location."

Harold frowned. "We are heading to Hoygul's home so that we can get the map and then get to Tate and Ariana."

"No," Zachariah argued. "I will now be able to get us directly to Tate."

Tiege's eyebrows shot up. The other male's words, combined with the ring, had realization dawning.

Walking over to Zachariah's right side, he looked at the mark on his bicep that had been made when he paired with Tate as her guardian. Before, it had been two red arrows crossed over each other, indicative of a pairing for protection. Now, the symbol was one of Tate's deep blue-green cinquefoils with a red arrow running diagonally through it.

An avowed marking.

"What the hell did you do?" Tiege asked.

"What needed to be done…brother."

Chapter 34

"IT SURE DOESN'T MAKE MUCH OF AN IMPRESSION," SOPHIA SAID.

To her mind, the small, worn-down cottage in the middle of the jungle was a less than spectacular culmination to the arduous hike through the jungle. Vines covered almost the entire surface of the walls, some of which appeared to be crumbling. There were holes in the roof, the windows were only partially covered with broken shutters and the door stood partly ajar. The only welcoming element to the Scultresti's home was the beams of moonlight filtering through the top of the tree canopy above them.

Melanthe waved a hand at Sophia's comment. "That is just what the illusion wants you to think."

Understanding, Sophia nodded. "Okay. Now what?"

"Now ye knock," Derian said.

Realizing that they expected her to take the lead, Sophia blinked in surprise. They had seemed so familiar with the Scultresti that she assumed they would at least pave the way with an introduction.

"Oh," she said, unable to think of another response. "Okay."

Squaring her shoulders, she walked up to the door that appeared to be dangling from its hinges. She couldn't help but consider the fact that at some point, her grandfather and Quincy had once taken these very same steps. That knowledge gave her the courage to knock.

"What is it?" came a male voice from the other side of the door.

"Um, hello. My name is Sophia. I wanted to—"

A hand suddenly reached out from behind the door, grabbed her upper arm and yanked her inside.

Her instincts almost had her shifting to protect herself, but she managed to control the impulse. She found herself standing alone in the middle of what was obviously *not* a poorly-maintained home.

She realized that a ball of light which hadn't been visible from outside bounced on the ceiling. With a quick sweep of her eyes, she spotted a kitchen to her left with a neighboring dining area, a bed and nightstand to her right, and floor-to-ceiling bookshelves straight in front her. Although she knew she should be focused on other things, her attention was captured by those books.

"Sophia, you said?"

The voice sounded from right behind her. She jumped and turned to face the Scultresti known as Hoygul.

He wasn't all that much taller than her, a fact that surprised her. She had gone through life thinking that every male on the plane was exponentially bigger than her. It was something of a relief to not have to crane her neck to meet the male's Scultresti-brown eyes. She noted that he wore a dark blue toga with brown sandals, and his strawberry-blond hair was pulled back into a ponytail. More importantly, his gaze was shrewd and assessing, but not aggressive.

She could do shrewd and assessing.

"Yes," she said at last. "I'm sorry to intrude."

"You are not sorry to intrude, or you would not be here," he argued.

"Okay, you're right. I'm not sorry to intrude, though I do regret any inconvenience I'm causing you by being here."

He studied her for a moment. "Very well. Continue."

Wondering briefly what he would have said or done if she hadn't given the response he sought, Sophia plowed gamely on. "I need the map to the library."

Hoygul shook his head and made a tut-tut sound with his tongue. Walking over to his kitchen, he said, "And up to there you were doing so well."

"I figured you would appreciate my honesty," Sophia said, hoping she hadn't already destroyed her chances of getting the map.

As Hoygul took a tea kettle and began filling it with water, he said, "Do you think I have no need or want for company?"

Feeling as though she was losing the thread of the conversation, Sophia looked around and said, "Well, I imagine you don't get many visitors out here."

"I receive plenty of visitors. Do you think those Mercesti out there know my location by mere happenstance?"

Sophia opened her mouth, but couldn't think of an immediate rebuttal. For lack of anything better to say, she offered, "They're a great group. How come you've never mentioned them to anyone?"

As he set the kettle over what appeared to be an unceasing flame in the small hearth beside the dining area, he said, "Will you mention them when all is said and done?"

Again, she floundered. Shaking her head, she said, "Only if they allow it."

"There you have it."

"Sir—"

"Hoygul."

"Hoygul," Sophia repeated. She struggled to catch up with him. Figuring it couldn't hurt, she said, "You once helped my grandfather. Do you suppose you could find it within you to aid me?"

Glancing at her, he said, "I was curious whether you would mention your obvious connection to Saraqael."

Hearing her grandfather's name had unexpected emotion flooding through Sophia. Her parents hadn't known her grandfather and she had always hesitated to bring her many questions to Quincy, the one person who knew him best. Finding herself in the presence of a being who had once met him had her moving into the kitchen and catching the Scultresti's gaze.

"What was he like?" she asked.

For once, Hoygul appeared less sure of himself. He placed a few containers that she assumed contained sugar, honey and cream on the table. Then he rested his hands on the back of one of the wooden chairs surrounding the table as he collected his thoughts.

"He was passionate," he said eventually, "which is more than I can say for most Estilorians. He knew he had exhausted all other options to save Kate and he found himself on my doorstep."

Tears burned Sophia's eyes. He remembered her grandmother's name. She knew he had probably been told about the results of his "gift" of the map to Saraqael, since he didn't seem surprised to see a female from a new class standing in front of him. But he said it so casually, as though in his mind Saraqael and Kate had been destined to be together, regardless of the tragic circumstances.

"Yeah. Quincy mentioned that," she said.

"Ah—the other Corgloresti." Hoygul nodded. "He was not passionate like Saraqael. I would never have given the map to him alone."

Although she wasn't sure why, Sophia found herself frowning over the comment. "Quincy's a very passionate male."

He made a sound of clear disagreement. "He had nothing resembling passion in him."

"You just didn't know what to look for," she argued. "Believe me, he's full of passion."

"Is that so?"

Feeling her cheeks heat under the Scultresti's pointed gaze, she nodded.

He turned to focus on a shelf of teacups. "Do you love him?"

"Yes." Despite the abruptness of the question, the response came quite easily to Sophia's lips…a fact that made her chest hurt. "I only wish I had realized it sooner."

Placing three cups on the table, he said, "How interesting."

This wasn't at all what she expected. She glanced around as Hoygul added tea leaves to the water, wondering if she could find clues regarding how she could get the map. She felt time ticking away like drips of water through a cupped hand.

"Please, sir—" she started to say.

"Why do you seek the map?"

Thrilled that they were finally on a pertinent topic, she answered, "There's a Mercesti trying to get to a piece of the Elder—"

"You know that the elders have already been here to communicate with me about this, do you not?" he interrupted.

"Um…yes."

"Then you might try a different approach, since theirs failed to sway me."

Feeling like an incompetent dolt, she held his gaze and scrambled to think of how she could possibly convince him to help her when the elders had failed to do so. Realizing that for the first time in her existence logic wasn't going to help her, she decided to throw it out the proverbial window.

"I need to save my cousin and my friend. I think they've been led to someone wishing them harm…most likely the same Mercesti seeking the Elder Scroll."

Hoygul studied her. "Then this isn't about saving the entire plane from someone bent on destroying it?"

"Not really," Sophia admitted. "Right now, I just want to save Tate and Ariana."

"Hmm."

Several minutes passed in silence as Hoygul stood beside the kettle waiting for it to boil. She couldn't help but sense that he was leaning in the direction of not helping her. After what Quincy had told everyone regarding his own encounter with the Scultresti, she realized that the rationale for sharing the map was rather specific.

It had her mind churning, and when he finally pulled the kettle from the flame and gave her a look that she sensed was a prelude to denying her request, she said, "Did you know that Penelope once styled my Aunt Amber's hair?"

The tea kettle rattled as he set it on the table on a round, brown disc that was meant to contain it. "Did she?"

"Yep," she said conversationally. "It was just before my Aunt Skye and Uncle Caleb's wedding."

"Is that so?"

Seeing the effect her words had on the otherwise unflappable male, she continued, "And did you also know that I'll be heading to Central soon to be paired with my very own Lekwuesti?"

Hoygul's sharp brown eyes met hers. "I see."

Not wanting the male to think that she was trying to manipulate him, she moved closer, her hands intertwined. "Hoygul, I'm happy to pass along any messages you might have for Penelope. Quincy mentioned that you asked my grandfather a question to which Penelope was the answer. Because I assume you're the hero, Odysseus, awaiting the connection with Penelope, I would love to see you reunited."

There was a very long pause, during which time Hoygul busied himself pouring tea into the cups. Sophia fought the urge to wring her hands as she awaited his next words.

Finally, he again caught her gaze. "Well? You see this table is set for three do you not? Go and get Melanthe."

Chapter 35

A BLAST OF PAIN PULLED ARIANA FROM SLEEP.

Her eyes popped open as she instinctively curled into the fetal position, protecting her vulnerable midsection. Panting over the blow, she glanced up and found a Mercesti staring down at her.

"Get up," he snapped. "We hunger."

Having learned long ago that delays resulted in more punishment, she hurriedly got to her feet and turned to face Eirik. The Mercesti leader had crouched beside Tate, who still appeared to be sleeping.

Rushing over, she asked, "What can I get you, my lord?"

When he looked at her, she reached down and vigorously shook Tate by the shoulders. Relief rushed through her when Tate stirred.

"A stew, perhaps?" she asked, careful to hold Eirik's gaze. "Maybe a—"

As Tate slowly levered herself up, Eirik reached out and seized Ariana around the throat. Grasping at his arm, she struggled to catch a breath.

"You ruined my fun," he said.

"I'm sorry," she wheezed, remaining as still as she could. She knew that flailing and carrying on only added to the punishment. "I only wanted to serve you, my lord."

He tossed her from him. She landed with a thud beside Tate, who had moved into a sitting position and was working on rearranging the mass of hair covering most of her face.

"You females need to serve all of us a meal. Then we will continue on."

"Yes, my lord," Ariana said, knowing that was what he wanted to hear.

The moment he turned to speak with the being masquerading as Kanika, Ariana cast a light and turned to Tate. "Okay, we must—"

She stopped when she got a good look at Tate's face.

"What?" Tate asked.

"You—you have red markings around your eyes."

With a look of disbelief, Tate instinctively reached up to touch her cheekbones. Her eyes shifted to the ring she now wore on her left ring finger.

"Holy crap," she said. "I thought we only did it in the dream."

Glancing around, Ariana realized there were some Mercesti focused on them. She hurriedly generated a soup tureen and began using her power to create a stew to fill it. When everyone appeared satisfied that they would be fed and turned their attention to other tasks, she looked again at Tate.

"What did you do?" she whispered as she created bowls and spoons.

Her eyes latched onto the glaring red arrows now lancing through Tate's cinquefoils. The mark of the Mercesti on Tiege's sister made her stomach churn. Glancing away to try and collect herself, she spotted Knorbis, whose gaze was centered on them. She gave him a look that told him just what she thought about their current situation as she awaited Tate's response.

"I avowed myself to Sparky," Tate responded. "He thought if we did it in the dream, he'd be able to hear my thoughts once we woke up."

Dropping the ladle she'd just created, Ariana gaped at her. "But you weren't physically touching. That's impossible."

"Apparently it isn't."

Not knowing what to say, as the evidence of the ring and the new markings indicated that Tate was right, she managed, "Have you lost your mind?"

Tate's gaze remained focused on the silver ring she wore. She appeared lost in thought. Then she murmured, "No."

Knowing they didn't have the luxury of time to discuss it any further, Ariana reached up to touch both sides of Tate's face. Praying she had enough ability to match Tate's skin tone, she generated the Lekwuesti form of a cosmetic to cover the red arrows around her eyes, as well as the symbol that surely marked her right shoulder blade.

"What are you doing?"

Eirik's voice had Ariana flinching and removing her hands from Tate's face. Her mind raced to come up with some kind of explanation.

"I asked her to get rid of the bags under my eyes," Tate said. "You seem to want to run us into the ground, but that doesn't mean we have to look the part."

Silence filled the clearing as they awaited Eirik's response. Finally, he said, "Finish serving us. Then you will take us the rest of the way to the remaining scroll piece." His gaze shifted between Tate and Ariana. "I do not care what it takes. This next trip, you had better get us to what I seek or you will suffer the consequences."

Ariana swallowed hard and nodded. Eirik once again turned away. The moment he did, Tate reached out and touched her hand.

"Ariana, you know we can't bring him to the scroll piece. Right?"

"Tate, I—"

"You can't do it," Tate insisted, holding her gaze. "There is more at stake here than the punishment he describes."

"But...you're the one he's going to punish," she whispered.

"I know."

Bertram sat among the branches of a tall tree, watching the Mercesti gathered around the old, abandoned cottage in the jungle. He observed one of the Mercesti—a female with golden-brown hair—enter the cottage not too long after the Kynzesti went inside. None of the others approached the structure.

It was difficult to believe that this place was their goal. After all, it had taken quite a bit of time to work through the complex ecosystem of the jungle. In Bertram's opinion, there should have been some kind of amazing prize at the end. Seeing it was nothing more than a derelict building was beyond aggravating. If this was the location for the supposed ransom exchange, it was an exceedingly odd choice.

He and Tycho had split up upon entering the jungle, seeing that these Mercesti were uncommonly cautious when it came to their travels. Bertram knew that in order to maximize their chances of catching the female Kynzesti without a guard, they needed to expand their coverage area. As it was, it had required quite a bit of moving and maneuvering on his part to avoid the Mercesti patrols on his own.

Just then, the cottage door opened. Bertram wished he was close enough to hear what was said as the Kynzesti and Mercesti females emerged, but he couldn't. He caught a glimpse of a small male in a toga beyond the door. Because it wasn't anyone he recognized, he reasoned that this wasn't actually where the ransom exchange was going to occur. Maybe they stopped at the cottage for supplies or something.

He had no way to know. All he could do, he decided, was follow the group as they departed. So he did so with the belief that the next time they stopped, he would have the Kynzesti in his grasp.

Tiege struggled not to sputter as he absorbed Zachariah's statement. "*Brother?*" he repeated. "That's ridiculous."

Zachariah crossed his arms over his chest. "Even presented with visual proof that I have avowed with your sister, you doubt it?"

"My second power is the power of illusion," Tiege countered, glowering at the cool-toned Mercesti. "I question everything I see. It isn't possible to undertake an avowing without touching the other being. More importantly, you have to actually *love* someone to avow with them. That means that you..."

He trailed off. Seeing the other male's bland stare, he wondered if this was really a direction he wanted to take this conversation, especially with commander Harold and a number of Waresti standing only a few feet away. But this was about his sister.

"The kind of emotion required to create an avowed pairing is unparalleled," he said at last. "Two beings have to love each other unequivocally. They have to be willing to commit their entire existences to each other...die for one another."

"Do you think me ignorant of that?"

"No, I think you incapable of it."

In the long pause that followed, Zachariah's expression never changed. Tiege waited for him to argue, declaring his love for Tate. Only after a couple of minutes passed did he realize that would never happen.

Anger festered, tightening his throat as he fought the urge to shout or punch Zachariah in the face. "This isn't like a Gloresti sacrificing himself for someone else out of a sense of duty and instinct. An avowing can only happen when a being feels as though his life is complete only if his avowed is a part of it. You'd have to—"

"Tate and I exchanged vows while connected in our dreams," Zachariah interrupted. "Our pairing carried through to consciousness. While I should think that this offers you enough clues on the subject, my feelings are none of your concern."

"None of my concern? Tate's my sister. I'm going to look out for her—especially when it comes to protecting her feelings—whether you like it or not."

"Tate is my concern now."

The words struck Tiege. A keen sense of loss hit him hard enough that he staggered back a step.

Zachariah stiffened. He lowered his arms and looked away, his gaze unfocused. Then fury darkened his expression.

"Fight, damn it," he snapped.

Tiege realized that the Mercesti was talking to Tate. Whatever he saw in his mind had him responding to her in more than just thought.

"What's going on?" Tiege asked, fear quickly replacing his anger.

Zachariah didn't reply. After a moment, he nodded to himself. Then another look entered his eyes…a look that had Tiege's heart dropping like a stone.

"Is it Tate?" he asked, his voice hoarse. "Tell me!"

Not responding, Zachariah turned so his face was no longer visible. He clenched his hands into fists at his sides, bunching the roped muscles of his forearms. Then he made a sound in the back of his throat. He suddenly extended his wings and took flight.

Tiege caught Harold's eye and brought forth his own wings. Confusion and alarm cycled through him as he rose into the air. He knew something was terribly wrong.

It was only a small consolation to realize in that moment, after seeing the first real emotion enter Zachariah's expression, that the Mercesti really did love his sister.

Chapter 36

ARIANA REALIZED THAT THE MERCESTI NUMBERS HAD GROWN WHILE SHE and Tate slept. Once again, Eirik had rallied his supporters to his cause.

She carefully avoided looking any of the Mercesti in the eye as she walked around and handed out bowls of stew. She had cautioned Tate to do the same and was relieved to see the other female acting docile and submissive as she also served the stew. Eirik's eyes moved between the two of them. He didn't speak and the group seemed eager to finish the meal and depart, which gave her hope that they would manage to escape this place without incident.

Even as that thought entered her head, a large hand swung out and knocked the last bowl of stew she carried. The hot contents splattered over several nearby Mercesti. Their loud curses filled the night air.

"You spilled the stew, Lekwuesti," said the male who hit her. "You need to clean us up."

Although anger burned her cheeks, she responded, "Yes, sir," and waved her hand, using her power to clean up the mess.

"I meant for you to clean it by hand," he said, grabbing her upper arm and turning her so that she had no choice but to meet his red gaze. "Now you must pay the pr—"

He cut off abruptly and turned to look behind him. Ariana spotted Tate and realized the other female must have tapped the male to get his attention. She held a bowl of stew.

"Here you go," she said. "No harm, no foul."

"Stay out of this," the male barked. His hold on Ariana's arm loosened as his attention shifted, but she didn't try to pull away.

"Hey, I'm doing what I'm told," Tate said with a small shrug. "We were ordered to feed you so we could get moving. I figured you didn't want to anger your leader by holding things up."

"You figured wrong," he said.

Then he released Ariana and used his fist to knock the stew out of Tate's hands. The rest of the Mercesti started edging closer while Eirik remained seated on a fallen tree. Ariana's heart pitched in fear. She saw Knorbis looking from Metis to Tate, indecision on his face.

"Don't fight, Tate," she warned. But it was too late.

What had seemed like an uneven match between a towering hulk of a male and the younger, smaller Kynzesti ended in astonishingly short time. He made one attempt to strike Tate. She evaded it, then took him down with five well-placed blows of her knees and elbows. Within seconds, he was an unconscious heap in the center of the group.

Unfortunately, that left the others. And Ariana knew they wouldn't let Tate's victory go unaddressed.

"Our turn," said another male as the Mercesti soldiers surrounded Tate.

The next few minutes were among the most horrifying of Ariana's existence. She and Knorbis were restrained before they could intervene. The male with mental dampening abilities stood close to the elder, his red eyes shining as he exercised his power to keep their thoughts and powers contained. They could do nothing but watch events unfold.

Ariana didn't realize she was screaming until someone stuffed something in her mouth to silence her. All she heard were the brutal sounds of the Mercesti's retaliation against Tate. Before long, Deimos started making his terrifying noises as he strained for escape, evidently scenting her blood.

"They're going to kill her!" Knorbis shouted at Eirik. His eyes glowed as his stronger mental powers overrode the dampening of the Mercesti. "Stop them, damn you!"

Eirik didn't even look at the elder, but he did raise a hand. A soft popping sound emitted from somewhere behind Ariana. She watched with her heart in her throat as a dart landed in the elder's neck. He dropped to the ground as his captors released him.

Eirik's gaze remained focused on Tate. She was now on the ground, trying to protect her head and midsection from the fists, heavy boots and weapons that rained merciless punishment on her. One of her wrists was clearly broken. Ariana had heard the snap of several bones so far. Blood glistened on Tate's pale skin. Hot tears coated Ariana's cheeks.

And then a dark shadow briefly blocked out the stars. A sinuous tail swept through the night, striking a number of the males hurting Tate. Those Mercesti hit the ground, instantly paralyzed.

Nyx had arrived.

Ceasing her struggles, Ariana watched the Mercesti stop their attack on Tate and turn to address this new threat. Eirik rose. He signaled again to the soldier with the blow gun. Ariana looked behind her and realized he was reloading with a different kind of dart.

When she whipped her head back around, she saw Eirik walk over to Tate and grab her hair, pulling her head up. Both of her eyes were nearly swollen shut. Blood from a likely broken nose covered most of her face and upper body. Still, she managed to look defiant rather than broken, something that Ariana knew would infuriate Eirik.

"Your pet kragen may have saved you once," he said to Tate, "but I am prepared this time. And you will be the reason the creature dies."

Ariana's eyes widened. She watched as Nyx made another pass, targeting Eirik. A second popping sound had Ariana issuing another muffled scream even as Nyx screeched in pain and protest.

The kragen vanished over the trees. Seconds later, there was a distant crashing sound as she hit the earth.

Ariana's heart wrenched over the expression that came over Tate's face. Although the kragen had always frightened Ariana, she knew the creature meant a great deal to both Zachariah and Tate. More tears blurred her vision over their loss.

With a fierce scream, Tate struck Eirik in the face with her unbroken hand. The punch had enough power that his head snapped back. She managed to yank one of his cursed krises from their harness as he recovered from the blow. Even as she got in a strike to his arm, however, he slammed his fist into her jaw. She fell and didn't move again.

The Mercesti holding Ariana released her as Eirik approached. Frozen and numb, she didn't even bother removing the gag from her mouth.

"You will get us to the scroll piece today," he said, his words striking her like blades of ice. "If you do not, the kragen will not be my only victim."

* * *

"Do not disturb anything in the jungle," Alexius warned Quincy and the others as they began their journey through the dense foliage leading to Hoygul's cottage. "Many beings have entered here never to return."

"Guess that's another reason why Hoygul didn't really feel like he needed extra protections around his home," Clara Kate mused.

Quincy nodded in agreement as they carefully navigated the thick brush and tall trees overgrown with clinging vines. It was especially challenging in the dark. He supposed there were any number of reasons that Estilorians didn't make it out of the jungle. The area contained hundreds of wild animals, poisonous insects and even deadly plants. One misstep could easily lead to harm. Without proper medicines or the ability to heal, an Estilorian taken off-guard by one of these things would likely not survive.

And then there were the stories of other, more mysterious elements of the jungle. Stories that humans had long ago chalked up to myth because the creatures tied to those stories transitioned with the Estilorians to this plane.

Although Quincy walked with his short sword in-hand, he didn't use it to clear a path or otherwise impact the environment. He knew the importance of heeding Alexius' words. Still, he had to be prepared to defend himself if needed. As his eyes scanned the trees and the ground in front of him, he kept a sturdy grip on the weapon.

It made him again think of Sophia out there somewhere, alone and unarmed. The thought squeezed his heart. When he glanced at Ini-herit as a matter of habit, the elder shook his head.

Still no word.

Sighing in frustration, Quincy returned his focus to the jungle. He saw a Waresti point to a low-hanging branch on a tree, so he glanced over and spotted the dim outline of a long python resting there. They all gave the serpent a wide berth.

Ini-herit's healing ability came in handy. A Waresti female was bit by a spider. A male brushed against some poison sumac. Another came into contact with a poison dart frog.

They had just resumed their trek after the last round of healing when Clara Kate tripped over a lapuna tree root. Quincy heard her gasp as she fell, but he lost sight of her behind the enormous tree's trunk. As he hurried forward to see whether she needed any assistance, he heard her shout.

Breaking into a run, he reached the other side of the trunk at the same time as Ini-herit. They watched as Clara Kate used one of her blessed butterfly swords to cut a vine that had somehow wrapped itself around her neck. The sharp blade scored the tree trunk as the vine fell loose.

Scrambling to her feet, she yanked the vine from around her neck and looked around a bit wildly. "Did you see that?" she demanded. "That plant was going to choke me!"

"Of course it was," Ini-herit replied. "That is a Death's Shade vine."

Seeing her eyes blaze over the elder's lack of concern, Quincy asked, "Are you all right?"

She ground her back teeth and nodded once. Then another expression crossed her features. Her deep blue-green gaze moved to a point between Quincy and Ini-herit's shoulders.

"Who's that?" she asked.

Looking over his shoulder, Quincy spotted Alexius standing not too far away. The commander watched them with obvious concern, his burnt orange eyes settled on Clara Kate.

"Who?" Quincy asked in increasing bafflement. "Alexius?"

"No...the lady in white standing behind him."

A thin quality had entered her voice, as though she wasn't really aware of what she was saying. Quincy exchanged a look with Ini-herit.

"Do you not see her?" Ini-herit asked.

Looking around again, Quincy shook his head. "No. There's no one like that around here."

"She's coming this way," Clara Kate said, unnaturally calm. It had Quincy's instincts flaring.

"C.K., there's no lady in white," he argued.

He started to reach for her, but she was suddenly propelled off her feet and thrown a far enough distance away that it appeared she had flown. While he froze in shock, Ini-herit ran after her. Quincy realized her complexion was slowly leeching of color.

He sprang forward. Several Waresti joined Ini-herit in swatting at the air just over Clara Kate, as though trying to ward off an attacker.

"What are you doing?" Quincy asked as he reached them.

"Trying to get this demon off of her!" Alexius growled.

"What demon?"

"Do you still not see her?" Ini-herit asked. Before Quincy responded, the elder leaned over Clara Kate. "You must not listen to her, Clara Kate. You must believe that you can fight her. Have faith."

His efforts weren't working. She grew so pale she resembled a human corpse. In the brief span of time that he watched his class elder try to aid her, Quincy remembered a legend about the jungle's guardian spirit. Many beings believed that if harm came to certain elements of this naturally sacred environment—particularly the aged lapuna trees—that the being who caused the harm would be hunted and killed by a demonic spirit.

That spirit often took the form of a lady in white.

Quincy's pulse raced in understanding. "Get out of my way," he ordered, shoving several Waresti aside. When he reached Ini-herit, he said, "You must move, sir."

The words had the elder looking up with a flash of something indefinable in his silver gaze. Quincy wondered over it even as Ini-herit obeyed and stepped away from Clara Kate. Going with instinct, Quincy dropped to his knees beside her. A frigid chill rushed over him, raising the hair on the back of his neck.

"C.K.," he said, looking directly into her sightless gaze. "There is no lady in white." Grasping her face in his hands and ignoring how terrifyingly cold her skin felt, he leaned closer. "Listen to me, Clara Kate."

She blinked.

"That's right." Continuing to let his instincts guide him, he pulled forth his Corgloresti power. "Look into my eyes. Believe that what I'm saying."

Tears filled her eyes. His power flooded him, making his own eyes light with energy. Much as he did when guiding the Kynzesti into the world, he used it to lure Clara Kate back from whatever precipice she teetered against.

"There is no lady in white," he insisted. "Come back to me."

He repeated the words countless times, his power at its height. When his energy flagged, Ini-herit reached over and used his healing energy to bolster his efforts. Gradually, her color returned. And finally, she blinked back to full awareness.

A loud shriek filled the air, causing several stalwart Waresti to cover their ears. The cold temperature dissipated. Apparently, the demon had given up.

Clara Kate studied Quincy as he continued to hold her. She seemed to be trying to figure out what had happened. Eventually, she said, "Thanks, Quincy."

Breathing a sigh of relief, he shook his head. “No, thank *you*. If you hadn’t come back to us, I don’t even want to think about what your father would have done to me.”

That made her gift him with a lopsided grin. “You’re right,” she agreed. “You’d probably prefer death by a demon.”

Chapter 37

URIEL MADE HIS WAY THROUGH THE DARK HALLWAYS OF KANIKA'S HOME as easily as another being made his way through a well-lit room. The ability to see in the dark ranged for the Waresti based on level of skill, and for him it was a non-issue. He had been able to see perfectly well without light for centuries.

Moving in complete silence, he headed for Kanika's bedroom. There was no one behind him. He wouldn't require backup.

When it came to his priorities as the Waresti elder, there was no greater need than the rescue of his fellow elders. In his millennia of existence, he could count on one hand the number of times when his skills were needed in this regard.

This was one of them.

When he reached the corridor leading to Kanika's bedroom, he lowered himself to the ground. Knowing Mercesti could see in the dark, he eased only part of his head around the corner. As his power had shown him, there were no more than five Mercesti outside the door leading to Kanika's bedroom.

Maintain your position, he sent to Enyo.

When he received an affirmative, he then thought, *Mal?*

Yes.

I'm outside the bedroom. You ready?

Yes. I think—I mean, I'll be able to contain the males in here with me.

Okay.

Taking her at her word, he gave the signal to his team. Then he surged to his feet with his sword drawn and laid waste to the Mercesti guarding the door. Knowing he made a lot of noise as the dying issued screams, he could only pray that Malukali had fulfilled her end of the arrangement and contained the beings around her.

When he dispatched the last guard in front of the door, he broke it down with a flick of his power and then raced down the hidden staircase he had identified from outside the dwelling.

Trusting that Malukali's power was strong enough, he plowed headlong into the chamber and began fulfilling his sword's purpose. One Mercesti after another fell beneath his blade until, at last, the room was empty of enemies.

When he completed his mission, he approached Malukali and took her hand. He had a Waresti among his group who could open any lock, but that female wasn't yet in the room.

"Thank you for coming for me," she said.

He didn't need to see the tears on her face to know the emotion that ran through her. Gently squeezing her hand, he said, "Tell your husband you're safe and we're going to bring you to him. Let him know he's free to use his power to the best of his ability. Tell him to get Tate and Ariana back home."

She nodded and closed her eyes. After a moment, her expression morphed into puzzlement and concern. She opened her eyes. Uriel instinctively connected to her thoughts.

Something's wrong. Knorbis isn't responding.

Sophia found the map guiding her to the library absolutely fascinating. Hoygul had eventually bestowed it upon her and Melanthe after they shared tea. She still wasn't sure why.

Once her new Mercesti friend joined them, the conversation centered around the Mercesti settlement and the various accomplishments achieved by Melanthe, Derian and the others. Hoygul treated Melanthe warmly, speaking to her as though they conversed on a regular basis. Based upon what she'd learned, Sophia figured they probably did.

Finally, Hoygul produced an intriguing glass disc. Sophia watched with rapt attention as the Scultresti murmured a few unintelligible words that caused the disc to glow Scultresti brown. Her eyes widened as an ephemeral map of the Estilorian plane appeared before her. She noticed a dark brown path leading from the cottage to another location. It took only a moment for the map to somehow imprint itself on her brain.

A gasp from Melanthe told Sophia that the process of sharing the map had somehow affected her, too. Before Sophia could plague Hoygul with questions, the Scultresti ushered them out of the cottage. Sophia hadn't argued. She knew she had to get to the library as quickly as possible.

"Please give me one more moment with Hoygul," she said to Melanthe. The Mercesti nodded and walked over to the others, and Sophia turned to Hoygul. "I wanted to get your message for Penelope before we leave."

He raised an eyebrow. "Is that why you believe I gave you the map?"

"No, sir. But I'll be visiting Central at some point soon. I would be honored to deliver a message on your behalf."

After studying her in silence for a moment, he turned and went back into the cottage. Sophia stood there for several minutes, wondering if he was actually coming back. She grew more anxious as the night faded to gray, heralding the approaching dawn. Just when Derian told her they had to leave, though, Hoygul once again emerged.

"Please give this to Penelope," he said, handing her a small bundle wrapped in fabric.

"I will," she said. Since she wasn't wearing a satchel, she'd have to ask Melanthe to carry it for the time being. "Do you have anything you wish to tell her?"

"The gift you bear will tell her everything she needs to know."

"Are you sure?" Sophia flushed and looked down at the small parcel, avoiding his gaze. "Sometimes a female just needs to hear the words to understand how someone feels about her."

Hoygul reached out and touched her shoulder, prompting her to look up. Then he surprised her with a smile. "Thank you, Sophia. But Penelope will know."

Clearing her throat, Sophia said her goodbye and set off with the Mercesti. The sun was fully cresting over the horizon as they reached the edge of the jungle. Although weariness had settled in her bones, Sophia took flight with the others, allowing the amazing map to lead them to their goal.

She had no idea what they would do when they got there. What if Eirik was already there? He'd managed to gather hundreds of soldiers before he reached the first scroll piece. They'd only managed to defeat him thanks to Tiege's illusions and the timely arrival of Waresti reinforcements. This time, she had about fifty Mercesti as her escort and no backup. The facts didn't add up to a conclusion that made her very comfortable.

They flew for a couple of hours before stopping to rest. Sophia sensed they were near the library and really wanted to press on, but she knew that the exhaustion she read on Melanthe's face mirrored her own. The moment they landed in a grassy field, Sophia sank to the ground.

"Can I offer you something to eat or drink?" Melanthe asked a few minutes later. She was making her way among the Mercesti, generating refreshments.

Offering her new friend a small smile, Sophia shook her head. "I'm about to head over to that lovely stream to get a sip of water and try to wash away some of this fatigue. Thanks, though."

Smiling back, Melanthe patted Sophia's upper arm and then continued making her rounds. Derian shadowed her, his stride casual but his gaze vigilant. When he passed Sophia, he said, "Do not go off by yerself."

Remembering a similar warning from Zachariah not even two days ago, Sophia fought a wave of remorse as she gave Derian an acknowledging nod. There were so many things she wished she had said and done differently. Sighing because there was nothing she could do about that now, she rose and headed for the stream only twenty feet away from the group.

Even as she kneeled to scoop water into her hands, she spotted a shadow blending with hers. Looking up—and then up some more—she realized Cleve had followed her.

Yesterday, this enormous male with his tattooed face and fearsome demeanor would have had her shaking in terror. Now, she found his presence comforting. Since he didn't talk, she continued her drinking and washing in silence. Then she stood up and glanced in the direction of the forest in the distance.

"I need a little privacy," she said. Her full bladder squelched any embarrassment she might have felt over the admission.

He surprised her with a friendly wink and started walking toward the trees. Relieved, she hurried to follow him. When they reached the tree line, she said, "I won't go far."

He nodded. She hurried into the forest, finding a small cluster of trees to use for cover as she saw to her personal needs. Thank goodness for Melanthe and her Lekwuesti abilities, she thought, not relishing the idea of having to use leaves.

She had only just adjusted her skirts back down when she sensed that she wasn't alone.

"Cleve!" she called out, trusting her instincts although she didn't see an immediate threat.

The sound of a weapon leaving its sheath had her diving to her left. She rose from her roll and found herself facing one of the Mercesti males who had tracked her as she chased Tate and Ariana.

"Tycho is taking care of your guard," the male said, telling her she now faced Bertram.

His words made her aware of the sound of weapons clanging. She briefly glimpsed the two combatants through the trees before Bertram swung at her with his sword. She jumped away, her heart flinging itself against her breastbone.

Surely the others were aware of the fight and would soon reach the forest, she thought. She narrowly avoided another thrust of Bertram's sword. Then her feet went out from under her.

A rope trap.

Disoriented and terrified, Sophia felt her second power surge out of her control. There was no stopping her shift. She fell back to the ground, this time in the form of a panther.

The cat's incredible center of gravity allowed her to turn mid-fall so she landed on her feet. Unfortunately for Bertram, he stood between her and the ground. She shifted and fell so quickly that he didn't even have time to raise his sword. Her animal instincts at their full height, she went for his throat.

When she next looked up, she found herself surrounded by Mercesti. Derian was the only one who dared to approach her.

"I told ye not to shift," he said.

She licked blood from her muzzle.

"Right." He looked down at what was left of Bertram's form. "Guess ye had the right of it then."

Chapter 38

THE SUN JUST STARTED LIGHTENING THE SKY AS QUINCY LAID EYES ON Hoygul's cottage. Much like it had when he first spotted it with Saraqael, the dwelling failed to impress. Now that he was aware of it, however, he sensed the heavy enchantments masking the cottage's true appearance.

Although covered in dirt and sweat and feeling ready to sleep for a week, he approached the door with purpose and determination. Not very long ago, Ini-herit received word that Uriel rescued Malukali. He also discovered that Knorbis wasn't responding to his wife's attempts to reach him. The reasons for that were limited and none of them were good.

Based on the second-hand information conveyed to Alexius by his commander, something had also happened to Tate. They learned that Zachariah had somehow avowed with her through their mental connection and something that he experienced through Tate's thoughts sent him into a tailspin. The Mercesti said only that he recognized where she was and he was leading them to her. Apparently, he had lost his connection to her.

The news shocked them on every front. An even stronger sense of urgency propelled them the last mile to the cottage. Quincy felt it with every breath as he knocked on the door.

When Hoygul reached out and grabbed his arm to pull him inside, Quincy didn't even flinch. The same thing had happened to Saraqael all those years ago. It seemed the Scultresti was a creature of habit. Once he had been pulled inside, Quincy steadied himself and faced the smaller male, prepared to battle it out to get the map.

"I am ready for this scroll piece to be found already," Hoygul muttered in greeting. "There has been far too much interest in the library map for my peace of mind. A male my age needs his rest."

Frowning, Quincy glanced around the tidy home. He noticed three teacups resting in the strainer beside the sink. "Who else has been here?" he asked. Looking again at Hoygul, he added, "Did you give them the map?"

"That I did. They left less than an hour ago." Hoygul tilted his head slightly to the side. "She mentioned you."

Something about the other male's tone and expression had Quincy feeling lightheaded. He took two careful steps closer to the dining table and grasped the edge of the closest chair. Bracing himself, he managed to ask, "Sophia?"

"Yes."

He sank into the chair. Emotion swarmed through him with such intensity that he had to press his palms against his eyes to stave it off.

Sophia was alive.

"You told her about your visit here with her grandfather."

Quincy could only nod.

"She is very courageous. I saw much of Saraqael in her. That same spark…the thirst for knowledge."

Taking a deep breath, Quincy lowered his hands and stared at the three teacups. A very foolish part of him wanted to know which had been hers so that he could touch it and feel more connected to her.

"Unlike her grandfather, however, it seems Sophia resisted the truth of her heart."

Now shifting his gaze to the Scultresti, Quincy wondered, "What do you mean?"

Hoygul shrugged. "I will merely say that she harbors regret. Assuming you make good time, hopefully she can remedy that."

Hope flared in Quincy's chest. "You'll give me the map?"

Producing the glass disc, Hoygul said, "Since Sophia and Melanthe have received both portions of the map, I will only share the library's location with you."

"Okay," Quincy said, getting to his feet. "I truly can't thank you enough, Hoygul, and I want to get out of here with all haste. But first, please answer me this: who on the Estilorian plane is Melanthe?"

* * *

Ariana didn't think twice about leading Eirik to the library. Tate had warned her multiple times not to do so. But now Tate was severely injured and being carried by a male who flew next to Ariana as a warning. Her friend's complexion had gone gray beneath the blood that covered her. Even with the wind in her ears, Ariana heard the rattle of Tate's every breath. She feared Tiege's sister wouldn't survive the flight to the library. She had yet to regain consciousness.

The Mercesti left Knorbis behind. Ariana overheard Eirik and Metis arguing over whether the elder was more of a risk to keep among them, and she guessed they decided that was the case. She had no idea if he was even alive.

Tears continued to fall unchecked down her cheeks. Fortunately, she didn't need to be able to see in order to follow the pull of her second power. Judging by the intensity of the pull, they would reach their destination very soon.

Metis had ordered the males keeping Deimos in check to fly near Ariana and Tate. The savage male continued to fight against his restraints, lured by the scent of Tate's blood. Normally, this would have shaken Ariana. Now, the depth of her anguish and hopelessness had her feeling almost blessedly numb.

So what if he killed her? Wouldn't all Estilorians be better off without her?

Knowing that she was Tate's only real chance for survival kept Ariana from doing anything rash, however. Despite her despondency, she wouldn't abandon another being like that.

Although she almost managed to convince herself she had done the right thing, when she sensed that they needed to land because they had reached the library, her stomach lurched. She was exactly where she wasn't supposed to be. The awful knowledge had her leading them in several wide circles to stall for time. Only when she knew he was onto her did she finally signal to Eirik.

The place where her senses led her looked like an expanse of barren land. There wasn't a thing around for at least half a mile in any direction. In the distance, she spotted the jagged edges of mountains on one side and, a bit closer, an expanse of forest on the other. The sun cast long shadows on the ground as it touched their forms.

Eirik walked over to the male carrying Tate. “Release her,” he said.

The male made quick work of unfastening the flight harness. Tate sank to the ground. Eirik looked at Ariana.

“Produce something to rouse her,” he ordered.

Swallowing, she nodded. She knelt next to Tate and gently smoothed her unruly, matted hair away from her battered face. Tears fell onto bloodied and bruised skin as Ariana generated the Estilorian equivalent of smelling salts and waved them under Tate’s nose.

After a moment, Tate turned her head from the powerful odor and moaned.

“Get up, female,” Eirik snapped.

“Tate, we’ve reached the library,” Ariana said, watching her friend struggle to open her swollen eyes. “They need you to dissolve the illusion surrounding it.”

Tate made a sound in the back of her throat. Ariana figured she was saying she understood. She carefully reached under Tate’s arms and guided her into a sitting position. Knowing she wasn’t strong enough to lift the larger female, she moved to one knee.

“Come on,” she said. “I’ll help you up.”

Though it must have pained her terribly, Tate put forth her best effort and managed to gain her feet. Ariana helped support her as Eirik moved to stand in front of them.

“Where is the library, female?” he asked.

Expecting Tate to look around so she could find the entrance, Ariana was puzzled when her friend just stood there staring at Eirik through her bleary eyes. Her jaw flexed as though she was trying to work up the energy to speak.

Then she spit in Eirik’s face, the liquid red with her blood.

“Find it your damn self,” she said.

Before he died, Tycho managed to slice open Cleve’s side with a well-targeted strike of his weapon. It took some time to repair the injury before again taking flight. Sophia thanked the Mercesti male numerous times for his heroism. He just nodded, offering her another wink.

A couple of hours later, she sensed that they were nearing the library. She motioned to Derian, who had asked her to let him know when they got close.

“Pay attention, all of ye,” he called out.

That was all the instruction needed. Fanning out, they all rose to a height that offered them maximum visibility of the ground below. It wasn't long before Derian saw something that had him signaling for them to land.

"What is it?" Sophia asked the moment they were all on the ground.

"The library is on the other side of this forest," he replied.

"How can you tell?"

"There are at least five hundred Mercesti gathered there."

"Five hundred?"

Tiege repeated the number stated by Harold as they gathered in the forest near Ariana and Tate's location. In his mind, the fact that they were standing there was nothing short of a miracle.

Not long after they left the wheat field, Harold managed to pry out of Zachariah that he recognized Tate and Ariana's location from Tate's thoughts. Because Zachariah had spent fifty years roaming the Estilorian plane and likely knew every shadowy crevice, Tiege didn't find that hard to believe.

Only when Harold received a thought from his elder that Malukali had been rescued and she could no longer connect to Knorbis did Tiege really grow concerned. Although he asked Zachariah multiple times for news about Tate and Ariana, the Mercesti didn't respond.

They reached a clearing in an ocean-side group of trees as the sun rose. The first thing Tiege noticed was Knorbis. The elder lay on the sandy ground. He had braced his hands beneath him and was shaking his head as if to clear it.

Zachariah didn't even pause. He landed, grabbed Knorbis by his tank top, jerked him to his feet and plowed his fist into the elder's face.

It took a couple of minutes for Harold and his men to subdue Zachariah. The Mercesti's eyes glowed red with the obvious want for blood. Tiege could hardly provide an argument to stop him. Still, he had been raised by an objective father and forgiving mother, so he placed a restraining hand on Zachariah's arm as he struggled to free himself.

"What would you do for Tate if you were in his position?" Tiege asked. When Zachariah yanked again in an attempt to get free, Tiege shifted so that the Mercesti had no choice but to look him in the eye. "You would sacrifice everyone—including yourself—to protect her."

Finally, the violence in Zachariah's eyes began to ease. His chest heaved with exertion as he stopped fighting for release. In the place of his fury, however, came an indescribable pain.

"But you don't know what they did to her," he said at last. "What he *watched* them do."

Stunned by the powerful emotion behind Zachariah's words, Tiege couldn't respond. He took a deep breath to try and subdue the excruciating ache that settled in his chest. Then he nodded at Harold, who held Zachariah's right arm. The commander gave the signal and let Zachariah go.

Rather than charge at the Wymzesti elder, who had been helped to his feet by a couple of Waresti, Zachariah walked over to a spot in the clearing. He dropped to one knee and reached out to touch the ground. That was when Tiege noticed all of the blood.

He was sure the Wymzesti elder felt every bit of his fury and anguish when he looked at him in disbelief.

"I can't undo what's been done," Knorbis said, his gaze haunted. "There will be no forgiving my actions. But I've reconnected with Malukali. Quincy has the map to the library and is conveying it to both of us. I will get you there." He reached into his pocket and produced a handful of vials. "And I can get us there quickly."

Zachariah rose. Tiege saw him put something in his pocket that looked suspiciously like one of Tate's curls. Then the Mercesti walked over to the elder and took the vials from him.

"*Archigos* Uriel can convey the map to commander Harold," Zachariah said without inflection. "You can assuage your guilt some other way. You will never again go anywhere near Tate. Ever."

Knorbis couldn't meet Zachariah's gaze as he nodded. They left the elder standing in the clearing with a few Waresti for protection, figuring he could fly to Malukali. Thanks to the potions, they made excellent time getting to the library's location.

They also learned of Sophia's survival and her Mercesti escort. Tiege was inordinately relieved by the news, even if the fact that she had been rescued by Mercesti came as a surprise.

Now, they stood near the edge of the forest and watched as the last of Eirik's crew landed. Tiege saw Ariana's lavender wings, but she was soon surrounded. He also briefly glimpsed Tate. Her hair covered much of her face because her head hung limply. But the marks and blood he saw all over her body made him want to fly back to the clearing and give Knorbis a few punches of his own.

He exchanged a look with Zachariah. He nodded once to convey understanding. Zachariah briefly returned the nod before once again focusing on Tate.

Harold's eyes flashed. Looking around, he said in a low voice, "Alexius' advanced scouts spotted activity just south of us. He believes it is Sophia and her escort. If we meet up with them and wait for Alexius to arrive with his team—"

"I am not bloody waiting," Zachariah interrupted.

"You must," Harold said firmly. "Just a few more minutes so that we can reinforce our numbers.

"If you don't, Tate and Ariana will surely die."

Chapter 39

EIRIK DIDN'T BOTHER TO WIPE THE SPITTLE FROM HIS FACE BEFORE HE drew his krises. He had been convinced by Metis to leave the Wymzesti elder alive in case he was needed to activate the Elder Scroll. But there was nothing preventing him from dragging this insolent female's nearly-dead form across this godforsaken stretch of land until she came into contact with the illusion surrounding the library and dissolved it.

She didn't even flinch as he raised his weapons to strike her down.

"No!"

The cry came from the Lekwuesti female. She moved so that she stood more in front of the weakened Kynzesti than beside her.

That was fine. She was no longer needed, either.

"There's a third piece to the scroll," she blurted.

Nothing else would have so effectively halted his attack.

"What?"

She paled at his tone, but didn't look away when she repeated, "There's a third piece. I lied to you before."

Eirik looked to Bain, his soldier with mental abilities. Although his dampening power was much stronger than his thought perception, he nodded to let Eirik know the female spoke the truth.

Bain would definitely pay for not catching the earlier lie. Eirik squeezed the grips of his krises so hard the handles creaked in protest.

"Metis," he ground out.

She moved forward. "Yes?"

"If you kill the Kynzesti, can you assume her second power to see through illusions?"

Metis gave the two other females a thoughtful study. "There is no way to know. I do not always assume the full abilities of those whose forms I take. I understand that Kanika had the ability to bring forth miscellaneous items with just her thoughts, for example, but I cannot."

His nostrils flaring, Eirik sheathed his krises. Turning to the Mercesti around him, he snapped his fingers. "Take the Kynzesti. Drag her along the ground until she finds the damn library."

Surprisingly, the female didn't resist as she was grabbed by multiple males and pulled, her boots kicking up dust as they moved along the ground. He supposed the fight had been beaten out of her after all. That didn't brighten his mood in the least.

But there was a way to make himself feel better, he realized.

"So, little liar," he said, stepping closer to the Lekwuesti. He enjoyed watching her eyes widen. "Let's discuss your punishment, shall we?"

By the time Quincy, Clara Kate, Ini-herit, Alexius and their group reached the forest beside the library, they were beyond weary. Although Hoygul had provided them with a helpful shortcut out of the jungle, they still had to fly as fast as possible without stopping for a few hours to cut the distance between them and the others.

Despite that, Quincy's adrenaline kicked into high gear as the forest entered his sight. He saw the streams of Mercesti milling around the barren section of earth housing the library. They landed out of the enemy's range of visibility and headed straight for the trees.

Quincy trusted that Alexius was conveying their arrival to Harold, who had met up with Sophia's group a few minutes ago. He hurried into the forest with the others right behind him.

He found himself facing a sea of beings. Some faces were familiar—the Waresti led by Harold who had traveled with Tiege, Zachariah and *archigos* Sebastian. Many were not. Ignoring the fact that there were a large number of strange, tattooed Mercesti staring at him, he hurried forward, searching for Sophia.

Then he spotted her. She stood beside Tiege, looking up at him and listening to something he said. She wore leather armor over her gown, something he had never seen on her before. Her beautiful hair had been pinned up in anticipation of the fight to come.

She looked like a Fae warrior standing among the sun-dappled trees.

Her gaze suddenly shifted to him. Everything inside him settled into place. He started toward her. She met him halfway at a run, throwing herself into his arms.

"I'm so sorry, Quincy," she whispered against his chest. "I was so stupid."

After breathing in her scent and squeezing her for an extra-long moment, he tipped her head up. "I'm sorry, too, Sophia. There are many things I should have done differently. But we'll get to all that. Right now, let's go and rescue Tate and Ariana." He gave her a small smile. "Then you can spend as much time as you want telling me how much you love me."

She pulled him down for a quick kiss. "Deal."

Ariana couldn't stop herself from backing away as Eirik drew nearer. She quickly bumped up against a group of Mercesti who weren't about to let her get away. Although he had asked her what she believed her punishment should be, she knew he didn't really expect a response.

"Be sure to keep her alive," Metis said, her eyes conveying no emotion as she focused on Ariana. "Deimos will be unhappy if you take away his prize."

In response, the evil creature began emitting his awful shrieks in a bid for release. This was just what it had been like the last time, Ariana realized, her gaze wheeling in panic and fear. She was surrounded by Mercesti trying to get to the item she wasn't supposed to have led them to, listening to the wild cries of a beastly monster that wanted to kill her.

But when Eirik's fist came at Ariana's head, she ducked.

Some things had changed, after all.

The male behind Ariana who took the punch crumpled to the ground. She used the confusion to open up her senses, seeking an escape. The instant a lavender path appeared in her sight, she took off running.

Evading the hands that reached for her, Ariana thought she just might make it. Then brilliant light blazed across the crowd. Deimos screamed in pain.

Ariana knew Tate had found the library.

And she knew she had to go back.

"Quincy, give me your short sword," Clara Kate said, drawing Sophia's attention.

Beside her, Quincy pulled his sword from its sheath and held it out to her cousin. Clara Kate touched the hilt, her deep blue-green eyes glowing as her second power surged. When she removed her hand, the weapon shimmered.

"There," she said. "All blessed. Should last for an hour or so."

"Thanks, C.K."

Sophia watched her turn to the closest Waresti so she could bless his weapon, as well. She was trying to get to as many as she could before they charged out and challenged the Mercesti. The only reason they were still sitting there was because Harold, Alexius, Zachariah, Tiege and Derian were conducting a quick strategy session.

"So…Mercesti, huh?" Quincy asked.

Since he leaned down to whisper the question right in her ear, pleasant shivers ran down her spine. She managed a smile despite the circumstances. "Yes. Quite an interesting class, I've found."

"What was Zachariah's reaction when he met others like him?"

Her smile faded. Derian and his team had greeted Zachariah with something akin to awe. She knew from what Melanthe said that Derian greatly respected his former commander. But aside from a cursory greeting, Zachariah hadn't turned his attention from the group out in the empty field. Sophia noticed something markedly different about his demeanor, but when she asked Tiege about it, he told her to let it drop.

"He didn't say much," she said at last. "He's focused on rescuing Tate."

A flash of light put both of them on alert. The time for conversation was over.

Ariana allowed herself to be hauled by a couple of Mercesti over to where Eirik and Metis now stood. They looked intently at the ground. She followed their gazes.

The entrance to the library was little more than a mound of dirt with a round wooden door covering it. It looked barely large enough for a being to enter, never mind house the entire ancient library. Even if it hadn't been enchanted, Ariana would have been hard-pressed to believe that anyone would willingly enter it. In fact, there was something distinctly repelling about it.

Eirik didn't seem to care. He reached down and lifted the door by its handle, wrenching it open with one hard tug.

"Let's go," he said, turning to the males holding Tate.

She was still being held by the Mercesti who had dragged her in order to find the library. Her head bobbed as she fought to remain conscious. Fresh blood glistened on her lips. If possible, her complexion looked even worse than it had before. Dark bruising had spread along her torso, Ariana realized, spotting a section of skin revealed by Tate's torn tank top. Although she was no expert, Ariana felt certain that Tate had endured internal injuries that would prove fatal if not treated soon.

She felt Eirik's gaze on her and lifted her eyes to meet his. "You'll never have the scroll if she dies," she said.

"Then I shall keep her alive…barely."

A surge of activity drew their attention to the forested side of the field. Ariana gaped as the sky filled with beings. Even from her distance, she saw orange, silver, deep blue-green and lavender wings among the red of the Mercesti.

"Tiege!" she cried.

Then she was yanked by the hair. Disoriented, she found herself flung toward the hole in the ground. She couldn't stop her forward momentum and fell headfirst into the library. Her breath left her lungs as she struck the hard floor.

When she heard them tossing Tate down after her, Ariana twisted and did her best to catch the other female. They ended up in a heap. Ignoring the pain resulting from the collision, Ariana struggled to her feet, reaching under Tate's armpits and pulling with all of her strength. She managed to get them both out of the way before Eirik and Metis entered the library. Deimos came down next, causing Ariana to stiffen.

Where were his handlers?

"Remember to behave yourself, my dear Deimos," Metis crooned, reaching out and stroking the creature's dark, filthy hair. "These are not your prizes…yet."

Eirik reached up and pulled the library door closed, sealing them in utter darkness without anyone else joining them. Ariana realized that there would now be no one restraining Deimos. She and Tate were trapped with the most vicious creature on the Estilorian plane.

And he wanted their blood.

Chapter 40

WHEN HAROLD GAVE THE SIGNAL TO ATTACK, TIEGE UNSHEATHED HIS blessed kamas and prepared to run from the forest to engage his first combatant. A strong hand grabbed his arm, holding him back.

He glanced over at Zachariah as everyone surged past them. "What are you doing?" he asked. "Let's—"

"Can you cast the illusion of invisibility?"

Blinking, Tiege responded, "Harold said their dampeners will clamp down on our second powers the moment we make ourselves known."

"Your sister refuses to listen to any rules or directions and you do nothing but abide by them. How is that possible?"

Feeling a flush building in his neck, Tiege frowned. His parents had always jokingly called him and Tate their "yin" and "yang" children. They tended to balance each other. But perhaps it was time to tilt things off their axis.

"I've never tried," he admitted.

"Was it against the rules?" Zachariah asked dryly.

"Shut up," Tiege muttered.

He glanced at the battle occurring just feet away. Flares of light flooded the field as blessed weapons met cursed ones. His cousins were out there risking their lives. But his abilities could allow him and Zachariah to get to Tate and Ariana more quickly than battling their way there.

"Keep them from killing me while I try," he said.

As Zachariah moved into position to defend him, Tiege put his kamas away. This illusion wasn't going to be the same as making someone believe they were seeing something that wasn't really there. This was making them *not* see something that was.

Closing his eyes, he tried to open up his second power. There was a definite damper in effect. He considered what to do. Tate and Zachariah had defied all kinds of logic in the course of their relationship, first through their mental connection to each other and then through their dream avowing. Whatever part of his sister had permitted that to happen also had to be a part of him.

He just had to believe that he could do it.

Conjuring Tate's image in his mind, he drew on his grandfather's Corgloresti ability of faith. He felt the dampening ease as his concentration and belief grew. He focused on making himself the illusion. What others saw would be the environment that surrounded him.

He opened his eyes. Zachariah was removing his tomahawk from the chest of a dead Mercesti, wiping it on the other male's clothes.

"Okay," Tiege said, feeling his power remain steady. When Zachariah looked up and glanced around as if searching for him, Tiege knew it was working.

"Good." Zachariah looked down toward Tiege's boot prints, then moved closer. "Can you extend it to me?"

Although he tried, Tiege couldn't get it to work. "I think I might have to touch you," he said.

"Fine."

He reached out and grasped Zachariah's upper arm. He sensed immediately that the illusion extended to both of them even though he could still see Zachariah.

"Okay, we're good to go," he said. "We should probably fly. Running through this field of bodies will be impossible. If anyone touches either of us, the illusion will dissolve."

"How the hell are we going to fly while you're touching me?"

Tiege considered that. "I don't have a flight harness and I doubt I'm strong enough to carry you. We'll have to hold hands."

The look Zachariah gave him clearly questioned his sanity.

"Do you see another choice? We're wasting time here."

Sighing, Zachariah harnessed his weapon and extended his wings. When Tiege also extended his wings and reached for Zachariah's hand, the Mercesti hesitated.

His gaze narrowing, he said, "You will speak of this to no one."

"I make no promises."

"Sure. *Now* you sound like your sister."

Sophia and Clara Kate, the youngest beings in the group and the ones with the least battle experience, were among the last to leave the cover of the trees. Tiege was supposed to be with them, but the moment Sophia had a chance to look for her cousin, she realized he was nowhere to be found.

There wasn't time to worry about it. They may have been the last out of the forest, but there were plenty of Mercesti to go around. Considering they were outnumbered two to one despite their combined forces, it seemed they were on an impossible mission.

They instinctively started battling in the air to meet the hundreds of Mercesti who took flight once they spotted the newcomers. But they soon realized the Kynzesti weren't properly trained for it. Wings couldn't be extended in the area of protection surrounding their homes, so they had only been trained on the ground.

Once they returned to the ground, Clara Kate's blessed butterfly swords whirled as she met opponent after opponent in their effort to reach the library. Ini-herit wielded a sword of his own, protecting her back. Quincy did the same for Sophia with his short sword and a shield he borrowed from Derian's crew.

Sophia also carried a shield, but her weapon wasn't made of steel or wood.

Because her ability to shift was a part of her genetic code, no dampener on the plane could prevent her from doing it. As a result, now curling from underneath the hem of her gown was her homage to Nyx: a kragen's tail with a paralyzing barb on the tip. She used it to strike the enemy anywhere they had exposed flesh, sending them straight to the ground.

Up ahead of them, Derian and Melanthe led their team in the primary ground assault as Harold and Alexius led the attack by air. Derian's lochaber axe left a wake of carnage that Sophia was sure would haunt her nightmares. Melanthe stunned Sophia with her ability to wield a bo. It was clear that she had received exceptional training. She and Derian worked so seamlessly that they had obviously practiced scenarios like this many times.

Sophia had feared that her new Mercesti friends would accidently get killed or injured by the Waresti, but she needn't have worried. Those Mercesti who didn't have colorful tattoos on their bodies wore face and body paint generated by Melanthe, distinguishing them from Eirik's followers.

There wasn't time to think. Her heart racing faster than she could ever remember, Sophia went from consciously considering her every move to acting entirely on instinct. She stretched her abilities. If Zachariah had taught her anything through his unconventional lessons, it was that she was capable of more than she ever imagined.

Even as she maneuvered her kragen's tail, she tapped into the predatory hunting instincts of the panther. Soon, she didn't really need her shield because she moved so effortlessly out of the way of weapons. She registered hundreds of details at once.

Including Clara Kate's fall, just as Sophia evaded the swing of a mace and struck an enemy with her tail.

Clara Kate slipped on the remains of one of the fallen. Her weapons flew from her grasp. Her enemy moved in for the kill. Ini-herit was busy dispatching two Mercesti and couldn't turn to aid her. Before Sophia or Quincy could intervene, Clara Kate flung out her hand. Fire blazed from her palm, engulfing the enemy.

Evidently, the Kynzesti elemental abilities couldn't be dampened, either.

Ini-herit helped Clara Kate to her feet. They battled on. It seemed they were making progress, but Sophia felt the passage of every precious minute.

She knew that the longer they were held at bay and unable to reach the library entrance, the greater the chances they would lose not only the scroll piece, but Tate and Ariana, too.

Ariana cast a light with a trembling hand, knowing she and Tate were the only two in the library who couldn't see in the dark. She realized they were in some kind of rectangular anteroom. The walls glowed with dark purple light, indicating the documents housed there had been created by the Wymzesti class…possibly even *archigos* Knorbis himself.

"Is the scroll piece in this room?" Eirik asked.

Her gaze moved nervously from him to Deimos, who licked his lips and bared his fangs when she glanced his way. She stammered, "N-no."

"Then get moving."

Her breath escaping in frightened gasps, Ariana kept Tate's arm around her shoulders and opened up her second power. The wash of lavender light led out of the anteroom and into the darkness beyond an arched entrance. She sensed the scroll piece was quite a distance into the library.

Not bothering to resist Eirik's demand, she moved forward, bearing as much of Tate's weight as she could. The wheezing of the Kynzesti's breath worried Ariana, as did the low-level moans she issued with each expansion of her lungs. Tate walked hunched over, unable to stand straight. The fact that she accepted Ariana's assistance without complaint told her how bad things were.

She guided them out of the anteroom as quickly as she thought Tate could manage, not wanting to invoke Eirik's wrath. Once she saw how massive the inside of the library actually was, however, her heart sank. She couldn't even see the end of it.

Her power told her the scroll piece was within the far reaches of the library's depths. Doing a quick guesstimate, she figured it could easily take an hour to walk to it.

Tate would never last that long.

A shove from behind had Ariana staggering further into the library. She barely kept Tate upright. When she heard Eirik draw his weapons and Deimos made one of his terrifying noises, she whimpered.

"It'll be okay," Tate said, the words barely audible. Her hand squeezed Ariana's shoulder, offering her support the only way she could.

Drawing strength from her dying friend, Ariana nodded and started forward.

Chapter 41

TIEGE AND ZACHARIAH HOVERED OVER THE ROUND DOOR TO THE library. All but the door itself was surrounded by Mercesti…and not the ones on their side.

"We both have to land on the door," Zachariah said. "If either of us misses, we will come into contact with one of the bloody Mercesti guarding it and lose the illusion."

Tiege nodded. It had been hard enough to make their way around the Estilorians in the air, but this was even more challenging. They both got lower to the ground and considered their options.

The noise was atrocious. Between the sounds of weapons clanging and hundreds of beings screaming in pain or intimidation, it was a wonder he and Zachariah could even hear each other.

When they were about twenty feet off the ground, Tiege said, "We'll have to extinguish our wings before we reach the heads of the soldiers, or we'll risk touching one of them."

"How the hell—?"

Tiege turned and flew right up to Zachariah, grabbing him around the waist in a form of hug. The Mercesti's expression was priceless, even if Tiege was as discomfited by the close contact as Tate's avowed.

"This is the only way we'll both land on the thing once we extinguish our wings," Tiege said. "Just do it and—for God's sake—don't think about it."

"You will speak of this to no—"

"Damn straight."

Without another word, Zachariah wrapped his arms around Tiege's waist so that they were as close as possible without their wings touching. They slowly lowered themselves into position. After counting to three, they extinguished their wings. Somehow, they managed to land together without falling.

"Stand on the edge," Zachariah instructed in a low voice as they quickly parted.

Tiege obeyed, keeping one hand on Zachariah's back to maintain the illusion and trying not to think about the Mercesti standing close enough to hit them with weapons if they so much as sneezed.

He felt exhaustion creeping in. The longer he maintained the illusion, the more drained his energy would become. He would hold it until he dropped, however.

"Damn it," Zachariah growled. "It's locked."

Tiege reached down with his free hand to pull at the door's round, metal fastening, hoping his combined efforts with Zachariah's might yank it loose. When it didn't budge, Tiege cursed, grateful for the sounds of battle keeping them from being overheard.

"Is there some kind of key?" he asked, searching for a keyhole.

"I don't need a bloody key," Zachariah replied, and he pulled out his tomahawk.

His brows lifting in surprise, Tiege watched as Zachariah lifted the honed weapon and began hacking at the wood. Worried someone might see what they were doing, he quickly extended the illusion to include the door, making it appear the way it normally did to anyone who chanced to look at it. The effort had his head throbbing. Fortunately, the surrounding noise masked the sounds of the chopping wood.

It was slow-going since the wood was so thick. After a while, Zachariah stopped and looked up. His face went ashen, his gaze sightless.

"No," he said in a choked voice.

Fear clutched Tiege's heart. He nearly lost the illusion as he realized something had gone horribly wrong. And when Zachariah's unseeing eyes gleamed with moisture, Tiege's knees buckled.

"Oh, God." Feeling like a hole had just been ripped in his chest, Tiege grasped Zachariah by both of his shoulders. "You need to tell Tate to hold on. Tell her we're coming. She can hold on for a few more minutes."

"She said she's sorry," Zachariah said hollowly, looking away and clenching his jaw. "She's held on for as long as she can.

"She just told us goodbye."

Quincy had never been so awed by Sophia's abilities. She moved with unparalleled grace and precision, drawing on every instinct within her to make her an unstoppable force. He realized that all of her years of weapons training may have enhanced her understanding of battle strategy, but that certainly wasn't keeping her alive now.

No...that was all her.

He'd gotten a couple of slices and a host of bruises thus far, but nothing life-threatening. Now that Clara Kate knew her elemental power wasn't dampened, she alternated the use of her butterfly swords with well-targeted fireballs to fend off her opponents. Although the resulting smell was an unfortunate side effect, it proved highly effective. Ini-herit kept pace beside her, swinging his sword up to meet attack after attack. As a group, they were making progress toward their goal.

"Melanthe has the map for when we're inside the library, correct?" he asked Sophia between opponents.

"Yes," Sophia answered.

He nodded and made a mental note to keep Melanthe in sight so they could follow her once they were in the library. Although they had only met briefly before the battle, he could tell that the former Lekwuesti had a good heart. Hoygul clearly knew what he was doing. If they couldn't easily track Tate and Ariana by the time they got into the library, she would lead them where they needed to go.

A couple of opponents later, Sophia asked, "Have you seen Tiege or Zachariah?"

Frowning and giving a quick glance around, Quincy said, "No."

"Where could they have gone?"

"I have no idea. But they better show up soon. I think our forces will reach that door very shortly."

Ariana knew within ten minutes of walking among the endless rows of books and scrolls filling the library that they would never make it to the scroll piece. Tate's breathing had grown shallower. Blood trickled from her nose. Her moans became more insistent. She started murmuring to herself. Ariana made out the names "Sparky" and "Tiege," something that brought tears to her eyes.

"Stay with me, Tate," she said. "We'll do this together."

"Hurry up," Eirik snapped. "How much farther is the scroll piece?"

"I can't tell," Ariana responded, maneuvering Tate around a pedestal housing a large book. She flinched when Deimos lurched at her, but Metis grabbed his arm to restrain him. Her voice wavered as she continued, "You know the limits of my ability."

"We will fly to it, then."

"But Tate—"

"I will carry the weak female. Give me no more excuses and extend your wings."

When he walked over and lifted Tate, Ariana knew she would have to fly. Their wings would disturb the books and scrolls, an act that was punishable by the Elphresti and one she would normally never do. Not seeing any choice, she turned sideways so that she could extend her wings and then lifted off.

Fear for Tate's life had her focusing her abilities with all of her concentration. She found what they were seeking within another few minutes.

They landed in an area housing numerous scrolls. As soon as they were on the ground, Eirik tossed Tate down without a care. The fact that the Kynzesti didn't make a sound of protest or move from her ragdoll position had Ariana's fear spiking.

"Tate?"

"Forget about the damned female," Eirik said. "Where is the scroll piece?"

Metis turned and started rifling through nearby scrolls as Ariana fell to her knees beside Tate. Deimos got closer to Ariana while Metis' attention was diverted, but Eirik used one of his boots to keep the creature at bay.

Just as Ariana reached with trembling fingers to check Tate's pulse, Eirik bent down and grabbed Tate by the arm. Appalled, Ariana watched as he dragged her friend's limp form across the ground by her wrist—her broken one—closer to the stacks of scrolls. He didn't care what condition Tate was in. He was going to use her ability to defeat the protections in place around the scroll piece.

Her fear vanished in a snap. Outrage flooded in. Boiled over. She opened her mouth to order Eirik to let Tate go, poised to strike if he refused.

Several things happened in that instant.

A series of booms, followed by the loudest crack she had ever heard, resonated throughout the tomb-like library.

White light exploded in front of her, telling her the illusion protecting the scroll piece had been shattered.

And Deimos used the opportunity to take her down.

Her breath left her as she hit the ground. Pain blasted through her as her head smacked into the stone floor. The loud noise and blinding light disoriented her. Terror seized her.

But when she felt Deimos on top of her, his hips between hers as he went for her throat, she knew exactly what to do.

The remembered image of Zachariah on top of her, talking her through the defensive moves, superimposed themselves on her mind as she rocked her lower body from side to side to dislodge Deimos. They flipped sideways. The moment her arm was free, she rammed her elbow into the back of the creature's head with all of her strength, catching him in the delicate tissue of his cerebellum.

His neck snapped. He crumpled like a sack of wheat. Metis shrieked, lurching over to fall by his side.

Hurrying to her feet, glancing wildly around, Ariana once again saw Tate on the ground near Eirik. She ran over to her friend while Eirik looked at a piece of parchment, probably ensuring it was what he sought.

"Tate," she said, reaching out to brush the curls away from her friend's cold face as her vision blurred with tears. "Tate, please…stay with me."

But she knew Tate could no longer hear her.

Chapter 42

TIEGE TOOK ZACHARIAH'S QUIET WORDS LIKE STABS TO THE CHEST. HIS lungs refused to work. He made a sound in the back of his throat that had a couple of heads swiveling in confusion. Fortunately, the illusion held.

He had been told Tate was dead once before. He refused to go through it again.

Because Zachariah kept his gaze averted, Tiege grabbed his arm to get his attention. His fierce grip had the Mercesti snapping his head around and glaring at him.

Perfect.

"Don't you dare give up," Tiege commanded. "You're the most hard-headed being I've ever met. If you want to be a part of this family, you need to earn the right, damn it. Share that stubborn strength with your avowed."

When Zachariah's frown faded, Tiege put his left hand on his shoulder and reached for the tomahawk with his right. "You're right," he said, hefting the weapon. "Tate never listens." He began hacking at the wood. "She deliberately goes against what she's told. So tell her that she's too weak to survive something like this. Tell her that you're not surprised Eirik managed to get the better of her. Tell her that I was always Mom and Dad's favorite, anyway. Tell her...whatever she needs to hear."

For once, the Mercesti didn't argue. Instead, he closed his eyes and concentrated. Tiege continued to pound the tomahawk into the door. Tate and Ariana were somewhere beyond this single boundary. He didn't care how long it took. He didn't care if he had to rip the wood apart with his fingernails. He would get through it.

As soon as that thought entered his head, he realized how close the sounds of battle had gotten. Someone screamed right behind him, but he couldn't afford to let it distract him.

Down went the tomahawk. Then back up.

Before he brought it down again, blood splattered over him and Zachariah. He felt the illusion dissolve even as he turned to see a Mercesti's head roll one way and his body fall the other.

With the glare of sunlight shining between his shoulder blades, Derian stepped over the body. He looked between Tiege and Zachariah, then down at the door.

"Seems yer in need of an axe," he observed as the battle raged around them.

"We have an axe," Tiege argued, waving the tomahawk.

Derian snorted. "Stand aside."

Since the Mercesti lifted his lochaber axe with the clear intent to swing it down, Tiege scrambled to abandon the door. Zachariah also moved out of the way. They watched as the Mercesti male lowered his weapon in a mighty blow.

The door to the library exploded.

"They have breached the entrance."

Ariana heard Eirik shout at Metis, but she didn't care. She knelt on the ground and lifted Tate's upper body, holding her close. Shock over what she had just done to Deimos clouded her senses. She barely realized where she was. All she could focus on was Tate.

The female she held was the twin sister of the male she loved, and she had contributed to her death.

There would be no going back after this. It didn't matter if Eirik and Metis left the library right then and never harmed a hair on her head. Ariana could never go back to Tiege now. He deserved someone far stronger than her.

"You must get us out of here, Metis," Eirik growled. "They have extended their wings. We have only a minute or two before they are upon us."

Not bothering to wipe her tears, Ariana clutched Tate to her, rocking back and forth. "I'm so sorry," she whispered.

"Deimos is dying!" Metis shouted, sounding as distraught as she ever had. "She's killed him."

"I do love Tiege," Ariana continued with a sob. "And I wanted to love you. But you loved a Mercesti, and I couldn't move past that."

"Then you must finish the kill and attempt to assume his abilities," Eirik said. "You created him, so perhaps you have a better chance of it working. Do it *now*."

Ariana's gaze grew unfocused as her thoughts pulled inwards. "You loved a Mercesti…one who saved my life as much as he did yours."

"It is you or him, Metis."

"And then he taught me how to save my own." Shame and remorse flourished as shock eased. "I let fear rule me."

There was a scream and flurry of movement. Ariana didn't watch as Metis grabbed Eirik's outstretched kris and brought it down to end Deimos' life. The horrifying sound of the weapon sinking into his chest barely registered. A wash of dark light, accompanied by the deepest chill Ariana had ever felt, crawled along her back as she curled over Tate's body.

"Ariana!"

Finally, she looked up. Tiege was within sight of them. When she blinked, releasing two tears, her vision cleared enough that she could almost make out the features of his face.

"Run!" he called to her.

But she wouldn't leave Tate.

When she felt Metis touch her head, she kept her gaze on Tiege in hopes he could see her more clearly than she saw him.

Then she whispered, "I'm sorry."

Sophia, Quincy, Clara Kate and Ini-herit were right behind Derian and Melanthe on the battlefield, so they all piled into the library after Tiege and Zachariah. Melanthe raced ahead of them, following the map inside her head.

"Wait!"

The order came from Quincy. Sophia staggered to a stop beside him, confused. When she got a good look at his face, she finally realized just how difficult this must be for him. He appeared to be having some kind of flashback. It had his complexion going pale and his silver eyes unfocused. Her heart wrenched over what had to be painful memories.

He explained, "Assuming they've reached the scroll piece, they'll be far from here...at least an hour by foot."

When everyone looked at each other, he extended his wings. "I remember now."

No one argued. Going against the rules of the Elphresti, they all took flight. Although she felt a strong urge to get ahead of everyone else and fly faster, Sophia stayed back with Quincy, Clara Kate and Ini-herit, letting Melanthe serve as the guide. Derian, Tiege and Zachariah flew beside her in a staggered pattern so their wings didn't touch. All of them had their weapons drawn.

Within a couple of minutes, they spotted Eirik standing with a piece of parchment in one hand and a black kris in the other. The low timbre of his voice carried to them, though they couldn't make out the words. Those were followed by a high-pitched voice that Sophia assumed was Metis. The female wasn't visible.

Neither were Tate and Ariana.

When she realized how far they still were from her cousin and friend, a surge of energy rushed through her. It wasn't unlike the one that had overtaken her when she killed Bertram as a panther. Her instinct to shift was nearly unstoppable.

But she knew Quincy wanted her to stay with him. Although they hadn't had much time to discuss it, she saw how much her disappearance had cost him.

She must have made a sound that alerted him, as he suddenly looked over at her. She could almost feel herself vibrating with the need to shift. The need to help Tate and Ariana. When she caught his gaze, she saw the glow of her eyes reflected in his irises.

"Do it," he said.

That was all the encouragement she needed. Diving, she headed straight to an aisle. A few feet from the ground, she shifted into a cheetah. Her clothes and armor fell into a forgotten heap as she surged ahead. She shot past stacks of books and scrolls. Elaborate bookcases passed in a blur. The only thing imprinted on her mind was the path to Tate and Ariana, and she knew she could get to them.

"Ariana!" Tiege shouted from somewhere far behind her.

She was nearly there. Just one more stack of bookcases...

"Run!"

The urgency in Tiege's voice had Sophia flinging herself around the last bend. To her left, she saw Eirik with his hand on Deimos' shoulder. Ariana sat on the ground in front of him with Tate's upper body cradled in her arms. Metis was missing, but Sophia couldn't worry about that. Deimos touched Ariana's head, his mouth moving as he chanted.

Even as Sophia leaped from the side with the intent of tearing into Eirik, she heard Ariana whisper, "I'm sorry."

Sophia's flight through the air didn't have her sinking her teeth into flesh, however. It had her crashing spectacularly.

Eirik and Metis were gone, and they had taken Tate and Ariana with them.

Chapter 43

"No!" Tiege's cry echoed through the vast library. Quincy felt the torment behind the single word.

They had come so close. But they had failed.

When they finally reached the place where Eirik had stood with the scroll piece, Quincy saw Sophia in her cheetah form investigating the large red stains on the ground. Some of them were Tate's blood, but the rest were all that remained of Deimos. Having been on the ground, she had missed the gruesome sight of Metis standing over the evil creature, absorbing his essence like another being would air in her lungs, until the stain was all that remained.

Squatting beside her, he touched her head and explained, "That was Deimos. Metis has assumed his form…likely so that she could get them out of here."

Melanthe approached. With a flash of red light, she generated a pile of clothing. "Sophia," she said in a soft voice, "I can aid you in dressing if you would like."

When the two females moved behind a series of tall bookcases, Derian walked along with them to stand guard. Since there was no one in the library outside of them, Quincy figured this was habitual for the Mercesti. As he got to his feet, he realized everyone was standing around as though in a state of shock. He supposed they were.

Moving closer to the pedestal that he once approached while Saraqael hunted for a solution to save the love of his life, he felt transported back to that moment. He had seen a glow from the pedestal, one that caught his eye and had him lifting up the parchment he found there and reading it. It was at that moment that a bright light flashed from where Saraqael sifted through scrolls. Quincy hadn't known it at the time, but his friend had just sealed his fate.

And in so doing, secured the futures of many others.

"This was where the scroll piece used to be," Quincy said after a moment. He lifted a page of the large book housed there. "Eirik definitely has it now."

He glanced up when he heard Sophia and Melanthe emerging from behind the bookcases. Just as he turned to face them, Zachariah shoved past him. With blazing red eyes, the Mercesti heaved the heavy stone pedestal with all of his strength. The book flew through the air, its brittle pages scattering like autumn leaves. Stone fell to the ground with a deafening crack.

Even as the sound careened through the library, Zachariah punched the closest bookcase, splintering the wood. Then he struck it again.

"Zachariah," Tiege said.

The Mercesti was beyond reason, however. He reared back to strike the bookcase again, his knuckles wet with blood. Tiege reached up and grabbed the other male's arm.

"Stop it! She wouldn't want this."

Using his larger size to his advantage, Zachariah shoved Tiege to the ground. Even as the Kynzesti fell, Zachariah went with him, ending up on one knee with his fist raised to strike Tiege.

"Sparky!"

That stopped him.

Quincy glanced at Sophia, who had spoken the word. She stopped next to him and took his hand, but her gaze was centered on Zachariah.

"Think about what you're doing," she said quietly. "You're not honoring Tate this way."

Zachariah released Tiege. His chest rose and fell as he caught his breath. The intensity of his gaze eased, even if his pain did not.

Staring at Sophia, he said, "Do not ever call me that again."

She nodded. Quincy gave her hand a squeeze. Then his gaze moved back to Zachariah, who remained on one knee even as Tiege regained his feet. The Mercesti braced his left forearm on his bent knee as he reached down to touch a small pool of blood with his right hand. After a moment, he bowed his head and covered his eyes with his left hand.

With a similar devastated expression on his face, Tiege reached out to touch Zachariah's shoulder. Seeing the gesture, Clara Kate put a comforting hand on Tiege's arm. Fascinated, Quincy watched his elder tilt his head in consideration. After a brief hesitation, Ini-herit tentatively touched Clara Kate's other hand. Without missing a beat, she wove her fingers with his. Sophia then reached out with her free hand to give Ini-herit a pat of appreciation for making the gesture.

Silver light flared. Quincy squinted against it, tensing as he wondered what was happening. When the brilliance of the light eased, he opened his eyes. What—or rather, who—he saw had his heart dropping into his stomach.

"*Saraqael.*"

The shimmering image of the dark-haired young man standing before them gave him a familiar smile. Sophia gasped upon hearing her grandfather's name. Zachariah got to his feet. Everyone stared at the image with a range of emotions on their faces. Quincy realized Saraqael was dressed just like he had been the last time they were in this library…a white shirt with dark pants and knee-high boots.

"Yes, my old friend," he said. His voice had emotion clogging Quincy's throat. "I have a connection with this place. It is so good to see you, even under such terrible circumstances."

"How…" Quincy trailed off, uncertain what to ask. What to say. His thoughts seized as he tried to accept what he saw.

"I am here because the six of you joined in touch and grief," Saraqael said, looking among them. "Your connection was powerful enough, you see."

No, Quincy didn't see. But Saraqael had settled his gaze on Sophia. His sharp silver eyes moved to where her hand connected with Quincy's. For the first time, Quincy worried what his best friend thought about his feelings for his granddaughter.

"Sophia," Saraqael said with another smile. "It is nice to meet you, granddaughter."

"Yes. Um, hello," she replied, clearly dazed.

"Your beauty and intelligence are just staggering," he said, bringing a blush to Sophia's cheeks. "It makes me wonder what you see in Quincy."

When Quincy's jaw dropped over the unexpected, playful dig, Saraqael winked at him. Then he looked back at Sophia and said, "It warms my heart to see the two of you together. Please allow me and your grandmother to congratulate you."

The words had the invisible band of emotion around Quincy's chest easing. While he had never expected to have the chance to ask his friend's blessing, it was a relief to have it.

"Oh," Saraqael continued. "I also thought you might like to know that your great aunt has blonde hair."

That had Sophia's eyes widening. "She does?"

"Yes. Your grandmother was not an only child, after all."

Quincy blinked in surprise. Before he could pursue that, Saraqael turned, crossed his right arm over his chest and bowed.

"*Archigos* Ini-herit," he greeted. "Thank you for all you have done to protect my legacy. I know that above all others, you have sacrificed the most to be here right now."

The elder lifted a chin in response, his expression revealing nothing.

Then Saraqael turned his gaze to C.K. "Clara Kate…my love's namesake and my firstborn grandchild."

"That's me," she managed.

"Your part in this journey has not yet begun, but you have done whatever you could to aid your cousins in theirs. I applaud you. You make all of us proud."

"What do you mean?" she asked, her eyebrows lowering in confusion. "Do you know what's going on here?"

"Of course I do." Here, he turned somber eyes to Tiege and Zachariah. "I am so sorry for your loss."

The words fell like hammer blows, causing everyone to grow quiet. Quincy couldn't think of a thing to say. Their failure to save Tate and Ariana weighed heavily on all of them.

"Loss?" Sophia echoed at last. She looked up and caught Quincy's gaze. He shook his head.

"Yes, of course," Saraqael replied. "Tate—"

"Isn't dead," Sophia interrupted. "I know the scent of death. Her blood didn't carry it."

Saraqael briefly bowed his head in acknowledgement before saying, "I was only going to say that Tate and Ariana are lost to you…for now. But you must get to them soon. Eirik will begin to piece together what the scroll contains and realize how much more of a role all of you will play in this."

Quincy's head reeled as he continued processing the fact that he was standing there having this conversation. Still, his voice freed up enough to ask, "Do you know what the scroll pieces say?"

"I know what the piece contained here says, but I do not know the location of the last piece." Saraqael once again smiled. "*Archigos* Ini-herit's map will help you find that one."

They all looked at the Corgloresti elder, who shrugged.

"The one you wear around your neck," Saraqael added.

Reaching under his shirt, Ini-herit pulled out the medallion he wore. Quincy had seen it many times. It contained a series of etched images in a variety of colors, resting on a silver background. None of it looked much like a map to his mind, but then again, he hadn't known to look at it in that light.

"You might have been willing to have the location of the scroll piece erased from your mind, sir," Saraqael said, "but you were smart enough to give yourself a backup plan."

Clara Kate nodded, clearly not surprised. "Okay. How do we read the map?"

"That, I cannot say."

Frowning, Tiege asked, "What did the scroll piece contained in this library say?"

"I will recite from the beginning that which I know:

"Should time and Fate both dictate
That nine Elders become eight
Let not their power and sway
Fade like the light of the day.

~ - ~

By this scroll may power flow
So another's skill may grow
And from eight will one become
Mightier than anyone.

~ - ~

To unfurl the force herein
Eight journeys must now begin;
Once separate and undefined

Different paths somehow align.

~ - ~

One most pure in blood and soul,
One with too much self-control,
One conceived of age and might,
One who dwells 'tween dark and light."

As Saraqael recited the scroll, his gaze moved among them line by line: Quincy. Ini-herit. Clara Kate. Zachariah. When he stopped speaking, he waited for them to look between each other while they absorbed the meaning of the words.

After a moment, Clara Kate cleared her throat. "You're saying that we're all part of the eight needed to unfurl the scroll's power?"

Her voice was thin, as though she had trouble accepting the words as they left her mouth. Quincy could hardly blame her. Even having been prepared for this by the guesses posed by Malukali and Knorbis, it still blew him away. But the scroll's descriptions did fit. He was also willing to bet his right arm that the last scroll piece would describe Sophia, Tate, Tiege and Ariana. Their fates had been unavoidably woven together from the moment Nyx first snatched Tate out of the sky and carried her to Zachariah as a gift.

"Yes," Saraqael replied. "You must get to Tate and Ariana as soon as possible."

They all exchanged looks. There had never been a doubt about that, though the question remained how they would ever find them. Metis could have transported them anywhere on the plane with her new ability.

"My time is done, and I must go," Saraqael said, pulling Quincy's attention back to him.

The words were surprisingly less painful than Quincy would have thought, though they did make his throat constrict. Sophia's fierce grip on his hand helped. When his friend gave him one last smile, Quincy finally got to say the words he'd never really had the chance to more than forty years ago.

"Goodbye, my friend."

Chapter 44

NO ONE SPOKE AS THEY ONCE AGAIN DEFIED THE RULES OF THE ELPHRESTI and took flight inside the library. Zachariah was sure to get in trouble for the destruction he caused, but they had much bigger things to worry about. First and foremost, they needed to come up with a plan to rescue Tate and Ariana.

They all had a lot to absorb. Sophia now knew she was one of the eight beings meant to somehow activate the power of the Elder Scroll. The pieces that Eirik currently held might not say as much, but it wasn't a huge leap of logic to conclude that she, Clara Kate, Tate, Tiege, Quincy, Ini-herit, Zachariah and Ariana were involved in this for a reason. Their connection to each other, rocky and uncertain as it was, had grown over the past couple months. Somehow, every step they had taken up until then felt mapped out…fated, as though it was all leading them to some significant point. Although she didn't have much evidence to support her deduction, she felt confident in it.

Her gaze continually moved to Quincy. Their interaction with her grandfather had shaken all of them, but him most of all. His expressions had ranged from shock to sorrow to joy as they communicated for the first time in nearly forty years. Now, he looked contemplative.

They all had to come to terms with what they had just been told. It would be up to them to embrace this destiny and do whatever was required to stop Eirik from using the scroll for his own evil purposes. Whether they could then destroy it to avoid this ever happening again was unknown. But Sophia knew they had to try.

When they reached the entrance to the library, Zachariah led the way out.

His expression was stony, but she had witnessed the pain he experienced over losing Tate. She had no doubt that he loved her. If his emotional reaction hadn't convinced her, the ring he wore and the changes to his pairing marking certainly would have.

Obviously, some events had occurred during her absence that she had yet to learn.

When Zachariah gave the all-clear, they exited out the small opening. Sophia looked around as she emerged, blinking against the sunlight. Although the day was fading, the light was still painful on the eyes compared to the energy balls they created below-ground.

She couldn't believe the carnage. Eyes wide, she watched the Waresti and Derian's Mercesti moving among the many bodies lining the ground. Enough time hadn't yet passed for the bodies to begin dissolving into colored sand. The extensive violence exhibited on the field around them had Sophia feeling weak in the knees.

Quincy reached out and put an arm around her. It gave her strength, as did the sight of Clara Kate and Ini-herit hurrying to see if they could assist the injured.

"You have your healing supplies?" she asked.

"Yes," Quincy replied.

"Then let's make ourselves useful."

They spent more than two hours moving from one being to the next, treating a range of injuries as Ini-herit's silver healing energy glowed. The elder couldn't heal Mercesti, so Quincy's skills were highly in need. Sophia had learned enough from him over the years to serve as an effective nurse. She found herself treating almost as many injuries as he did.

Once they made a complete round of the field and did what they could to help, they headed back toward the library. Zachariah and Tiege stood with Derian, Melanthe, Harold and Alexius, consulting over an ethereal map of the plane generated by the Waresti commander. Sophia also spotted Verrell, Alys and Oria among the group and figured they must be strategizing. She wondered why Cleve wasn't with them.

When Melanthe looked up and caught her gaze as they approached, Sophia knew.

"No," she said, shaking her head as Melanthe met her and took her hands. "Not Cleve. Please tell me he's okay."

"I'm sorry, Sophia. Cleve has fallen," Melanthe said, her eyes shining with tears. "Verrell had the bodies of our brethren brought into the forest so he could honor them with a brief tribute while we were in the library."

When Sophia would have sunk to the ground, Quincy grabbed her and pulled her against him. She barely registered it. One thought overrode all others.

"It's my fault," she said, the words barely audible. "It's all my fault."

Quincy lifted her and carried her away from the others. "Don't say that," he argued. "None of this is your fault."

"He was injured protecting me from Bertram and Tycho," she said as they stopped and he once again set her on her feet. Tears came in a hot, painful flood. "If he hadn't been injured—"

"No, Sophia." Quincy's voice was firm. He forced her to meet his gaze. "The only being at fault for what happened here today is Eirik. He's the one who orchestrated all of this. Cleve wouldn't have been forced to protect you if not for Eirik. Don't ever lose sight of that."

She wanted to argue, but his logic was irrefutable. Instead, she allowed him to pull her close, pressing her cheek to his chest as she cried.

Eventually, her emotions leveled out. Anger and determination met pain and loss. She would grieve, there was no denying that. But she wouldn't let the sacrifices made by Cleve and the other fallen Mercesti and Waresti warriors go unaddressed.

Eirik and Metis would be brought to justice for what they had done, and she looked forward to being one of those who ensured that happened.

Tiege knew the news about their significant losses would impact Sophia, and wanted to help her if she needed it. Once he confirmed that Quincy was taking care of her, he returned his attention to Zachariah.

"The medallion appears to contain some kind of coded image," Zachariah said, studying the map. "When *archigos* Ini-herit is done healing the last of our wounded, we can better determine what it is. I only got a quick glance at it."

"*Archigos* Uriel is nearly here," Harold said. "When he arrives, we can discuss strategy. We are gathering every available Waresti so that we can send out scouting patrols. They might get lucky and find Tate and Ariana before we do."

Tiege saw that Zachariah had mixed feelings about this. He wanted Tate found, yes. But he wanted the pleasure of killing Eirik himself. It was a conflict Tiege well understood.

"We can assist ye," Derian offered, looking at Zachariah. "There are many like us. We know how to reach them. Ye'll find no better resources for information about things happenin' on the mainland."

"This is not your conflict," Zachariah said, his gaze moving to Melanthe. "You have already risked enough. There is no need to sacrifice more."

"Eirik has your avowed, commander. Is that not right?"

Derian's words made Zachariah flinch, though Tiege thought he was the only one who noticed the subtle reaction. Whether it was the reminder of his former Gloresti title or the mention of Tate, Tiege could only guess.

"Yes," he answered stiffly.

"That serves as reason enough."

Before Zachariah could argue further, their attention turned to the sky. Tiege spotted at least a hundred Waresti…and one pair of dark purple wings. When Clara Kate and Ini-herit joined them, Tiege shared a look with his cousin. They knew that, especially in light of his current mindset, Zachariah wasn't likely to react well to the arrival of the Wymzesti elder. Tiege couldn't imagine why Knorbis was pressing his luck by showing up right then.

Then he realized that Knorbis carried Malukali.

When the group landed, Tiege couldn't tear his gaze from the Orculesti elder. She appeared to be in as bad of shape as Tate. Her face was almost unrecognizable. Bruises, some of them yellow with age, mottled her entire body. Deep wounds covered with fresh scabs lined the backs of her arms. Although her back wasn't visible, Tiege suspected it was covered in similar lines. Whip marks.

Ini-herit hurried forward. Knorbis continued to hold his wife as the Corgloresti elder used his healing ability to help her. They all watched in silence until the silver light faded. When Ini-herit stepped back, Malukali was fully healed.

She touched the side of Knorbis' face and held his gaze for a moment. He slowly lowered her to the ground. Then she took a few steps closer, her gaze on Zachariah.

"We don't seek your forgiveness," she said. "But we do seek your understanding."

Tiege looked at Zachariah, figuring the Mercesti was equating Malukali's condition with Tate's and knowing he would have done the same thing as Knorbis if their positions had been reversed. Eventually, Zachariah looked from Malukali to Knorbis and gave a brief nod. It was all they would get from him right then.

"Thank you," Malukali said, her dark green eyes glistening. "We will do everything we can to get Tate and Ariana back. And you'll have the help of another friend, too."

She glanced back at the forest. Tiege squinted as the sun faded to deep orange to try and see what friend she meant. The shadows appeared to move. Then he realized that he wasn't looking at shadows at all.

He was looking at Nyx.

The kragen emerged from the forest, her formerly graceful stride hindered by a notable hitch. After a frozen moment, Zachariah pushed past Derian and ran into the field, meeting Nyx before she had moved ten feet. No one disturbed the reunion, knowing the Mercesti wouldn't welcome it.

"How did she survive?" Tiege wondered. "Eirik seemed certain the poison he used would kill her."

"It nearly did," Knorbis said, his gaze on the kragen. "When you left me, I wandered for a bit as I waited for Uriel to bring Malukali so we could get her to Ini-herit. I found Nyx. She had been struck by a dart." He rubbed his neck, likely remembering that he'd also been shot. "I wasn't sure what form of poison Eirik used, but I carried an inoculation that I thought might work to reverse it."

Sophia stiffened. "What?"

Flushing, the Wymzesti elder admitted, "I stole the altered antitoxin that you created before we left your homeland. I wanted to be prepared for any eventuality and I knew Zachariah would send Nyx after me when I…took Tate and Ariana."

Everyone exchanged looks as the elder's actions once again fell into a harsh light. Then Malukali reached over and took her husband's hand.

"The enhanced antitoxin created using Sophia's DNA worked to revive the creature," Malukali said.

Blinking, Sophia shared a look with Quincy, who nodded. "The part of your DNA that allows you to shift into animal form must have bonded with Nyx's. Since the formula you created worked on Nyx, I would guess that the poison used by Eirik was probably similar to her natural toxin."

Tiege took a few steps away from the others as they discussed the scientific reasons behind the vaccine's success. The sun vanished to little more than a sliver on the horizon as he focused on Zachariah, who rubbed his friend's neck and spoke words he couldn't hear. All around them, forms of the dead began dissolving, a reminder of the brutality of the afternoon.

But Tiege had to take the miraculous survival of the kragen as a positive sign. She was proof that even when things seemed at their bleakest, there was a glimmer of good things to come if one only looked for it. As the dark settled around them, he knew that the new day would dawn, and it would dawn with hope and promise.

Epilogue

"WHERE HAVE YOU BROUGHT US, METIS?" EIRIK ASKED.

He scanned the dark room, not needing any light to make out even the smallest details. It appeared to be some kind of laboratory. He spotted a large work table and numerous scientific implements. A cot rested against one wall. Books lined shelves along every other.

"Somewhere we will not be found," she said.

Hearing her speak with Deimos' voice struck him as odd. She had explained that her base form was that of a female, but she could assume both genders. He dismissed the odd conflict as unimportant right then and continued his study of the space. In one corner of the room was a cage large enough for several Estilorians. He grabbed Ariana and hauled her to it, tossing her in. The Lekwuesti didn't issue a sound of protest, a fact that disgusted him. She would serve her purpose and lead him to the final scroll piece, and then he would kill her.

When he turned after securing the cage, he saw Metis hovering over the Kynzesti. Her red eyes glowed.

"You will not succumb to that creature's blood lust," he ordered, striding back across the room. "You will draw upon the Scultresti abilities you mentioned and heal this Kynzesti's life-threatening injuries."

Metis licked her lips. "I do not think that I can restrain myself. She smells delicious."

Grabbing her by the neck, he squeezed until she yelped and fought for release. Only when her eyes dimmed did he bother loosening the hold. "Do what I said," he snapped.

She collapsed beside the Kynzesti and gasped for air. Her hands went to the dying female's chest, where it was obvious the most severe injuries had occurred. Murky brown light flowed from Metis' hands into the Kynzesti's still form. She closed her eyes and concentrated, causing the light to strengthen.

A long while later, Eirik gazed down at the still-unconscious Kynzesti, taking note of the red pairing markings Metis had uncovered through her efforts. Apparently, Tate would have a few questions to answer once she awakened. For now, she would join her companion in the cage. Her injuries had been healed enough for her to survive and that was all that mattered.

He sat at the work table with Metis, studying the scroll piece. "It describes very specific individuals," he observed. "How are we to know to whom it refers? Even once we find these individuals, how will we know how to imbue the scroll?"

"Perhaps the last portion of the scroll will make everything clearer."

Eirik's eyes gleamed. "It had better. One way or another, I will complete the scroll and use it to become the next elder. No one and nothing will stand in my way."

Quincy found Sophia sitting on a large boulder at the edge of a glade within the forest. Moonlight filtered through the treetops to bathe her in a soft halo. Once again, he was struck by her remarkable beauty. He took a moment just to watch her.

Nearby, where the memorial had been held for the fallen, an abundance of orange and red flowers bloomed. A converted Scultresti created them as a way to honor the dead. Sophia twirled a red flower between her thumb and forefinger, seemingly mesmerized by the action. He hesitated to disturb her, wanting to give her this time to process everything.

"Do you suppose Cleve might one day be able to project himself here like my grandfather did?" she asked, jarring him.

Moving closer to her, he replied, "I believe anything is possible."

"You really do, don't you?" She caught his gaze and surprised him with a brief smile. "I can see why my grandfather asked you to accompany him on the most important mission of his existence."

He couldn't think of a thing to say, so when she got to her feet and walked up to him, he just stared at her.

"When it comes to an impossible task, who better to have along than someone whose mind and heart are open enough to accept any possibility?" She reached up to touch the side of his face, making his heart flip over in his chest. "He was so lucky to have you with him, Quincy. Just as I'm lucky to have you. I love you so much. I don't know how I didn't understand all of this sooner. I'll kick myself about it for years to come."

He started to reply, but she pulled him down for a kiss. Any words in his head vanished. His hands moved up to her silky hair, cradling her head and rubbing his thumbs along the sensitive skin of her jaw. When she parted her lips, he eagerly took the chance to explore her, indulging in her taste and essence.

The kiss lasted forever, yet not nearly long enough. Only when he knew he was losing his control did he break away from her. The ragged sounds of their breathing filled the clearing.

She leaned back after a moment to catch his gaze. "I feel guilty for enjoying that so much when Tate and Ariana are out there somewhere, suffering."

"I know," he said, feeling the same way.

"It's because of these terrible circumstances, though, that I've finally come to realize how much I love you...and how incredibly important your love is to me. I don't want another day to pass without you by my side."

Her words were everything he had ever dreamed. Yet he discovered what she said next surpassed them.

"I want to avow myself to you, Quincy."

The statement filled him with such joy that he nearly lost his composure. Grinning, he said, "Leave it to you to steal my opportunity to ask you first."

She returned the smile, but her eyes were somber. "We're facing so much right now. I'm sure the others will think we want to do this because of our current situation. But you and I know it's because I finally understand my own heart. I'd like to see if *archigos* Sebastian will craft us rings so we can avow ourselves before the morning."

"That won't be necessary."

Frowning, she watched as he reached into his pocket. When he pulled out a pair of rings, her eyes went wide. Her reaction made him laugh, something that surprised him.

"It seems your parents knew our hearts better than we did," he explained. "They had these rings made last year, knowing I would be staying at the homeland as we awaited the births of the new Kynzesti. When I told them that I loved you before I left, they gave these to me. We have their blessing…as long as we have a proper wedding when we get back home."

With every word he spoke, her face brightened. Then she threw her arms around him with a combination between a gasp and a laugh.

"Come on," she said, taking his hand. "Let's end this day by giving everyone a reason to smile. We'll face our next challenge in a few hours when we leave to find Tate and Ariana."

"Yes…and most importantly, we'll do it together."

Coming soon........

Elder

Book three of the Firstborn Trilogy

Turn the page for a preview of *Elder*, from the mind of Raine Thomas.

Elder

"Let me get this straight. Your dad is Gabriel? As in, *the* Gabriel mentioned in the Bible?"

"Yep."

"And he and I were once the equivalent of best friends?"

"Yep."

"Holy crap."

Clara Kate stifled a laugh as she watched Ini-herit process this news. His gray eyes were wider than she'd ever seen them. The only sound was of the rain pelting the roof of the large tree house located in the backyard of their guardian, Mrs. Clara Burke. Despite the fact that they were eighteen and the tree house was meant for younger kids, it was a place they visited whenever they wanted some time away from everything else. They'd even camped in it a few times.

Now, they sat against one wall with their legs sprawled in front of them and their hands joined. He studied her carefully for a moment. When she just quirked an eyebrow, he let out a long breath.

"Wow."

Her lips curved upwards. "You believe me."

He continued to look at her without responding. She knew his features as well as her own after these past few months spent with him on the human plane, but that didn't make her less interested in gazing at them. His aristocratic nose, long-lashed eyes and full lips would have made him what others called a "pretty boy" if not for the rough, honed edges of his cheekbones and jaw line. He wore his dark hair longer than Mrs. B would have liked, but he usually pulled it back into a ponytail out of deference to her. At the moment, he had it unbound and it brushed his shoulders in beautiful waves.

"I do believe you," he said at last. "Though heaven knows why."

"Well, you're the Corgloresti elder. It's a class founded on faith. Even though your Estilorian self has been suppressed while you re-learn human emotions, you retained your core characteristics."

"So, when I call you Angel, it's not so much a nickname as a fact."

Shaking her head, she nudged him with her elbow. "I told you we're Estilorians, not angels."

"What if I want to be an angel?"

"Oh, you're no angel," she said. He grinned wickedly, making her heart work overtime. "Angels are just one of the mythical creatures humans created based on their memories of Estilorians. When we separated the planes a couple of thousand years ago, humans documented their experiences with us in a variety of ways. Art, literature, music…you name it. In essence, we became human myths and legends."

"Being a legend doesn't sound so bad." He paused, looking thoughtful. Then he asked, "And I'm how old?"

"Oh…several thousand years."

"Get out."

"It's true," she said, laughing at his expression. "On the Estilorian plane, you'll look about the same age you are now, though. Maybe a few years older. Estilorians don't age, and many of the elders are the youngest in appearance."

"You said I'll look different when we transition. How different?"

She was pleased by his apparent acceptance of what she'd shared with him. They had been discussing this for hours, ever since she received word that they had to return to the Estilorian plane. She knew she wouldn't be commanded back unless something big had happened. Maybe her mother had gone into premature labor or something. Whatever the reason, she couldn't refuse the command.

"I don't know," she responded. "We don't have photographs on the Estilorian plane, and you left right before I was born. I've never seen your Estilorian form."

"Well that kinda sucks."

"Why? Do you think you'll end up looking like Brent?" She batted her eyelashes at him.

He shoved her shoulder. "Ha. You can have that blond Viking with the IQ of a sock puppet. Who needs enough muscles to lift a car, anyway?"

"Yeah." She sighed dramatically. "Who needs 'em?"

He rolled his eyes and swung an arm over her shoulders. She felt the taut muscles there and knew he didn't really have a complex about Brent's steroid-induced physique. It was Brent's unwanted attention toward Clara Kate that had brought her and Ini-herit closer together, so he was a frequent butt of their jokes.

"But you'll look the same?" he asked.

"Yes," she said. She'd already discussed this, but didn't mind reviewing it if it helped ease his worry. "I've been able to transition between the planes without changing forms since I was three."

She didn't bother describing the uproar she'd caused the first time she did it. She barely remembered the experience. One moment she'd been sleeping in her bed at home. The next she was in a hospital on the human plane answering a million questions from the humans who found her. As a result of her impromptu transition, the protections around her homeland had been strengthened considerably.

"You'll look similar to how you do as a human," she explained. "*Archigos* Zayna, the Scultresti elder, did her best to mimic your Estilorian features in your human form to make the transition less psychologically stressful on you. Your eyes will be more silver than gray, and you'll have a bunch of silver markings on your body from past pairings with Gloresti. I believe your hair will be longer, too, based on what I've heard."

"Based on what you've heard?" he repeated. He reached over and traced the line of her jaw, causing her to shiver. "You were curious about me before you ever came here, weren't you?"

"Yes," she said a bit breathlessly. His touch always did this to her. "I couldn't wait to meet you."

"And now that you have?"

"You're everything I ever dreamed of and more. You know that by now. I love you, Harry."

He leaned down and kissed her. It was every bit as potent as the first time.

She reached up with her left hand and wove her fingers through the soft hair at the nape of his neck. Her tongue pressed eagerly against his as he deepened the kiss. Bliss such as she had never envisioned coursed through her.

Eventually, he pulled away from her. They both had to catch their breath. His eyes were dark with passion.

"I love you, too, Angel."

Her heart soared. This wasn't the first time he'd said it, but it never got old. She caressed the side of his face, enjoying the feel of stubble beneath her sensitive fingertips.

"What will we tell Mrs. B?" he asked.

She sighed. "We'll have to tell her some form of the truth. She won't see you again…at least, not in this form. She went through this nineteen years ago with my parents. She'll understand."

"I'm worried about her," he confessed.

"I know," she said. "Me, too."

They'd both observed how tired their guardian seemed lately. She had told them that she was retiring once they left for college in the fall. She'd been a foster parent for nearly forty years, ever since her beloved husband, Henry, was killed in the line of duty when she was twenty-eight. She'd been unable to have her own children, so she decided to raise those kids who needed a good home. But the time had come, she said, to hang up her hat.

"She's been going to the doctor more frequently," he said, running his fingers through her hair. "She won't tell me what they say."

"We'll get some answers after we transition," she promised. "We have contacts in the human medical field. My friend, Quincy, will probably be coming back here soon to harvest more souls. He usually transitions after the Kynzesti are born. I'll ask him to look into it."

"Okay."

They sat in silence for a moment. Clara Kate rested her head on his chest, listening to his heartbeat. "We have to leave soon," she said eventually. "Within a day or two."

"That soon?"

She nodded. "There's something going on. They wouldn't tell me what, but we're both needed right away."

"Wow."

"Yeah." Lifting her head, she looked again at his lips, then caught his gaze. "Harry, when we transition...things might be different. We'll both have responsibilities, and I'll have my family around me every moment of the day. And, well...I've decided that I want our last bit of time here on this plane to be memorable."

He lifted a dark brow. "Memorable?"

"Yeah." She shifted and ran one hand slowly up his chest, following the lines of his well-toned midsection through his T-shirt. When he drew in a sharp breath, she smiled. "Memorable."

About the Author:

Raine Thomas is the author of a series of young adult fantasy/romance novels about the Estilorians. She has a varied background including such professions as wedding planning and mental health…two fields that intersect more often than one would think. Residing in Orlando, Florida with her husband and daughter, Raine is hard at work on her next books about the Estilorians.

You can get more info about Raine, her books, and her upcoming releases by visiting her at the following sites:

http://RaineThomas.com
http://twitter.com/Raine_Thomas
http://facebook.com/RaineThomas

Made in the USA
Middletown, DE
01 December 2022